REMEMBER TUESDAY MORNING

Other Life-Changing Fiction™ by Karen Kingsbury

Bailey Flanigan Series
Leaving
Learning
Longing (Fall 2011)
Loving (Spring 2012)

9/11 Series
One Tuesday Morning
Beyond Tuesday Morning
Remember Tuesday Morning

Lost Love Series
Even Now
Ever After

Above the Line Series
Above the Line: Take One
Above the Line: Take Two
Above the Line: Take Three
Above the Line: Take Four

Stand-Alone Titles
Oceans Apart
Between Sundays
This Side of Heaven
When Joy Came to Stay
On Every Side
Divine
Like Dandelion Dust
Where Yesterday Lives
Shades of Blue
Unlocked

Redemption Series
Redemption
Remember
Return
Rejoice
Reunion

Firstborn Series
Fame
Forgiven
Found
Family
Forever

Sunrise Series
Sunrise
Summer
Someday
Sunset

Red Glove Series
Gideon's Gift
Maggie's Miracle
Sarah's Song
Hannah's Hope

Forever Faithful Series
Waiting for Morning
Moment of Weakness
Halfway to Forever

Women of Faith Fiction Series
A Time to Dance
A Time to Embrace

Cody Gunner Series
A Thousand Tomorrows
Just Beyond the Clouds
This Side of Heaven

Children's Titles
Let Me Hold You Longer
Let's Go on a Mommy Date
We Believe in Christmas
Let's Have a Daddy Day
The Princess and the Three Knights
Go Ahead and Dream
Brave Young Knight
Far Flutterby (Fall 2011)

Miracle Collections
A Treasury of Christmas Miracles
A Treasury of Miracles for Women
A Treasury of Miracles for Teens
A Treasury of Miracles for Friends
A Treasury of Adoption Miracles
Miracles — a Devotional

Gift Books
Stay Close Little Girl
Be Safe Little Boy
Forever Young: Ten Gifts of Faith
for the Graduate

KAREN KINGSBURY

NEW YORK TIMES
BESTSELLING AUTHOR

REMEMBER TUESDAY MORNING

Previously published as *Every Now & Then*

ZONDERVAN.com/
AUTHORTRACKER
follow your favorite authors

ZONDERVAN

Remember Tuesday Morning
Copyright © 2011 by Karen Kingsbury

Previously published as *Every Now and Then*
Copyright © 2008 by Karen Kingsbury

This title is also available as a Zondervan ebook.
Visit www.zondervan.com/ebooks.

This title is also available in a Zondervan audio edition.
Visit www.zondervan.fm.

Requests for information should be addressed to:

Zondervan, *Grand Rapids, Michigan 49530*

Library of Congress Cataloging-in-Publication Data

Kingsbury, Karen.
    Remember Tuesday Morning / Karen Kingsbury.
        p.   cm. — (September 11 series)
    ISBN 978-0-310-33414-9 (softcover)
    1. Fire fighters — Fiction. 2. Life change events — Fiction.
3. September 11 Terrorist Attacks, 2001 — Psychological aspects — Fiction.
4. Ecoterrorism — California — Fiction. I. Title.
PS3561.I4873R47   2011
813'.54 — dc22   2011007206

Published in association with the literary agency of Alive Communications, Inc.,
7680 Goddard Street, Suite 200, Colorado Springs, CO 80920. www.alivecommuni
cations.com

Cover design: Gearbox
Cover photography: ©gettyimages/Veer®
Interior design: Michelle Espinoza

Printed in the United States of America

11 12 13 14 15 16 /DCI/ 21 20 19 18 17 16 15 14 13 12 11 10 9 8 7 6 5 4 3 2 1

DEDICATION

To Donald, my Prince Charming . . .

How I rejoice to see you coaching again, sharing your gift of teaching and your uncanny basketball ability with another generation of kids — and best yet, now our boys are part of the mix. Isn't this what we always dreamed of, my love? I love sitting back this time and letting you and God figure it out. I'll always be here — cheering for you and the team from the bleachers. But God's taught me a thing or two about being a coach's wife. He's so good that way. It's fitting that you would find varsity coaching again now — after twenty years of marriage. Hard to believe that as you read this, our twentieth anniversary has come and gone. I look at you and I still see the blond, blue-eyed guy who would ride his bike to my house and read the Bible with me before a movie date. You stuck with me back then and you stand by me now — when I need you more than ever. I love you, my husband, my best friend, my Prince Charming. Stay with me, by my side, and let's watch our children take wing, savoring every memory and each day gone by. Always and always . . . The ride is breathtakingly beautiful, my love. I pray it lasts far into our twilight years. Until then, I'll enjoy not always knowing where I end and you begin. I love you always and forever.

To Kelsey, my precious daughter . . .

You are nineteen now, a young woman, and my heart soars with joy when I see all that you are, all you've become. This year is a precious one for us because you're still home, attending junior college and spending nearly every day in the dance studio. When you're not dancing, you're helping out with the business and ministry of Life-Changing Fiction ™ — so we have many precious hours together. I know this time is short and won't last, but I'm enjoying it so much — you, no longer the high school girl, a young woman and in every way my daughter, my friend. That part will always stay, but you, my sweet girl, will go where your dreams lead, soaring through the future doors God opens. Honey, you grow more beautiful — inside and out — every day. And always I treasure the way you talk to me, telling me your hopes and dreams and everything in between. I can almost sense the plans God has for you, the very good plans. I pray you keep holding on to His hand as He walks you toward them. I love you, sweetheart.

To Tyler, my lasting song ...

I can hardly wait to see what this school year will bring for you, my precious son. Last year you were one of Joseph's brothers, and you were Troy Bolton, and Captain Hook — becoming a stronger singer and stage actor with every role. This year you'll be at a new high school, where I believe God will continue to shape you as the leader He wants you to be. Your straight A's last year were a sign of things to come, and I couldn't be prouder, Ty. I know it was hard watching Kelsey graduate, knowing that your time with your best friend is running short. But you'll be fine, and no matter where God leads you in the future, the deep and lasting relationships you've begun here in your childhood will remain. Thank you for the hours of music and song. As you seize hold of your sophomore year, I am mindful that the time is rushing past, and I make a point to stop and listen a little longer when I hear you singing. I'm proud of you, Ty, of the young man you're becoming. I'm proud of your talent and your compassion for people and your place in our family. However your dreams unfold, I'll be in the front row to watch them happen. Hold on to Jesus, Ty. I love you.

To Sean, my happy sunshine ...

Today you came home from school, eyes sparkling, and showed me your science notebook—all your meticulous neat sentences and careful drawings of red and white blood cells and various bones and bacteria. I was marveling over every page, remarking at the time you'd taken and the quality of your work, and together we laughed over the fact that neither of us really cares too much for science—but that it still matters that we do our best. You smiled that easy smile of yours and said, "Wait till you see Josh's—his blows mine away." You didn't know it at the time, but I was very touched by the tone in your voice. You weren't envious or defeated by the fact that Josh—in your same grade—might have managed to draw even more detailed pictures in his science journal. You were merely happy that you'd done your best, earned your A, and could move on from seventh grade science proud of your effort. I love that about you, Sean. You could easily sulk in the shadow of your brother, a kid who excels in so many areas that the two of you share. But you also excel, my dear son. And one of the best ways you shine is in your happy heart, your great love for life and for people, and your constant joy.

Sean, you have a way of bringing smiles into our family, even in the most mundane moments, and lately we are smiling very big about your grades. I pray that God will use your positive spirit to always make a difference in the lives around you. You're a precious gift, Son. Keep smiling and keep seeking God's best for your life. I love you, honey.

To Josh, my tenderhearted perfectionist ...

So, you finally did it! You can beat me at ping-pong now, not that I'm surprised. God has given you great talents, Josh, and the ability to work at them with the sort of diligent determination that is rare in young teens. Whether in football or soccer, track or room inspections, you take the time to seek perfection. Along with that, there are bound to be struggles. Times when you need to understand again that the gifts and talents you bear are God's, not yours, and times when you must learn that perfection isn't possible for us, only for God. Even so, my heart almost bursts with pride over the young man you're becoming. After one of your recent soccer tournaments, one of the parents said something I'll always remember: "Josh is such a leader," she told me. "Even when he doesn't know other parents are looking, he's always setting an example for his teammates." The best one, of course, is when you remind your teammates to pray before a game. What a legacy you and your brothers are creating here in Washington State. You have an unlimited future ahead of you, Josh, and I'll forever be cheering on the sidelines. Keep God first in your life. I love you always.

To EJ, my chosen one ...

Here you are in the early months of seventh grade, and I can barely recognize the student athlete you've become. Those two years of home schooling with Dad continue to reap a harvest a hundred times bigger than what was sown, and we couldn't be prouder of you. But even beyond your grades, we are blessed to have you in our family for so many reasons. You are wonderful with our pets—always the first to feed them and pet them and look out for them—and you are a willing worker when it comes to chores. Besides all that, you make us laugh—oftentimes right out loud. I've always believed that getting through life's little difficulties and challenges requires a lot of laughter—and I thank you for bringing that to our home. You're a wonderful boy, Son, a child with such potential. Clearly, that's what you displayed the other day when you came out of nowhere in your soccer qualifiers and scored three goals. I'm amazed because you're so talented in so many ways, but all of them pale in comparison to your desire to truly live for the Lord. I'm so excited about the future, EJ, because God has great plans for you, and we want to be the first to congratulate you as you work to discover those. Thanks for your giving heart, EJ. I love you so.

To Austin, my miracle boy...

I smile when I picture you hitting not one home run, but *three* last baseball season—all of them for Papa—and I feel my heart swell with joy as I think of what happened after your second home run, when you had rounded the bases one at a time and accepted congratulations at home plate from your entire team. You headed into the dugout, and a couple of your teammates tugged on your arm. "Tell us, Austin... how do you do it? How do you hit a home run like that?" That's when you smiled and shrugged your shoulders. "Easy. I asked God for the strength to hit the ball better than I could without Him." Papa must be loving every minute of this, Aus. I'm sure of it. What I'm not sure of is whether missing him will ever go away. I can only tell you that our quiet times together are what I love most too. Those, and our times of playing give-and-go out on the basketball court. You're my youngest, my last, Austin. I'm holding on to every moment, for sure. Thanks for giving me so many wonderful reasons to treasure today. I thank God for you, for the miracle of your life. I love you, Austin.

And to God Almighty, the Author of Life, who has—for now—blessed me with these.

ACKNOWLEDGMENTS

One night when I was putting the finishing touches on this book, Austin crawled into bed next to me and stared at my laptop screen. "You know, Mom," he said, "I've been meaning to ask you about writing books. I have a couple questions." I smiled at him and asked him what he wanted to know. "Well," he said, "you know those beautiful covers on your books? They're so nice, with just the right colors and pictures. So, do you do those? Do you make the covers?"

I shook my head. "No, buddy. I don't have anything to do with the covers, really. The publisher has these wonderful designers. They take care of coming up with a cover."

He seemed a little disappointed for a few seconds. Then his eyes lit up. "I know, how about the design inside the book, the way the letters line up just so, and those little swirly things that make the first page of every chapter so nice?" He scrunched up his face, slightly baffled. "Do you do that part?"

Again I shook my head. "No, honey. Actually, there are designers at the publisher that make sure the book looks nice on the inside." My smile turned a little sheepish. "They're the ones who do that."

His shoulders sank, and after a slight pause, his brow raised, hopeful once more. "I know, how about the bookstores! Are you the one who gets all those books to the bookstores, so they can be there on the shelves for the people?"

Feeling the clear sense that I was disappointing him, I shook my head and managed a weak smile. "No, Aus, I don't do that either. The publisher has a sales staff who handles getting the books to the bookstores. After that, other people at the bookstores open the boxes of books and put them on the shelves. I don't have anything to do with that."

"Wow." He climbed back down, but before he ran off he shrugged his shoulders. "You don't really do that much, do you?"

Austin had a point. No book comes together without a great and talented team of people making it happen. For that reason, a special thanks to my friends at Zondervan Publishing who combined efforts to make *Remember Tuesday Morning* all it could be. A special thanks to my dedicated editor, Sue Brower, and to my brilliant publicist Karen Campbell, and to Karwyn Bursma, whose creative marketing is unrivaled in the publishing business.

Also, thanks to my amazing agent, Rick Christian, president of Alive Communications. Rick, you've always believed only the best for me. When we talk about the highest possible goals, you see them as doable, reachable. You are a brilliant manager of my career, and I thank God for you. But even with all you do for my ministry of writing, I am doubly grateful for your prayers. The fact that you and Debbie are praying for me and my family keeps me confident every morning that God will continue to breathe into life the stories in my heart. Thank you for being so much more than a brilliant agent.

A special thank-you to my husband, who puts up with me on deadline and doesn't mind driving through Taco Bell after a basketball game if I've been editing all day. This wild ride wouldn't be possible without you, Donald. Your love keeps me writing; your prayers keep me believing that God has a plan in this ministry of fiction. And thanks for the hours you put in working with the guestbook entries on my website. I look forward to that time every day when you read through them, sharing them with me and releasing them to the public, praying for the prayer requests. Thank you, honey, and thanks to all my kids, who pull together, bringing me iced green tea and understanding about my sometimes crazy schedule. I love that you know you're still first, before any deadline.

Thank you also to my mom, Anne Kingsbury, and to my sisters, Tricia, Sue, and Lynne. Mom, you are amazing as my assistant—working day and night sorting through the mail from my reader friends. I appreciate you more than you'll ever know.

Tricia, you are the best executive assistant I could ever hope to have. I treasure your loyalty and honesty, the way you include me in every decision and exciting website change. My site has been a different place since you stepped in, and the hits have grown tenfold. Along the way, the readers have so much more to help them in their faith, so much more than a story with this Life-Changing Fiction™. Please know that I pray for God's blessings on you always, for your dedication to helping me in this season of writing, and for your wonderful son, Andrew. And aren't we having such a good time too? God works all things to the good!

Sue, I believe you should've been a counselor! From your home far from mine, you get batches of reader letters every day, and you diligently answer them using God's wisdom and His Word. When readers get a response from "Karen's sister Susan," I hope they know how carefully you've prayed for them and for the responses you give. Thank you for truly loving what you do, Sue. You're gifted with people, and I'm blessed to have you aboard.

A special thanks also to Will Montgomery, my road manager. I was terrified to venture into the business of selling my books at events for a couple of reasons. First, I never wanted to profit from selling my books at speaking events, and second, because I would never have the time to handle such details. Monty, you came in and helped me on both counts. With a mission statement that reads, "To love and serve the readers," you have helped me supply books and free gifts to tens of thousands of readers at events across the country. More than that, you've become my friend, a very valuable part of the ministry of Life-Changing Fiction ™. You are loyal and kind and fiercely protective of me, my family, and the work God has me doing. Thank you for everything you're doing, and will continue to do.

Thanks too, to Olga Kalachik, my office assistant, who helps prepare our home for the marketing events and research gatherings that take place there on a regular basis. I appreciate all you're doing to make sure I have time to write. You're wonderful, Olga, and I pray God continues to bless you and your precious family.

I also want to thank my friends with Extraordinary Women — Roy Morgan, Julie Clinton, Beth Cleveland, Charles Billingsley, and so many others. How wonderful to be a part of what God is doing through all of you. Thank you for making me part of your family.

Thanks also to my forever friends and family, the ones who rushed to our side this past year as we lost my dad. Your love has been a tangible source of comfort, pulling us through and making us know how very blessed we are to have you in our lives.

And the greatest thanks to God. The gift is Yours. I pray I might use it for years to come in a way that will bring You honor and glory.

Forever in Fiction®

A special thanks to the Northern Cross Foundation and the Spica family who won Forever in Fiction®* at the Grand Rapids annual "Making it Home" Auction. The Spica family chose to honor their friend Dave Jacobs, age 58, by naming him Forever in Fiction. Dave is a pillar in his community, a man with many friends and much integrity and faith. He spent his younger years in social work, but then became involved in the Home Repair Services business — a venture devoted to helping the less fortunate in various Michigan neighborhoods.

Dave has won many awards for his philanthropic efforts, but remains deeply humble and committed to making life better for the people around him. His greatest accomplishments include his marriage to his wife, Lois, and their four children. He loves woodworking and bird-watching, and when he travels to the Upper Peninsula of Michigan with his family, he tries to do a little of both.

Dave's character in *Remember Tuesday Morning* is that of the generous developer whose Oak Canyon Estates are the subject of threats by a radical environmental group. I could see Dave working in that role, commanding a team of construction workers and still finding time to be with family and friends, and making a difference in his community.

I pray that the Spica family sees their friend Dave deeply honored by their gift and by his placement in *Remember Tuesday*

---

*Forever in Fiction is a registered trademark owned by Karen Kingsbury.

Morning and that they will always see a bit of Dave when they read his name in the pages of this novel, where he will be Forever in Fiction.

For those of you who are not familiar with Forever in Fiction, it is my way of involving you, the readers, in my stories, while raising money for charities. To date Forever in Fiction has raised more than $100,000 at charity auctions across the country. If you are interested in having a Forever in Fiction package donated to your auction, contact my assistant, Tricia Kingsbury, at Kingsburydesk@aol.com. Please write *Forever in Fiction* in the subject line. Please note that I am only able to donate a limited number of these each year. For that reason, I have set a fairly high minimum bid on this package. That way the maximum funds are raised for charities.

REMEMBER
TUESDAY
MORNING

ONE

Smog hung over the San Fernando Valley like a collapsed Boy Scout tent, filling in the spaces between the high-rise office buildings and freeway overpasses. The Pacific Ocean hadn't produced a breeze in three weeks, and by two o'clock that August afternoon temperatures had long since shot past the century mark.

Alex Brady didn't care.

He picked up his pace, pounding his Nikes against the shimmering asphalt. Salty sweat dripped down his temples and into the corners of his mouth, but he kept running, filling his lungs with the sweltering, stifling air. Something about the sting in his chest made him feel good, stirred the intensity of his run. The intensity of his existence. If chasing bad guys on the streets of Los Angeles didn't kill him, he wasn't going to keel over on the Pierce College running track. Whatever the weather.

Five miles and ten hill sprints every off-day, that was his mandate. And he never made the trip without Bo.

They were alone on the track today, no one else crazy enough to push this hard in the suffocating heat. He glanced at the German shepherd keeping pace alongside him. His dog, his partner for every on-duty call. His best friend, his only friend. "Atta boy." The dog wasn't even breathing hard. Alex slowed long enough to pat Bo's deep brown coat. They both needed a drink. Alex's ribs heaved as he ran to the bleachers and slowed to a stop. He grabbed one of his water bottles from the lowest row and downed half of it. Bo found his bowl a few feet away and lapped like crazy. This was a two-bottle day if ever there was one.

Alex slammed the bottle back down on the bench and kicked his run into gear again. His dog was a few seconds behind him, but he caught up easily. "Alright, Bo … let's get this." Alex could feel the workout now, feel his legs screaming for relief the way they always did when he had a mile left.

Bo's earnest eyes seemed to say he would stay by his master whatever the pace, whatever the distance. Alex wiped the back of his hand across his forehead and squinted against the glare of the afternoon sun. Without question, Bo was the best police dog in the Los Angeles Sheriff's Department. Every bit as fit as Alex, and with a resumé of heroism unequalled among K9 units.

Another lap and Alex noticed something on the surface of the track. His running shoes were leaving an imprint. The asphalt was that hot. Good thing Bo was running on the grass. *Push through it*, he ordered himself. *Dad would've done this without breaking a sweat.*

And then, like it did at least once a day, a rush of memories came over him so hard and fast he could almost feel the wind from its wake. His dad, Captain Ben Brady, New York City firefighter. His hero, his best friend. Suddenly it was all real again. The sound of his voice, the feel of his hand … firm against Alex's shoulder when he lost the big game his junior year … running alongside Alex when he was six and learning to ride a bike … or even before that, when he lifted Alex up into the fire truck that very first time.

Two more laps, Brady. You can do it. Alex clenched his teeth and pushed himself, but the memories stayed. There was his dad, hovering over his bed that September Tuesday morning, placing his hand against the side of Alex's face. "Buddy … time to get up. You gotta ace that math test … we'll talk about the other stuff when I get home."

The other stuff. Alex blinked and the hillside that surrounded half the track appeared again. The other stuff was Alex's determination to parlay his years as a fire cadet into an immediate position with the FDNY. As a teen, Alex could already see himself in the uniform, rushing into burning buildings, climbing atop blazing rooftops, rescuing families and putting out fires. His dad saw things differently. College would be better. His grades were good, his SAT scores in the top ten percent. Why battle fires in Manhattan when you could work in an office with a view of Central Park? Alex was sure that was the message his dad was going to deliver that night.

Only the message never came.

The terrorists ... the terrorists picked that day to —

Alex found a reserve of energy for the last lap. "Come on, Bo." He could feel the heat in his face and neck and arms, but he pushed ahead. Of course he hadn't gone to college, and he hadn't spent another day desiring a job with the FDNY. He'd done the only thing he could do. He moved as far away from New York City as he could and threw himself into earning a sheriff's badge. That way he could consume himself with the one job that mattered after September 11. Get the bad guys.

Didn't matter if they were drunk drivers or gang thugs, bank robbers or terrorists plotting the next big attack, Alex wanted them off the street. That desire was all that drove him, the only purpose he felt born to fulfill. Get rid of the evil. He and Bo. So that some other high school senior wouldn't have to sit in his Shakespearean English class and watch his dad murdered on live television.

He took the last ten yards at a sprint, his heart bursting from his chest, and then he dropped back to a walk. The smog didn't pass for oxygen, and he couldn't catch his breath. But he'd been here before. He knew how to work with the heat and dirty air. He pursed his lips and blew it all out, emptying his lungs, making space for his next breath. "Go on, Bo ..." He followed the dog to the water, and by the time he reached the bleachers he was breathing again. Ready for the hills.

He downed the rest of the first bottle and paced a few yards in either direction. Bo stayed by his water bowl, but his eyes moved from Alex to the hill at the other end of the stadium. "Give me a minute." He grabbed his towel from the bleachers and buried his face in it. The hills were the best part. For a few intense minutes, he could feel what his father had felt, the way he must've pushed himself up the stairs of the North Tower, looking for victims, seeking the wounded and trapped on one floor after another.

He tossed his towel on the bleachers and stretched hard to the right, lengthening his core muscles and bringing relief to his tired body. The left side was next, and when he finished he nodded to the dog. "Come on." He jogged to the base of the hill with the German shepherd on the grass at his side. Then, without waiting, he lowered his head and dug into the hillside. The ground was steep, all craggy dirt clods and forgotten weeds, but his footing stayed sure and steady.

Move it … push harder, he ordered himself. Halfway up the hill the burning began and Alex welcomed it. Again his surroundings faded and Alex could see the stairwell, the way it must've looked as his father climbed higher and higher. People rushing down the stairs, firefighters rushing up. He would do this as often as he could, every day when he didn't don the uniform, and he would remember everything his father stood for. Everything that drove him and gave him purpose in life.

Bo made it to the top of the hill ahead of him, tongue hanging from his mouth halfway to the ground. But even then the dog was ready for the downhill, ready for the next nine trips back up. *Faster … don't let up.* He wiped the back of his hand across his wet forehead and focused on the path back down. At the base of the hill he glanced at his watch. He needed to push through this thing. He still had to grab a shower and run a few errands before dinner at the Michaels' house. And he wouldn't miss dinner.

The evenings with Sergeant Clay Michaels and his wife, Jamie, were the only social invites Alex received. Most times he didn't really want to go, didn't want someone worrying about him or probing around in his personal life. But he promised himself he'd show up every time Clay and Jamie asked. Otherwise, he'd become a machine, an unfeeling robot whose sole purpose in life was to round up crooks and lock them away. Alex squinted at the hill and attacked it a second time. Not that he minded being a machine. He sort of liked the idea. But if he lost touch completely with people, he might forget one very important aspect of his job—

The pain of it.

A driving force for Alex was the way people were hurt by bad guys, because there was way too much mind-boggling sorrow out there. Deep life-altering sadness like the kind that had ripped into him and his mom on September 11, 2001. If he lost track of the human suffering, he could just go ahead and hang up his gun, because the hurt was why he was here in the first place. So yeah, he would keep his dinner invitation tonight and anytime Clay and his wife made room for him at their table. Because being around them kept alive what was left of his heart. That and times like this, when his workout actually allowed him to think beyond the next few minutes.

The workout did something else, too—if only for a few hours.

It made him forget the girl he'd left back in New York City, and all the reasons he'd walked away from her. A girl whose indelible fingerprints stayed on his heart and whose contagious laughter and easy smile had a way of catching up to him, no matter how hard and fast he ran.

A girl named Holly Brooks.

TWO

Clay Michaels reached into the pantry of his Calabasas, California, home, pulled out a plastic pitcher, and handed it to his wife, Jamie. "Everyone here?"

"Not yet." She took the pitcher and filled it with three scoops of powdered lemonade. "We're waiting on Alex. Everyone else is out back." She leaned close and gave him a quick kiss. "Time for you to work your magic."

He caught her by the waist and eased her close to him. "You mean …" he kissed her again, long enough to take her breath away, "…like this?"

She took a step back, starry-eyed, and inhaled sharply. "Later." She glanced over her shoulder at the window that separated the kitchen from the backyard. "They're hungry." She straightened her shirt, spun around to the fridge, and pulled out a tray of raw burgers. "This magic."

Clay took the tray and grinned at her. "Where's Sierra?"

"In the garage with Wrinkles," she frowned. "That cat's been sleeping all day."

"Yeah, well," Clay made a silly face and balanced the tray of burgers on the palm of one hand. "With a three-year-old running around, sometimes I think we could all use a nap in the garage."

Clay's brother Eric opened the slider door and stayed beside him while the burgers cooked. Not far away on the patio, Jamie sat with Eric's wife, Laura, across from Joe and Wanda Reynolds. The six of them did this regularly, getting together at one of their homes for a weekend barbecue.

Eric was talking about a deal at work, an acquisition of some kind, but Clay was catching only every other word, distracted by Michael Bublé playing in the background and the happy voices of the kids on the swing set across the yard. Three-year-old CJ was running his Hot Wheels car on the slide with Joe and Wanda's little boy, Will. The two looked like miniature versions of their fathers—one blond and blue-eyed, one black with sparkling brown eyes, the best of buddies. On the nearest swing, Eric and Laura's little red-headed girl, Lacey, was giggling at them.

Clay turned his attention to the burgers. "Looks like they're just about ready."

Eric peered inside the grill. "I'll get the buns."

"They're inside on the counter." Clay surveyed the scene again. The thick smell of burgers mixed with the warm summer sweetness from the gardenias, the ones Jamie planted along the back of the property the week they moved in. Clay breathed in deeply. He wanted to freeze the moment, wrap his arms around it, and never let it go.

Times like this, he could almost forget the pressure of his job, the responsibility he wore like a heavy yoke when he headed off to the LA sheriff's Monterey Park headquarters. Tonight he wasn't a sergeant with the Special Enforcement Bureau or one of the most respected men in the department. He wasn't training the next group of SWAT guys or worrying about threats from local environmental terrorist groups a few weeks shy of what could be the area's worst fire season ever.

No, tonight he was a married man, longing to stretch out the weekend hours. He was a daddy who didn't mind wearing a jester hat when the kids played dress-up and a friend who had stayed faithful through too many highs and lows to remember. He was a brother and an uncle, a God-fearing family man who prayed daily for the people in his life. Most of all—no matter what work threw at him—he was a believer.

All the things he feared Deputy Alex Brady might never be.

He was sliding burgers off the grill and onto the open buns on the tray in Eric's hands when he heard someone at the patio door. He turned in time to see Alex walk through the door, his expression marked by an unspoken apology. "Traffic on the 101," he shrugged as he set his keys on a table just outside the patio door. He wore a white T-shirt and jeans, his short dark hair streaked with a few blond highlights and styled more like a contemporary pop star than a sheriff's deputy. Alex gave Clay a half-grin. "Your famous burgers again, huh, Sarge?"

"That's why they call me 'Magic.'" He kept his tone light. Alex came for dinner once a month or so, and usually they never got past shoptalk. But Clay had a feeling about tonight, that maybe they could find their way to something deeper, like why it was Alex had trouble connecting with any other human being. "Did you bring Bo?"

"He's out front. Tied him up on the porch."

"We'll save him a burger."

The men headed to the table and Clay called the kids. Eric and Laura's son Josh came in through the side gate, a basketball tucked beneath his arm, his face damp with sweat. He was fifteen now and almost as tall as Eric. Behind him were Joe and Wanda's older two—both in middle school and fascinated with basketball.

"They're good." Josh waved his thumb at the Reynolds kids. "I barely beat 'em."

"Yeah right." The oldest of the Reynolds kids rolled his eyes. He used his tank top to wipe his forehead. "He schooled us again." The three older kids took their plates and headed out front once more.

As the younger kids finished eating, they ran to the swings, leaving the seven adults sitting around Clay and Jamie's patio table. Joe took a long drink of his lemonade and sat back in his chair. He shaded his eyes and watched CJ, Will, and Lacey. "The miracle babies are growing up."

Clay smiled at the term. *Miracle babies.* That's what the couples had called their youngest children ever since the three of them arrived — all within a year of each other. Lacey was the baby Eric and Laura never would've had if not for a fateful business trip on September 11, 2001. If Eric hadn't spent three months in New York City recovering from his injuries and learning how to be the father and family man he had never been, their marriage wouldn't have survived.

Joe and Wanda's marriage had been over as well, their love for each other lost in the aftermath of heartache when their firstborn son was hit and killed by a car. Years passed with the two of them living separate lives on opposite coasts, but then Joe dragged Clay to New York City for police training and something more — a chance to reunite with Wanda.

Joe was laughing now, telling a story about little Will. Clay studied his friend. There were no signs of the near-fatal gunshot wound he'd gotten while on that New York trip. All that mattered was he'd come back with Wanda ready to start over again. Their son Will was proof that God could bless even the most broken people with a second chance.

And, of course, his and Jamie's own little CJ. It was still hard to believe that on that same New York trip, Clay had connected with Jamie — Jamie Bryan, the very woman who had nursed Clay's brother, Eric, back to health in the months after 9/11. Love for them had been sure and fast — beauty borne of ashes. By then Clay had all but given up on marrying and having a family, and Jamie never for a moment thought that someday her daughter, Sierra, would have a sibling.

But here they were, all of them — embracing life and raising their miracle babies.

Joe nodded toward the kids. "Lacey's definitely in charge." He was holding Wanda's hand, the two of them relaxed and happy together. Little Will had his mother's milk chocolate skin, and his father's sense of humor. The boy loved nothing more than to tease the lone girl who rounded out their trio.

"I'll tell you what," Wanda made a jaunty snap of her fingers, her eyes still on Lacey, "that little girl's going to run a corporation someday."

Eric and Laura both laughed, and Eric anchored his elbows on the table. "She'd probably be good at it."

"You ever think about it?" Laura wore sunglasses, but now she took them off, her eyes thoughtful. She looked at the others around the table. "None of them would be here if it weren't for 9/11."

"We wouldn't be here, either. Not together." Joe brought Wanda's hand to his lips and kissed it. He held her gaze for a long moment, then looked back at Laura. "Yeah, we think about it. Every now and then, anyway."

At the mention of the terrorist attacks, Clay shot a quick glance at Alex. He'd been quiet until now, mostly eating his way through three burgers and listening to the conversation about the children. But with the talk of September 11, a shadow fell across his expression, and his eyes grew dark. He wiped his mouth with a napkin, pushed back from the table, and turned to Clay. "Thanks for dinner." He smiled, but it didn't move past his lips. "Great as always."

"Wait a minute, young man." Wanda was on her feet, her hands on her hips, laughter in her voice. "You see those apple pies in there? I worked my tail off making those, and far as I can tell your skinny backside could use one all for yourself … so sit back down."

"Yes, ma'am." Alex chuckled, but his body language was stiff. "Gotta check on Bo. He's tied up out front."

"Okay, then," Wanda waggled her finger at him. "You come right back, and bring that appetite of yours."

Clay waited until Alex had walked back into the house and shut the patio door behind him. Then he crossed his arms and caught Joe's eyes. "I'm worried about him," he told his friend.

A heaviness settled over the table, and Joe released a weighty sigh. "Anytime 9/11 comes up, it's the same way." He squinted in the direction where Alex had gone back into the house. "Kid's eighteen again, hearing the news for the first time."

Laura's shoulders sank forward and she looked at Eric, and then the others. "I'm sorry. I shouldn't have said anything. I forget he's still struggling."

"The man's not *struggling*. He's consumed." Joe shook his head. "Completely consumed."

"He doesn't have family in the area, does he?" Eric looped his arm around Laura's shoulders. "No girlfriend?"

"No family. And he hasn't talked about a girl." Clay uncrossed his arms and reached for Jamie's hand. She gave his fingers a gentle squeeze. "He lost his dad when the towers came down. Finished high school, took off for the West Coast and left his mom back in New York City. She remarried some time later. Alex rarely talks to her, from what little I've gathered." He looked back at the patio door. He didn't want Alex to find them talking about him. "There might've been a girl back then. Don't know where she is now or what happened to her, but there doesn't seem to be anyone now."

"That's why we include him in our barbecues." Jamie's eyes held a knowing look, an understanding that came from having walked the same path Alex was still walking. "Otherwise he's alone."

"If anyone can feel for the guy, it's us." The teasing was gone from Wanda's voice. A decade ago, after she and Joe divorced, Wanda moved to Queens and married a firefighter. He was killed in the Twin Towers, same as Jamie's first husband, Jake, and Alex's father, Ben. Yes, this was a group Alex could relate to, but there was one big difference between Alex and these couples.

Alex hadn't moved on, not by a long shot. Because of that, the people around the patio table had never shared with Alex their personal connections to 9/11. It was enough that their common ground instilled a deep compassion from the group, without getting into the details of the past. Someday, Clay hoped to dig a little deeper with the young deputy, but based on Alex's quick exit to check on his dog, that conversation probably wouldn't happen tonight.

They heard the slider again, and Alex walked out carrying a pie in each hand. He slid the door shut with the toe of his work boot and brought the pies to the table. "Alright, Wanda," the shadows were gone, but the walls around his heart remained. The flatness in his eyes was proof. "Let's check out these pies of yours."

She waved her hands at him and flopped back in her seat. "You do the honors, and make mine the smallest. Last thing I need's a big ol' slice of pie after that dinner!"

The children scrambled to the table for a taste of the dessert, and after a little while the older kids stopped their game long enough to finish off what was left. Jamie made coffee, and the women went inside to check out some vacation spot Laura wanted to show them online. Only the men remained around the table, drinking their coffee and watching the little ones.

"Congratulations on that award you got." Joe raised his brow at Alex. "You earned it."

"Thanks." Alex shifted in his seat. "Anyone could've won it."

Clay knew that wasn't true. The award went to the K9 team with the most arrests, and the fact was, no other team was close. "Your humility is admirable, Brady, but it's a fact. You and Bo are the best," Clay gave a firm nod. "The department's lucky to have you."

"Yeah, well ..." Alex gripped the arms of his chair and turned to Clay. He seemed anxious to change the subject. "So ... what do you hear about the REA?"

Clay exchanged a quick look with Joe. The SWAT division was hearing a lot about the group and the threat they posed to Los Angeles this year. Radical Environmental Activists, they called themselves. REA. Clay was newly in charge of the department's monitoring of the group, and Alex and Bo were one of the K9 teams specially trained to deal with the group's activity. Even so, Clay was careful how much he said. "We're watching them."

"They're trouble." Alex's answer was sharp. "We need to be proactive next time."

"There never shoulda' been a first time." Joe leaned on one forearm. "We had 'em on our radar back when they were just thinking up bad stuff." He flexed the muscles in his jaw. "I'm with you, man. We need to take 'em out."

"They're smart." Clay, too, wanted to round up the members and throw them in prison, but that wasn't possible. Not yet. "They're elusive and cunning. New members come alongside them all the time—like the REA is more of a mind-set than an actual group."

"Oh, they're an actual group." Alex's eyes hardened. "Eight of them, at least." He hesitated. "I found out where they meet."

Clay stared at the young deputy across from him. This was why he didn't want to say too much. Alex was driven to get the REA more than any other criminal group on the streets. He was a good deputy, worthy of the honors he'd received. But if he became obsessed, Clay would have no choice but to recommend Alex be taken off the case. He raised an eyebrow at the young deputy. "We've talked about this."

"I'm doing it by the book, Sarge." He didn't blink. "I'm just saying I have the information. When SWAT's ready, let's take this thing. The evidence is there." He took a swig of his coffee. "I've heard it from a lot of places."

They needed more than conversational evidence, and Alex knew it. Clay gritted his teeth and resisted the urge to continue with the topic. Of course the Special Enforcement Bureau knew about the REA—their headquarters and the scope of what they planned to do. But they didn't have a thread of physical evidence linking the group to previous acts of ecoterrorism. K9 deputies weren't intended to be part of the investigation—not until the time came for a search and arrest. Whether he was on the case or not, Alex had to be careful about spending his free time conducting quasi-investigations. He allowed the intensity to ease from his voice. "We're on it, Brady. We're watching."

Alex was quiet, his eyes locked on Clay's. "They're gonna hit Pasadena, the hills overlooking the city, right? That's the talk?"

Clay's heart skipped a beat, but he worked hard to keep his expression from giving anything away. Alex Brady was good. He might not have been in on every meeting, but he knew the department's deepest concerns. Almost as if he was getting information from the inside. Clay finished his coffee, relishing the few grounds at the bottom of the cup. "With the publicity they got last fire season, it's a sure bet there will be fires this year. The REA has fans even they don't know about."

"I think SWAT's wrong. I don't think it'll be Pasadena, Sarge." He lowered his voice and shifted his look to Joe. "They've got their eyes on Malibu, on that new development off Las Virgenes and Lost Hills … Oak Canyon Estates. The gated custom homes up there."

Even with temperatures in the nineties, a chill worked its way down Clay's spine. In meetings, the entire SWAT division had considered just about every possibility for the sites where fires might be set by the radical members of REA. The Oak Canyon Estates were certainly mentioned, but no one took the idea seriously. The gates would keep out arsonists after hours, and even a group as crazy as the REA wouldn't set fire to custom homes while people were around.

"Not possible." Clay heard his work tone kick in, the voice he used when he was training SWAT guys. "Wherever you're getting your information, forget about it, Brady. Let us follow the leads. When it's time to make arrests, you'll be there." Clay reached over and gave Alex a hearty pat on his shoulder. "This is your day off, man. Relax."

Alex nodded, slowly, thoughtfully. "Okay." He stood and looked first at Joe, then at Clay. "I need to go. Got to get Bo home." He mustered a stale smile as he turned and headed for the door. "Thanks for tonight."

Frustration poked at Clay. This was hardly the breakthrough he'd asked God for. "Be right back," he muttered to Joe. Then he stood and followed Alex to the patio door. "Wait."

Alex turned around, his smile gone. "Who am I supposed to tell, huh?" His voice was intense, but he kept it low so the conversation stayed between them alone. "I'm sure about this, Clay. Dead sure."

"There's an order to things in the department, Brady." Clay was more sorry than angry. "Let us take the lead. We're on it; I promise you."

Alex studied him a moment longer. "What if you're too late? Have you thought about that?" He gestured toward the hills. "Every bit of that canyon is filled with homes. People could die this time. A lot of people."

Again Clay didn't want to say too much. He could hardly tell the young deputy that the scenario he'd just hit on was the exact one the department brass were concerned about. Instead, he took hold of Alex's upper arm and held it, the way a father might hold onto his son. "We know that. Trust us on this."

Alex didn't try to pull away. He must've heard in Clay's voice that the conversation was over, and he looked down at a spot on the grass.

"Listen, Alex, what's eating you? The anniversary? Is that it?"

"No." Alex lifted his eyes, and they flashed with a sudden intensity. "September 11 is just another day. It's the next anniversary, man." He jabbed himself a few times in the chest. "That's what's eating me."

"Okay." Clay released his hold on the deputy. "I'm here, Brady. If you need to talk, I'm here."

Alex took a few seconds for his anger to dissipate, and then he managed the briefest smile, just enough to convey that his determination wasn't directed at Clay, but at the bad guys. He left and Clay watched him head through the house, stopping just long enough to thank Jamie and tell the other women good-bye. A few minutes later he heard Alex's truck start up out front, and the slight squeal of tires as Alex pulled away.

By then Joe had joined him beneath the covered patio. The two faced the children, who were chasing each other through the grass in small circles, giggling and falling down every few steps. "You know what it is, don't you?"

"Sure." Clay felt the full weight of his defeat that night. He'd hoped to invite Alex to church, talk to him about getting involved in the singles ministry. But the guy was a world away from that sort of invitation. "Kid's full of pain."

"That's only part of it." Joe crossed his arms tightly in front of him. "For Alex Brady, it's still September 11." He gave a strong shake of his head. "He's still stuck on that dreaded Tuesday morning."

Long after they'd moved the children into the house and slipped in a Jana Alayra music video, and even after the couples gathered around the nearby card table for a game of Apples to Apples, Clay couldn't shake what Joe had said, how perfectly he'd nailed the trouble with Alex Brady. The deputy had never moved on, never found his way to a life without his father. Sure, he was three thousand miles away from New York City, but not in his heart. And Clay had the feeling that on every call the kid felt the impact again, the Twin Towers crashing down, the bad guys winning bigger than ever before.

As the night wore on, for the first time Clay began to understand Alex's near obsession with the REA. In some ways the group wasn't that different from the people who had killed Alex's father. It was a sobering thought, because the REA was really nothing more than a group of terrorists whose weapon was fire. The same weapon used by al Qaeda. A weapon that could create utter chaos and destroy massive structures in a matter of minutes, one that actually could do the one thing Alex feared might happen:

Take innocent lives in the process.

THREE

The round of cards was finished for a few minutes, and Jamie walked back to the kitchen to make another pot of coffee. Around the table everyone was still laughing about how no one should play the game with Clay and Joe at the same table. The two could read each other without words or table talk.

Wanda was talking louder than the others. "I mean, please! We girls never have a *chance* at winning with you two around."

Jamie smiled to herself. She loved Wanda's spirit and Laura's quiet assurance. The three of them balanced each other, but even with all the excitement over the game, Jamie hadn't been able to stop thinking of one very memorable moment from earlier in the night. The look in Alex's eyes when the subject of 9/11 came up.

She moved to the fridge, took out the bag of fresh ground coffee, and measured the right amount into a new filter. Alex's eyes had looked both haunted and familiar, the same look she'd seen hundreds of times before in the eyes of visitors at St. Paul's Chapel—the little church that stood on the border of Ground Zero, the church where Jamie had volunteered her time for three years after her first husband Jake died in the terrorist attacks.

The stream of sorrow and heartache never ended at St. Paul's, and it would've never ended for Jamie if Clay hadn't walked into her life. She was better now, better here in Southern California, far from New York City with its scarred skyline.

Even still, the details were always close enough to touch. It was that way for anyone whose life had been changed by September 11. The tragedy created a bond that would remain among the survivors as long as they lived. So maybe God had brought Alex Brady into her life for a specific reason. She had moved on from St. Paul's Chapel, but she would always have a heart for people hurt by 9/11. If she could talk to Alex, perhaps find a minute alone with him, he might open up about his feelings.

The condition of Alex's heart reminded Jamie of something that happened to CJ last week. Their young son had run in from outdoors, whimpering about a pain in his toe. Jamie took off the child's shoe and sock, and there on the bottom of his big toe was a red area, hot and infected. At the center, with skin grown over the top, was a splinter that was causing all the trouble. Jamie performed minor surgery on CJ that afternoon and removed the offending piece of wood. After a day, CJ's toe was healed and whole again.

It was that way with matters of the heart. Alex would find no healing, no ability to move on and live again or love again until he dealt with the splinter of hurt and anger that clearly festered inside him. Maybe that's where she could help.

Show me how, God ... Give me an opportunity and I'll talk to him.

No distinct answer resounded in her heart, but Jamie felt an assurance. Somehow, in the coming season, she had a strong feeling God would indeed use her in the life of Alex Brady. Now it was up to Him to show her how that would happen.

She removed the old coffee filter, tossed it in the trash, and refilled the machine with fresh water. Even after meeting for dinner a dozen times, Alex didn't know the details about Jamie's first husband, Jake. He didn't know about Wanda's FDNY husband, either. Clay hadn't thought the information was necessary, at least not in the early attempts at friendship with the young man. But now it had been nearly a year since the first time Clay invited Alex over for dinner.

Jamie flipped the switch, and the coffeemaker began gurgling and spewing. She turned around just as her brother-in-law entered the kitchen, his coffee mug in his hands. For the smallest fraction of a second, she caught herself thinking Eric was Jake. The resemblance was still so strong, so uncanny. She had long since come to accept the fact that she would have that fleeting thought at times—the same way that once in a while Sierra would make a particular play on the soccer field or come home with an A on an essay and Jamie would catch herself making a mental note to tell Jake.

"You look a world away." Eric came closer and leaned against the kitchen island counter, opposite her.

"Thinking about Alex."

"Hmm." He crossed one ankle over the other. "Me too. He hasn't dealt with it."

"Not at all." Jamie pushed herself up onto the counter next to the coffeemaker. "That's why he's a deputy. Trying to make sure no one else suffers the kind of loss he's gone through."

"The job's bigger than he is." Eric's voice was marked by a familiar concern. "He needs to find a life outside work. The job'll destroy him otherwise." Eric set his cup down. "I know what you're thinking."

"What? You're a mind reader now?" Her voice was lighter than before, proof that she wouldn't linger in the past.

He could still look deep into her heart, and he did so now. "You think you can help him. The way you helped all those people at St. Paul's."

From the other room, the group was laughing again, but Jamie was quiet, letting the possibility drift in the air around them.

"Be careful." He angled his face, his eyes shining with a tenderness that underlined the connection they shared. "God moved you on from St. Paul's. Maybe Alex is supposed to be Clay's project. Clay and Joe's."

"Why?" She didn't feel defensive, but his thoughts surprised her. "Why not me?"

"Because it can consume you, Jamie. The way it did before." He paused. "You and Clay, you have something very special. You deserve to live outside the shadow of the Twin Towers."

The coffee finished percolating. Jamie slid her feet back down to the floor, took Eric's mug, refilled it, and handed it back to him. As she did, she met Eric's eyes and held them. "I'll never be completely out of that shadow." Her smile felt sad and small. "You should know that."

Empathy flooded his face. "I do." He touched the side of her arm. "Just be careful. Don't risk what you have."

His concern was genuine, and the warning hit its mark deep within her. "Thanks. I'll watch myself. I'm just not sure someone like Clay or Joe can reach him, someone who doesn't share that loss."

Eric took his coffee and moved back toward the living room. "You'll do the right thing, Jamie." He left her with one last smile. "You always do."

Jamie returned his smile, then grabbed hold of the fresh coffee. She carried it out to the others, refilled the cups of her husband and friends, and found her way back into another round of cards. But through the remainder of the night, as the game ended and the couples gathered their kids and said their goodbyes, even later as she washed her face at her bathroom sink, she couldn't shake the look in Alex's eyes, or the warning from Eric.

Would it really hurt to give the young deputy a chance to open up about his loss? Alex had no family in the area from what Clay knew, and even though Jamie was too young to be Alex's mother, she could take on the role for a short season, right? Or was Eric's concern valid, that she might become consumed once more with righting the wrongs meted out on 9/11?

Jamie pressed the warm washcloth to her face, wiping away the remains of her light makeup. The thoughts in her head all started because of the look in Alex's eyes ... A look of deep loss and pain mixed with a determination to find justice. Whatever the cost. The same look she'd seen in the eyes of the people who came through the doors at St. Paul's.

That's where she could help a guy like Alex. Because Jamie knew that sometimes the cost was too high, that a person could lose themselves in the quest to live for someone else, to devote one's days to redeeming the loss of someone you loved more than life. And that's what Alex was trying to do, at least it seemed that way. Live his life as a memorial to his father. Along the way, he was losing himself, and Jamie could certainly relate to that. Now if only God would show her the right time and place to share that truth with Alex.

Before his heart was so hard he wouldn't hear her anyway.

FOUR

Holly Brooks turned onto the steep gravel road and slipped her transmission into the lowest possible gear, the way she did every day at this hour of the morning. Sales at Oak Creek Canyon's newest phase of development weren't exactly overwhelming, but with the summer heat letting up and September right around the corner, her office was busier than usual.

Brightly colored red and yellow flags waved in the wind as she made her way up the mountain road to the single paved street half a mile up. No matter how many times she made the drive, the view from the summit never got old. Holly parked her Durango and stared at the panorama spread out before her. The view skimmed along the tops of several smaller peaks and then ended with the Pacific Ocean spread out in the distance.

I know, Lord ... the created things are proof You're really there. She tried to remember what it felt like to believe, to accept the things of God as easily as she drew her next breath. But life was complicated now, and when she tried to remember that sort of faith, she felt empty and flat. As if she no longer knew how to believe. She grabbed her leather bag and a stack of work she'd taken home last night and looked once more at the sight before her. The heaviness that resided in her heart swelled. *Okay, so if You're real ... why can't I feel You anymore?*

The quiet whisper echoed through her soul and died there. She dismissed the thought and checked her face in the mirror one last time. As she climbed out, the wind grabbed her thick, blonde hair, whipped it across her face, and blew it in a dozen different directions. Wind meant one dreaded thing. She hesitated and checked the horizon for smoke, for any signs of fire. The developers had held a meeting last week expressing their concern about the coming fire season. She might only have lived in LA for a few years, but she was well aware of the Santa Ana winds and the danger faced every fall by Dave Jacobs and anyone with a personal or financial investment in the hillsides of Southern California.

Holly pressed her way through the wind to the front door of the middle estate. Her office was set up in the front room of one of the most beautiful models in the new development. The house was enormous—more than seven thousand square feet—with no luxury spared. She slipped her key in the front door. The developers were here somewhere, overseeing construction on one of the eight spec homes being built up and down the spacious street on either side of the model.

It was an honor working for Dave. He was six-foot-two, with a presence that inspired loyalty and made other people want to catch his vision. And his vision was a great one. Never mind the criticism from environmentalists that was bound to come when a person spent his days developing the hillsides of Southern California. Away from his development company, Dave was involved in more charities than Holly could count. Every year he provided the material and labor for the construction of three houses for homeless families in the San Fernando Valley, and without fail he was the recipient of a number of philanthropic awards. With all that, his greatest moments were with his family—his wife, Lois, and their four children. With his wealth, he could've traveled the world. But his favorite vacations were simple and profound—trips to Michigan's Upper Peninsula where Dave would bird-watch and return to his work full of nature stories. No, his critics—especially the environmentalists—didn't have a clue who Dave Jacobs really was.

Holly set her things down. She would see Dave and his son, Ron, around lunchtime, but until then she would work alone. Something she liked least about her job.

She flipped a few buttons on the keypad just outside her office. Immediately, something by Rod Stewart worked its way from speakers hidden discreetly throughout the estate. Holly liked this radio station. It played the oldies her mother listened to, music that reminded her of home back on Staten Island. Holly turned up the music and sang along.

"Have I told you lately, that I love you ... Have I told you, there's no one else above you ..." The song reminded Holly of her dad. Long before his heart attack two summers ago, he seemed to know he didn't have long to live. He had called her up one day and told her that whenever he heard this song, he thought of his family. Holly turned her attention to her work. Two years might've passed since his death, but his memory still moved her to tears. It always would.

Just not here at work. She steeled herself against the loneliness and began filing the work she'd brought. She was twenty-five and single, heading toward a serious relationship with the developer's son, Ron. But nothing about her life was how she pictured it when she was in high school, back when she knew without a doubt that she and Alex would be married and having babies by now, back when nothing could've torn them apart.

Back before 9/11.

Holly hurried herself along. She had four appointments today, not counting walk-ins. Each would require a detailed tour, paperwork, and a discussion on financing. On top of that, there were follow-up calls to make and more documents to file. She was checking her calendar when a black Mercedes sedan drove up. Holly hadn't seen the car before, so she could only assume the obvious. Prospective buyers. She glanced at the decorative flags that marked the walkway to the front door. They weren't flapping as hard. Good. The wind had died down some.

The two men climbed out of the car and headed up the walk, both of them with straight backs and tailored suits, sure signs of their status in the business world. Holly met them at the front door, introduced herself, and welcomed them in. "How can I help you?"

"Actually, you can help *me*. My brother's just sort of along for the ride." The taller of the two pointed an elbow toward the bald man with him. "We work together and met for coffee this morning. I decided to show him what I'd found up here."

Holly tried to place the man. Anyone who had been through the model home or toured the neighborhood had to go through her. When she wasn't giving tours, the gates were shut at the base of the road, and no one could gain access up. "Have you been through before?"

The man chuckled. "Not officially." He held out his hand. "I'm Sam Baker. My wife and I drove by last weekend, but there were six other couples taking up your time." He grinned. "I told her I'd come check it out today, and if I liked it I could bring her back later."

Holly was surprised and slightly uneasy, but she didn't show it. Not once in the past few weeks had she been too busy to give a potential buyer the tour. There might've been one other couple walking the grounds, or even two, but six? Not lately. Still, she motioned for the men to follow her. "Let's take a look at the site map." She led them to a dramatic, glass-covered model of the development. "As you can see, only two of the homes in Phase Two are sold." She crossed the room and led them to a second detailed model. "The previous phase was larger. Twenty-five homes." She pointed to a cul-de-sac area. "Five homes remain for sale in that phase, but none of them have the views of Phase Two." *Or the sticker price*, but Holly didn't mention that.

The men stared a little closer at the second model and talked quietly between themselves. Holly was used to this, giving her customers plenty of alone time to talk openly about their likes and dislikes. But as the men talked, Holly noticed the shoes of the taller man. He wore beat-up tan loafers—the kind more suited for Dockers or jeans. *Strange*, she thought. Most business men shopping for homes in this price range wore the right shoes. Dark wing tips, fine Italian leather. She let the observation pass. "I'll go put together a packet for you." She smiled at the other man. He wore his baldness in an intentional sort of way. "Would you like one also?"

"Uh," he looked at his brother and shrugged, "sure. If you don't mind."

"Absolutely not." She returned to her office, but as she was putting the two packets together, her strange feeling about the men remained. She picked up her radio, the one that would signal the developers that she needed their help if any trouble arose in the model home. She clipped it to her belt and tried to get her mind around what it was about the men that bothered her. Maybe the one named Sam was trying to impress his kid brother, make it seem like he was on the verge of purchasing a five-million-dollar home. She'd certainly caught people lying about being in this affordability bracket. Whatever the reason, she was sure of one thing.

She'd never seen him up here before.

Holly returned to the men and handed them each a packet. By then they were fairly focused on the newer phase. "I don't have an appointment for another hour." She looked from Sam to his brother. "Do you have time for a tour?"

"Definitely." Sam smiled. "Tell me, what protection do these homes have against fires? The bigger brushfires?"

Something about the way he asked the question sent a chill down Holly's back. "Well," the question was a strange one, not the usual curiosity about square footage and lot sizes. But maybe because of the wind … "We have a sprinkler system around the perimeter of the development, and fireproof tile roofs on every house." She led them toward the front of the house. "Homeowners' dues will provide for brush clearing on an annual basis. That sort of thing."

She chastised herself for letting the man's question distract her. "Let's take a look through this estate first." She moved toward a sweeping staircase, marked by distinctly designed cherry wood and set against an entire wall of wainscoting and detailed high-end molding. "We call this model *Bella Noche*." For the next twenty minutes she led the men through the house, describing more than a hundred features, forcing them to linger in the rooms with the most breathtaking views.

The whole time she felt strangely nervous. Maybe because the men hadn't had an appointment, or because of the question about fire or the way the taller man's shoes didn't work with his look. Whatever it was, something about them didn't add up. She kept her hand close to her radio, ready in case the men threatened her in any way. But as the tour came to a close, Holly felt herself relax. The men were talking like any other potential buyers, going on about the benefits of being up here in the hills versus on the valley floor closer to the freeways, and wondering about whether this model or the one next door would better suit their needs.

"You have children?" Holly held her clipboard to her chest as they walked slowly toward the front door.

"Three, and they need all the space they can get." He rolled his eyes. "They don't exactly like each other."

"That's an understatement." His bald brother gave Holly a knowing look. "What is the square footage in the other models?"

"They range from sixty-five hundred to just under ten thousand." She felt proud of the fact. Not that she'd ever be able to afford anything close to the homes she sold, but the developers had done a brilliant job with Phase Two. Each estate took advantage of the limited flat land, and included oversized windows that let in every possible view.

Holly still had time, so she led the men outside and along the walkway that ran in front of the entire street of homes. At the end she pointed to the largest of the homes, one that was just being framed. "That's *Bella Grande*, the most spacious property in this phase."

The men seemed to take careful note of the place. "Sits right in the hillside." Sam seemed impressed with the fact.

"The developers made the best use of the natural topography, while maintaining a building pad large enough to include half-acre front and side yards."

"You have a picture of the place?" Sam's brother opened the packet he'd been carrying and thumbed through the glossy material inside.

"Yes. You'll find every model represented in the brochure." She pointed down the street. "The homes at that end will be finished first. The others have a completion date of next spring."

With that, the brothers seemed satisfied. Holly was walking with them back to the black Mercedes when Sam turned to her as if he'd just remembered a final thought. "I'd like to bring my wife up. How late are you here?"

"This is my long shift." She caught her hair in one hand so the wind couldn't whip it against her face. "I'll be here until nine o'clock, same as the late work crew."

Sam smiled. "Very good. Look for us sometime after dinner." The men left, and five minutes later Holly's first appointment showed up — a couple in their late fifties, with their realtor in tow. The hours melted away, and it was two o'clock before she knew it, the time each day when the developers took a break and met at the model home for lunch and an update on the sales prospects.

Ron Jacobs was the first through the door, followed by his father and a team of assistants. He found Holly in her office organizing a stack of follow-up sheets. "Hey ..." she stood, her voice soft. "How's the building going?"

He leaned against the doorframe of her office and smiled at her. "With everything my dad's built in these hills, this is it, Holly. The crown jewel. Best of the best." He came closer and reached for her hand. His fingers felt sweaty, the way they often did. "You were busy this morning."

She told him about the two brothers and about the others who had come with appointments. "The one guy, Sam Baker, will be back tonight with his wife."

"Good." Ron gave her hand a quick squeeze and released it. "That's what we're looking for. Return visits." He leaned down and kissed her cheek. "You're beautiful." He brushed a strand of hair off her face. "The windblown look suits you."

Her cheeks warmed under his gaze. "I'll be out in the kitchen in a minute."

"I have a few subs to check on, but we can spend the last few hours together. If you don't get too many walk-ins."

Holly nodded and waited for him to leave. As he did, she exhaled and stared at the pile of papers on the desk in front of her. Ron was a generally attractive man. Kind and diligent, a churchgoer who didn't ask more from her than she was willing to give. But he was a decade older than her and never married, a man for whom work and helping others came before anything else. Every other night there was a charity auction or benefit dinner, something that drew the attention of both father and son.

The one difference between Ron and his father was that Ron had never wanted marriage and a family. Development was his true love, something even he joked about. Holly had known Ron since she'd been hired by the company, but in the past year he'd shown a change of heart in his priorities. He'd stay late just to talk to her, and sometimes on slow afternoons he'd tell her that he was beginning to believe there had to be more to life than building beautiful homes and attending charity events.

Indeed.

Holly pulled a rubber band from the top desk drawer, gathered her hair behind her, and pulled it into a ponytail that hung halfway down her back. She cared about Ron, she did. No one else had come along, and there was no point living in the past, so maybe this was it — the man her parents had prayed for all those years when she was growing up. She wiped her still-damp hand on her black dress slacks and sighed.

At the same time, something caught her eye, a photo on the front page of the *Times'* Metro section. Even from this angle there was something familiar about the build of the man in the picture. Earlier she'd been too busy to even glance at the headlines, but now she rolled her chair to the left a few inches and as she did, the photo came into view. She gasped before she could stop herself.

Her lungs couldn't process the breath and again she tried to breathe while her heart dropped to the floor. The picture showed a stern-faced sheriff's deputy standing at attention, a trophy in his hand. Beside him was a stoic-looking German shepherd, his ears forward, body rigid and alert. Holly let her eyes fall to the caption beneath the photo because she had to see it, had to read his name in print before she could actually believe it. And there it was.

Los Angeles Sheriff's Deputy Alex Brady and his K9 partner, Bo, receive an award for excellence at a recent ceremony. Her eyes moved back to his, and she felt her heart limp slowly back to place. If it weren't for the distinct angles of his face and the way he held his broad shoulders back, she wouldn't have had a clue who he was. His eyes were so hard it hurt to look at him.

She brought the paper a little closer and studied him. *Oh, Alex ... you never made it back, did you?* Tears blurred her vision, and she blinked so she could read the rest of the caption. It wasn't long, not even a complete story. Just the fact that Alex and Bo had made more arrests than any other K9 team in the department for the second straight year. The only quote from Alex was a brief one. "I'm doing what I love."

Holly looked at him once more. The eyes of the Alex Brady she had known had been filled with light, same as his face. That Alex had spent his Sunday mornings at church and his weekends taking her on long walks, laughing over *Fresh Prince* re-runs, and whispering on the phone until late at night ... No one could dampen the life that spilled into everything they did together. Holly allowed herself to remember those years like she rarely remembered them anymore. There had been a time when she could look into Alex's eyes and easily know who he loved and what he loved and how much he loved.

But now? No matter what he said to the reporter, Alex's expression told a different story. That he didn't love anything or anyone at all. She took a last look at the paper, folded it carefully in half, and slid it into her bag for later. Still, even as she tried to tuck the memories away into the shadowy corners of her heart, they came back to life.

As vivid as they'd been in the days after 9/11.

FIVE

As far as Holly could tell, the change in Alex happened as soon as he got the news about the Twin Towers collapsing. Alex became a different person overnight, as if a piece of him had been buried in the rubble of Ground Zero.

She went to his house the morning of September 12, and his mother answered the door. The two of them hugged and cried, muttering about how maybe Alex's dad was alive, and maybe he would be rescued any minute. Finally, Holly took a few steps back and looked into the other room. Alex was sitting on the sofa, staring at the television. His eyes were red, his cheeks tearstained. Holly looked back at his mother. "Can I … can I talk to him?"

"You can try." She dried her cheeks, her tone weary. "He found out this morning that he wasn't allowed down there." She turned in his direction. "So he's watching it on TV."

Holly was heartbroken for him, but even so, she never expected the reaction she got that day. She went to him and sat beside him on the sofa. "Alex …"

"I can't talk." He didn't look at her. "Sorry, Holly … I have to watch this. I have to know." He stood and walked closer to the screen. "He's alive in there somewhere; I can feel it. They just need to get to him."

The pain in his voice frightened her, and she slid back deeper into the sofa. For two hours she stayed, wanting to help or hug him, trying to offer him some sort of comfort. But he was driven by the action on the screen, as if by watching carefully he could somehow will the rescue workers to find his father.

Alex stayed that way all day and for the next several days until the captains in charge of the rescue operation declared that the work had become a recovery. No one could possibly have survived the collapse of the towers and still be alive so many days later.

Again Holly went to him, but this time Alex met her at the door. "I can't talk." His eyes were dead, closed off in a way they'd never been to her. "My mom and I have a lot to work through, Holly. Try to understand."

She tried, and at first she figured he was in shock, the way most of the country and particularly the people of New York City were. But as the horrible days turned into weeks, his distance from her and indifference toward her remained.

Whereas before the attacks Alex had spent most of his free time with her, afterwards he wanted only to come home and study, or run at the track. He finished senior football season with his best numbers ever, but he seemed to find no joy in playing or in anything else.

"I'm worried about him," his mother admitted at one of the home games when Holly sat beside her. "He told me he doesn't believe in God anymore. Not if God could let all those firefighters die."

The weeks became months. Over Christmas break, Alex talked to her just once. "I've been a jerk, Holly. I know it." He looked at her, but not really. Not the way he used to. "It's like I can't feel anything anymore. Like I'm stuck or something."

Holly remembered one time that spring when they happened to meet after school in the 400 Building. He saw her from the other side of the hallway. Of course, he saw her. But he barely looked at her, and he never even slowed as he approached her.

"Alex." She called his name, and that was when he finally stopped and really noticed her.

"Hey…"

Holly felt strangely awkward, the way she had never felt around Alex. "Wanna go get something to eat? We need to talk."

His eyes never softened, never showed even a hint of emotion. "No, thanks. I have to get to work." He started walking away from her. "See ya, Holly."

So many times that year she had wanted to shake him, stop him in the school parking lot or in the cafeteria, and yell at him in front of the whole student body, if that's what it took. Because Alex Brady wasn't the only one suffering from the disaster of 9/11. At their school alone, nearly half the kids knew someone who died, someone who was hurt or grieving the loss of a loved one.

Support groups began meeting after school, and counselors were available for kids who couldn't shake their sorrow. But Alex was different from any of those. As far as Holly knew, he never once went for counseling or met with one of the support groups. Whatever he was feeling, he never voiced his sorrow or grief. Instead, he simply let the Alex Brady he had once been die. At the graduation party when school ended, he pulled her aside and gave her more of a window into his new life than he'd given her all year. "I'm moving," he told her. His look still wasn't the clear-eyed one she had known before, but his tone was kind. "I wanted you to hear it from me."

She asked him where he was going, and when he explained that he was headed out West to fight crime, she suddenly understood. His life, his heart, his days ... all of it had become taken up by one single focus — taking out the sort of criminal that had killed his father. A year later when she went to LA, she was sure he would've found his way past the hurt and anger. If he wasn't seeing anyone, she expected him to welcome her with open arms and apologize for how he'd acted. But not once since September 11 had she seen him look even remotely like the guy she used to love.

She had talked to his mother several times — mostly in the first few years after the terrorist attacks. "He's hurting, Holly. He won't deal with it, so the pain stays in his heart where it's killing him."

"Does he really think he'll find healing by seeking revenge?" Holly still loved him. She would've done anything to reach him, but she no longer knew how.

"It isn't revenge." Alex's mother sounded pensive. "He cares about the bad guys as much as the victims. Before he settled on law enforcement, he even thought about going into counseling. So he could help people change for the better — before they were capable of hurting society."

It was as if Alex was trying to become a real life Batman, a person incapable of sustaining relationships in his quest to right all the wrongs in the world. And for some sad reason — even though everyone who loved him could see the futility in his driving determination — Alex couldn't see it.

He still couldn't see it.

"Holly, you coming out?" Ron's voice rang out from the dining room on the other side of the house.

"Almost." She kept her tone upbeat because she needed this time, these few minutes. If for nothing more than to catch her breath.

She walked to the full-length window at the far end of her office and gripped the frame on either side. For just a few more minutes she wanted to live there again, in the past, back when she and Alex had all the world figured out, all eternity too. She could feel him beside her, hear the smooth richness of his voice as they walked along the path through Central Park on warm spring evenings. She could smell his cologne, the way it came off better on him than in the bottle and how it mixed with the mint of his favorite gum.

"I think I found a favorite Bible verse ..." he had told her on one of those days. "*For I can do everything through Christ, who gives me strength.*' That's gotta be one of the best."

Holly had heard it a hundred times before, but in that moment — with all the future stretched out before them — she might as well have been hearing it for the first time. After that, the verse belonged to both of them. Never mind the struggles that faced so many high school kids. They believed with God's help the two of them could do all things, absolutely anything.

His faith had been unshakable back then, and hers too. She closed her eyes and tried to hold onto the memory, the way his hand felt around hers, the easy way their steps fell at the same time as they walked side by side. *Alex, what happened to us? How did we let it slip away?*

Ron was talking to the other guys, and his loud voice interrupted the moment. The answer was obvious, of course. They didn't let it slip away. What they shared — the love and laughter, the quiet walks and determined faith — all of it came crashing down right alongside the glass and steel and bodies in the collapse of the Twin Towers. Alex had refused himself the joy of loving and living ever since then.

She heard Dave asking about her in the other room, and she blinked herself back into the present. Two years ago, seeing Alex's picture in the paper might've prompted her to find him again, call him, and at least reminisce about the beautiful days they'd left behind. But the eyes in the picture on the front page confirmed what she had only guessed before today. That there was no point ever contacting Alex again for one simple reason:

The Alex Brady she had known and loved no longer existed.

Six

Alex liked driving the Los Angeles freeways, whatever the gas prices. He didn't spend money on much else, so he could afford to drive. Besides, he wouldn't have traded his truck for anything. He drove a black Dodge Ram mega cab with a HEMI V–8—the kind of ride any environmentalist would hate, not that Alex would do anything about that. The truck was perfect for him—enough height to see over the LA traffic, power to go off-roading after work, and plenty of room for Bo in the back.

Still, Alex never once drove the truck to headquarters in Monterey Park. The last thing he wanted was for the bad guys to mark his Dodge and make him a target in his off-hours. Everyone knew the K9 deputies were headquartered at Monterey Park. So he did what a lot of deputies did. He parked his squad car at the Lost Hills station, eight miles from his condo. Every day he and Bo would get in his Dodge and drive to Lost Hills, where Alex would change into his uniform and share a few words with the local guys. The added driving was a good thing, more time to think about the calls behind him, the day ahead.

From Lost Hills, he and Bo would take his specially outfitted K9 squad car into headquarters. There was another benefit. If he saw someone suspicious, he might find a stolen car or a person with a warrant. The freeways belonged to the Highway Patrol, but if he caught someone tailgating or speeding, weaving in and out of traffic, or driving with expired plates, and if Alex had a suspicious feeling about the driver, he could run the plates. If the check turned up any sort of warrant, he could make a stop. He would leave Bo in the backseat with the air conditioning on, and quickly get to the heart of the matter.

He was halfway to headquarters, merging onto I–10 east when he spotted an older model Cadillac, deep orange and low to the ground. The car looked familiar. It took him a minute, but then he remembered. He'd seen it parked out front of an East LA drug bust a few weeks ago. Alex stayed with the car and after a quarter mile, he was convinced the driver was under the influence of something. He ran the plates and sure enough — the driver was wanted on a drug charge. He radioed in that he was pulling over a possible suspect and that he needed a CHP officer backup.

At first it looked like the driver of the Cadillac might gun it. But then the car swerved to the side of the road, and the driver slammed on his brakes. Alex pulled up behind him and left Bo in the car. The smell of alcohol hit him before he reached the guy's window. He was asking a few preliminary questions when, there on the floor, he saw a Ziploc bag of what looked like cocaine.

Alex radioed in the find, and in a few minutes two CHP cars pulled up behind his squad car. Half an hour later, the orange Cadillac had been impounded and the suspect was being hauled off — caught driving drunk and in possession of coke. Another drug dealer on his way to being locked up, and all before his shift even began.

It was the kind of morning that would've made Alex's father proud.

All told, Alex worked four overtime hours before his regular shift taking Bo through a couple of Compton area high schools and conducting three interviews at headquarters with TV reporters trying to learn more about the award he had earned. Alex didn't mind reporters. Any positive print was a good thing for K9 officers, helping the public understand the dogs and their high degree of training. More knowledge meant less fear and more public approval—all of which equated to the financial support the department needed to continue growing its K9 division.

His real shift started at four that afternoon, and for a while things picked up. A few drug arrests and a backup call on an unarmed suspect chase, one that ended with an arrest. But the late hours were unusually quiet. At midnight Alex checked out, and he and Bo headed back to the Lost Hills station.

Traffic was light, and after Alex made the transition north on the Ventura Freeway, he glanced over his shoulder. "You okay, Bo?"

The dog gave a single, sharp bark and moved about on his backseat.

"That's my dog. Good boy, Bo."

Alex kept his eyes on the surrounding lanes. No lawbreakers in this crowd, not that he could tell, anyway. He was sailing toward the San Fernando Valley when he clicked on his iPhone, glanced at the page of recent numbers, and felt the familiar thrill as he saw a missed call that read REA. He'd been waiting three days for this call.

He tapped the entry, and on the other end the phone began to ring. A quiet voice answered almost immediately. "Owl, here. Danny, this you?"

"The one and only." Alex rolled his window up tightly so he could hear every word. "Did you get the information?"

"I need a code, man. You know the routine." The man spoke in fast, jerky sentences. As if someone was holding a gun to his head.

"Green Night." Alex felt his body tense up. "Now tell me about the meeting."

"It's next week. Third Wednesday of August. The boss says we have to avoid headquarters for now. Thinks we're being watched." He laughed, but again it sounded strained, like he was high or something. "We're looking hard at OCE, did I tell you that?"

"You did." Alex swallowed, containing his fury, controlling it. "I've got the matches. Just tell me where and when."

"Go to the meeting. Nine o'clock at Chumash Park. First picnic table off the parking lot." He cleared his throat. "Gotta go."

Alex wanted more. "You got other ideas, Owl, or just OCE?"

"Too many questions. Don't miss the meeting." There was a click and then silence.

He cursed under his breath and tapped the End Call bar. His communication with someone deep in the organization at the REA had started two weeks ago. On his day off, Alex had pulled an overtime shift at the men's jail—something he was always looking for. The work gave Bo a day of downtime at home, and it helped Alex keep his ear to the ground. Pretty much the whole day was spent talking with other deputies, gleaning information about new gangs or wanted felons.

But that shift, Alex hung around a nineteen-year-old custody assistant, a skinny kid with dreams of being a deputy. The kid had a lot to say about one of his inmates—a guy who identified himself as a member of the REA. Apparently, the inmate had been talking, spilling his guts on everything the group was about. Alex wasn't surprised. One of the commonalities of ecoterrorists was that they were openly unrepentant for their actions. The more militant members saw themselves as righteous soldiers in a cause to save the earth, and often they didn't mind talking about their ideas.

"I listened." The custody assistant lowered his voice. They were sitting at a desk, but he clearly didn't want any of the inmates to hear him. "I think the con thought I was on his side, ready to sign up."

"I have a feeling you won't be a C.A. for long," Alex's heart beat faster. He hoped the compliment would make the kid talk. "So tell me about it ... what did the guy say?"

When the C.A. realized Alex's interest in the inmate, the kid shared everything he knew. Probably trying to impress Alex. When he left that day, Alex had a phone number and a code word—Green Night. He didn't expect much to come from the tip. He doubted it was even valid. But that afternoon he made the call and had his first brief conversation with Owl, as the REA guy called himself. After their second conversation, Alex was convinced the tip was legitimate. He told Owl his name was Danny, and he explained that he had a compelling desire to join REA. "I hate watching people rip through the world's resources like they're never going to run out," he told Owl.

Whatever else he said, Alex must've been convincing. Owl started talking, and before long he mentioned the Oak Canyon Estates. The information about the OCE had slipped, as far as Alex could tell. But it confirmed what Alex had feared all along.

The custom home development was next on the list for the environmental terrorists. Alex set his phone down on the console and stared at the empty stretch of freeway ahead of him. He reached back and scratched Bo's ear. "We're gonna get 'em, right, Bo?"

The dog whined his approval and nuzzled Alex's hand.

"You tell 'em. No one sets a fire on our shift." Alex sped up.

Environmental terrorists were not your typical street thugs, and they defied the definition of any other gang. They were educated and articulate, with an average income close to six figures. REA members didn't wear turbans or bandanas or heavy chains. They didn't shave their heads or tattoo their gang insignia on their arms. Instead, they drove hybrid or electric cars, rode their bikes to work, and kept mulch piles in their backyards. They shopped at Whole Foods, recycled everything from cereal boxes to plastic wrap, and wouldn't touch an apple unless it was organic. By day they held jobs at banks and advertising firms, tech corporations and telecommunication companies.

In other words, in a city like Los Angeles, they were absolutely mainstream, their agendas invisible and insidious. Most of them had started out as environmentalists, honorable people intent on being responsible and teaching responsibility in regards to the world's resources. Something everyone should be mindful of. But the members of the REA had allowed their devotion to the planet to become an obsession. A sick obsession.

Alex tried to picture the group meeting in clandestine locations, plotting the destruction of millions of dollars of other people's property and possessions. Not even concerned for the human life that might get in the way. He felt the familiar pain, the fact that he'd been unable to stop the al Qaeda terrorists from killing his father. But he could stop these terrorists. His father's memory was worth that much.

That anyone could be so crazed as to think that torching SUV's and burning down custom homes could ever help the environment. The idea was ludicrous. Alex tried to imagine what would happen if the members of the REA waited until a stiff Santa Ana wind and then set fire to a development like the one at Oak Canyon Estates. The mountains surrounding Las Virgenes Canyon would explode into flames, and, yes, lives could be lost.

Firefighters and civilians. Alex shuddered to think just how many.

Once he was in his own truck, he didn't head south the way he would've if he were going home. Instead, he took the freeway a couple exits the other direction and turned off at Lindero Canyon Road. He knew where the REA headquarters were, another tip from the custody assistant. Alex had been up here three times already, and again the tip checked out. The house was definitely a meeting place for the group.

Of course, Alex had tried to pass the information along to his sergeant, but the man wasn't interested. "We can only apply the law where people have broken it, Brady," the man told him. He was older and strictly by the book. "There's plenty of law breakers out there to keep you busy."

That's why Alex had tried to explain the information to Clay and Joe at dinner last weekend. Clay was overseeing the department's efforts against the REA, and Alex had a feeling Clay already knew the whereabouts of the group's headquarters.

But then why weren't they working harder to find enough evidence to make the arrests?

Alex had seen Clay and Joe in the break room at the Monterey Park headquarters every day since their barbecue last weekend, but the couple times he'd tried to bring up the REA, he'd been shot down.

"Don't get hung up on this thing," Clay finally told him.

"Do we have to wait for a fire?" Alex had to control his tone. "Is that what this is about?"

"You know the drill, Brady. We have to wait for a threat, at least. Like I said, they're on our radar."

Alex's patience on the matter was wearing thin.

He worked his truck up Lindero to the place where it veered to the right. The house he'd been watching was at the top of a winding gravel road, well into the brittle brush and dry grass that made up the Southern California hillsides. This was Alex's fourth visit up here, and each time he wondered why a group of fire starters would make their headquarters in a house that stood right in the path of fire danger.

Maybe the REA didn't care if their headquarters burned down. Less evidence that way. Alex felt his determination double. There weren't enough days in a lifetime to round up all the terrorists who would ever threaten the United States, but Alex would spend his life locking up the ones he could. And that included the members of the REA. He turned off his lights, same as last week, and took his truck off-road to a spot behind a covering of ten-foot-high wild shrubs. The kind of ground cover that made this fire season so volatile.

From behind the brush, he could still see through a small clearing. He angled himself so he could scratch Bo's ears with one hand while he held the pair of high-powered binoculars in the other. His heart reacted to what he was looking at. They were meeting tonight, same as last week. Wednesday night, well after midnight. Last week Alex happened to call at this time and hear voices in the background. Instinct told him he'd hit upon the group's secret meeting time, and sure enough, here they were.

He scanned the bumpers of the seven cars parked in front of the house. All of them had removed their license plates for the gathering—same as last week. Alex figured they probably stopped at separate spots on their way up, removed their plates, and didn't put them on again until they were headed back down the hill. He leaned against the headrest. This was a smart group, no question. They left no trail, donned none of the usual environmental bumper stickers. They were middle- and upper-class crazies who masqueraded as businessmen by day, terrorists by night.

He pulled out his phone again and clicked his way to the section of YouTube clips stored there. He'd bookmarked a dozen news videos about last year's brush fires later deemed to have been deliberately set, and now he called up one of the worst—a canyon fire started last year at a development in San Diego. Alex turned the volume down so Bo wouldn't wake up, and he let the clip play.

"Police believe the environmental terrorist group REA is responsible for the loss late last night of four model homes at a north San Diego hillside development," the announcer stated. The visual switched from the reporter to a wall of flames tearing through a series of homes. "Thankfully, the homes were empty at the time of the attack. A white flag was left in the front yard of one of the homes with spray-painted green letters that read REA." The shot switched to the jagged edges of a homemade flag fluttering in front of a raging inferno. The camera view changed again, and the screen showed four fire trucks on a dirt road with flames ten stories high on either side. "Firefighters narrowly escaped being caught in the ensuing brush fire," the announcer continued. Alex slid his finger across the video's progress line and watched that part again, and then a third time.

That must've been what it was like for his dad and the other emergency workers, trying to rescue people forty, sixty, eighty floors up in a building exploding with flames. He lifted his binoculars and stared at the tops of the few heads he could make out. If he'd had this type of bead on the al Qaeda terrorists before September 11, he would've called for the entire department to back him up, and together they would've brought down the group before a single plane could be hijacked. He felt the satisfaction of the imaginary scenario.

But then, before 9/11 he wouldn't have had any idea the destruction that could come from a meeting like the one taking place in the house up the hill. Life was one carefree day after another, and never for a single minute did he or anyone else think a morning would come when more than four hundred firefighters and police would go to work and never come home again.

He clicked off his phone and crossed his arms, holding down the memories fighting their way to the surface. When he could no longer keep them at bay, he stopped trying and let them come — wholly and completely, like ghosts from the past. On a night like this, the memories reminded him why he was fighting this war in the first place. But remembering, for Alex, wasn't something warm and comforting the way it was for some people.

It was a pain almost more than he could bear.

Seven

There was a place deep in the stony heart of Alex Brady where it would always be September 10, always that day before his dad left for work and never came back. Alex didn't go there often, but when the memories rushed at him the way they did now, he had no choice.

Holly Brooks lived down the street from him, and back in their elementary school days she was the yucky girl who tried to include herself with his group of friends on the way to class each morning. Alex would never forget the day that changed. He came in from a middle school football scrimmage, and Holly and her older sister were sitting at the kitchen table with Alex's mother.

"How was practice?" His mom stood and poured him a glass of milk.

Alex stood there — his helmet in one hand, shoulder pads in the other. He wasn't quite sure what he was feeling, except that his legs no longer felt attached to the rest of his body, and he couldn't force himself to look anywhere but at Holly. When had she grown up? And how had her hair gotten so long?

His mother seemed to notice he wasn't acting himself, so she laughed a sort of chuckle intended to put everyone at ease. "Holly and Heather were locked out of their house. Their mother had a doctor's appointment and forgot to leave the key."

Holly smiled at him. "Your mom said we could stay here." Her voice was soft and melodious, and in that single moment Alex felt his world slide off its axis. He nodded at her, downed his milk, and headed for the shower.

Things didn't change right away. But after that he would catch himself walking a longer path to get from one class to another just so he could say hi. By the time they were freshmen in high school, Holly was walking home with him every day. Her mom had a full-time career that fall and her older sister had a job after school, so Holly had nowhere to go but Alex's house.

That was the year when everyone else knew what neither of them was ready to admit. They were crazy about each other. Sometime that winter, Holly went to church with Alex's family for the first time, and that led to an all-night phone conversation that kept the two of them awake in their own beds, whispering to each other until the sun came up.

"So, what your pastor said about God being your friend? You really believe that?" Holly whispered.

"Of course." He stifled a laugh so his parents wouldn't hear him. "You can talk to Him anytime. Just like you talk to me."

The memories grated against his soul like splintered wood. Alex stretched his legs to the passenger side of his squad car. The irony of the long-ago conversation with Holly made him certain he'd never forget it. He hadn't talked to God since the September morning when rescue workers gave up the search for survivors. But before then, nothing could've rattled his faith. It was as rock-solid as the Twin Towers themselves.

Holly had questioned him some more, asked him about the Bible and how he could know without a doubt that what he was reading was true. It wasn't that Holly didn't believe in God. Her parents took the family to church on Christmas and Easter, and somewhere in the house there was a dusty old Bible handed down from Holly's great-grandfather. They believed like lots of people believed. That working in the background was a God who created everything. But believing never got more personal than that. Being with Alex, being his friend their freshman year, changed everything for both of them. Especially the way Holly thought about God.

That summer, the two of them went to a Young Life camp, and they grew even more serious about their beliefs. Late one night when campers were supposed to be in and cabin doors locked until morning, Alex met her out by the massive maple tree near the back of the camp. The night was warm, and frogs carried on a noisy battle in the distance as they sat side-by-side staring at the stars and holding hands.

"Someday we'll fly to a foreign country a million miles away and be missionaries. So we can share everything we're learning about God," Holly's eyes sparkled in the moonlight.

"Let's make it a country with a beach and warm water." They both laughed, and the air around them remained innocent. There was no kissing then and not for the next few months. Not until his family had a New Year's Eve party their sophomore year, and Alex found Holly looking at pictures in his family's living room.

"There you are." He brought her a glass of sparkling cider. "Come on, everyone's playing charades." He took a step toward the doorway. "You have to see my dad act out a chicken crossing the road. He's hilarious."

But she carefully picked up a framed photo of Alex's parents, arms around each other, laughing in some moment that belonged only to the two of them. "This is real, isn't it? The way they love each other?"

Her question caught him off guard. He looked from her to the photo and back again, confused. "Of course it's real." Only then did it hit him, the reason she was asking, the reason she never invited him to her house, but rather spent all her free time here. He closed the distance between them. "Your parents ... aren't like that?"

"No." Her smile was overtaken by the sadness in her eyes. She stared at the picture again. "Never." She hesitated, as if she wasn't sure how much to say. "They fight all the time, and my mom ... drinks a lot." She put the photo back on the shelf and turned to

Alex. "It's nothing major, I guess. Just …" she looked past him to the laughter in the next room. "… not like your parents."

Alex tried to think of something to say, some way he could fix the situation for her. Maybe if her parents talked to his, or if their two families started going to church together. He opened his mouth to tell her what he was feeling, but before he could say anything, the moment passed. Her sorrow lifted and she took his hand. "Let's go see your dad be a chicken."

They were hurrying from the room when they spotted a piece of mistletoe hanging from the doorframe overhead. Alex was never sure who stopped first, but suddenly there they were, standing under the mistletoe, giving each other a look that was half teasing, half scared to death. Alex made the first move. He put his hand on the side of her face and tenderly touched his lips to hers. Neither of them knew the first thing about kissing, so the moment was over as soon as it began.

But as they headed back to the living room, as they sat together on the sofa and watched his dad strut around the room making chicken noises, they shared a secret that belonged to them alone.

He tried to release the memory, but he wasn't completely successful. Behind his seat, Bo stretched and did a noisy yawn, and Alex turned to his K9 partner. He was moving his paws in his sleep—something he did often, especially on days when he hadn't gotten enough running, or when he was anxious for some work on the job. "I'm with you, Bo …" he looked back at the house where the REA members were still gathered. "I'd love a little action right now."

But the men didn't seem to be leaving anytime soon, and the memories fighting for his attention weren't either. He leaned forward and rested his arms on the steering wheel. Things between him and Holly never really tipped into the physically complicated territory most kids found themselves in. The two of them hardly ever kissed, and when they did their kisses were quick, more like an act of friendship. Almost as if they knew from the beginning they couldn't have it both ways. They could choose a sweet love rooted in faith, or the steamy backseat affair their friends were all about. The former gave them a friendship much stronger than the transient relationships of their peers, and by the time they reached the summer before their senior year, the summer of 2001, Alex and Holly were inseparable.

By then her parents must've seen what Alex's family shared, or the fact that their youngest daughter preferred being at the house down the street rather than at home. Whatever it was, Holly's parents began coming to church each week with Alex's parents, and Holly's mother stopped drinking. The two families were together often.

Alex closed his eyes and whispered her name, the way he hadn't said it in years. "Holly, girl … I hope you found someone better than me …"

Suddenly, there he was in the Adirondacks hiking the trail around Elk Lake with his parents and Holly and her family. The July humidity hadn't been as bad as back on Staten Island, and the forecast of thunderstorms never materialized. It was the third Saturday of the month, and Alex had that wonderful feeling summer would go on forever.

The parents were up ahead on the trail, and Holly's sister was with them. Alex slipped his fingers through Holly's and slowed his pace. "So … seniors this year."

"Shhh." She giggled at him, her blue eyes dancing. "That's against the rules, silly."

"What rules?" He loved this about her, the way she kept their relationship fun and full of laughter.

"You can't talk about school when we're right in the middle of summer. Otherwise it'll disappear …" she pulled away from him, her eyes bright with teasing, "like this!" She darted down a tree-covered hillside off the main trail, daring him to follow her.

"Hey!" He ran after her, but with so many trees he lost her almost right away. He was about to call her name when she jumped out at him from behind a huge trunk and grabbed his waist.

"Gotcha!" Her giggle was quiet, muffled by the canopy of branches and trees. She shifted herself so she was in front of him, then put her finger to his lips. "No more talk about school."

"Okay." His heart was pounding, his breathing fast from the chase and the electricity between them. He searched her eyes, her face, and watched as the humor fell away and left behind a longing that had always been there, a longing so deep Alex wasn't sure he could draw his next breath without her. "Holly ..."

She could feel it too ... her smoky eyes told him that much. "We ... we need to get back on the trail."

"All I need," he drew her closer and kissed her, "is you." The headiness of that kiss, the intoxicating way it felt to have her in his arms alone in a place where only God could see them, left him no choice but to tell her how he was feeling. He let himself get lost in her eyes. "I love you, Holly."

"I know." Joy filled her face and she took the slightest step back, giving the passion between them a chance to dissipate, allowing a way back to familiar ground. She giggled and turned around, running back up the hill toward the trail.

"Wait!" He ran after her and when he'd nearly caught her, she faced him again and he searched her eyes. "What do you mean ... *you know?*"

"Because ..." Her hair framed her tanned face, and she'd never looked more beautiful. "... I've loved you since that day in middle school at your parents' kitchen table." She tilted her head, only partly serious. "Same as you." She was off again, back onto the trail where they were in view of the others, safe from the power of their feelings.

But before the camping trip ended a few days later, Alex and Holly walked to the lakeshore one night and sat together on a tree stump, watching the moon on the water. Alex avoided kissing her, because out there … well, out there if he started he wasn't sure he could stop. Instead they talked about a Bible verse from Jeremiah 29, and how God knew the plans He had for His people.

"You know what I hope?" Holly's voice mixed with the breeze off the lake and washed over him in a way he could still remember.

"What?" He couldn't take his eyes off her. "What wonderful thing do you hope for, Holly Brooks?"

She smiled. "I hope God's plans for me always include you."

"They will." His answer was as quick as it was certain. "Because I meant what I said a few days ago." He touched the side of her cheek, wanting her to see the seriousness in his eyes. "I love you, Holly."

For a long time neither of them looked away, and with indelible ink the moment wrote itself across Alex's heart. Finally Holly touched her fingers to his, her eyes seeing deep inside him. "I love you too. So don't ever leave me, okay?"

"I won't." He pulled her close, and she rested her head against his chest. Alex was never sure how long they stayed there that night. The fact was, in some ways no matter how much he tried to let go of her memory, she was still there. Sitting beside him in the moonlight in the Adirondacks, knowing they would never leave each other for anything.

Alex took a deep breath and again willed the memories to leave. He squinted at the house ahead of him. Still no movement, so maybe tonight wasn't the night to catch them in the act. But that didn't discourage him. As long as he knew their meeting place, he'd be back, and their meeting would break and he'd follow them down the hill until they put their plates back on, or maybe he'd come on a day that wasn't Wednesday and the house would be empty and he could look around, maybe stumble onto something that gave him probable cause to search the place.

He turned the key in the engine, kept his lights off, and slowly pulled out of his hiding place in the bushes. Bo stirred in the back, and Alex heard him scramble to a sitting position.

"It's okay, Bo ... we're going home." Alex waited until he was halfway down the winding road before he turned on his headlights and picked up speed.

The thing that bothered him most about Holly was that he'd hurt her. Even after his dad died in the terrorist attacks, the last thing he'd wanted was to harm her in any way. He tried to explain it to her, that when the terrorists had killed his dad, they'd killed something inside of him too. He couldn't love like he'd loved before.

He wanted to live his life as a memorial to his father, and that left no room for relationships. Holly didn't believe him at first. She figured all Alex needed was to work through his anger and loss, and they could be fine again, the way they'd been before. But she was wrong. The part that laughed and loved and trusted God wasn't broken inside Alex; it was gone. Forever gone. And he could never subject Holly to a lifetime with someone who was no longer capable of those kinds of feelings.

He reached the on-ramp and sped up as he entered the Ventura Freeway again, this time south toward his townhouse. He hadn't talked to her in many years, and that could only be good for Holly. By now she would've met someone kind and trustworthy, someone with the faith he'd walked away from. He tightened his hold on the steering wheel. Yes, she was probably married and starting a family, smack in the middle of a life she perfectly deserved.

His precious Holly.

Because it wasn't that he no longer cared about her, and that's the part he never could get her to understand. No one would ever take Holly's place in his heart. He would die for her right now if it meant assuring her happiness, giving her the life she had dreamed of having all those years ago on that moonlit night by the lake. No matter how he tried to explain himself, Holly couldn't see that his care for her was what forced him to leave, what drove him to load up his car and move as far away from New York as possible. She didn't understand that releasing her was maybe his greatest and final act of love, because it nearly killed him to do it. But in the end he had no choice. The part inside him that could've made Holly happy the rest of his life was no longer there. It was dead.

In its place was a gritty, larger-than-life determination to take out the evil around him. If God was going to stand by and watch while four hundred firefighters and police officers lost their lives on 9/11, then Alex would use every waking hour he had making sure it wouldn't happen again. He would do the job himself. He wouldn't fight the fires; he would protect the firefighters. He would protect the whole city, for that matter. Taking down one bad guy after another was his single focus. Alex Brady and Bo against the world; that was his life now, and it left no room for anyone else. Not his mother, who had remarried some guy Alex didn't even know, not his friends back in New York or the God he used to trust. And especially not Holly.

Even if her memory haunted him as long as he lived.

Eight

Clay was at the Monterey Park department headquarters about to work through a series of tactical drills with a dozen SWAT officers when the call came across his radio. Hostage situation at a bar in East LA, two fatalities confirmed, eight people trapped inside with the gunman. But the detail that grabbed Clay's heart and made him jerk his radio from his belt so he could hear more clearly was this one: The standoff was taking place across the street from an elementary school, where more than five hundred students were in session.

Joe must've heard the call at the same time, because he jogged over from the group he'd been working with, his eyes wide. "Captain's made the call. He wants both our units on the scene immediately."

"Got it." He welcomed the familiar rush of adrenaline, the way his heart pounded into action as he signaled his men and explained the situation. In a hurry, Clay's and Joe's groups both ran the distance across the field to the station, where each man made sure he was doubly armed, and in less than five minutes they were in a convoy of squad cars racing through the streets. Halfway there, Clay heard the call for the closest K9 unit to respond, also.

A moment later Alex's voice came over the radio. "Ten-four. On my way."

Dispatch updated them with the latest details. Four squad cars were already at the scene, and communication had begun between them and the gunman. The guy was heavily armed, threatening to kill the eight hostages in the building, then hit the school.

Clay gritted his teeth. If the guy ran, he'd be taken out in a matter of seconds, but maybe not before he sprayed a load of bullets at the school. He added his voice to those crossing the police radio waves. "We'll send a couple of our cars to the school. Make sure the kids are rounded up on the other side of the building, away from the shooter."

"Ten-four, Sergeant Michaels. We'll contact the school principal and tell them you're on your way."

"ETA three minutes," Clay barked. His sirens were on and he was in the lead, clicking the stoplights so they'd be green as the line of squad cars reached each intersection. His mind raced with possibilities. What if the gunman wasn't working alone? If he was making threats about the school he could have one or several accomplices ready to take hostages in the building. The school was in lockdown mode, but that didn't protect the teachers and kids inside from an aggressive attack, from bad guys willing to bust through windows or shoot their way through doors.

Clay picked up his radio again. "Reynolds, you copy?"

"Copy, go ahead."

"Have your guys surround the school. Every side. We don't want anyone getting in that building."

"Roger that." Joe didn't need an explanation. He and Clay handled the big calls like they were thinking with one brain. Together they were known as the smartest SWAT officers in the department. It was the reason they'd both been promoted to sergeant, in charge of training the new guys.

But a call like this one would test everything they knew about police work. As they rounded the corner, they saw the squad cars ahead and the barricaded traffic barriers, and Clay did what he always did at this point in a call. "Please, God, be with us ... give us Your eyes and Your wisdom, Your strength and Your protection."

He could hear the adrenaline in his raspy, whispered voice. "Go before us, God … in Jesus's name, amen."

For a fleeting moment he thought about Jamie, about how well she handled his job and the possibility that on any given day Clay could take a call like this one and lose his life in the process. But as soon as the thought hit, he dismissed it. He and Jamie lived their lives based on trust in God. Life was His to give, and one day it would be His to take. For every person walking the earth. As for this specific call, Clay believed he was coming home at the end of the night. God was with him; he could feel His presence, His guidance.

He screeched his squad car to a stop, using another parked squad car as a cover. The other men did the same thing, creating a series of objects they could hide and duck behind as they worked to surround the front and back doors of the bar. In his peripheral vision, Clay watched Joe and his men whip around the opposite corner and head for the front of the school. In two minutes the building would be surrounded, and the danger to the students would be almost entirely eliminated.

Clay focused on the volatile situation at hand. The bar was a small single-story brick building with dark windows and a limited parking lot. Six civilian cars sat in the lot, three facing the establishment, three facing the road and the school across the street. From what he could tell, the three facing the bar were empty, but he wasn't sure about the others.

"Benson," Clay nodded to the SWAT officer nearest him. "Keep an eye on the cars facing the road. Look for an accomplice."

"Yes, sir." Benson stayed low and scrambled to the last row of squad cars, his gun pointed in the general direction of the parked cars facing the road.

One more threat down.

Clay needed to work his way around to the left side of the building, the corner closest to the front door. That was where a deputy now hovered, gun drawn, using a bullhorn to talk to the gunman.

"I said, 'Put your guns down and come out with your hands up,'" the deputy shouted the words, and they echoed loudly through the parking lot.

There was no response, but at that moment Alex's squad car squealed to a stop a few feet from where the initial deputies were gathered, at the left corner of the building. In seconds, he was out of the car with Bo on a leash and ready to go. He positioned himself adjacent to the officer with the bullhorn, gun raised in one hand, Bo's leash tight in his other. Clay watched Alex give his dog a command, and immediately the dog began barking, straining at his leash.

Suddenly, there was an explosion of glass as the gunman kicked his foot through the front window of the bar. "Hey!" he screamed. He used his elbow to push out the rest of the windowpane, and at the same time let loose a string of expletives. "Get the dog outta here or I start shooting!"

Clay was the sergeant in charge of the scene, and he signaled to Alex. Instantly, Alex uttered another command to his K9 partner, and the dog stopped barking and sat stone still at Alex's side.

The gunman waved an assault rifle through the broken window. "I want a thousand dollars, you hear me?" he shouted. His voice was wired and crazed — the guy had to be high on something. "Hear me? I want a thousand dollars."

One of the deputies took the bullhorn and brought it to Clay. He was still using a squad car for cover, his gun in his hand, finger on the trigger. He had a direct shot at the guy, but he wouldn't shoot unless he had to. He raised the bullhorn. "This is Sergeant Michaels. You're surrounded by SWAT officers. The game's over, so put your gun down and come out of the building with your hands up."

Another string of cuss words came from the guy. "I'll kill every one of you!"

"No, you won't." From the corner of his eye, Clay saw Alex stay low with his dog, moving from the cover of one squad car to the next. Clay wasn't sure where the deputy was going, but he hadn't been ordered to move. He raised the bullhorn again. "Put your gun down and come out with your hands up."

Deputies were in place all around the building, but they needed to wait, take their time. They couldn't rush a hostage situation like this, not when innocent lives were on the line inside the building. Clay was about to give the gunman another directive, when from behind him he heard a car door and a round of gunfire. A man started, "I've got the school ... I've got the school!"

A bullet grazed the side of Clay's vest as he took cover low between two squad cars. He turned in time to see the entire drama unfold in a handful of seconds. Alex had maneuvered himself to a position behind the row of parked civilian cars, so when the second gunman leapt from one of them and started shooting, Alex was in position to take him down.

The commotion brought the first gunman scrambling out the broken front window, shouting for his friend, gun raised. But before he could spray the scene with bullets, Bo burst across the parking lot, flew over the hood of a single parked car, and landed on the perpetrator, biting hold of his arm and flinging him to the ground. His assault rifle fell to one side, and the man screamed for help. All the while Bo continued to bite, wrestling with the man and keeping him away from his weapon.

With the situation stable, the SWAT team immediately surrounded both gunmen and Alex ran to his dog. Once the first gunman was cuffed, Alex called out to Bo. "Release!"

Instantly, the dog relaxed his bite hold on the man and returned to Alex's side, panting and ready to make another attack if necessary. Clay watched the entire scene from his place with three other SWAT members, all of them with guns drawn and aimed at the second gunman. The man had lost his weapon, and he was bleeding out, too injured to be a threat.

"We need an ambulance," Clay radioed. "We have a gunman down."

In a hurry, paramedics came for the second gunman, and another pair tended to the bite wounds on the arm of the first guy. After that, deputies loaded the less-injured gunman into a squad car and took him to the men's jail. By then, Clay and several of his men had rushed the building and released the hostages. The coroner's office came for the two bodies inside the bar – both employees. Each of the hostages had to be questioned, so Clay assigned four detectives to the task. By then Clay had already informed Joe that the situation was diffused. Joe promised to lead his men in a complete check of the school and then give the principal the okay to call off the lockdown.

Only after all that was finished did Clay find Benson talking with the other SWAT guys. Clay pulled him aside, frustrated. "What happened back there?"

"I didn't see him, sir. I was watching the cars like you told me, but I had to keep an eye on the gunman too." Benson blinked, apologetically. "I … I didn't see him."

Clay touched his fingers to the side of his uniform, where an indentation on his vest told him how close he'd come to taking a bullet. Alex had saved his life today, and possibly the lives of every SWAT officer whose back was to the second gunman. But he'd done it by breaking protocol, by leaving his post and handling the scene his own way. Again. Clay scanned the crime scene. "Where's Brady?"

"In his car, sir." Benson clearly felt terrible about the situation. He hadn't done anything wrong, specifically, and he wouldn't be written up. But missing the second gunman was a big mistake. Clay strode across the parking lot to the place where Alex's squad car was still angled next to the left side of the building. Alex was sitting in the driver's seat, door open, his feet on the ground. Inches away sat Bo, still ready if he was needed. Water dripped from the dog's jowls, and a half-empty bowl sat next to him on the ground.

Clay studied the young deputy, the emptiness in his eyes, and he thought he understood what the guy might be thinking. The reprimand could come later. "He's still alive. For now, anyway." Clay leaned against the building so the two were facing each other. "You had to shoot him."

Alex didn't respond, didn't blink. He looked like he was too far away to connect with the moment.

A sigh came from Clay, his body drained from the intensity of the scene. "I've been there." He lifted his eyes to the smoggy pale blue sky overhead. "It was a day like this one, routine traffic stop on the Ventura Freeway. Turned out to be a carjacker wanted for murder." Clay remembered the incident like it was happening still, right now, before his eyes. "I pulled him over, but before I could leave my car, he was running toward me, firing at me. I had no choice but to return fire, and that was that. The guy died there on the side of the road."

Alex seemed to return to the present. He patted Bo between the ears and looked hard at Clay. "One less bad guy on the streets, right?"

His answer was understandable, but it didn't sound like Alex, and it didn't match the deep pain in his voice. No matter how many bad guys he arrested or took out, their loss of freedom or life would never bring his father back.

Clay leaned against Alex's squad car. "You didn't have permission to leave your location. No one told you to take Bo to the other side of the parking lot."

"I had a feeling." There was no apology in Alex's eyes. "I saw something move in one of the cars, and I wanted to be ready."

"In police work it's not about what *you* want. Orders are meant to be followed." Clay struggled with the reprimand. After all, it was Alex's instinct and feelings that prevented a tragedy today.

"I was following orders, sir." Anger flashed across Alex's face. "I was instructed to provide backup. Me and my partner did that."

Clay thought about that. Alex had a point. He hadn't specifically been assigned to any one area, only to provide backup. The fact that he'd moved from one spot to another without exact orders wasn't — on its face — a violation of instructions.

Three SWAT guys passed by then, and one of them — Benson — pointed at Alex. "Bravest police work I ever saw, Brady. Way to go."

Alex nodded his thanks at the guy and returned his attention to Clay.

Futility washed over Clay regarding the situation. Any discipline now would be little more than a joke. Everyone on the call that day would've agreed with the comment from the SWAT deputy. Alex and Bo had acted on instinct, yes, but they were heroes for their actions that day. Nothing less.

Clay massaged his temples and released an overdue sigh. "You know the book. You'd established position, and because of the danger in the situation, you needed to receive permission or instruction before moving."

"I saw something suspicious in one of the parked cars." Alex knew the book, knew it well enough to know that by stating he'd seen something suspicious, he created cause for leaving his implied post. For all his passion and determination on the job, he never broke the rules.

Clay narrowed his eyes. "Tell me something." He hesitated, as if he was trying his best to read Alex's mind. "Did you see the suspect's gun before you opened fire?"

Alex held his stare but only for a few beats. When he looked down, the answer was obvious. "I saw a gun." He looked up. "Yes, sir."

Clay didn't want to push the issue, didn't want to force Alex into a corner that would leave neither of them a way out. Alex was well aware of the rules, no question about that. But the thing with police work was that sometimes the rules didn't quite fit. He took a step forward and put his hand on Alex's shoulder. "You worry me, Brady. You rely a little too much on instinct." He thought about the conversation they'd had the other night over dinner, the one about the REA. But this wasn't the time to bring up examples. "I will say that in this situation, Benson is right. You acted on your instincts and you saved lives." He patted Alex's back. "Mine included. You did good today, Brady. Very good." He stooped down and patted Bo beneath the chin. "You too, Bo. Good work."

The dog cocked his head to one side, but he stayed otherwise motionless at Alex's side.

Alex spoke to him. "Down, Bo." The dog cast loyal eyes in Alex's direction, then he stretched out his front paws and laid down on the asphalt, at ease.

"That's a heck of a dog you've got there." Clay had been around K9 units every day for the past three years, the entire time since he'd been promoted to SWAT sergeant. Always, the connection between deputy and dog was a strong one, but the bond between Alex and Bo was in a category all by itself. "How did he know to go for the other gunman, the one standing in the window?"

"I already had the guy in the parking lot." Alex stroked his hand along Bo's back. "We're a team."

"Right." Clay felt his heart go out to the young deputy. The guy was such an island, so cut off from everyone but his dog and his job. Clay took a step back. "Well, anyway, regardless of how it happened, you made the department proud today, Brady. I mean that." He hesitated. "Just be careful."

Alex peered up at him, squinting in the midday sunlight. He didn't smile, and none of the emptiness from before faded even a little. "Thanks, Sarge. I appreciate that. I'll try to look for permission next time."

It was the right answer, but that's all it was. Clay understood. The thing that drove Alex Brady to fight crime lived deep within him, not on the pages of a sheriff's department handbook. He gave Alex a final pat on the shoulder. "Get your dog some lunch, Brady. See you back at the station."

Clay finished with his paperwork and made sure the detectives had everything they needed. Then, after every other SWAT deputy was released back to the station, Clay walked to his car and left the scene. The whole drive back he tried to put his finger on exactly what was bothering him about the call that day, why he wasn't as in awe of Alex's work as everyone else.

He rolled down his window and rested his arm on the door, letting the warm late summer breeze wash over him. *Help me, Lord ... am I being too critical?*

A Bible verse flashed in his mind ... one he'd come across last week in the early hours of the morning, the time of day when it was just him and God, getting ready for another shift. The verse was from Proverbs, chapter 14. *There is a way that seems right to a man, but in the end it leads only to death.*

What did the verse mean in relation to the prayer he'd just uttered? Clay focused on the road and sorted through the possibilities. Certainly the Scripture applied to the bad guys. It described everything about them. But how did it work for someone like himself, or Alex? Clay slowed his car, wanting to stretch out the trip back. When it came to Alex, Clay had avoided talking about the one way the young guy could find peace — a rock solid faith in Christ. Clay was waiting for the right opportunity, the barbecue when Alex didn't seem so intense, or the moment when talking about God felt somehow appropriate.

But what if that moment never came? There was a way that seemed right to man, but in the end it would lead only to death, right? So the verse certainly applied to the young deputy. Clay doubled his determination. He would find a chance to talk to Alex about his beliefs, even if the timing didn't feel right. Even if it created the most uncomfortable moment in Clay's entire life. Certainty girded up his determination. He would seize the next possible opportunity.

Because the way that seemed right to Alex was whatever his heart told him, possibly even taking the law into his own hands. Everything Alex did, the way he was courageous on a crime scene, the way he worked with his dog, and the stony look of determination in his eyes — all of it told anyone watching that Alex Brady had one way that was right to him. He was responsible for eliminating any crime he came across without the help of anyone. Not even God.

That would never work, of course. One of these days, Alex was going to reach the end of himself, because no man could eliminate all the evil around him. Dealing with evil was something only the Lord could do, and in His timing He most certainly would deal with it. Clay was sobered by the truth, as if a new awareness had dawned on his understanding of Alex Brady. As he finished the drive back to headquarters, he prayed fervently for Alex, that the ways that seemed right to the young deputy would indeed take him to the end of himself, and that when he reached that place he would not find death.

But life, the abundant life God planned for him.

NINE

Jamie took CJ to preschool that morning and stayed to read to the children. She didn't know about the hostage situation or that Clay was on a SWAT call until that afternoon when she and CJ were driving home from the supermarket.

"Cookie, Mommy?" CJ patted the back of the passenger seat and strained against his belt so he could see her. "So hungry, Mommy!"

"We'll have a snack at home, okay buddy?" She turned and patted his chubby hand. "Mommy will slice up an apple for you."

Jamie turned up the radio and caught a news reporter mid-sentence. "— the situation on the hostage crisis earlier today. What we now know is that shots were fired at members of the LA County SWAT team. Two people are dead, and the two shooters are in custody. We'll update you as we gain more information on the —" Jamie slammed the radio off and grabbed her phone from her purse. *Not Clay, God ... please, not Clay.*

I am with you, Daughter ... I am here.

The blessed assurance was instant and all-consuming. She had lived in fear each day being married to Jake Bryan, worried sick that every call would be his last, refusing to believe in a God who would allow firefighters to die. Only after he was killed on September 11 did she finally make peace with God and realize the great ocean of strength and peace that came from putting all of her life in His hands. She could hardly pick up her old habits now.

"Mommy? What's 'a matter?"

"Not now, baby …" she held her finger to her lips. "Give Mommy a minute."

She exhaled. *Thank You, God … I hear You. I feel You here with me.* Her hands were shaking, but she felt stronger than before, ready for the news. Whatever the news. She was about to slide open her phone and call Clay when the ringer went off. A glance at the screen told her it was her husband, and relief rushed over her. She answered the call and held the phone to her ear. "Clay, is that you?"

"Yes, baby."

His voice worked its way through every cell in her body. "Thank You, God." She was breathing fast. "I just heard the news."

"This was the soonest I could call. I'm on my way back to the station."

"What happened … two people were shot?" She couldn't will herself to ask if the victims were from the department.

"It was bad. We were all out there, Joe and his men too. None of the guys were shot, but it was close." He breathed deeply. "A couple of crazed gunmen."

"The news said a K9 deputy got one of them."

"Alex. He and Bo were closest to the scene when the call came in." He sounded worn out. "I'll give you the details later, but Alex shot one of the guys just as he fired at our backs. At the same time, he released Bo to get the other one."

Jamie wasn't surprised. "Oh, Clay, I am so glad he was close by."

"Definitely." Clay hesitated, but only for a few seconds. "He saved lives, for sure."

"Is he okay?"

"Physically, yes. I can't vouch for his heart, though. He looked almost like he was in a trance after the shooting." The frustration was audible in his tone. "He won't let anyone inside, not even me."

Jamie exhaled slowly, allowing her heartbeat to return to a more normal pace. "I'm just glad you're okay. We can talk about Alex later."

They spoke another few minutes, and Clay had to go. By then, Jamie was just pulling into the driveway, and as she cut the engine, she turned around and smiled. CJ had fallen asleep, and why not? He had no worries, no concerns. He was with his mommy, and whatever was wrong, she would take care of it. Jamie held the picture for a few seconds. It was exactly how God wanted her to feel, safe and secure in His loving care—no matter what happened.

She took CJ from his car seat, carried him upstairs, and placed him in his new big-boy bed. His favorite blanket was spread out near the wall, and Jamie tucked it in around him. He still took two-hour naps, and she was glad he'd fallen asleep. Jamie sat on the edge of his bed and gently brushed his white-blond hair off his forehead.

Six months after she and Clay married, when she found out she was pregnant, Jamie came to grips with a very real possibility. The baby could look like his uncle Eric—distinctly different from Clay—the way babies sometimes favored one side of the family over another. And since Eric shared that uncanny resemblance with the husband Jamie had lost, he would look like Jake, like the son she and Jake never had. It wasn't something she dwelled on, and not once did she share that particular thought with Clay. As it turned out, she hadn't needed to worry about the issue. CJ was his daddy's son from the moment he was born—complete with Clay's blond hair and round face.

But he looked like Jamie too, enough that CJ and Sierra were clearly brother and sister. Sierra was an amazing big sister, playing with CJ every afternoon when he came toddling down the stairs after his nap. Sierra would take him out back and run through the sprinklers with him, letting him catch her and swinging him around until his laughter filled the yard.

Jamie smiled at him, then leaned over and kissed his cheek. For today, they were all well and whole. Sierra happy at school, CJ safe in his bed, and Clay alive after another dramatic day of police work. Nothing about tomorrow was promised to them; Jamie understood that. But as long as God gave them the gift of today, she would cherish it with all her heart.

She stood and left the room, quietly shutting the door behind her. As she did, she remembered Alex and what Clay had said about him, how he wouldn't let anyone inside. Jamie leaned against the stair railing, and slowly an idea formed. Alex's dad was FDNY, same as Jake. Jamie knew the last names of the firemen her husband had worked with, and Brady wasn't one of them. Odds were the two men rarely crossed paths, but the possibility remained. On the bigger calls, more than one station always responded. Maybe Jake had known Ben Brady.

It had been a year since she'd pulled Jake's old journal down from the top shelf in the hall closet. She lived with the wisdom Jake left behind, so she didn't need to look at the journal more often than that. Besides, Clay had suggested that looking at the book too often might not be healthy for her. Jake was gone, and this was her new life now. With him and CJ and Sierra. Jamie agreed wholeheartedly and she understood. Clay wasn't jealous of her dead husband. He only wanted her to be healthy about where she was now, where they were as a couple.

But this was different. The house was quiet, and Sierra wouldn't be home for another hour. She didn't want time alone with Jake's memory; she wanted to see if by some chance he had known Ben Brady. Jamie gave herself permission to check. She took soft steps toward the hall closet, opened the door, and carefully got the book down.

Often when Jake wrote in his journal, he talked about incidents at work, firefighters he'd come across, and what his conversations with them had stirred in his own mind. There were, of course, a number of entries where Jake talked about his best friend, Larry Henning. The two had died together in the Twin Towers, that much they knew. Their helmets were found in the same section of rubble more than a month after 9/11.

But what about Ben Brady? Was there a chance Jake had ever met the man or written about him? Jamie took the journal to a bay window seat where the afternoon sun was streaming in just so. Despite the warm afternoon, the news about the gunmen had left her cold inside. She took the seat, and warmth radiated through the window and into the muscles along her back.

She put the journal on her lap and opened the first page. Reading one entry after another would get her nowhere today, and it would leave her in tears. The way it always did when she allowed herself to go back to her life before September 11. No, this would be more of a scanning, an exercise of her left brain. In case the name Ben Brady was somewhere in the pages of Jake's extensive writings.

The pages weren't exactly ancient, but they had a brittle feel to them now. Jamie took great care as she opened the book and allowed herself to read the first page.

Jake Bryan, the inscription read. *A journal for notes and observations, a trail so that someday my Jamie might look back and read, and that by doing so she might* "believe that Jesus is the Christ, the Son of God, and that by believing you may have life in His name."—*John 20:31.*

Jamie read the words a second time. It was always strange and uncanny what Jake had written, as if he had somehow known he wasn't going to survive his days with the FDNY, and more, that the words in his journal, the words etched into the borders of his beloved Bible, might one day lead Jamie to the faith he had always prayed she would find. Which was exactly what had happened.

The slightest remorse seized Jamie, and once more she wished she'd found that faith while Jake was still alive. But this way, her change of heart would give them one more reason to celebrate someday when they were reunited in heaven. She steadied herself and turned the page. In keeping with her determination, she resisted the temptation to read each entry. Instead, she ran her finger down the page, searching for just one word.

Brady.

She was nearly fifty pages into the book and unaware of how much time had passed when suddenly the name practically jumped out at her. She gasped and let her eyes find the beginning of the entry. It was almost impossible to think Jake had known him, or that the name truly represented Alex's father. But there it was, right in front of her. The entry started on the previous page and was dated a month before 9/11.

Sometimes I come across someone in the department who personifies courage and commitment, the sort of firefighter people talk about with words like bravery *and* loyalty, strength *and* honor. *That's the way I feel about my friend Ben Brady from the station a few blocks from mine. We worked a call together yesterday, and I found myself watching him, the way he took charge of the blaze and set an example for the men from his firehouse. Ben and I know each other. We've talked a number of times. But yesterday we talked on a deeper level, about what drives us.*

Jamie could hardly believe what she was reading. Not only had Jake known Alex's father, but also he knew him well and even looked up to him. She kept reading, drinking in every word.

I wasn't surprised when he told me he was a Christian. "I take God with me on every call," he said. I liked that. It's the way I feel, the way I live. But I guess I never heard it put that way before. He said something else too. He told me he knows he can only do so much to keep the city of New York safe from fires. "When you live with constant danger," he told me, "you have to remember John 16:33." He winked at me. "That's what keeps me sane. John 16:33."I was familiar with the verse, so I understood. Jesus used that part of

Scripture to tell his friends a simple, profound message: "… in me you may have peace. In this world you will have trouble. But take heart! I have overcome the world."

He also told me he hoped one day his son would embrace the verse. "So far, my family has had very little trouble. Life is good, love is sweet, and time seems like it'll last forever." His eyes held a bittersweet shine. "We all know that isn't true. Especially working for the FDNY."

His words stayed with me all day and even now, as I write, I can hear them in my heart. He's right. Today is like that for me and Jamie and Sierra. Life is good, love is sweet, and time seems like it'll last forever. But it won't. It never does. And so we stay strong in the hope of John 16:33 … because in the end, Christ has overcome the world. That's what I have to tell myself every now and then.

Jamie let the final words of his entry fill her, consume her until she could barely breathe. *Every now and then.* The way they all needed the words from John 16:33.

And what about the connection with Ben Brady? Jamie had known the young K9 deputy for a year, known all that time that his firefighter father had died in the collapse of the Twin Towers. But never had she even considered looking in Jake's journal, checking to see if, by some strange act of God, the two men might've known each other. Even then, she never could've imagined a find like this one — an entire entry about Jake's admiration for Ben Brady and his thoughts on Ben's wisdom.

An urgency came over her, the same urgency she'd felt each day when she reported for her volunteer work at St. Paul's Chapel. In her years in that position, God had used her to help hundreds of men and women find a way out from under their anger and grief. With God giving her wisdom, she had helped people learn to live again. She was finished with her days at St. Paul's, but now here was Alex Brady. A part of their everyday lives. Or at least a part of Clay's.

She read the journal entry two more times, and goose bumps flashed across the length of her arms and legs. Once more, God had provided her with the wisdom she'd need to help someone find peace after the pain of 9/11. The journal entry would give Alex a window to his father that he'd probably never had before. And maybe in the process it would slice through the barriers that stood between Alex and the rest of the world. Maybe the news would whittle away the walls and allow him to find the life and love in Christ that had clearly marked his father's every breath. Yes, that's what God wanted her to do with this information. She could hardly wait to show Clay the journal entry. Certainly he would agree with her, that God had brought Alex into their lives for this exact moment, for this specific reason.

Now she only had to pray for the right timing.

She truly intended to put the journal away. After reading through the entry about Ben Brady the third time, she was about to close the cover when another line caught her attention, something about Sierra and how their daughter had worked her way so quickly into his heart. Jamie settled in over the page and clung to every word. One entry led to another, as she did what she hadn't planned to do this afternoon.

Made her way back to her old life.

When the front door opened, she barely heard it, caught up in something Jake had written about one of their weekend trips to the beach and how it felt to ride their WaveRunner across the harbor with Jamie at the controls, pushing the machine to its limit, and how—

"Jamie?"

She straightened, lifting her eyes to the sound of Clay's voice. Something wet was rolling down her cheeks, and her eyes felt thick and heavy. She was crying, and she hadn't even known it. "Clay." She closed the journal and set it on the window seat beside her. "You're home early."

"Captain told us to come home and get some rest." He wasn't looking at her, but at the journal. Slowly he came closer, the hurt in his eyes so raw the pain radiated from him. He stopped and turned to her. "What're you doing?"

Jamie wiped at the wetness beneath her eyes and sniffed. "It's not like it looks." She didn't have to defend herself, but Clay had a right to wonder. She stood and went to him. "I wondered if maybe Jake knew Ben Brady, you know, if maybe he might've written about him in his journal." She slipped her hands into the back pockets of her black jeans.

"Thousands of men work for the FDNY," his tone was kind, but wounded. "Don't use that as an excuse to —"

"I found something." She turned back to the window seat and brought the journal to him. She flipped through the pages until she found the right one. "I didn't believe it either, but it's there. Read it."

Clay released a heavy breath, but then he took the book in his hands and read the entry. His expression changed, and when he finally spoke to her, a sense of wonder filled his voice. "That's amazing." He closed the journal and handed it back to her. "I can't believe you would even think to look."

"God must've put the idea on my heart." Her cheeks were nearly dry now. "When the time's right, I want to share this with Alex. This could turn things around for him."

A skeptical look flashed across Clay's face. He framed Jamie's face with his hands and ran his thumbs lightly beneath her eyes, wiping away what remained of her tears. "Seeing you like that, sitting here crying, reading his journal," his voice was not much more than a whisper. "It breaks my heart, Jamie. It makes me feel …" he looked away from her, at the fraction of sky through the same window where she'd been sitting. "Like I'll never be more than second-best."

In the nearly four years they'd been married, Clay had only brought up this terrible feeling of his one other time — when he'd found her outside their house, lost in thought on what would've been Jake's birthday. What she'd told him then still applied today. She tried to find the right words to express her heart. "Clay," she waited until she had his complete attention again, "Jake was a part of my life for twenty years." Her tone was kind, begging him to understand. "You can't ask me to walk away from that."

He looked like he might say something in response, or try to debate her on her decision to spend the afternoon reading Jake's journal. But instead he took the journal from her and set it carefully on the floor beside them. Then he pulled her close and smoothed his hand along the back of her head. "I'm sorry. It's hard for me."

She held onto him, gripping his strong body to her own as fresh tears filled her eyes. "I don't know what to say, baby. It's hard for me too."

From the far end of the house they heard the happy voice of Sierra, home from school. "Mom? Dad? I aced my math test!"

Jamie pulled back and wiped her eyes again. "Time got away from me. That's all." She reached down, picked up Jake's journal, and took a few steps toward the stairs. "I'm sorry, Clay. Really."

He held her eyes a few seconds more, nodded, and turned to intercept Sierra. "All right! Did you bring it home?"

"Yeah, it's in my backpack."

Jamie realized what Clay had done. By going to meet Sierra, he'd given her unspoken permission to collect herself, to return the journal and find her way back to the here and now, and she loved him for it. But even as she hurried up the stairs and set the book back on the top shelf of the hall closet, even as she ran a washcloth over her face and pulled a brush through her dark hair, she had to ask herself if this wasn't what Eric had warned her about. That by taking up the cause of Alex Brady, she might wind up lost somewhere back in yesterday—a place she had a hard enough time leaving four years ago. At the time, she'd thought little of his warning, but now she didn't have to ask if the possibility existed.

The tearstains on her cheek told her all she needed to know.

TEN

The memories of Holly had hung around longer than usual, through the night and waiting there in the wings while Alex had shown up on the hostage scene and quickly taken matters into his own hands. Poor Clay hadn't known what to make of him, sitting in his squad car with Bo on the ground beside him, barely saying more than a few words about the incident.

What was he supposed to say? He hadn't liked seeing the bad guy lying on the ground bleeding out, but someone had to stop him. This was what he'd committed his life to doing, getting criminals off the street, making his father proud. Doing his part to keep families from being ripped apart the way his had been.

Sure, he'd acted on instinct, taking Bo and slipping toward the back of the parking lot. But he'd had a feeling about the parked cars, and as he made his way closer he was sure he saw someone move inside the middle one. By the time the second gunman sprang from the car shooting his gun, Alex was ready.

The way he'd been ready since the moment he was sworn in as a Los Angeles County sheriff's deputy.

Clay had thought Alex was quiet because of the shooting, but that was only partly it. The shooting was a necessary act, proving he had been right where he was supposed to be. He felt bad about taking the guy down, but what sort of crazy person would dare leap from a hiding place and start shooting at the backs of SWAT team officers? Crazy guy like that wouldn't think twice about killing again, whenever the system let him out.

The distance in his eyes had been about more than the shooting. The reason he didn't have much to say was because of Holly's memory, because the act of taking out the criminal was the very reason he'd given her up. Normally he could push her memory away, tuck it safely back into a cold, airless vault in his heart where it would never see the light of day. But this time her memory hung around, her voice talking to him as he drove into work that morning, the feel of her hand in his so strong she might as well have been sitting beside him as he went out on patrol. The only time he didn't catch himself thinking about her was during the call, while he sped to the scene to provide backup, and while he took care of the bad guys. The minute the danger had passed, she was back again, her clear blue eyes burning a painful hole in his heart.

Now it was noon Wednesday, and he was heading to work again. His sergeant had told him maybe this wasn't a good day for overtime, what with the drama from the day before. But Alex wanted as much overtime as he could get. Every hour on the job helped push memories of the past a little further away, back where they belonged.

He parked his squad car, climbed out, and let Bo free from the backseat. They were into September, and the Santa Ana winds were picking up. He searched the mountains that ringed the area looking for signs of a brushfire. There were none. "Come on, Bo. Let's get it." Together they walked in, and from the moment he entered the meeting room he knew something had happened. Guys were talking in whispers, getting their coffee, and finding their folding chairs without the usual loud joking and relentless ribbing.

"Somebody wanna tell me what's going on?" Alex stopped, and Bo immediately heeled at his side. Alex looked at the faces of the guys around him. "Anyone?"

Clay rounded the corner and stopped. He was the first guy to make eye contact with him since he'd walked through the door. "Brady … we need to see you in the office."

Alex racked his brain, trying to imagine what might've happened to cause this sort of reaction among the special forces teams. Had someone seen him parked outside the REA headquarters? Was his job on the line for breaking department protocol?

Inside the office, Clay and Joe leaned against one wall, and behind an oversized desk sat three of the department's highest-ranking brass. Clay shut the door behind them, and Alex remained standing. One at a time, he looked at the eyes of the men in charge. He waited until one of them spoke.

"Brady, we have bad news." One of the department's captains pressed his lips together.

Was it about his mother? He talked to her every few weeks, but never for very long. Her new husband had money, and the two of them were always going out or heading to some fundraiser or benefit dinner. She was an escrow officer now, busy with her own life. She understood how he felt about his job, how it was everything to him. But now had something happened to her too? His thoughts raced through his mind at breakneck speed.

"The suspect you shot at yesterday's standoff?" the captain frowned, his voice deeply serious. "He died this morning. We just got word."

Alex felt the loss of life instinctively, in a part of his soul where death of any kind would always hurt, always chafe against the ideal. He cleared his throat and stood a little straighter. "I'm sorry to hear that, sir."

"This means an investigation, of course. Purely standard procedure." The commander in the group folded his arms across his chest. "And for you, Brady, it means two weeks' leave." Alex felt like he'd been kicked in the gut. "Two weeks, sir?"

"Two weeks to clear your head, man." Joe slid one foot up the wall and leaned on his knee. "It's a good thing, Brady. Believe me."

"We'll keep you posted throughout the investigation. It's pretty open-shut. We'll let you know when the final results are put into a report." The captain motioned toward the door. "That's all, Brady."

Clay led the way, with Joe and Alex right behind him. The three walked down the hall to a different spot, a debriefing room with a small table and only six chairs. Again, Clay closed the door behind them, and the three of them took seats. Alex planted his elbows on the table and raked both hands through his hair. His remorse was quickly becoming something more like anger. "Did I ask for a vacation?" He spat the words at Clay and Joe, then tossed his hands and slammed himself back in his chair. "I shot to kill, like I've been trained to do in that situation. I don't like it, but I had no choice. So why punish me?"

"Calm down." Clay was usually the levelheaded one, but there was a simmering anger in his voice now too. "This is standard procedure when a deputy kills a suspect. You know that."

Alex released a hard breath through clenched teeth. "It doesn't make sense. I save a bunch of guys from getting bullets in their backs, and I'm kicked out for two weeks. How's that fair?"

"It's a vacation, Brady." Joe laughed, but he sounded incredulous. "Make the most of it. Go see your mom or something."

"I can't leave Bo."

"So fly Mom out here. Wouldn't hurt you to spend a little time away from the office." Joe bent down and patted Bo's head. "Bo here feels the same way, right, Bo?"

The dog cocked his head to one side, and his ears came forward. But he didn't bark. He wouldn't without a command from Alex.

"Look, I'll have the most input on the report." Clay's anger was gone now, and in its place he sounded tired. "Obviously, I'll explain that you saw movement in a car at the other side of the parking lot, and you pursued the situation as part of your command to provide backup."

Alex raised one eyebrow. "What about my implied assignment by the side of the building?"

"That was before you saw movement in one of the parked cars." Clay said the words like they were fact, and they were. But the way he was wording his description of what happened meant there was no danger of Alex being reprimanded for acting on his instinct rather than by the book. Basically, Clay was going to bat for him in the biggest case of his career to date. Clay wasn't finished. "I'll explain that while you were pursuing the movement in the parked car, a suspect burst from inside the car and began shooting at the backs of your fellow deputies. At that time," Clay's look grew more intense, "and only after you saw the suspect start shooting, did you fire your gun."

Joe watched the exchange between the two, doubt never once flickering in his expression. "You K9 guys have two choices. Shoot 'em or dog 'em. This time you had to do both." Joe shrugged one shoulder. "Captain's right. Open-shut case. Take the two weeks, then throw yourself back in the saddle."

Alex was still reeling from Clay's description of the events. They weren't false, and they didn't exactly stretch the truth. Everything happened so fast that day, he really wasn't sure whether he saw the suspect's gun first, or heard the gunfire first, or whether they both shot at the same time. In any case, his actions had been entirely warranted.

"I'll finish my part of the report by confirming that a number of SWAT deputies could've lost their lives that day if not for your quick and accurate shooting." He motioned to the others in the next room. "Every one of them on the scene would say the same thing."

"Thank you, sir." Alex kept up the formality because the matter was serious. But he had never felt Clay's friendship more than at that moment. Bo pressed in against his leg, as if to say it was all going to be okay. They could take two weeks off and survive. "How am I supposed to spend my time?"

"I have an idea." Joe took a folded sheet of paper from his back pocket. "LAPD's doing a session on K9 training all next week, noon to four. I called, and they'd love to have you."

"Tell him what they said." Clay allowed the hint of a smile as he stretched his arm around the back of his chair.

Joe chuckled. "Apparently, the LAPD's heard of you, Brady. The guy told me maybe you'd like to *teach* the course."

The compliment hit its mark. It felt better than Alex might've imagined and took away some of the ache of knowing his bullet had killed a man. He didn't bother containing the grin that tugged at the corners of his lips. He and Bo were building a reputation among good guys and bad. *Don't mess with a deputy and his dog.* The fact made Alex hungry for patrol time, anxious for the next backup call. "Training's good, but …" he had to be careful with his words. "I'm concerned about the REA. I have a few leads, guys. I think we can catch them before they strike."

"I thought I talked to you about that." Clay sounded like a weary older brother. "SWAT's aware of the REA. We're watching them, Brady. We know where they're meeting. Leave it to us."

Alex stopped himself from saying anything more. This was the beginning of fire season, and the REA was primed for a hit. He'd been in contact with Owl, but the meeting had been postponed till tomorrow night. Alex still planned to go. What he did on his off time was up to him, as long as he didn't break any laws.

"Do me a favor, then. Keep an eye on the Oak Canyon Estates, will you? A fire there would be huge."

"*Brady* …" Clay didn't need to say anything else.

"Yes, sir." Alex worked his jaw one way and then the other. "Am I allowed here at headquarters?"

"Not until we get the report in." Joe felt bad for him, Alex could tell. "Look, man, don't you surf?"

Alex worked to control his frustration. "I do. A few times a month ever since I moved here."

"So go to the beach." Joe shrugged his shoulders. "A little K9 training, a little time in the sun. Doesn't sound that bad if you ask me."

Clay's face softened some. "Come for dinner Saturday, okay? Jamie's cooking her world-class lasagna."

"We'll be there for sure. The kids love Jamie's lasagna." Joe headed for the door and slapped Alex on the shoulder. "Come on, Brady, stop pouting. It's just two weeks."

"So?" Clay followed Alex, but he stopped at the door. "You'll be there?"

Alex reminded himself of the promise he'd made, that whenever he was invited, as far as it was possible, he'd say yes. So that he wouldn't lose himself completely. He nodded and tried to let a little kindness into his voice. "Yeah, Sarge, thanks. I'll be there." He felt the resignation come over him. "What should I bring?"

"A suntan." Clay grinned once more as he and Joe left the room.

Alex realized he'd been holding his breath, and he exhaled long and slow. A guy was dead because of his gun, and that would stay with him. But he hadn't had a choice, and it wasn't fair that he was being taken off the streets—even for two weeks. What if a showdown happened with REA? If anyone should be in on the arrest of a bunch of cowardly arsonists, it was he and Bo. He looked out the window at the tree branches blowing in the distance. The wind had let up, but not for long. It just took one strong day of Santa Anas and the REA could make their move.

He stood, defeated. "Okay, Bo, let's get going."

The memory of Holly didn't find him again until he walked through the front door of his townhouse. She'd been here to his place, but just once. The summer after he left the East Coast, she followed him out here, determined to find her way back to his heart. She'd gotten the address from his mother, and she'd come unannounced.

Alex flopped down on his sofa, and Bo curled up in a ball on the floor beside his feet. "Good boy, Bo." The dog lifted his eyes, and utter loyalty filled his features. He would've destroyed anyone who tried to harm Alex, no question about it. Every breath he drew had one purpose—to protect Alex and the other members of the department. Alex rubbed the spot under the dog's chin. "Get some rest, Bo. We'll run later." The dog settled back down, and Alex stared at his front door, remembering what it had been like to see Holly that summer day in 2002.

That was before Bo, back when he lived here by himself. He'd just gotten home from a run at Pierce College, and he had four hours before he had to report to his job as a custody assistant at the men's jail. He was headed for the shower when the doorbell rang. Alex hesitated, suspicious of anyone who would come to his door. He knew no one and had no friends in the area. He was convincing himself the caller must be soliciting one thing or another when he opened the door, and there she was.

Holly.

Like something out of his unrelenting dreams, she stood there, more beautiful than she'd been at their senior grad party—the last time he'd seen her. Older and with more wisdom in her eyes. It took him half a minute before he rebounded enough to say something. When he did, he was still trying to make sense of her standing there. "Holly … what are you … how did you …?"

She laughed, but it sounded more nervous than funny. "Hi." She didn't make a move in his direction. "Your mother told me where you lived. I flew in this morning and rented a car."

The Holly he'd known was confident and charismatic, with a charm and joy that could take over a room. But she was only nineteen, and she seemed overwhelmed by what she'd done. He felt the same way. After all, she'd flown here by herself from New York, rented a car, and navigated the LA freeways all in an attempt to find him. Even knowing that he clearly hadn't wanted to be found.

Her laughter faded, and she locked eyes with his. "Can I come in?"

"Yes." Alex could have kicked himself. He didn't have room in his life for a relationship with Holly, but he had no reason to be rude. "Sorry." He stepped aside and motioned for her to come in. That's when he realized he was wearing only the scrap of a muscle shirt and running shorts. He must've smelled horrific.

She looked around the dark living room, and he saw it for the first time through the eyes of a visitor. Dishes were stacked on the coffee table, and newspapers were scattered along the sofa. Dirty socks and an occasional towel lay on the floor. Alex managed a weak smile. He couldn't believe she was here, let alone try to reckon with the condition of his condo. "I wasn't expecting company."

"Apparently." She slid a stack of newspapers off the couch and onto the floor and sat down. "Go shower, Alex. We need to talk."

He didn't say anything, just followed her directions and hurried himself down the hallway and into the shower. The respite gave him time to collect his thoughts and form a plan. Never mind that his heart hadn't beaten normally since he first saw her standing on his doorstep, or that seeing her had a way of making him forget 9/11 ever happened. The fact was, he had different passions now—the all-consuming desire to make his father proud, to prevent other innocent lives from being lost. She deserved more than he could offer.

By the time he was dressed and ready to face her, his emotions were firmly in check. He found her standing near his bookcase, looking at a photo of his parents. The same one that had caught her eye when she was a freshman in high school. For a moment he remembered how it used to be, how much he'd loved her. But his heart wasn't wired the way it had been back then. The only thing that drove him now was school and the idea that one day he would be protecting others from the pain he'd been dealt. He couldn't ease up long enough to love or laugh or let down his guard.

She must've sensed him there behind her, because she spoke without turning around. "They really did have something special, Alex." She returned the picture and turned to him. "Death can't change that."

He didn't cry, hadn't shed tears since that horrible day after the terrorist attacks. But in that moment he had to swallow hard to stuff his feelings. "I know." He motioned for her to take her seat again, and he took the chair closest to her. What he needed to say was very important, and he didn't want her to misunderstand. For a while he only looked at her, letting himself remember how it used to be between them. Finally, he cleared his throat and tried to round up the right words. "But death changed a lot of other things. For me, anyway."

"You told me that last year. When you said good-bye." She slid to the edge of the sofa and reached for his hand.

He wanted to resist her, but he couldn't. She was his friend, and he wouldn't hurt her anymore than he had to. He let his fingers be drawn between hers. "So, why are you here?"

"I gave you a year." Tears made her eyes shine. "I figured if I gave you enough time, you'd work through all this." She lifted her free hand and let it fall to her lap again. "The pain you have about losing your dad, and whatever else you're dealing with."

She didn't understand at all. "What happened on September 11 isn't something I'll ever work through." His voice was tender, desperate for her to grasp what he was saying. "It changed me." He released her hand, stood, and paced to the far window. "It changed how I feel about God and family and myself."

"And me, Alex?" She was on her feet and when she reached him, she put her hand on his shoulder. "The attacks changed how you feel about me?"

He looked deep into her eyes, and lifted his fingers to her face. "Holly ..." For a precarious moment he wondered if he might kiss her, if he might welcome her back into his life. Then before he could cross that line, he forced himself to answer her question. "Yes. They changed that too." He moved his hand from her cheek and pressed it to his chest. "Inside me, something died that day, and it won't ever live again. Not ever." Once more he brushed his knuckles against her feathery soft cheek. "I couldn't do that to you, ask you to stay with me when I'm ... I'm not the same as I was back then."

"But you are." Her tears came harder then. Clearly this wasn't the response she'd expected to get by coming all the way to LA to see him. "Deep inside you, you're the same, and one day you'll wake up and wonder why you threw it all away, why you couldn't bring yourself to move on like everyone else who lost someone that day."

Her words steeled him to her, made the rest of the conversation easy. He took a step back, his heart hurting and cold. "It's over, Holly. I'm sorry." He grabbed his keys and his wallet and looked at her one last time. "I'm leaving, and when I come back you need to be gone."

"That's it?" She yelled at him then, tears streaming down her face. "No good-bye, nothing? I come all the way here to tell you I still love you, and this is all the time you'll give me?"

He was dizzy from the guilt tearing into him, but he couldn't stop himself. He took gentle hold of her shoulders and silenced her with an embrace, a hug that lasted nearly three minutes. The whole time he let her cry, let her sobs shake both of them, until finally he could feel her regaining control, accepting his words even if they all but destroyed her.

Finally, he drew back and spoke to her for the last time. "Good-bye, Holly. I'm sorry." He left without looking back, and for the next three hours he drove the LA freeways, forcing himself not to turn around and run to her. She deserved better, he kept telling himself. He had no room in his life for a relationship when all he wanted was to fight crime. When he returned home that night, she was gone.

That was the last he'd seen or heard from Holly Brooks.

He blinked and stared at the window, the place where they'd shared their last hug. He could still see her standing there, the questions in her eyes, the love in her heart. He groaned out loud and ran his fingers hard through his hair. He could usually go a whole day without thinking about her, and when he was swamped at work, even a handful of days, or a week. But lately she seemed to creep up from her place in his heart more often.

Sometimes it was his mother's fault. She would bring Holly's name up once in awhile, but Alex always stopped her. "I want to talk to you, Mom, but you gotta keep her out of this. She's probably married with kids by now, the way she should be. It doesn't help me stay focused when you keep bringing her up."

Bo was running in his sleep again. Alex leaned over and stroked the dog's head. He'd done the right thing, sending her away. He was not living the life he and Holly had dreamed of back when they were high school kids, back when he actually believed God had plans for His people.

For a fraction of an instant, he almost let himself return to that awful Tuesday morning, to the place where his life truly changed forever. But he stopped the memories before they could come to life. He stood up and headed to his bedroom. The place was clean now. At least he'd learned that much about living on his own. He grabbed a T-shirt and a pair of shorts, and ten minutes later he and Bo were headed off to Pierce College. If he ran the hills hard enough, maybe he could escape not only Holly's memory, but also the memory of the terrorist attacks themselves. Because some things from his past didn't only haunt him.

They threatened to destroy him.

ELEVEN

Holly was about to leave her office for the day when Dave and Ron came through the door in a hurry, their voices intense. She settled back down at her desk so she could hear them better. Whatever they were discussing, Dave sounded upset with his son.

"You can't take that sort of thing lightly." The older man was pacing.

"I'm hardly taking it lightly. I called the police, didn't I?"

"A threat of arson? We should have the whole sheriff's department down here patrolling the place. Someone could get hurt."

Ron was clearly trying to keep from fighting. His voice fell a notch. "Take a deep breath, Dad. Seriously. It was one phone call."

"At a time when environmental terrorists are plotting against people like you and me." Fear welled up in Holly. She stood and moved hesitantly into the next room. "You received a threat about fire?"

Ron gave her a pacifying look. "It was nothing. Sounded like a bunch of kids."

"Kids don't make those kinds of threats." Dave had a pencil in his hand, and he tapped it against the edge of the table. His expression made it clear how serious he was. "When did you call the police?"

"As soon as I hung up." Ron leaned back in his seat. If he was worried about the call, he didn't act like it. "They've made a record of the threat, and they promised to patrol up here more often than before."

"The thing is, we have the gate and the security system." Holly didn't want to take sides, but she'd always been comforted by that fact. "No one's going to start a fire while we're here. And the gate's half a mile down the road."

"Right." Ron smiled first at her, then at his father. "If they drove through the gate or hoofed it up the road, they'd set off the silent security sensors. The sheriff's department would be here before they reached the top of the hill."

"It'd be easier to find a development they could drive up to." Holly didn't wish this sort of thing on anyone, but it terrified her to imagine it happening here.

"Exactly." Ron gave his father a reassuring look. "Come on, lighten up. We've thought this through. We have a hundred grand in that gate and security system. We're safe up here, no matter who made the call."

Holly listened, desperate to believe him. The way the homes lay right along the canyon, a fire would pick up speed and barrel down the mountain, taking anything in its way. She'd watched footage of last year's brushfires, and she knew then that if not for the gate, someone could walk right in and wipe out all of Oak Canyon Estates with a single match — both the previous phase and this one. And the firestorm they would create in the process could take out entire neighborhoods at the base of the hill.

If the fire started at night, there might not be time to warn the residents down below, and then ...

She closed her eyes, refusing to think about the possibility.

Ron was saying, "Listen, Dad, tell you what." He left the table and crossed the room. "Holly and I are going to check the security fence around the back of the property. Just to be safe."

Dave seemed to relax at the idea. "Good. I'll call the alarm company and make sure everything's working fine on their end."

When they were outside, the door shut behind them, Ron offered her his arm. She took hold of it, and they found an easy pace as they started up the street toward the largest model. "Maybe the stress is getting to him." He gestured toward the row of homes. "The economy's still soft, and … well, everything he has is wrapped up in these houses."

"They're insured, right?" Holly didn't worry herself about such details. Her concern was about their safety and the safety of homeowners in the area. Beyond that, her job was to sell houses, and she was ahead of projections, even with the weak economy.

"We have insurance, but the deductible's pretty high." He made a face like he was calculating something. "If we lost all these houses, the subs would get paid. But it'd put us under. Dad knows that."

The wind had died down, and only a gentle breeze rolled down from the top of the mountain through the high canyon development. Holly swallowed hard. "That won't happen. That's why the security system and the gate were such good ideas."

"Thank you." He straightened his shoulders and gazed down at her.

She hadn't meant it as a compliment, but if he took it that way, fine. They reached the end of the street, and he jogged up along the craggy dirt at the front of the end lot to a post that anchored the security fence along the backs of the houses. While he checked it, Holly studied him. He was soft around the middle, but tall with broad shoulders. Most women her age would've found him attractive — if not overwhelmed by his physical presence, then because of his kindness and confidence and great success in business. Holly didn't know exactly how much Ron Jacobs was worth, but it was a lot. Aside from his father, he owned several developments on the Valley floor, and a house that overlooked the ocean.

But the money didn't matter to Holly. In fact, it was more of a detriment. Ron had clearly become comfortable in his life, satisfied with conquering the business world and acquiring houses and cars. A man like that could never really need her. Not the way she'd been needed once, a lifetime ago.

He jogged back to her, and as he reached her, he must've seen the doubt flickering in her eyes. She looked away, but it was too late.

"What're you thinking?" He held out his arm again, and she took it.

This was how he always walked with her, the way cultured people showed affection, maybe. But it made Holly feel like she was pretending to be someone she wasn't. She breathed in the sweet smell of the canyon and thought about putting him off, telling him she wasn't thinking about anything. But the solitude of the moment and the beauty of the setting sun made her feel more transparent than usual. She lifted her eyes to his as they kept walking. "I guess I'm thinking that you must not need very much." She smiled, keeping her tone even. "Since you already have everything you ever wanted."

He didn't react to her statement other than with the hint of a smile that played on his lips. He looked straight ahead, self-assurance spilling into his voice. "I have much, that's true. Wealth and property." He shrugged in an attempt to look humble. Then he stopped and faced her. "I earned everything I have, and I worked hard to get it. But lately," he touched her chin. So far he hadn't kissed her, and he made no attempt now. "Lately, all that pales to how it feels when I'm with you." The breeze lifted the front of his hair and exposed his receding hairline. "Sometimes I feel like you're the one, Holly."

She tried not to squirm beneath his stare. "Really?"

"Yes." He ran his thumb along her brow. "The one with whom I can share all I've built, all I've made of myself."

What about her *feelings?* she wanted to ask him. Had he thought about that? She silently warned herself that she was doing it again. Being critical of Ron for no reason. She smiled at him. "I like when you share your feelings with me."

"See, that's what I mean." He grinned and continued walking, his elbow still extended for her. "You say something like that, and I feel like I'm alive." They checked the post at the other end of the street, and when they reached the front door of the model home again, he turned to her. "This weekend, Holly? Can I take you out?"

Though Holly could see this offer coming, so far they hadn't been on a date. They'd walked together and spent time at work together, and she could sense his interest. But this was the first step. She swallowed and tried to think fast. There wasn't a single reason why she should tell him no. She felt her smile become shyer than before. "What did you have in mind?"

"How about I surprise you?" He leaned close and kissed her forehead. "Whatever I come up with for Saturday, how about you come with me to church Sunday morning?" He stepped back. "The eleven o'clock service?"

"Uh …" What was wrong with her? Ron was perfect, right? Able to care for her beyond her wildest dreams, and he didn't only want a date with her, he wanted to take her to church. What more could she ask for? "Yes, Ron … that sounds lovely."

But from that moment until her drive home that night, she wanted to wash her mouth out with soap. *That sounds lovely?* Had she really said that? There was nothing lovely about taking in a church service. Who was she kidding? That wasn't how she talked or how she felt at all. The idea of going to church with Ron felt as phony as the picture of her walking alongside him, clinging to his elbow. If she couldn't be herself around Ron, the weekend was doomed already.

She pressed the clicker on her car's visor, and the security gate at her townhouse complex opened slowly. Holly tried to relax.

Usually she liked coming home, liked leaving the demands of Oak Creak Estates behind her for an evening.

She had earned her degree in business and taken a job with Jacobs Development her senior year. Now she earned a considerable income, and she'd been able to purchase one of the new condos off Las Virgenes Road, just before Malibu Canyon. The view was pretty—though not the breathtaking panoramas she worked around every day. Mostly it was a great investment, a safe place to live close to work and with all the amenities she wanted in a home—security, a swimming pool, tennis courts, and a private gym. All that and her mom had a unit right around the corner from her.

But that night as she stepped into her house, she felt as empty as her feelings for Ron Jacobs. The phone rang just as she kicked off her heels, and she answered it on the third ring. "Hello?"

"Hi, honey." It was her mother. "How was your day?"

She and her mom were closer now than they'd been back when she was growing up. Because of Alex's parents, her mom had stopped drinking years ago and found what they'd been missing as a couple. But they only shared that special time for a few short years. After her dad's sudden heart attack, her mother had been left alone. Holly's older sister married five years ago, and she lived in Maryland with her husband and two sons. Finally, when it became clear to Holly's mother that Holly wasn't moving back to the East Coast, she sold her house in Staten Island and found a townhouse in the same development as Holly.

Her mom's training was in nursing, and she found a position in the Neonatal Intensive Care Unit at Humana West Hills Hospital. Between her job and her involvement at church, her mother kept busy. But there was still time for daily conversations and regular dinners throughout the week. Holly kicked back in her leather love seat and closed her eyes. "We had a threat today, someone saying they were going to set fire to the estates."

"Holly, that's terrible!" Her mother's alarm was right up there with Dave's.

"I know, but Ron reported the call to the police." She tried to convince her mother and herself there was nothing to worry about. "Besides, we have the gate and the security system."

"True." Her mother sounded a little more at ease with the reminder. "So tell me about Ron? Anything coming of his attraction?"

"I think so." She could talk to her mom about any topic, and Ron was no exception. She kept her voice upbeat, because she needed to give the idea of Ron a chance. She'd always been able to talk to her mom, and this was no exception. "He asked me out this weekend."

"Really?" There was a smile in her mother's tone. "And you said yes?"

"I did. I don't know where we are going. He said he wants to surprise me."

They talked a few minutes more about her conversation with Ron, how he was beginning to wonder if maybe she was the one he was supposed to share his life with. She worked her way through all the details, but when she was finished, there was silence on the other end. "Mom?"

"I don't hear it. The excitement in your voice."

Holly felt the rush of defeat. "You know me too well." She let her sigh linger over the phone line. "I should feel something, right? Wouldn't you say?"

"Well, that's just it, honey. In the movies and in storybooks, love comes at us all at once, like a stunning rainbow across an otherwise dreary sky. But that's not always how it is in real life." She hesitated. "In real life, love takes time. You need to get to know Ron and see his strengths, his weaknesses. Sometimes women in their mid-twenties are busy holding out for the magic of first love and missing the fact that they need to work at the relationships around them. Real love takes a lot of work, Holly."

She didn't know why exactly, but her mother's talk depressed her. They made a plan to talk the next day, said their good-byes, and hung up. Without making a conscious decision, Holly wandered through the house to the place at her kitchen bar where she kept her leather workbag. The newspaper article was still tucked inside, and now she pulled it out. She opened it and spread it on the counter.

"Alex … why can't I stop thinking about you?" she whispered, as if by doing so she could keep from admitting the truth to herself.

The lighting was better here than it had been in her office, and she could make out his face more clearly than before. Not just his face, but his eyes — or the empty hard glint of darkness where his eyes used to be. She looked more closely. Those weren't the eyes of the boy she'd fallen in love with. Not even close. She walked to the kitchen sink and poured herself a glass of milk.

Alex was right to send her away when he did. He was different then, and he still seemed different now. Changed forever by the tragedy of 9/11. She drank the milk and allowed her mother's words to ring again in her mind. *In real life, love takes time …* She set the glass down by the sink and stared at her image in the mirror that hung on the wall. Was that true? Did love really take time? Wasn't it still possible that two people would meet and share a look or a smile that in a moment's time would change both their lives?

She dismissed the idea. Her dishwasher needed unloading, and she set about the task. What else had her mother told her? Real love takes a lot of work, right? Wasn't that it? She unloaded the glasses, moving them one at a time into the empty space in her cupboard. The trouble was, love hadn't been that way between her and Alex. Not when they were kids. Love took no work whatsoever. Relationships, yes. The logistics of blending two lives into one, and finding the beauty and laughter in the ordinary—that part took work for anyone.

But love?

With her and Alex, love had been everything her mother said only happened in movies and storybooks. It had come all in a rush and left the most brilliant rainbow behind. A heaviness settled over her heart. The house was too quiet. She crossed the living room and slipped in a Barry Manilow CD. Her father's favorite. The first haunting strains of "Even Now" filled the empty places not only in her townhouse, but in her heart. *Even now ... when I have come so far ... I wonder where you are ... I wonder why it's still so hard without you ...*

Tears stung her eyes and made it hard for her to see the newspaper still spread across her kitchen counter. She didn't miss the man Alex had become, whoever he was. But her heart was still ripped apart over losing the boy he'd been. Because somewhere deep inside him, that boy was still alive. Holly would bet everything on that fact, but there was one problem.

She would never have the chance to find out.

TWELVE

Only two days had passed, and already Alex was going crazy without his job. He understood the department's policy. Being responsible for the death of another human being was something that weighed on him more than he could've known. No matter how badly he wanted to rid the streets of crime, he didn't want to kill anyone.

So maybe a little time off was a good thing. But still he couldn't get past the fact that he felt like he was being punished.

He was almost to Clay and Jamie's house, ready for a night of lasagna and listening — which was what he liked best about these dinners. By listening, he had learned to feel for the families who gathered at the Michaels' house, and by feeling he could keep his focus. Fighting crime, so that one more person wouldn't feel the pain of losing someone to another lousy bad guy.

The sun was still bright in the sky, and Alex wore his darkest Oakleys. He tried to imagine how different life would be this very night at Clay's house if the gunman had killed him, if the shot had hit him in the neck or if it had pierced his bulletproof vest. Jamie knew nothing of the pain that would've consumed her that day if Clay had never again walked through the front door. Her heart would've been torn apart by a bullet fired half a city away, and the kids? Neither Sierra nor CJ would ever be the same again.

Satisfaction warmed his veins and cast a calm over the stormy seas in his soul. He never intended to kill a suspect, but in this case Clay was still alive because Alex had taken the right action.

His determination to keep people from the pain that had torn his family apart was working.

He steeled his gaze at the road ahead of him.

While he was off work, he would keep an eye on the REA. The meeting was tonight—after another delay, according to Owl. Alex could hardly wait. He would have dinner with his friends, and then leave earlier than usual. He had his disguise in the trunk—dark sweatshirt and sweatpants, a ski mask, and an ankle holster so he could add a third gun to the ones he'd be wearing around his waist and thigh.

The others were all there when Alex parked his truck and took Bo from the backseat. As the two of them headed up the walkway, he could hear them already laughing, sharing stories about kids or something funny that had happened. Alex wrapped Bo's leash around the porch post and hooked it so it was secure.

Bo gave him a tired look, as if to say, "Really? I'm staying out here by myself again?"

"Not for long, boy … just an hour or two." Alex sat on the step beside the dog and patted his head. Light from the setting sun made it easier to see the small missing piece in Bo's ear, the place where a bullet had nicked him during a drug bust a few months ago. Neighbors had reported drug activity, and two squad cars had been dispatched to the scene.

The missing piece wasn't much, maybe a quarter-inch. But it told the story of Bo's uncanny ability as a police dog, and his unending loyalty. Alex ran his knuckles against the side of Bo's face. Two years ago when the dog had come home from the Netherlands, green with only basic training, his eyes were forever earnest and willing, always giving Alex the same message. Sort of an, "Okay, boss … tell me what to do … tell me what to do."

But that look had long since been replaced by one of utter control and confidence. Alex trusted Bo with his life now, no question. He and Bo had spent more than eight hundred hours training together, finding bad guys in empty buildings and alleys, tracking would-be perpetrators through chest-deep marshes and thick swamps and dense brush. Since Bo had no police training in Europe, his training was all in English. But for every verbal command, he was equally adept with a hand signal or physical cue.

Alex looped his arm around Bo's neck and leaned against him. A K9 officer never went anywhere without his dog, so after two years the bond between them only intensified the effectiveness of their training. It was part of what made them so good at catching crooks. Alex had read somewhere that for a K9 deputy, his dog was his friend, his partner, and his defender. For Bo? Alex rubbed the dog's ear again. For Bo, Alex was his life, his leader, his everything.

After 9/11, Alex withdrew from people, all people. Working with a police dog was the only crime fighting Alex ever wanted to do—from the moment he made his decision to be a deputy. Not only did the job give him a reason to be a loner, to focus on the bad guys, but also K9 teams were always on the frontlines, the first guys into a building or chasing down a suspect. No deputy could have a better partner. Alex's intense training on his off hours, his determination and focus, were sometimes only an attempt to match Bo's complete devotion.

The smell of lasagna drifted onto the front porch. Alex patted the dog one last time as he stood. "You're a good boy, Bo. Good dog."

Bo wagged his tail and, at Alex's hand command, stretched out his front legs and lay down on the porch. He watched Alex walk to the front door and inside the house, and Alex smiled to himself. Whether he was in the house a few minutes or a few hours, Bo would keep his eyes on that front door the whole time. Watching for him, waiting.

Alex found Clay in the kitchen slicing garlic bread. "Brady, look at you." He tried to look serious, but there was a light in his eyes that belied the fact. "You're turning into a slacker."

"Sir?" Alex leaned against the nearest kitchen counter and crossed his arms.

"Your suntan." He took a nearby dish towel and flicked it in Alex's direction. "You asked me what to bring, and I told you." He shook his head in a mock show of disappointment. "So what'd you do, spend the last two days thinking about the REA?"

Clay was kidding, so Alex didn't dare tell him that he was dead-on. He forced a yawn. "You know, Sarge ... caught up on my sleep, lazed around in the recliner."

Clay raised an eyebrow. "Why do I doubt that?"

A buzzer went off near the stove, and Clay tossed Alex a pair of hot pads. "Get the lasagna." He carried the plate of sliced bread to the dining room. "Set it on the stove."

As Alex took the glass dish from the oven, he caught a glimpse of Jamie and Sierra in the backyard. They were talking to the others, showing off something in their vegetable garden. Funny, Alex thought. Sierra could easily be Eric's daughter, something about the shape of her face, or her eyes, maybe.

The lasagna needed a few minutes to cool, and after everyone had served their plates they gathered in the backyard again. This time Jamie had set up a card table for the smaller kids, and another one for the teens. Someone always prayed before the group ate, and tonight Clay took the lead.

"Dear God, we gather here as friends and family, grateful for Your love and provision. Thank You for this food and the hands that prepared it." He paused. "And we ask You, Lord, to help us lean on You and not on our own understanding. In everything we do. Amen."

A round of hearty *amens* followed, but Alex had the sudden urge to excuse himself from the table and spend the meal out front with Bo. Why had Clay added that last part? Alex had a feeling the words were directed straight at him. He lifted his eyes slowly, glancing at the others and making sure no one was staring his way. Only then did he let the words hit their mark. They had to be intended for him. Everyone else around the three tables already relied fully on God. He was the only one who leaned on his own understanding.

Alex took a piece of lasagna and kept his thoughts to himself. Clay had never talked to him about God, not directly, anyway. Probably because it was clear where Alex stood—he wasn't interested. Either way, he didn't want Clay using tonight to get into a discussion about dependence on God. He was two hours from meeting the Owl, something he'd worked out all on his own. A talk about needing God was the last thing he wanted.

There were no awkward silences with this group, which was one reason Alex liked coming. As soon as everyone was served, the conversations around him picked up. Josh Michaels was boasting about taking on the rest of the group in the basketball game Around the World, and laughing about the unlikely possibility that Sierra would make it past the first two shots. To her credit, Sierra was holding her own, giggling and promising to show them all wrong.

At the adult table, Joe was launching into a story about little Will and the family goldfish bowl. He dragged a napkin across his mouth. "So all along we've known Will has a fondness for fish, right?" He kept his voice low enough that Will and the other little kids couldn't hear him. "I mean a real fondness."

"He regularly drags his blanket from his bedroom and curls up for a nap right beside the fishbowl." Wanda made a face that suggested Will was a few crayons short of a box. "The sort of fondness where he talks to the fish, you know what I'm saying?"

"Anyway, so yesterday Wanda and Will come in from a trip to the market, and the goldfish are gone."

"Both of them?" Laura set her fork down, taken in by the story.

"Both." Wanda waved her hand in the air. "Disappeared."

"So Wanda looks at Will and points to the fishbowl, and Will walks a little closer." Joe leaned in so the others could hear. "Then he turns those big brown eyes back up at her and smiles. 'Fish sleeping,' he says."

Jamie jumped back and bit her lip. "No!"

"Yes!" Wanda glanced at Will, busy eating his dinner ten feet away.

"Those fish were sleeping, all right."

"So Wanda marches Will upstairs, and sure enough, there were the goldfish right smack on Will's pillow, blankets pulled up all nice and snug."

For the flash of a moment, Alex caught himself yearning for the life these three couples shared. He glanced at Will and CJ and Lacey and imagined what it would be like if he were a father, if one of the little ones at the next table belonged to him. Then, without warning, a memory came to life. He and his dad, sitting beside each other at the table after dinner one Thanksgiving. His mom must've been in the other room, because it was just the two of them, and his dad leaned back in his chair and put an arm around Alex's shoulders. "Of all the things I'm thankful for," he messed his fingers through Alex's hair and grinned at him, "you're at the top of the list. You know why?"

"Why?"

"Because I love being a dad." His father's eyes grew more serious. "I love being *your* dad."

Even with night falling and the smell of sweet wildflowers in the late summer air, even with the reassuring pressure of the gun against his waist and the sound of the voices all around him, Alex could still see the way his dad looked at him that Thanksgiving Day. He blinked and tuned back into the conversation. Clay was asking if Will understood, if he'd learned anything from the fish tragedy.

Wanda rolled her eyes. "Yeah, we all learned something. Apparently, we need to read that boy the book of Genesis. The part where God created water so the fish would have a place to live."

A round of muffled laughter passed over the table, and Eric looked from Wanda to Joe. "Let me guess, the Reynolds house has a couple of new goldfish."

"Wanda took Will to pick 'em out, so that she could show him how all the fish in the store were in water — not wrapped in blankets."

Alex smiled at the story and pushed his fork through his salad. The food was good, but he wasn't hungry, and he was struggling to stay focused on the conversation. What if Owl somehow knew he was a cop? The meeting could be a setup, and in his zeal to catch the REA, he could walk straight into a trap. He had to consider the idea, the way he'd been trained to consider all possibilities.

He took a bite of lasagna and looked up. As he did, he caught Jamie looking at him. Not just with a curious glance or incidental look, but really studying him. As if she knew he wasn't truly there tonight. She locked eyes with him for a second or two, and then she turned back to the conversation. Something about Laura and Eric's little girl, Lacey.

Between Clay's prayer and Jamie's strange way of watching him, Alex had a feeling about tonight. The group wasn't just including him in another dinner; they were worried about him. Loner sheriff's deputy Alex Brady, unable to process his feelings about shooting a bad guy. Alex finished his meal and quietly surveyed the others. Or maybe not. Maybe the things he was feeling were only in his imagination. But either way, he didn't belong here tonight.

He had an appointment to keep.

The meal was still going on, and Alex didn't need to leave for another half hour, but he needed time alone, time to think about the task ahead of him. As soon as the timing felt right, Alex excused himself and went out onto the porch with Bo.

He sat next to his dog and stared into the fading sunset. What was it about being here, the way it both drew him and confused him? No matter what fleeting thoughts had descended on him during dinner, he didn't want to be a father. Far from it. There was no room in his life for that kind of love. First, because he was incapable of loving that way, and second because he was driven to fight crime with every breath, with all his time and energy.

He ran his hand along Bo's side. Being here stirred feelings in him he never had otherwise. Questions about what it would've been like if he hadn't sent Holly away. Because if his ability to love was truly dead, then how could he explain the sensation that surrounded him even in this very moment — the feel of his dad's arm around his shoulders?

Thirteen

All through dinner, Jamie watched the young deputy at the opposite end of the table, and when he stood and excused himself, she took his action as her cue. She silently prayed, asking God for wisdom and the right words. Then at the next break in the conversation, she put her hand on Clay's shoulder. "I'll be right back."

He didn't have to ask where she was going. His eyes told her he already knew, and that he was hesitant about her determination to help Alex. Hesitant, but not opposed to it. They had talked a few more times about Jake's journal, and whether the situation with Alex was drawing her heart back to the grief she'd known after the terrorist attacks. Jamie had been honest with him, because she wasn't really sure if that was happening.

"I just know I have to help him," she'd told Clay last night. "Please … understand, okay?"

In the end he gave her his promise. If she felt God was leading her to talk to Alex, to share what Jake had written in his journal, then so be it. She had his blessing. But his expression now told her he also had his doubts. Jamie would talk to him later. She tucked that assurance into the corner of her heart as she reached the front screen door and stared out. On impulse, she grabbed her camera. Photography was a new hobby for her, and she'd always wanted to take pictures of Bo. She made sure the camera had a fresh battery and an empty memory chip.

Alex was sitting against the house, one knee pulled up, his eyes distant and focused on some unseen person or place, as if he wasn't really there, but somewhere far, far off. His dog lay on the porch beside him, his head on his paws, and they both looked at her as she stepped out. Jamie lowered her camera and resisted the desire to turn and head immediately back to the table, back to the safe conversation about goldfish and children.

Help me, God … give me the words. She took a step closer. "I got a new camera." She gave a lighthearted shrug. "Can I take a few pictures of you and Bo?"

Surprise registered in Alex's eyes. "Uh … sure, I guess." He smiled, as if maybe he was relieved that she wasn't going to ask anything deeper.

She made casual talk about dinner and the kids as she grabbed a dozen shots of Alex with Bo, and of Bo by himself. "He's a beautiful dog."

"The best ever." Alex patted Bo's back. "No dog like him anywhere."

Jamie's heartrate picked up speed. Picture-taking could only last so long. She opened the door and set the camera down on the table just inside. When she came back out, she slipped her hands in her back pockets. "Can I join you for a minute?"

Alex looked immediately uncomfortable with the idea. Jamie knew he had no intention of letting his guard down around her, but she needed to try. It was a job she felt compelled by God to do.

Bo yawned and set his chin down on his paws again. Alex watched him, and then gave Jamie a nervous look. "Uh, actually … I was coming back in. Just checking on Bo." He seemed to realize that his excuse sounded weak in light of the way she'd found him. "I guess … I don't know, I got distracted."

Jamie's confidence grew. She lowered herself to the porch and sat cross-legged, facing him. "I'm sorry … about the shooting."

"Yeah. It happens." Alex stroked the top of Bo's head, his eyes on his dog. "I don't really need time off, you know."

She thought about her years at St. Paul's Chapel, how driven she'd been never to miss a day in her quest to bring meaning to Jake's death. A car drove by and the distraction gave Jamie time to gather her courage. When it passed, her voice filled with a depth that hadn't been there before. "I understand, Alex. More than you know."

He looked at her, his eyes narrowed just enough that his unspoken question was as clear as if he'd said the words.

Jamie held his gaze. "I know about your father. How he died."

Alex's expression hardened. "I'm over it. A lot of people died that day."

"Including my first husband. He was FDNY." It still hurt to say the words. "He died in the Twin Towers."

For the first time since he had come into their lives, the walls around Alex's heart crumbled just a little. Jamie could see the change in his eyes. "You ... were married to a firefighter?"

"Yes." She drew up her knees and hugged them to her chest. "His name was Jake Bryan."

"How come ..." he turned his eyes straight ahead again. "... Clay never said anything?"

"Wanda too. Her husband was a firefighter in New York."
Alex sat straighter, his back rigid, eyes wide and unblinking. "I never ... I had no idea." Slowly he regained some of his composure. "Why didn't anyone tell me?"

"The guys thought it would scare you off." Jamie could feel the sadness in her half-smile. "Too much pain."

He was quiet, processing the information. "So why tell me now? What brought you out here?"

Jamie breathed in slowly, allowing God to turn her thoughts into words. "For a long time, I've wondered whether your father might've known my first husband." She looked out past the rooftops of the houses across the street. "Wanda and I have talked about it, and there was no connection between her husband and Jake. But I wasn't sure about your father."

"What would it matter?" The muscles in Alex's jaw flexed. "They would still be gone."

Bo must've heard a change in Alex's tone. The dog lifted his head long enough to size up the conversation. When he was satisfied everything was okay, he stretched out again.

Jamie's heart pounded harder than before, and she tried to find the right words. She wanted to tell him it mattered because the terrorists were still waging war seven years later, right here in Alex's heart and soul. But she didn't want to make him run. "My husband kept a journal. For years while he worked for the FDNY, he wrote about his thoughts and … and the people he met." She felt Jake's loss like a knife that never quite dislodged from inside her. "He had a very strong faith."

Alex released a quick, angry-sounding sigh and stood, restless. "Ma'am? I guess I don't get it. Why are you telling me this?"

Bo lifted his head again, alert and ready, his eyes locked on his master.

"Call me Jamie." Her tone remained kind, unshaken. She dropped her knees back to the cross-legged position. "Please sit back down. I have something to tell you."

He paced a few steps toward the walkway, and then back again. "Ma'am … Jamie …" He stopped, his struggle clearly intense. He spoke through tight jaws. "I don't do this. I don't talk about him."

I feel You, God … be with him, please. A quiet strength came over her, and she watched him, undeterred. "It won't take long." She motioned to the spot where Alex had been sitting. "Please."

For a few seconds, it looked like Alex might call his dog and run off without another word. Instead he breathed a few times through his nose, the battle playing out in his expression until finally he came closer and slowly lowered himself back to his spot beside Bo. He pulled up both his knees and rested his forearms there. "Go ahead."

She tried to imagine the massive twist of anger and pain that tied up the heart of the young man across from her. The same anger and pain that bound the hearts of countless people Jamie had talked to at St. Paul's. She leaned closer. "The other day I looked through Jake's journal. It was a long shot, but I had to know—whether Jake knew your dad or not. Whether they'd ever talked."

Alex looked down at his dog and waited.

"I found an entry, an entire page about your dad." She held her breath. "They knew each other. But more than that, Jake wrote that—"

"Please." His eyes flashed, his tone sharp. "I don't want to hear it. There's nothing he could've written that would change anything now." His voice softened. "I'm sorry, I just ..." He let the air gather in his cheeks, and he released it in a rush. At the same time, he pushed his fingers through his hair, his frustration tangible. After half a minute, he shook his head and made a sound that was half-groan, half-cry.

She didn't know whether to apologize or argue with him, so she stayed quiet, watching him.

"Don't you see?" His expression begged her to understand. "It's different for you." He motioned to the front door. "You have Clay and your kids. You have a life." He stood and unhooked Bo from the porch post. "I have a job to do." He waited until Bo was up and at his side. "I'm not looking for healing." He took a step back. "Thank you for dinner. Tell the others good-bye for me."

She stood and dusted her hands on her jeans. "Alex?"

He was already at the end of the walk, but he turned back to her. "Yes?"

"We're praying for you."

The sharp intensity in his gaze barely let up. He hung his head for a moment, and then nodded in her direction. "Thank you."

That was it. He opened the back door of his truck, waited while Bo scrambled up, then climbed into the front and drove away. Jamie leaned against the post and watched him go. *Well, God, that didn't go very well.*

Prayer is a powerful thing, precious Daughter . . . be strong, and do not give up.

The answer resonated deep within her, like a silent roar across the hills and valleys of her soul. Jamie's knees trembled, and she leaned harder into the post so she could keep her balance. Rarely did she feel the Lord's response so clearly. But the thought that echoed within her was exactly what she'd read in the Bible that morning. She'd known Alex was coming for dinner tonight, and she'd been wrestling with whether she should approach him about the journal entry or wait for another time—after his two-week leave, maybe, when the shooting was farther behind him. But her devotion time had been in Galatians—one of Jake's favorite New Testament books. In Chapter six, one verse stood out. *Let us not become weary in doing good, for at the proper time we will reap a harvest if we do not give up.*

Of course, God would whisper those very words to her now, when she felt ill-equipped and unable to reach the hurting young man who'd just driven away. The fruit of her concern for Alex would come if she did not give up. And she wouldn't. She would get the journal entry to Alex one way or another, because that was the right thing to do. Even Clay agreed on that much.

Jamie went back in the house and returned to the dinner party. The others seemed concerned about Alex's early departure, but after a few minutes the laughter and lighthearted talk continued. When their guests were gone, and after CJ was in bed,

Sierra found Jamie and Clay in the kitchen. Her face was drawn and worried. "Wrinkles looks sick."

"She might be tired." Clay wiped his hands on a towel. He was the parent in charge of pet issues. It had been that way from the beginning. "It was over a hundred degrees today." He thought a minute. "Or maybe she got into another fight."

"I don't see any cuts on her. And her eyes look funny." She held her hand out to him. "Please, Daddy, come check her with me."

Jamie watched the way Clay took hold of Sierra's fingers and walked with her toward the back patio. She followed, but only because it never got old, hearing Sierra call Clay "Daddy," and knowing that he so perfectly fit the description. She stood in the doorway and watched her husband and daughter tend to the old cat, still curled up on the nearest patio chair.

Clay ran his hand along the cat's back, and when he reached the base of her tail, Wrinkles jerked away and let out a pained meow. "Hmmm ... this might be the trouble." He gently took hold of the cat and parted the fur near her tail. "Sure enough. Looks like she was mixing it up with the neighbor cat again."

Sierra's worry turned stern. "Wrinkles! What did we tell you about fighting?" She crossed her arms and frowned at the cat. "We should never let you out again!" The cat almost seemed to be listening, and Sierra lowered her face so Wrinkles had no choice but to look straight at her. "Remember when you used to play dress up, Wrinkles? You were a lady back then!"

A grin tugged at Clay's lips but he hid it by looking at Jamie. When he had more control, he cleared his throat. "How 'bout you hold her and I'll get some hydrogen peroxide?"

"Wrinkles!" Sierra looked indignantly at the cat. "Thank you, Daddy. Wrinkles appreciates that very much."

Clay was chuckling as he passed Jamie, went into the house, and came out with a spray bottle of the clear liquid. Wrinkles needed a lot of hydrogen peroxide lately. Clay returned to the place where Sierra was holding onto her cat. "Here …" He aimed a few long sprays at the troubled area and stepped back. "You can let her go. If it doesn't look better tomorrow, we'll take her to the vet."

"Maybe she should be in time-out someplace." Sierra still sounded put out by the cat's actions. "What'cha think, Daddy?"

Jamie angled her face, touched by Clay's obvious concern. He was such a wonderful dad, so good to the kids. No one ever would've known that he wasn't Sierra's biological father. His adoption of her simply made official what anyone else could easily see. Sierra was his daughter, no doubt.

"Well," Clay bit his lip, again doing his best to stay serious. "Maybe we could give her another chance. She might've learned her lesson this time."

Eventually Sierra agreed, and they left Wrinkles to wander off to the back of the yard. Half an hour later when Sierra was in bed, Clay and Jamie headed to the kitchen. "So," he faced her. "How'd it go with Alex?"

A sigh slipped from her. "He wouldn't let me tell him what I found." She was still disappointed, but the holy encouragement she'd received earlier stayed with her. "I told him we'd pray for him."

Clay came to her and took her in his arms. "You still think this is a good idea?"

"I think God wants me to keep at him."

Quiet surrounded them, but Jamie could almost hear what Clay was thinking, as she sensed his deep love and understanding. "Then you do that." He kissed her, tenderly and with a confidence that told her he was doing all he could to stand by and let her make Alex her project. "I'll pray for him. And for you."

Peace soothed the jagged edges leftover from her conversation with Alex, and as she did the dishes and Clay cleaned up the backyard, she analyzed the few glimpses Alex had given her of the battle that raged inside him. What stuck out most were his final words. *You have a life … I have a job to do.* And the last part, where he'd told her he wasn't looking for healing. Jamie ran the hot water over another plate. Alex was telling the truth. He wasn't looking for healing.

He was looking for revenge.

But that sort of angry hurt wouldn't just consume him; it would kill him. It would drive him so hard that one day he'd make some dangerously heroic move on a call and get shot in the process. If not, he'd die on the inside, long before his heart stopped beating. Either way, spending his life seeking revenge would destroy him.

Jamie set another few glasses into the dishwasher. Somewhere in the life Alex Brady lived before the terrorist attacks, he must've had someone. His mother, for one. Perhaps he'd even been in love. Jamie felt the flicker of hope light the dark path ahead of her. That was it. She needed to contact his mother and find out who Alex had cut himself off from.

Maybe then she'd find the missing pieces that would better help her understand not only who Alex Brady was—

But also who he used to be.

FOURTEEN

Alex took Bo home, gave him food and water, and settled him down for the night. He needed to run, but since he didn't have time for a workout before the meeting with Owl, Alex had just one choice. Let the road take him somewhere far away. He drove his truck onto the northbound Ventura Freeway and exited at Las Virgenes Road toward Malibu. No specific destination drew him, but he had to put distance between him and the conversation with Jamie Michaels. Alex turned off his air conditioning, rolled down all four windows, and let the canyon air fill the truck.

Forget about it, he ordered himself. *She was only trying to help.* But everything about those fifteen minutes on the porch stayed front-and-center in his mind. How was it possible? Jamie and Wanda had both lost firefighter husbands in the terrorist attacks. The idea that he'd been coming to Clay's house every month for a year without knowing about their connection was more than Alex could take in. He laughed one time, a bitter, ironic laugh. What had he just told himself? If Clay hadn't come home from the hostage call that day, Jamie wouldn't have known what to do, right? Wasn't that it? He had guessed she and the kids would've been decimated by that kind of tragedy.

But no. Jamie Michaels had been through it all before. He drove with one hand, wishing he had a reason to open up his engines. The wind caught him square in the face, whipping his hair and filling his ears with the sound. But it did nothing to stop his mind from racing through this new reality. Jamie had been dealt the same tragic hand as he had, but somehow she'd found peace and healing.

Suddenly, he thought of something else. Sierra, their oldest daughter. If Jamie's first husband was killed in the terrorist attacks, then ... that meant the child had been four or five when she'd lost her daddy. The reason she didn't look like Clay was because her real father was dead.

Alex sucked in a sharp breath. The information was more than he could process. Joe and Wanda's story must've been different. Very different. He'd heard them talk about the younger days, so the fact that she'd been married to a firefighter didn't really add up. He'd have to find out more about that later. But either way he was surrounded by 9/11 survivors.

And as if that wasn't enough, Jamie's husband had kept a journal? Notes about his days as a firefighter? FDNY guys were either loud and full of surface talk or quiet and tight-lipped — at least the ones his dad used to bring around the house. Other than his father, Alex hadn't thought there was another New York firefighter whose passion for the job came from a tender, transparent heart. But if Jamie's husband had kept a journal ... he must've been very much like Alex's dad.

Then when Jamie got to the part about finding a journal entry that mentioned his father's name, it was all a little too far out there. Like she was making the story up as she went along, or like she was trying to crawl into a place inside his heart that he had long since convinced himself no longer existed.

He clamped his jaw tight and made the sweeping right curve that put him at the beginning of Malibu Canyon. What did it matter if Jamie's husband had written about Alex's dad? Nothing in the guy's journal could've added a single detail to what Alex had known about his father, what he'd admired about him.

His dad was a hero long before he died in the collapse of the Twin Towers. He sat next to Alex at the kitchen table every weeknight from middle school on, teaching him how to find the circumference of a circle or the chemical names for salt and carbon dioxide and water. Testing him on the *Bill of Rights* and helping him edit his essay on George Orwell's *Animal Farm*. He took him to the park to throw a football and taught him how to shave two seconds off his sprint time in the hundred-yard dash. He was there every single time Alex needed him — right up until the morning of September 11.

Angry tears poked pins at his eyes, but Alex blinked them back. Crying wouldn't help. His dad was gone and he wasn't coming back. Period. Even so, the memories remained. Like with Holly, Alex didn't allow time for reminiscing, otherwise the pain would paralyze him. He didn't need heartbreak; he needed determination. Drive, not grief, was what saw him through every shift with the LA Sheriff's Department. The sort of drive that could keep him on his game sixty or eighty hours a week, so that no more creeps could steal the happy life from some other unsuspecting family.

He slowed down, taking the curves with expert care. His dad might as well be riding shotgun. That's how clear his father's image remained in Alex's mind, his tall and handsome dad, the smile in his eyes, the laughter in his voice. The man never once thought of himself, not at work and not at home. His last morning alive, he'd only been concerned that he and Alex talk about Alex's future, about him being a doctor or a lawyer or a salesman. Anything but a firefighter.

"I'm concerned for you, Son," his dad had told him. "You're driven and competitive. Fighting fires can take over a person's life and leave him nothing for the people back home."

His dad's final concern as he left for work that Tuesday was that Alex might find a career that would allow him an amazing life. *Others.* That's what drove his father in everything he did. Of course, he'd be racing up the stairs of the Twin Towers when everyone else was running down. His dad wouldn't have had it any other way.

Alex dug his fingers into the steering wheel. He tried his best never to go back to that horrible Tuesday morning. But here, winding through the canyon toward the beach, he couldn't stop himself. He'd been sitting in his Shakespeare class, first period, watching the door for the moment when Holly would pass by like she did every day at that time. Some kid from across the hall ran in and shouted something about a plane crashing into a building in the city.

There were TVs in every room, and almost instantly the footage was being broadcast throughout the school. All around him people were talking, saying things like, "Man, that's crazy," "How could a plane do that?" or "Look at that fire ... wickedest fire ever!"

Alex tuned out every noise but one: the sound of the announcer giving updates. Let everyone else wonder about why a plane would fly into a building or how many people must've been killed. Alex was the son of a firefighter. Looking at the first footage from the city's financial district told him that across Manhattan, fire trucks were being dispatched, racing into the streets and heading south to the Twin Towers. And within a handful of minutes, those same firefighters would be trekking their way up seventy stories into an inferno in the sky.

Don't do it, Dad ... don't go, he thought. *Be with him, God ... please. He's too good. Don't let him get hurt. Please, God ...* The frantic pleading ran constantly in Alex's mind from the moment he saw the flames. He was still catching his breath, still wishing he could get a message to his dad when another plane appeared on the left side of the screen and flew straight into the second tower.

No, God ... not again, please ... no ... The horror of the scene brought Alex to his feet, coursing through him and urging him to run, to find his dad and help somehow. But there was nothing he could do, nowhere to go. He didn't need the TV announcer to state the obvious: Someone had flown the jets into the buildings intentionally.

On purpose.

Alex couldn't find a place in his imagination to relate to the evil that would've done such a thing, so he watched, too stricken to move, until finally Holly raced into the room and took hold of his arm. "I talked to my mom," her face was pale, her eyes wide with terror. "She and your mother, they both want us home."

The images on the television drew him, but he needed to get home. His car was at the shop that day, so Holly was his best option. He grabbed her hand and raced with her toward the school parking lot. Maybe there was something they could do. If they could make it into Manhattan, maybe they could catch his dad and get him home. Before he reached the Twin Towers. They were irrational thoughts, all of them. As they drove home, they listened to the radio, and when Holly dropped him off, tears were streaming down her face. "What's happening? It's like the world's gone crazy."

Alex didn't know what to say, but he wanted to get inside, needed to see for himself again that the Twin Towers were really on fire. That he hadn't dreamed it. Needed to hear the reports about whether firefighters were actually being sent in to fight what looked like unbeatable fires. He promised to call Holly later, and he tore from her car, racing up the sidewalk and into his house.

His mother was sitting there, stone still, watching the TV, and . . .

Alex stopped himself. Stopped the memories cold right there. He couldn't take another minute of remembering. His heart was pounding so hard he could hear it, and his face felt flushed from the searing pain of the images in his head. He exhaled and tried to slow his heartbeat. The fear and agony and shock of that day was as real inside him now as it had been seven years ago.

Ahead of him, the ocean came into view, spread out beneath a hint of remaining daylight. With no plan, and no way to stop his racing heart, Alex took the easy route. At the light where Malibu Canyon ended at Pacific Coast Highway, he turned left and then right into the parking lot for Malibu Beach. A few surfers hung out near the showers, rubbing down their boards, peeling off wetsuits. They didn't notice him, another guy in a truck.

He parked in a spot that gave him a clear view of the water, and again he exhaled long and slow. The events of 9/11 were too agonizing to relive, and he could do nothing to change the outcome. So why remember it at all, except to let it motivate him? The criminals on the streets of Los Angeles County? They might as well all have been members of the al Qaeda. People who plotted evil were all the same, and someone needed to take care of them.

Someone other than God, because He didn't seem to be doing it.

Alex looked at the clock on his dashboard. It was just after eight. He didn't want to risk being late to the meeting, so he put his truck in reverse and pulled back into traffic. He missed the beach, missed surfing the way he'd done so often when he first moved here. The power of the waves beneath him was for a few seconds like wrestling his loss, like finding relief from it.

He would bring Bo here tomorrow, after his workout at Pierce College. That way he could surf and Bo could watch, and by the end of the afternoon he'd be one day closer to wearing his uniform again.

Shadows danced between the mountain peaks as Alex turned right onto Malibu Canyon. A sick part of him wanted to go back and retrace the day of the terrorist attacks, but he couldn't let himself think about that now, with the job ahead of him. Fear needed to be far from him, because this was his chance. An inside look at the insidious ways of the REA.

The meeting spot remained the same. Chumash Park. A sixteen-acre oasis of sloping hills and trees at the base of the Santa Monica Mountains. Alex pictured the park. He'd been aware of the place before, but in the last two weeks he'd cased it from every angle. Agoura High School sat to the east, and each of the other three sides was framed with cozy cul-de-sacs and two-story homes.

The beginnings of an adrenaline rush worked through his veins. He entered the Ventura Freeway, north again to Kanan Road, just a few miles away. The meeting place didn't surprise him, because it was smack in the middle of the sort of reclusive, high-end neighborhood that might house a member of the REA.

Once he'd been assigned to the taskforce on studying the REA, Alex had tried to climb into the REA mind-set by reading an interview with ecoterrorist Jeff Luers, a bespectacled guy with the look of a computer techie. Luers described himself as a militant, a radical who enjoyed civil disobedience. True to his passion, a year before the Twin Towers were attacked, the then-twenty-one-year-old Luers set fire to a number of SUV's on an Oregon car lot and was sentenced to more than twenty years in prison. The sentence brought Alex deep satisfaction, but there was something even more maddening.

After his arrest, Luers created a magazine called *Heartcheck*, in which he wrote this message to those who would come after him: "Smash it. Break it. Block it. Lock it down. I don't care why you do it or how you do it, but stop it. Get out there and stop it." Worse, in the same publication, Luers said, "It's a beautiful thing to see the financial district of a major city smashed to pieces." He went on to say that what happened on 9/11 "wasn't totally wrong," and that the World Trade Center was a legitimate target.

The idea that there were members of the REA who actually believed and thought the same way was enough to push Alex even in his off-hours. He focused on the center line stretched out before him. Did the members of the REA ever think about the people who put the fires *out*? Luers actually said in his interview that in order to stop consumerism and overuse of the environment, a loss of life might be necessary.

Of course, not every extreme environmental group behaved like the REA did. Some had even issued statements condemning the idea of violence as a means of achieving environmental goals. But not the REA.

Alex exited at Kanan Road, turned right, and drove a mile toward the hills. A left turn at Thousand Oaks Boulevard put him just a few blocks from Chumash Park. His heart beat out a hard and steady rhythm, and he was glad he'd left Bo at home. The dog would've sensed something big was about to happen, and since he couldn't be involved, it would only frustrate him.

Besides, Alex needed to be as inconspicuous as possible. No police dog, and no way he could let Owl or any of the others see his truck. A guy interested in joining the REA wouldn't think of driving a Dodge Ram. If anyone from the group suspected he was an infiltrator, they'd guess right away he was a cop. Everything he'd been working toward, the knowledge of the REA's headquarters, their plans for burning down custom homes, all his work would be gone in a single instant. His life could even be in danger. That's why he'd cased the area. At first he'd thought about parking in the strip mall at the corner of Kanan and T.O. Blvd. but at this hour the shops would be closed, leaving his truck way too visible.

Instead, he'd gone on Google Earth and found the perfect spot, a paved area nestled between the trees at the south end of the football stadium at Agoura High. Alex turned right on Argos Street and there it was, Chumash Park on his right, the high school on his left. The meeting spot was on the far side of the park, so even if Owl and the others were there, they would be near the picnic tables—out of view from his driving route down Argos.

Here we go, he thought. *Don't make a mistake.* He turned left into the school's back service road and wound his way up toward the stadium. The spot was perfect. A person couldn't see the truck from five feet away, let alone from across the street. He killed the engine and rehearsed his plan again. While he did, he slipped a pistol into his ankle holster and made sure his other guns were in place. Then he donned a hooded navy sweatshirt and slipped out of his work boots. He'd brought old leather sandals for the occasion—so he'd look the part a little better.

Finally, he pulled a miniature tape recorder from his glove box. The thing could pick up a conversation from twenty yards away. Alex had no doubt it would do the trick tonight. He needed proof of the meeting, so he could share it with his superiors. The information might never be admissible in court, but at least it would help Clay and Joe get the SWAT team on these guys. Before they lit a match to start their next fire.

He climbed out of the truck, shut the door, and slid his way through a few yards of brush, over a fence, and over a hill. Just like that, he was back on Argos. The street was empty as he jogged across and stayed to the right, cutting across the top of the park and then down Medea Valley Drive toward the picnic area. Alex slowed his pace, slipped his hand in his pocket, and started the recorder. At the same time, he checked his watch. Five minutes till nine.

Calm, Alex ... be calm. This is a war ... no room for hesitation. He exhaled and lifted his sweatshirt hood into place just as the first picnic table came into view. Sure enough, there were three men sitting at the table. Alex felt his heart skip a couple beats, then slam back into some kind of hyperrhythm. *Calm ... calm ...*

One of the men shifted his attention toward Alex, and the other two did the same. Alex forced himself to play the role, pretend he was truly interested in connecting with the REA. He kept his hands empty and at his sides as he approached the table.

"Danny?" The closest of the three men stood.

Alex glanced over one shoulder, then the other, and suddenly it occurred to him that he'd made a colossal mistake. So he was armed, so what? He was meeting with crazed felons in a dark park without backup of any kind, without a cell phone or a radio. What if this was an ambush? Alex refused to give the possibility further thought. It was too late for that. He motioned to the bald man. "You Owl?"

A slight breeze rustled the leaves of the trees overhead. The man shifted nervously, and behind him the backs of the others tensed. The short guy shrugged. "You need more than that."

More than that? Panic tried to grab at Alex, but he dodged it. "Green Night."

The man held out his hand. "Owl." He stopped short of smiling.

"Danny."

"Glad you could make it."

He wasn't sure whether to sit or not, so he stayed standing. If for some reason this *was* an ambush, he'd have a better chance on his feet. With a quick glance at the others, he noted everything he could about their appearances—everything he could determine at a dark picnic table in a matter of seconds. Owl had a week's growth on his unshaven face, and he was easily the youngest of the three. Of the other two, the shorter one was completely bald, and the taller one had neatly combed short dark hair and wire-rimmed glasses. Alex had no guarantee about this meeting or how long it would last. His observations needed to happen fast.

"Why the REA?" the one with the glasses nodded at Alex. His eyes looked hard and unflinching.

Alex needed to think fast, think like an ecoterrorist. "The REA's not really a group, right? I mean, it's a mind-set." He hooked his thumbs into his front pockets and stayed confident. "The more of us who act, the greater the chance people will notice." He gave a shrug that said the things he was explaining were obvious. "Civil disobedience has been a part of societal change since the days of the Boston Tea Party."

The air around them was still tense, but he saw the two at the table relax their posture a little. "We don't have long." The bald guy focused hard on Alex. The chip on his shoulder seemed only slightly smaller than his ego. "We're looking for people to run reconnaissance for us. A few housing tracts."

Alex could hardly believe he was taping this conversation. "Owl tells me you're looking at the Oak Canyon Estates."

The two on the table looked at each other—then at Owl. They wore buttoned-down oxfords and dark slacks—like they'd just gotten off work at a bank or an insurance office.

"Danny guessed." Owl's lower lip twitched, and his voice rose a notch. "Not like I just brought it up."

The tall bespectacled man was still looking at Alex. "Owl talks too much." He leaned closer. "You talk and we kill you. Get it?"

Alex ignored that. "So it's the OCE, that's what's next?"

"The OCE is ours. You'll start small. Find the next possible targets."

"Right." The bald one piped in. "You'll report to Owl."

"What am I looking for? Homes only, or SUV's?" Alex's heart pounded harder, fueled by a combination of fear and thrill. "I could take out an SUV every night after work."

"The REA is more methodical than that." The tall guy bristled. "You'll do only what we tell you to do."

His buddy nodded. "Or it isn't the REA."

Owl looked nervous, uneasy. Alex had the suspicion that maybe Owl wasn't as committed as the other two, as if he was maybe in over his head here and didn't know how to cut himself free. If he was right, Owl could be a help to him down the road. Alex was about to ask what they'd already accomplished and how long it had taken to plan those attacks, when a small sedan drove slowly by the park, along the street closest to them.

Immediately, Owl took a step back, and the other two stood. "Meeting's done." The guy with the glasses started walking in the opposite direction of the car.

The driver of the car was either part of the REA or someone undercover, a detective from the sheriff's department watching them. Either way, the three said nothing as they left the picnic table and hurried through a cluster of trees. Alex took a different route, straight across the field toward the far end of the park. He wasn't sure what happened to the slow-moving sedan, but he heard no sounds of a car. Was he crazy to be out here when he was on mandatory leave? He reached into his pocket and clicked the tape recorder shut so it wouldn't pick up his racing heart. If the information he'd gathered tonight was ever going to be used, he would really have to work to convince people why he'd done this.

When he was sure he wasn't being followed, he crossed the street, pushed his way through the bushes, back over the fence and climbed into his truck. The service road he'd driven in on led back to the freeway a different way, so that he could avoid crossing paths with any of them.

Alex was halfway to the freeway when he finally caught his breath. *Stupid, Alex ... so stupid.* A cop should never make himself that vulnerable. He grabbed a piece of gum from the center console and shoved it in his mouth. It was one thing to be driven to get the bad guys, to protect the citizens of the city in a way that would've made his father proud. But it was another to be so careless that he got himself killed. He'd have to keep his discussions with Owl to the phone. He could tape those conversations a lot easier.

It was just after ten o'clock when he pulled off the freeway and drove the last few miles home, and only then did he think once more about Jamie Michaels and the things she'd told him, the sad truth about her first husband and the bit about his journal. But more than that, something else she'd told him weighed heavily on his mind. The part about her praying for him. Not because he wanted to think about God or allow himself to believe again, but because if there had ever been a time when he could almost sense that someone had been praying for him, it was tonight.

FIFTEEN

Jamie found the woman's phone number by contacting a few of her friends back in New York—Jake's former captain, Aaron Hisel, and her good friend, Sue Henning. As it turned out, Sue had spent time with Linda Brady at an FDNY wives' support group in the first few years after 9/11. Back when Jamie spent all her spare time at St. Paul's. She had dialed the number as she sat at the Lazy J Park and watched Sierra and CJ play on this early October afternoon. The conversation with Sue was long overdue, the way it was when best friends let half a year pass between hellos.

"I'm seeing someone." Sue's voice was brimming with the sort of hope and new life that hadn't been there since her husband Larry's death. "He's a police officer. We met at church." She paused. "We're talking about getting married."

Jamie listened as she sat on a bench close to where the kids were playing, enjoying the sun on her face. "Ah, Sue … I'm so glad." She didn't need to comment on the fact that they'd both found police officers, or that God had a way of knowing which women could be married to men who put their lives on the line every time they went to work. That much was obvious. She pictured her friend, sitting near the front window of her house in Staten Island. "How are the kids?"

"Katy's eleven, same as Sierra. She still talks about her and has that BFF photo of the two of them on her dresser."

"Sierra has hers too." Jamie smiled. "What about little Larry?"

Sue's lighthearted laughter filled the phone lines. "He doesn't like the little part, anymore. He's eight now. Tallest kid in the second grade."

"We need to get back there, get everyone together." Jamie meant it. Sue and Larry had been her and Jake's best friends before 9/11. The couples spent their free time together and had everything in common. After their husbands were killed, Jamie wasn't sure she would've survived without Sue.

"How are you and Clay?"

"He's wonderful … so patient with me." She took in a long breath and went into the story about Alex and his determination to keep people out of his life. "I feel like Alex is part of Jake's legacy, somehow. Like Clay and I are supposed to reach him and tell him about God, you know? Help him find the healing he's missing."

They talked for another ten minutes about Sue's new guy and Jamie's love for Clay, and about the kids.

"I think Katy's starting to forget." Sue's voice was tinged with a sorrow she'd long since made peace with. "She doesn't talk about Larry like she used to, and when we see a picture of our family back then, she squints at it, like she can't really place the details."

"It's that way with Sierra too. I noticed the changes a few years ago — the details aren't crisp like before."

"Still," Sue drew in an encouraging sigh, "God is good. He's taught us all how to live with our losses, and He's given us new people to love."

"Yes, He has." Jamie liked the way that sounded. *New people to love.* Healing was definitely happening when people could find their way out of the dark clouds of grief to love again. Further proof that Alex hadn't gone more than a few steps on the mile-long journey to healing.

The two made a plan to talk again, sooner this time, and Jamie made Sue promise to send an invitation if there was, indeed, a wedding in the works. Before they hung up, Jamie pulled a pen and piece of paper from her purse and jotted down Linda's number. When the call was over, Jamie spent a few minutes relieving Sierra, pushing CJ in his swing while Sierra took the swing beside them.

"Higher, Mommy! So high, okay?"

"Okay, buddy." Jamie grinned at Sierra. "He could swing for an hour and never get tired."

"Tell me about it." Sierra dropped her shoulders forward, as if she was already exhausted from pushing CJ for the past ten minutes. Then she straightened and her eyes began to dance. "Did I tell you the boys are chasing us at school again?" She made a face, but the sparkle in her eyes remained. She was in fifth grade, and already the talk between them turned to boys fairly often. "We four girls found a hiding place, though. On the other side of the school by the baseball field."

"That's good." Jamie studied her daughter, the way her face still held a strong resemblance to Jake's. "Boys can wait awhile."

Sierra giggled. "That's what Daddy says."

Jamie smiled, because with Sierra's words, Sue's statement came rushing back. The part about God giving them new people to love. The fact that Sierra would have not one, but two wonderful fathers in her lifetime was more than Jamie could have asked for.

"Slide!" CJ pointed to the climbing structure and a couple of built-in slides across the sandy play area. "Out, Mommy! Peeeese!"

She lifted him from his swing. "Can you go with him, Sierra, sweetie? I have one more phone call, okay?"

"Sure." She stood up from the swing and took hold of CJ's hand. "I like the slides too, right, Ceej?"

"Yay!" He strained forward, pulling her along behind him. "Come on, Sissy ... come on!"

Jamie made her way back to the bench, all the while watching her kids as they walked toward the nearest slide. She found the phone number on the slip of paper and punched in the numbers on her cell phone. As the phone began to ring, she uttered a last-minute prayer, asking God to help her reach Linda Brady, and that, in the process, some sort of wisdom might come of the conversation, wisdom that might help her and Clay reach Alex.

The woman answered the phone almost on the first ring. "Hello, this is Linda." She sounded upbeat and lighthearted.

Jamie leaned back against the hard park bench. "Linda, this is Jamie Michaels, formerly Jamie Bryan. I think our husbands used to work together for the FDNY."

"Who?" A short pause filled the phone lines. Then Linda sucked in a quick breath. "Oh, wait. Jamie Bryan ... Jake's wife. Sue Henning told me about you. Sue's Larry and your Jake were at the same station."

"Right." Sudden tears stung Jamie's eyes, and she dabbed at them with her wrist. When it came to losing Jake, there was an ocean of tears in her heart, and whether she liked it or not, she was never more than a few minutes from the beach. She sniffed silently and composed herself. "Did I catch you at a bad time?"

"Not at all. I'm a nurse now, and I work later today, but not for a while."

Jamie felt herself relax. "Okay, good." She wasn't quite sure where to begin. "Did Sue tell you I remarried?"

"No." A smile filled Linda's voice. "I haven't been to a support group meeting for years now. I think a lot of us are remarried."

The news surprised Jamie for some reason. "You're remarried?"

"Three years ago." Some of the joy in her tone fell off. "Not that life is ever normal again."

"No." Jamie smiled at CJ, just about to go down the slide. "It's beautiful, but never really normal." She slid to the edge of the bench, willing herself to get to the point. "Anyway, I live in LA now, and my husband is a sergeant with the LA Sheriff's Department. His name is Clay Michaels. He works with your son, Alex."

It took a moment before Linda responded. "Your husband knows Alex?"

"We both do. Alex has been coming to our house for dinner once a month for the last year."

"I ... I had no idea." A hint of bitterness now colored her voice. "He doesn't tell me anything about his life in California."

Jamie kept her eyes on Sierra and CJ, still on the play structure. She didn't figure now was a great time to tell the woman about Alex's role in the hostage situation, or the fatally shot suspect. "He's still very hurt. Very closed off."

"Yes. He hasn't moved past the loss of his father. That's why he's out there fighting crime. Just him and his dog." She hesitated. "Is he ... is he seeing anyone? He never talks about that with me."

"Not that we can tell." Jamie told her about Jake's journal and how she'd found the entry about Ben. "I guess he and Jake were talking about Ben's favorite Bible verse."

"John 16:33." Linda didn't hesitate. "Did you tell Alex about the entry?"

"He wouldn't let me." The defeat was still there in Jamie's voice, but it was tempered by a new sense of hope. Certainly his mother would be able to shed some light on the young man. "He told me that getting past 9/11 was different for me because I have Clay, and that made me think ... was there someone for Alex ... a special girl? Before the terrorist attacks?"

Linda sighed. "There was. Her name was Holly Brooks. She and Alex dated from their freshman year on, right up until that awful day during their senior year of high school."

"And then?"

"I don't know. A part of Alex died that day. The part capable of trusting and loving."

The thought was so sad. Again, Jamie felt her eyes grow damp. "Do you still talk to her?"

"Actually, she moved to LA. Works for a developer, at least she used to. I have her information written down somewhere." Linda's cheerful tone was all but gone. "Alex loved that girl with his whole being. I always thought if someone could find the old Alex in the pile of debris left after the collapse of those towers, it would be Holly. She went to LA because of Alex."

The flicker of hope in Jamie burned a little brighter. "Then they've talked."

"Just once, as far as I know. Alex turned her away. Told her he could never give her the life or the love she deserved. His only purpose in life was his police work. Making his dad proud, doing his part to prevent the murder of other people's fathers."

Jamie's heart hurt listening to the details. No wonder Alex's eyes were full of so much pain. He'd lost more than his father; he'd put aside his girl and his future ... everything that had mattered for the first eighteen years of his life. "How did Holly take it?"

"I haven't talked to her in a year or so. She left me a message a few months ago that she's seeing someone, trying to move on. The whole thing's so sad."

Jamie's mind raced. "You said you had her information somewhere? Do you think you could give it to me? Maybe she could help Clay and me understand him better, the way he used to be?"

The slight chuckle that came from Linda was more hopeless than humorous. "It's too late for that, but ... well, I don't think she'd mind if you had her information. At least her work number."

This was what Jamie had prayed for, a breakthrough, some new way she could reach Alex. She silently prayed while Linda looked for the details.

"Here we go." Linda sounded doubtful. "She works for a developer named Dave Jacobs." Linda rattled off the girl's work number. "I'll say this … if you and Clay care enough about my son to do this, then my husband and I will be praying. That's all I can do for him anymore." A crack in her voice betrayed the depth of her heartache. "Seven years ago, I lost my husband and my son, all on the same day. Since then I've prayed for a breakthrough and maybe … maybe somehow this is it."

The phone call ended with Jamie promising to keep in touch with Linda, and to pass along updates about how Alex was doing or if he was making any progress. When Jamie slipped her phone back into her purse, she thought about this Holly Brooks, a girl so in love with Alex she had moved across the country to follow him. Suddenly, in the warmth of the afternoon sun, Jamie was convinced of two things: First, God was indeed leading her to work on behalf of Alex's healing, as a part of Jake's legacy and her own. And second, she needed to make a call to Holly Brooks, to see if she could help them understand Alex a little better. At the same time, maybe Jamie could determine whether Holly had moved on and found love elsewhere. Because maybe, Jamie suspected, just maybe, she was still longing for the striking young deputy who had captured her heart when she was just a girl.

Sixteen

Holly was having trouble focusing. She'd given three tours that day and closed the deal on the sale of the largest home in the current phase—the one at the end of the street. It was early afternoon, and she still had two more appointments, but not for another hour. The break gave her the chance to grab a cup of coffee and settle in at her desk for some paperwork.

But her heart wasn't interested in numbers and spreadsheets. She pushed the pile of papers back and leaned on her elbows, her eyes on the brown hills adjacent to the development. The sky was bluer up here above the valley, and today especially so. The Santa Ana winds hadn't materialized into anything too strong yet, and it had been a week since anyone had mentioned the fire danger posed by the phoned-in threat.

Life should be wonderful, but there was a heaviness in Holly's soul that made every breath a struggle. Something caught her attention, and she looked across the street and over one homesite to see Dave and Ron examining the framing of a spec home that they'd just broken ground on. Ron's confidence was like a force around him, something she could feel without seeing his face or hearing his voice. It was what had attracted her to him the first time they met.

So what was the problem? Holly released a heavy breath and covered her face with her hands. She and Ron had gone out twice now, two Saturdays in a row. The first night he'd taken her to LAX where they boarded a plane and flew to Vegas for dinner at Andre's in the Monte Carlo hotel. They sat near a grand fireplace and ate exquisite French food by candlelight. After dinner a limo met them out front and whisked them to the Hilton where they had stage seats for Barry Manilow.

Holly had never been on a date like that in her life, never even dreamed of such a thing. The whole time, Ron was attentive and proud of himself for coming up with something so creative. They caught a red-eye back, and he dropped her off at her townhouse just before three in the morning. Holly dropped her hands back to the desk and looked up at the pair of champagne glasses sitting on the top shelf of her office bookcase. They were souvenirs from the concert. Their seats were so close they had the chance to shake Barry's hand during one of the songs.

Once she realized how extravagant a date he'd planned for her, Holly worried about his expectations. When Ron wanted something, he got it. But on the flight home he simply took her hand and looked into her eyes. "I hope you don't mind getting home so late."

"No," Holly's answer was quick. How could she mind? He'd just given her a night fit for a princess. "I'm fine ... the night was," no other word seemed to fit, "it was lovely, Ron."

"Good." He gave her hand a squeeze. His palms were dry this time. "I wanted to get you home before morning. So you wouldn't question my intentions."

With that he launched into a dissertation about faith and his moral compass and maintaining integrity in every area of life, including his relationships. Holly agreed with everything he said, but he never asked for her input, and for some reason the whole bit came across like a lecture or a speech — impersonal and more about Ron than something intimate and special the two of them might've shared.

When he drove her home, he hopped out of his BMW, walked around the front of the car, and opened her door. She'd been curious about whether he'd kiss her, but before she had time to think about it, he moved in close and pressed his lips to hers. It was quick and to the point, then he took a step back and patted her arm. "Thank you, Holly. I had a wonderful evening."

She resisted the temptation to say the word *lovely*. Instead she smiled and thanked him, and that was that. When she went inside, she walked around her empty townhouse trying to understand why she felt so let down, so alone.

Holly stood and walked to the bookcase. She took one of the champagne glasses and held it by the stem. The date should've been a dream come true, but instead it reminded her of something she'd read in a magazine once about a certain pop star's wedding. The couple had spent more than a million dollars on everything from a dress handmade in Vienna to a cake whose price tag was in the five figures. Holly read the article, and rather than longing for something similar, she caught herself feeling sorry for the couple. Could love ever find its way into a ceremony so lavishly wasteful, so grossly materialistic?

She set the glass down again. This past Saturday had been simpler. A drive to the beach and dinner at Gladstone's. But by the time he'd brought her home and efficiently kissed her goodnight, she finally figured out the problem. Both times they went out, Ron had the entire evening scripted. There seemed to be a schedule to keep, an agenda. Though in some ways he seemed the most spontaneous guy she'd ever met, the spirit of spontaneity was completely missing on their dates. It was like he was in a hurry to check things off the list.

Dinner … conversation … even the kiss.

She wandered back to her desk and sat down again. Or maybe that wasn't it at all. Maybe it was all about the newspaper article, about seeing Alex after so much time. Holly couldn't stop thinking about him. She breathed in deeply and checked her watch. She still had half an hour before her next appointment. She rolled her chair a few feet to the computer and placed her hands over the keyboard. Without really meaning to, she typed his name into the Google search line. Alex Brady. Then she added the keywords she already knew would work. *LA Sheriff's Department ... award ... K9.* The story with his picture was the first thing that popped up.

And there he was, the stern-faced deputy who had once been the boy she loved. The photo showed him accepting an award, but it might as well have been a cry for help. His expression was so closed off. The phone began to ring, and in a rush Holly closed the Internet site. But before she could reach for the receiver, Ron and Dave stormed through the front door. Ron stuck his head in her office. "We need you out here." His expression was all business. "It's urgent." He continued into the house after his father.

She glanced at the Caller ID, in case the call was from one of her appointments. But the window read *Michaels*—a name she wasn't familiar with. She would have to let the machine take the call. She hurried past the computer, where the image of Alex's face remained. "Coming," she announced. She found them sitting at the dining room table, poring over a piece of paper. Whatever the problem, they both looked stricken. She hesitated as she reached them. "What's going on?"

Ron's face was several shades paler than usual. "Remember the phone threat we got the other day? The one that said we would be targeted for a fire up here?"

"Of course." Holly's heartbeat doubled. She sat slowly in the chair opposite them and looked at the paper on the table. "What about it?"

Dave handed the paper to her. "One of the framers found this tacked to the back of the house across the street."

"I didn't think the threat was serious before." Ron wasn't panicked, but he was definitely concerned.

Holly took the paper and studied it. The person had typed the brief letter, and Holly scanned it quickly, wanting to get to the point.

Developer:

Since you have chosen to violate the natural resources of our canyons and hillsides, and since you persist in creating homes that meet the gluttonous needs of the over-indulgent in our society, we are hereby giving you notice. Tear down your homes, or they will be burned to the ground. Don't think your gate can keep us out. We're everywhere.

The letter was signed only, "*The REA.*"

Holly felt sick to her stomach. There were often nights when she worked later than the others, up here alone. Day or night, she was terrified at the thought of being here when a fire might be set. "Have you called the police?"

"Of course." Ron took the letter from her. "They've promised increased security, but still ..."

"They found a way to get up here and tack that threat onto one of our homes." Dave's forehead glistened with a faint layer of perspiration. He'd never looked this upset in all the time Holly had known him. "That could just as easily have been a match, and—"

"And there's no telling how much we would've lost." Ron stood and walked to the window at the back of the room. For a while he stared out at the hills behind the development. Then he turned back to them. "We're surrounded by dry brush."

"Which we've known about from the beginning." Dave sounded as if he were trying to calm himself down. "Every hillside home stands in the line of fire danger. Same as homes in the Midwest stand in the line of tornado danger. People buy these houses knowing that. But an arsonist?" He stared at his son. "We never planned for this."

Holly was grateful they'd included her in the meeting. The danger was as much hers as theirs, but neither of them was looking to her for comments or thoughts on the matter. She sat back in her chair and listened, trying not to give way to the anxiety building up inside her. "We have the gate, don't forget. And the security fence." Dave stood and paced to the nearest window and back. "That's gotta be worth some sort of protection."

Ron waved the paper at the front door. "Neither one did us any good last night, or whenever this was left here."

Dave anchored his forearms on the table and uttered a heavy sigh. "Tell her what the sheriff's department said."

Ron shifted his attention, and for the first time — maybe the first time ever — he had genuine concern in his eyes. "They said we need to be very careful. Report any suspicious activity ... be aware of people wanting tours and then not following through. That sort of thing."

"Not following through?" Holly felt overwhelmed at the idea. "I've given tours to hundreds of people. We've sold only a handful of homes." She felt bewildered, and her nervous laugh conveyed the fact. "So everyone who comes up for a tour is a suspect?"

Ron maintained his concern. "They told me we can't be too careful. That's all I'm saying."

"They're afraid someone'll start a fire in the middle of the day? With the gates wide open?"

"That's why we wanted you in on this." Dave tapped his knuckles on the table, his voice tense. "This is very serious. Every person who makes it up that road must be greeted. We must get names and addresses. Phone numbers." He shot a questioning look at Ron. "Maybe even license plates and descriptions."

Ron jabbed his finger in the air, and his eyebrows lifted. "I like that." He looked at Holly. "You could do that, right? I mean, there's not that much traffic up here."

Holly didn't mind, certainly, but she had her doubts. "Most of the time that would work, but ... I have to say that on the weekend there are times when I can't get to everyone. Some people come up, drive around, and maybe get out of their cars for a few minutes. They leave before I can get to them."

Dave and Ron seemed to think about that for a minute. "That should be okay." Ron walked back to the table and sat down. "No one would start a fire when it's busy, when people are all around."

Holly tried to imagine an arsonist coming up the hill. They might avoid the crowded days, but they would hardly want to be the only visitor here, either. Catching a lone visitor would be easier than catching someone who slipped into a crowd. But before she could say so, Dave threw his hands up, his tension high. "Crowded or not, it doesn't matter. The point is we need license plates and descriptions. Some way of tracking the people who come up. I can't stand the thought of someone getting hurt in our development."

They talked about the idea of a guard station and decided it might be a good idea — at least when the gate was open. That way, every car up the hill would be accounted for.

"Paying a security guard to screen every visitor would cost considerably less than the damage a fire would cause." Dave seemed to settle down some. "I like the idea."

The conversation wrapped up, and Dave and Ron congratulated Holly on closing another deal that morning. "There'll be a bonus in your next paycheck," Ron told her. "You're really quite good at what you do, Holly."

Holly wished his compliment made her feel warm and special inside, but it didn't. The way he delivered his lines — even to her — made him sound like a college math professor declaring some sort of algebraic theory.

Ron and Dave left to check the progress on a home at the far right end of the street, across from the large model they'd just sold. After they were gone, Holly returned to her office. She was terrified at the thought of an arsonist. No matter how the note had gotten tacked to the back of the new house, a fire setter could do his work alone or with people all around. The idea was way too possible.

She sat back at her desk and positioned herself in front of the computer again. But what scared her more than a fire in the hills was the possibility of settling for a man she didn't love. A nice guy with a nice faith and a nice job who knew how to take her out on the town and show her a nice time. A guy who hadn't once dug deep enough to know her heart, and who seemed to handle dating like another to-do list. Settling for just okay, when once upon a high school romance she'd had a love that seemed to have slipped right from the pages of a storybook.

That scared her.

Holly stood and stretched. She needed fresh air, needed to clear her mind before she could focus on selling houses again. A quick look through the window told her the development was pretty quiet for now. Light work crews at either end of the street, but otherwise no one in sight. She stepped out the front door and breathed in deeply. The canyon had a sweet smell, mesquite mixed with wild grass and clear air. She sauntered down the walkway, out of the shadow of the house and into the sun. Her mind drifted to the situation with Ron. The right girl would fall over backwards trying to win the attention of a guy like Ron Jacobs.

But maybe that girl had never hiked along a deep blue lake in the Adirondacks beside a tall handsome boy who could see straight to the center of her soul. She was about to turn around and head back in the house when something caught her attention. She turned toward the movement in time to see a shiny, full-size black pickup truck spray gravel as it headed back down the hill.

She caught just a glimpse of the driver's profile before the truck disappeared behind a clump of brush, leaving only a cloud of dust to mark its place. There was something strangely familiar about the guy, but Holly wasn't sure why. She felt her stomach tighten. Maybe he'd been up here before, casing the development. She could get his license plate number. She took a few running steps toward the place where the truck had been before she stopped herself. It was too late for license plates. The guy was probably halfway down the hill. She needed to tell Ron and Dave. What if the driver was part of this whole fire threat thing? This was when a guard at the gate would've been perfect. She could've radioed him to stop the truck and ask the driver a bunch of questions.

She hurried inside, her heart racing ahead of her, and radioed Ron. After she explained what she'd seen and how the guy had seemed in a hurry to leave, Ron calmed her down.

"An ecoterrorist wouldn't drive a full-size truck Holly, my dear. Definitely not." The sound of loud hammering and men's voices made it hard to hear him. "Probably just someone curious about what's up here."

He had a point. She finished the conversation, turned off the radio, and stared out the window. What was it about the driver, the way he'd looked familiar? A few seconds passed, and suddenly it hit her. Her heart thudded in response, and her breathing became fast and shallow. She slid her chair over to the computer and moved the mouse, bringing the screen back to life. The picture was still there, the deputy and his dog, the award. The image was the same as the one in her head, but it couldn't be him. Alex would have no idea where she worked, and certainly if they were going to send a deputy up to look around for anything suspicious, they'd send one in a marked car.

The resemblance was all in her head, and what did that say about her feelings for Ron? She could tell herself she needed time, or that her mother was right — real love took work. But her mind must've had other ideas. There could be only one reason why a quick glance at a perfect stranger in a truck she'd never seen before would remind her of Alex Brady:

Her heart had never forgotten him.

SEVENTEEN

Alex had to will himself to slow down, because if the rush of urgency in his veins had its way, he'd be flying a hundred miles an hour. He'd done what he set out to do today. He'd gone to the Oak Canyon Estates to check out for himself the danger and layout of the property.

What he'd found had shot terror straight through him.

He and Bo weren't there long, just enough time to drive to the end of the street and back down again. But that's all it took to tell him what a fire would do this high up in the hills. It wouldn't work its way down the street—it would explode through it. The wood-framed homes and construction materials would go up like so many fireworks, and the hillside would be instantly on fire. Alex didn't need fire training to understand that such an inferno would roar down the steep, sloping brush and become a firestorm in minutes.

"It'd be a fire like nothing LA's ever seen." He spoke the words out loud, and from the back Bo whined. "It's okay, Bo ... we won't let it happen. We'll get the bad guys."

At that, Bo released a single sharp bark—the way he was trained to do on command whenever Alex mentioned bad guys. It was one more thing that set Bo apart. He shared Alex's passion for getting the job done. At the base of the hill, Alex made two quick rights into a housing tract literally carved into the mountain. The homes sat on lots barely larger than the footprints of the houses, with maybe ten feet between them. At this afternoon hour, the neighborhood had kids everywhere—riding bikes along the narrow street, playing basketball in the driveway of a house that backed up to the hillside, and walking with their parents along the neatly manicured sidewalks.

Alex took the road through the development, driving slowly enough that he could see a handful of cul-de-sacs that branched off on either side of the street. He was stunned at the danger the place posed. There were tons of homes bunched together on maybe six or seven acres, and there were only two ways out. Two exits for the entire neighborhood.

He pulled out of the development and realized his hands were shaking. Sure the homes had tile roofs, but roofing wouldn't stop a tidal wave of fire barreling down the hillside. Add winds to the formula, and a neighborhood like the one at the base of the mountain could be swallowed whole — taking dozens of lives with it. Hundreds, even. He rolled down all four windows so he could breathe. From the backseat, he heard Bo walk to the window and stick his face out — the way he loved to do.

The faces of Owl and the other two came to mind, and he felt the anger again, felt it driving him to do something. Anything but sit back and let Oak Canyon Estates become victim to the REA. At the next stoplight, he grabbed his iPhone, swiped his finger across the lock bar, and dialed Clay Michaels.

Clay picked up just before the call went to his voice mail. "What's up, Brady?" His voice was raised above the noise of what sounded like a restaurant.

"Something big's about to happen, Sarge. I had to call."

"Hold on." There was a pause, and the background noise dimmed some. "There. I can hear now. Say it again?"

"We're on the verge of something big … I had to call. Somebody's gotta be on this."

Clay uttered a muffled groan. "A wave, you mean? A big wave? Tell me you mean a wave, Brady, 'cause you're supposed to be on a beach, remember?"

"Sarge, I'm serious." Alex expected this, the reminder that he had a week left before he was even supposed to be thinking about police work. But he had to get the information to the department one way or another. He was using his Bluetooth, so he had both hands on the wheel as he talked. "I met with the leaders of the REA."

"What?" Clay raised his voice, and then quickly brought it back down again. "What do you mean? Like you put on a green T-shirt and pretended to hate trucks?"

"For a few minutes, yes." Alex wasn't worried about getting in trouble. He hadn't represented himself as a deputy, and he hadn't done anything illegal. "Remember I told you about Owl, how I was talking to him?"

"Brady, you're crazy. Deputies don't infiltrate into terrorist gangs on their off-hours. Nobody does that, and if they do they—"

"Wait! This is important." Alex had never taken a sharp tone with Clay, but in this moment he came close. His breathing came faster than before. "They didn't know I was a deputy. We met at a park off Kanan Road. I taped the whole thing. Had a recorder in my pocket and got it all."

"You *what*?" This time Clay shouted the question. "What if they'd found it on you? They could've killed you, Brady." He was seething. "Besides, that won't be admissible, you know that."

"I'm aware of that." Respect returned to Alex's voice. "I'm not trying to build a case; I'm trying to stop a tragedy before it happens."

Clay was quiet at that, as if maybe, finally, Alex's words hit their mark. "Okay … what'd you learn?"

"A lot. They're gonna hit the Oak Canyon Estates." Alex worked to regain control of his emotions. He was halfway down Las Virgenes Road now—headed for Malibu. He had his surfboard in the back, because he really did plan to hit the waves tonight. The trip to the Oak Canyon Estates had been on the way, and he just couldn't resist checking out the development.

"They said that?"

"In so many words." Alex reached back and patted Bo, but he kept his eyes on the curves of the canyon. "Check it out. Please. See if anyone from the development has called the department. My guess is the REA is making threats. That's sort of their calling card."

"So you're sure."

"Absolutely. I just drove up to the development. Sarge, it's terrible. The houses sit right in a clearing surrounded by sky-high brush. And at the base of the hill are a hundred homes. I mean, if the winds are right, we could lose the whole neighborhood and half the people living there."

This time Clay was quiet for several seconds. "You know what I thought when I saw your name on Caller ID?" He sounded suddenly tired. "I thought, 'Well look at that. Alex Brady is taking time out of a stroll with his mother through Central Park to call me on my birthday.'"

Alex remembered the restaurant sounds. "It's your birthday?"

"It is."

"Oh." Alex put both hands on the steering wheel again. Traffic was light in the canyon, but he liked full control for the last curves. "Happy birthday."

"Thanks." He sighed. "We've gone over this before. Fire danger is high all around LA this season, and everything you're hearing could be nothing more than false tips."

"It doesn't feel that way."

"Okay. So ... you want me to check for complaints from the developer, and then what? Tell Lost Hills to send out a patrol every hour to keep an eye on the place?"

"Something like that." Alex didn't smile. There was nothing lighthearted about the situation.

"I'll tell you what, Brady. I'll check into it if you work on one thing." The background noise was getting loud once more.

"What's that?"

"Your suntan." He had to talk above the sounds around him. "No more detective work on your off time, Brady. You could get yourself killed. You get that?"

"Yes, sir."

"Okay, then. I'll let you know if I hear anything."

When he'd clicked his phone off, Alex's overwhelming alarm eased some. Clay was good for his word. If he said he'd check into the situation, he would. And if he found that calls had been made from the developer expressing concern about arson, combined with Alex's tip, then they could justify sending a deputy up every hour. Whatever it took to protect the homes and the hills and the residents.

And the firefighters who would be forced to deal with the conflagration when it happened.

He reached Pacific Coast Highway and turned right this time. Malibu was too crowded this time of the day, so he headed north to Zuma Beach and parked facing the farthest part of the beach from the entrance. He surveyed the empty stretch of sand and the waves rolling in. It was just after three o'clock, the perfect time to surf. He helped Bo out and attached a chain to his collar. Bo was completely reliable without a chain, but if anyone walked by, a German shepherd of his stature could be very intimidating. The chain helped.

Alex peeled off his T-shirt and grabbed his surfboard. It was in the high nineties, even at the beach, so he grabbed a gallon jug of water and a bag with Bo's bowl and a towel. Clay didn't have to worry. He was already tan from spending the last two afternoons here. The beach was helping pass the time, but he was going to go crazy waiting another week before he could get into his uniform.

Bo loved the water, just not over his head. So after Alex set his things down close to the shore, he walked his dog to the ocean's edge and unhooked him. Bo frolicked along the foamy surf a few yards, and then padded back to Alex. His eyes were raised as if to say, "Come play with me."

Laughter flexed the muscles along Alex's bare stomach. "You wanna play, is that it, boy?"

Bo barked once. The way he held his mouth made it look like he was almost smiling.

There were no people in sight, so Alex balled up the chain and tossed it onto the damp sand. Then he took off after Bo, toward the shallow water. Every few steps he splashed the dog, and Bo would turn around and chase him. The game ended when Alex spotted a bikini-clad girl coming their way. He lowered himself and held his arms out to his dog. "C'mere, Bo."

Immediately, he wagged his tail and walked right into Alex's arms. Alex hugged him and gave him a hearty pat on his back. "Good boy, Bo." He stood. "Heel."

Bo fell into place at Alex's side, and they walked up the beach to the chain. Once it was on, Alex dropped to the sand and leaned back against his hands.

"Hi."

The sound of her voice caught him off guard. He turned and shaded his eyes to find her standing a few feet away. "Hi." He tried to use his tone to tell her he didn't want company.

"What's your dog's name?"

Alex felt the muscles in his jaw tense. "Bo."

"He's beautiful." She walked around in front of him and reached toward his dog. "Does he bite?"

If she only knew. "He's fine."

She was probably in her early twenties, a bleached blonde with a pale blue string bikini that matched her eyes. "I love German shepherds."

He didn't say anything. Other than a subtle admiration, Alex felt no thrill from her presence.

"I live down the beach a ways. Just seemed like a good day for a walk."

Alex squinted at her. "I guess."

She patted Bo a little more. "You want company?"

He smiled at her as politely as he could. The condition of his frozen heart wasn't her fault. "Honestly?"

"Sure." She tilted her head, her eyes catching the sunlight.

"My board's up there on the beach. I sort of wanted a few hours alone in the water."

Something in his voice must've hit its mark, because she straightened and took a step back. "Okay, then." Her smile told him she considered the move his loss. She shrugged one shoulder. "See you around."

"Yeah." He put one arm around Bo's back and felt his smile fall flat. "See ya." He watched her go, and for the few seconds it took the next set of waves to crash to the beach, she wasn't some stranger hitting on him, she was Holly, walking away. Leaving him for the last time, without looking back.

He stared at the distant horizon at the far end of the ocean. Wherever she was, he hoped she'd finally figured out how to make a break with the past. His mom insisted she was still in Los Angeles, working in real estate. But Alex doubted that. She had probably moved back to the East Coast by now, met some great guy who could love her wholeheartedly, the way she deserved to be loved. He'd certainly given her no reason to wait around for him in LA.

Alex looked down the beach again. When the blonde girl was far enough away, he walked up to the crest of sand, chained Bo to his bag, and poured him a bowl of water. The waves looked strong, bigger than before. He grabbed his surfboard, slipped off the shorts he wore over his swim trunks, and ran down the sand to the water. He could already feel the waves beneath him, and as he stretched onto his board and paddled out, he thought again of the REA. How could they believe setting a fire to anything would further their cause?

He moved past the first line of breakers to the place where the waves were three and four feet high and waited. Driving by the Oak Canyon Estates had been a good idea. Now he understood even more the urgency of the pending disaster. The firestorm would be like nothing this area had ever seen. He angled his board out to sea. A wave was forming, rising up out of the water and coming toward him. Alex paddled hard, positioning his board in just the right spot as the wave began to curl.

The thrust of power never got old. He kept himself tight, compact until he was sure of the ride. Then slowly he straightened his knees and gave himself to the wave. The wind and ocean spray blew against his face as he flew along, tucked into the curl of water as he raced toward shore. In those few seconds, he experienced the same thing he felt when he ran hills at Pierce College. Relief from his driving passion for ridding the city of crime.

He surfed for nearly two hours, attacking the waves until he felt a relief he wasn't sure he understood. He ran his board back to the place where Bo was sleeping on the sand, grabbed his towel, and rubbed it over his arms and legs and through his hair. He and Bo were back in his Dodge heading out of the parking lot and south on Pacific Coast Highway when he thought of the REA again.

Never mind what Clay said. It wasn't against policy or illegal for him to keep an eye on the REA's headquarters. In fact, that's exactly where he would go tonight, after dark. He would drive up and watch, maybe place a call to Owl and tell him about some bogus tip the REA might like having. Then he'd ask about the Oak Canyon Estates, whether he could help or be a lookout. Something. He would work the guy, have a conversation, develop that crucial trust he'd need if he were to keep getting information.

Alex couldn't think of a better way to spend the night. If he couldn't wear a uniform, he could at least keep an eye on the bad guys. If there was danger in that, then so be it. His connection to the REA gave him a window to the group's activities. Because of what he'd learned, he could see the tragedy before it played out, the houses at the base of the hill in the path of the potential fire, the children who lived in the neighborhood. The death and destruction that could so easily lie ahead. He could imagine the firefighters rushing to the scene, running into the fire while everyone else ran out.

Just the way they'd done in the Twin Towers.

If only someone had been given a window before 9/11. Someone could've been looking for the al Qaeda terrorists at airports across the country, or even been aware of which airports they were planning to take off from that Tuesday morning. The terrorists could've been caught, and the Twin Towers would still be standing.

His father would still be alive.

Alex blinked back the dampness in his eyes. But there had been no window, no way Alex or anyone else could've helped his dad and the hundreds of others from the FDNY. That's what made the situation with the REA so intensely urgent. This window was real, and it belonged entirely to Alex. He felt himself tense up, holding tighter to the steering wheel. He would make sure these terrorists didn't cause the death of a single firefighter. He would watch them and be ready for them, and he'd keep Clay and the others updated. He would do what he hadn't been able to do for his father, protect innocent civilians and firefighters. He would stop the REA, whatever it took.

Or he would die trying.

EIGHTEEN

C lay had a strange feeling when he woke up, an uneasiness that Alex was right—that something big was on the brink, some drug bust or hostage situation. Or maybe the fire Alex was worried about. In his years of working in law enforcement, a number of times God had impressed upon him an urgency or higher degree of alertness when he was entering a day that would require his very best. As he ate breakfast with Jamie and CJ and Sierra and as he dressed in his olive green uniform, he had that feeling today.

Or maybe it was just the wind.

They were a little more than a week into October, and sometime before dawn the Santa Ana winds kicked up with a vengeance. All morning he could hear them rushing through the trees out front, the haunting whistle signaling the sort of wind that could rip tree branches and down power lines. Once he hit the road for work, the force of the wind became easy to see. Strong and relentless, the steady gusts powered their way through the trees, bending them to one side and pushing against his car. Already some debris lined the gutters and sidewalks.

Unless the wind let up, there would be fires today. Anyone who had lived in LA more than a few years knew that much. Some might come from careless cigarettes tossed from passing cars or from a campfire left untended. Others would be set by kids messing around. But without a doubt, this was a day that could easily attract the REA.

The feeling of something big was still with Clay when he reached work, so he did something he often did after he parked just outside headquarters. He took the small Bible from the console between the front two seats and opened it to the last place he'd been reading. Proverbs. So much about life in that book. Clay was constantly amazed at the simple lessons provided in every chapter. He read a few paragraphs from chapter eighteen, then he turned back to the fourteenth chapter, to the place where he'd found the verse that had shouted to him about Alex Brady.

There is a way that seems right to a man, but in the end it leads only to death. He still hadn't shared the verse with Alex, but if the REA chose today to act on some of their threats, this was one day they could all use wisdom from God. Especially Alex. Clay looked at the verse once more. The kid was crazy, infiltrating into a volatile gang like the REA. The members weren't known for their violence against people, but if they figured out Alex was a sheriff's deputy, who knew what they might do? Whether he was armed or not, they could've overtaken him, found his recorder and his guns, and used them on him.

Today was Alex's first day back at work. Clay exhaled slowly and closed his Bible. Alex meant well. The guy was already a legend in the department, a hero by any definition of the word. He had a passion for solving crime, catching crooks, and eliminating a problem before it came to pass. All admirable qualities for a deputy. But Alex had to be careful not to take his passion to an obsessive level. If Clay could find a minute alone with him today, he'd tell him about the verse, about the fact that he'd been praying for him to find the kind of peace that couldn't come from any amount of fighting crime.

Clay went inside and found Joe in the break room adding sugar to his coffee. Alex wouldn't be in for another few hours—since K9 guys mostly worked the later shifts. Clay lifted a cup from the stack and was filling it when he heard the radio in the corner crackle and an urgent voice come through the speaker.

The call was an APB to all departments. A fire had been set at a new housing development. Two homes were on fire, igniting a blazing section of brush. Ten acres already. There were reports of people being evacuated in neighborhoods near the fire, and of at least three residents trapped by the flames. All fire stations in the area were responding. Witnesses described a light green Honda hybrid leaving the scene and heading south on the Ventura Freeway.

Clay and Joe moved closer to the radio. "All deputies be on the lookout," the voice ordered. "Suspect driving the Honda appears to be a Caucasian male, medium build with …"

The description went on, but Clay could hardly focus. He felt his heart skip a beat and then slam into double-time. Had the REA finally acted on its threats and attacked the Oak Canyon Estates? Clay stood motionless, waiting for more information while his mind raced.

"Alex warned us." Joe leaned his shoulder into the wall and stared at Clay. "You followed up on it, right?"

"Of course." Clay sat on the edge of the closest table and tried to think if he'd missed anything. He'd checked for reports from the developer and found several — each one claiming a threat of arson. Clay had personally assured the guy that the department was aware of the danger, and that they'd have deputies drive by often to keep an eye on the place. He rested his forearm on his thigh, frustrated. "I talked to Lost Hills and asked them to patrol the area. Not much else we could've done."

Before Joe could add anything, the radio came to life again with the address of the development, a new neighborhood in the hills west of Pasadena. The woman rattled off a few other details and finished with the one that told the most:

A flag had been left at the scene with the letters REA.

Clay took a deep breath and stood again. He silently prayed that one of the deputies would catch the guy, but he couldn't keep himself from feeling somewhat relieved. To have a fire set in broad daylight at a location where they'd already been warned would be frustrating and embarrassing, both. "So much for Alex's tip."

"Not a surprise, really. They might've noticed the extra patrol at Oak Canyon Estates. Maybe changed their target because of that."

"True. Or maybe they never trusted Alex from the beginning. Told him the wrong location on purpose."

The SWAT guys had talked about the fire threat — not just from the REA but from all sources. There was no way to patrol every remote area or every hillside cluster of homes — not with crime still breaking out on the valley floors.

Clay walked to the window and stared toward the west. Already the tell-tale smoke darkened a section of the distant sky. If the wind here was similar to the conditions up on the mountain, it would be a long day for firefighters. Joe came alongside him. "Kind of eerie, the wind today."

"The fire's gonna be a big one, hard to contain." He tried to imagine the sick strategy of a group like the REA. "There could be more targets today."

"Got that right." Joe breathed in sharp and slipped his hands in his pockets. "Make a call to Lost Hills. Be sure they send a deputy up to patrol the Oak Canyon Estates." Concern showed in his eyes. "With half our firefighters up in Pasadena, what better time to hit it?"

The wind howled outside, and in the distance the cloud of smoke grew. Fire danger hadn't been this high in two decades, and across the city firefighters and law enforcement had prepared for what could be devastating fires. With a group like the REA out there, there was a citywide awareness that the devastation could be worse than anything they'd seen before. Clay had a feeling that wherever Alex was, he knew about the fire by now, and he was probably already on his way in.

Looking for a light green hybrid Honda as if his life depended on it.

When Alex woke up and heard the wind, he immediately called his sergeant and asked for an okay on overtime. He'd already shared with him his taped conversation with Owl and the other two REA guys. His sergeant wasn't as concerned as Clay had been. After all, Alex was part of the task force assigned to the REA, and he'd done the research on his own time, not as a representative of the sheriff's department—so he hadn't needed permission. There wasn't enough information for an arrest, but if a case was ever built around the ecoterrorists, the tape could help.

The sergeant sounded grateful for his call. "It's already busy around here, Brady. Get in when you can."

Wind made people do crazy things. Not just setting fires, but committing bank robberies and assaults. As if the whipping of the trees and the driving gusts didn't only set people on edge, but pushed them over. In addition to the threat of fires, there would be more of the common troubles today, for sure.

Alex parked his truck, changed into his uniform, and he and Bo climbed into the squad car just after nine in the morning. As soon as he turned on his radio, he heard the news. A fire had been set at a housing development—but not Oak Canyon Estates. Some place outside of Pasadena. The part that mattered, though, was that witnesses had seen a suspect leave the site of the arson.

He was halfway to the estates when he got a call for backup. An elderly woman in Calabasas had been calling 9-1-1 all morning needing help with about a hundred soldiers who were milling about her backyard and wouldn't leave. He and another deputy were closest to the woman's house, so the call was theirs.

Alex huffed his frustration. The woman had called in the same complaint before. Everyone at the Lost Hills station knew about her and the delusional concerns that drove her to call for emergency help. Cats covering her roof ... aliens landing in her kitchen ... plants overtaking the house ... and now this. He'd never responded to a call at her house, but from what he heard in the Lost Hills break room, the deputies never accomplished anything, never solved the problem.

He flipped on his lights and sped down the 101 Freeway a few exits. A call like this was a waste of time when the arson risk was so high. He drove as fast as he could, and in ten minutes he reached the small, neighborhood home where the old woman lived. One of the Lost Hills deputies was already there, waiting in his car. Alex left the air conditioning on for Bo, cracked the window, and went to meet the other deputy, one of the newest in the department, a guy named Scheidel.

"You know the old girl. She's loony," Scheidel shrugged. "Not sure what we can do but check it out."

Alex felt his stress level double. He wanted to be back on the road, looking for the suspect, driving up to the Oak Canyon Estates before the REA struck again. He steadied himself and nodded for the deputy to join him. "Let's do it."

They didn't quite reach the door when it flew open. Standing there was a frail, white-haired woman, her face stricken with fear. She clung to her oversized house jacket, and her arms and legs shook. "They're everywhere! Everywhere, I tell you!" She stepped onto the porch and grabbed hold of Alex's arm. "Help me, young man! Please help me!"

Alex stiffened and started to take a step back. Nobody touched him on a call, not for any reason. But then he stopped himself. The woman wasn't going to hurt him, and something about the terror in her face touched him. The feeling was strangely unfamiliar, and he couldn't help but wonder how his father would've handled the situation. "Ma'am, calm down." Alex put his hand on her shoulder. "What seems to be the problem?"

"Soldiers! They're everywhere!" She was panting now, on the verge of hyperventilating. "Get them out!"

His partner stepped up. "Show us where they are, okay?"

"This way." She remained at Alex's side, clutching him, her whole body trembling. They walked through a cluttered living room to a patio door off the kitchen. The woman waved her hand at her backyard, a patch of overgrown grass and weeds surrounded on all sides by a rotting wooden fence. "See?" She tried to hide behind Alex. "Soldiers everywhere!"

"Ma'am, come here right now." Scheidel's tone grew stern, his patience pressed. When she peered out from behind Alex, he motioned for her to come closer. "Now, ma'am." He jabbed his finger at a spot on the floor beside him. "Right here."

The woman seemed stricken at the idea of leaving Alex's side, but she took three shaky steps toward Scheidel and cast frantic eyes at him. Her voice was a pathetic whine. "Make them go." She clutched at Scheidel now and squeezed her eyes shut. "Please, make them go!"

Scheidel shook his arm free. He pointed to the backyard. "Ma'am, open your eyes and look out there."

It took her a few seconds, but finally she opened her eyes the slightest crack. As if she were really seeing something, her eyes darted from one side of the yard to the other. "They won't leave!"

"Ma'am," Scheidel lowered his voice to the methodical, patronizing tone typically reserved for young children and dogs. "There are no soldiers in your backyard. Not one single soldier."

She was shaking harder now, her gaze glued to the things her mind was seeing in the backyard. "Yes ... a hundred of them." Her frantic eyes found Scheidel again. "I counted."

Something about the scene tugged at Alex, the way most calls never did. She looked harried and helpless, like the victims walking the outer edges of a disaster. The way people looked after

9/11. Suddenly, he had an idea. He touched the woman's shoulder again. "I'll get rid of them, but I need your help."

The first sign of hope softened her features. She was still out of breath, panicked by whatever she was seeing.

"Follow me out here onto the patio."

She started to shake her head. "But they —"

"Ma'am, if you want them to leave, you need to help me."

The woman seemed to summon all the courage of a lifetime. Alex walked outside first, and slowly she followed. When she was on the patio with a clear view of the yard, Alex stopped her. "Stay right here."

"Brady …" Scheidel held up his hands as if to tell him not to feed into the woman's craziness.

But Alex signaled the deputy that he had the situation under control. Then he took a few determined strides onto the grass and put his hands on hips. "All right, men, listen up! I want all of you in a straight line right now." He barked the orders loud enough that his voice carried across the yard. Again, he could almost feel his father's approval as he shouted, "First soldier over here!" He pointed to the left, where a wobbly gate provided the only exit. "The rest of you fall in behind him. Everyone!"

From the corner of his eye he saw the woman put her hand over her mouth, her eyes wide.

"Okay," Alex walked to the gate, carefully opened it so it wouldn't fall off its hinges, then returned to his spot near the woman. "When I give the command, you march out that gate and don't come back. I'll count you off. Ready …" He pointed to a spot near the open gate. "One … two … three. Keep it moving, men. Four … five …"

The woman turned her head with each number, watching the imaginary soldiers slowly leave her yard. Alex kept counting, through the twenties and thirties and on into the seventies and eighties. As he reached the end, he forced his tone to sound even more stern. "Ninety-eight … No stragglers! Ninety-nine … one hundred." He went back to the gate and yelled, "Don't come back, or I'll arrest every one of you."

He walked to the woman and found her gripping Scheidel, who had stepped out onto the patio beside her. She was weeping openly, the fear and trembling gone. As Alex came to her, she reached out and touched him, her wet eyes shining with admiration. "Thank you, sir. You saved me! Thank you!"

They spent another couple minutes reassuring her, then went back to their cars out front. The whole thing hadn't taken more than ten minutes, and Scheidel chuckled as they walked. "That was brilliant, man. Absolutely brilliant."

"Figured maybe it would help if someone took her seriously." He shrugged one shoulder. "You'll make the report, right?"

"Should be a keeper. A hundred soldiers cleared out. Mission accomplished."

Before he left, Alex saw the woman waving at them from her front porch. Again, his heart went out to her. He waved back and took off toward the freeway. A few minutes later, he heard the report. Another fire was burning at a housing development — this one in Malibu. The hills adjacent to the area were already burning, and firefighters as far as three hours north in Santa Maria were being called in to help. Arson was suspected again, and this time there were no witnesses. The fires were far apart, which would stretch the fire departments in the area, and with the winds, the dangers that day were only just being realized.

He drove as fast as he could without sirens and lights to the winding road that led up to the Oak Canyon Estates. Without hesitating, he drove up and onto the main street, the one where all the houses in this phase sat. He turned right and cruised slowly to the end. A few work vans were parked outside one house, and a pair of well-dressed men with hard hats were talking to a construction worker. Alex nodded at them as he drove by, and at the end of the street he turned around and drove to the other side. The model house in the middle had just one car parked out front, and past that were more work trucks.

Alex fought back his frustration as he headed back down the steep road. The place should have a guard, at least. Someone to screen visitors. He'd checked with Clay, and the suggestion had been talked about with the developers. Apparently, they were in the process of hiring a security company. Alex scanned the horizon and saw the two gray-black areas that marked the separate brush fires. The wind kicked up a dust cloud in front of him, and he squinted to see through it.

Sometimes he felt like the old woman from the earlier call, shouting for someone to believe him that the fires this year could kill people. They could kill firefighters. But after today, he was bound to feel the same relief the woman felt. Because based on the way the day was going so far, no one could argue about whether the REA was setting fires in new housing developments. They could argue just one thing:

When was it going to happen at Oak Canyon Estates?

NINETEEN

Jamie could hardly sleep, and when she woke Thursday morning only one thought filled her mind — this was the day she was going to meet Holly Brooks. She'd found the girl at the work number Alex's mother had passed along. Their initial conversation was brief since Jamie wanted the heart of their discussion to happen in person. She'd told the young woman only that the two of them shared a New York connection, and she'd like a chance to meet with her this week if possible.

The meeting was set for nine o'clock that morning when Holly had no other appointments. Jamie had been praying about it almost constantly.

As she drove the kids to school, she turned the radio to a news station for an update on the brush fires still burning along two separate mountain ranges. The Santa Ana winds had died down in the past twenty-four hours, and the smoky skies had cleared some, but the last Jamie heard, the fires were still burning.

The announcer was talking about baseball, with breaking news coming up on the hour. Jamie wasn't concerned with who was ahead in the World Series, so she turned the volume down and glanced at Sierra, sitting in the passenger seat of their Trailblazer. "Ready for your math test?"

"Ugh!" Sierra made a face. She was in sixth grade, and much like when she was younger, she had an opinion about everything. "I wanted to talk to you about that." She angled herself so she could see Jamie better. "I love writing and reading and art and music and PE and—."

"And soccer!" CJ leaned his head as far forward as his car seat would allow. "You love soccer, Sissy."

"Right." Sierra flashed him a grin. "I love a lot of things, but I don't love math. So I was thinking, it doesn't seem right—once a person knows the basics … adding, subtracting, division, multiplication—that she should have to take math in school unless she loves it." She grabbed a quick breath and kept on with her rapid-fire pace. "I mean, I don't want to be a math teacher, Mom. So math's a waste of time for me, and by the way, I had this talk with Josh, and he feels the same. We're thinking of starting a petition, passing it around my school and then through his high school classes, and since we're not part of the public school system, maybe we can get rid of math except for those kids who love it." She blinked. "Isn't that a good idea?"

Jamie raised one eyebrow, a smile tugging at her lips. "Nice try." She reached over and patted Sierra's knee. "But I'm pretty sure no amount of signatures will convince the board at King Christian School to eliminate required math."

Sierra looked out the window, no doubt working up a retort.

"I have school today, right, Mommy?" CJ asked the question in a happy voice. With Sierra around, he'd learned to talk early and often, and his vocabulary was beyond that of most three-year-olds.

"Yes, honey. You have preschool two days a week, and today's one of those days."

"Goody!" He shouted his enthusiasm. "'Cause I love school, Mommy!"

"I love school too," Sierra jumped in. "Just not math."

"I like math 'cause we count with jelly beans." CJ bounced up and down. "Jelly bean math is yummy!"

"Yeah, I'd like that math too, buddy." Sierra grinned back at her brother. "Wait till you get to sixth grade." She held up empty hands. "No more jelly bean math."

"No more?" CJ sounded alarmed.

The commercial on the radio ended, and the news report came on. Jamie turned up the volume, and the kids quieted to listen. "Fires in the hills surrounding Los Angeles are seventy percent contained, a spokesperson for the fire department said this morning."

Jamie was grateful about the containment. She listened for the rest of the report.

"Officials have confirmed that the two separate blazes, which both began at the construction sites of custom hillside housing developments, were apparently intentionally set by the environmental terrorist group REA," the reporter's voice grew somber. "No arrests have been made, and a statement released by the sheriff's department today warned that with more winds in the forecast later this week, the danger for additional fires is high."

A shiver of concern ran down Jamie's arms. Clay and Joe both expected more fires in the weeks to come, and with the tinder-dry hills, the department feared the situation could grow much worse.

"We've gotten off easy so far," Clay told her last night. "Five unoccupied new homes and a few thousand acres of brush. The chance for a huge disaster still exists."

The news was over, so Jamie pushed the button, turning off the radio.

"I don't understand people setting fires on purpose." Sierra pulled down the sun visor and looked at herself in the mirror. She pulled lip gloss from her backpack and applied it. "I mean," she smacked her lips a few times, "how can it be good for the environment to have all that smoke clogging up the sky?"

"It doesn't make sense." Jamie kept her eyes on the road. "They're a bunch of bad guys who like the attention. They can talk about the environment, but you're right, honey. Destroying hillsides and homes … that's not the sign of people who care."

"Someone should tell them about Jesus." Sierra marked the statement with a tone of finality. "Then they could see how wrong they are."

In the backseat, CJ launched into an off-key rendition of the song he'd learned last week in preschool. "Jesus loves me, this I know ... for the Bible tells me so!"

Jamie grinned. She loved this about Sierra and CJ, that they so fully and naturally embraced their faith. Clay had a wonderful way of incorporating talk about the Lord into their everyday conversation, so moments like these were completely natural. She pulled into the school parking lot and entered the drop-off line. King Christian School required a drive each morning, but it was well worth the effort. The school had a waiting list of kids hoping to get in, and its academic standards made it one of the top-ranked schools in the state — especially in math.

When it was their turn, Sierra leaned over and kissed Jamie's cheek. "Bye, Mom. Love you." She grabbed her backpack. "Have a good day! And pray about my math test."

"I will. Love you too." Jamie hugged her daughter and then watched her run off toward her peers. Three girls from her class hurried over to her, their faces lit up as the four of them headed toward the front doors.

"My turn!" CJ's voice was pure glee. "You can see my turtle, Mommy! Okay? 'Kay, you can see my turtle!"

"Sure, buddy. I can't wait to see it." Jamie eased out of the line and found a parking spot on the far end of the lot, adjacent to the separate building that housed the preschool. She unbuckled CJ, and he held her hand, skipping as they walked up the path to the right classroom.

Inside, half the kids were already there, and the teacher was helping them with some oversized crayons and construction paper. "Hi, CJ!" She waved. "We're drawing pumpkins today!"

CJ smiled big. He tugged at Jamie's hand. "Over here, Mommy … my turtle's over here!" He led her to the far wall where an extended family of paper turtles was tacked to a display area. He pointed to one with purple spots across its back. "That's it, see! My turtle has polka dots!"

Jamie admired her son's work, and after a few minutes she swung him up into her arms and kissed his forehead. "I love you, buddy. Have a good day."

"Okay. Love you too." He wrapped his arms around her neck and hugged her for a long time. "You're my pretty Mommy."

"Thanks, Ceej." She set him down, and he ran off toward the others at the coloring table. Preschool lasted only three hours, and CJ loved every minute of it. But the fact that he was so well-adjusted was bittersweet. Just a year ago, he wouldn't leave her side, and now … well, he was growing up and needing her less.

She didn't dwell on the fact as she left the classroom. She had to hurry if she was going to be on time to her appointment with Holly. The young woman had sounded pleasant but guarded during their phone call yesterday. Once they agreed on a meeting time, Jamie took down the address where Holly worked. She had searched online for it this morning on the way out the door and now, before she pulled out of the parking lot, she glanced at the piece of paper.

The directions took her back to the Ventura Freeway south toward Las Virgenes, and then up into the hills. *Strange*, Jamie thought. Most real estate offices would typically be on the valley floor, in the more populated areas. It took ten minutes to get to Las Virgenes, and another eight before she found the right road. She turned right and immediately saw the grand entrance to a housing development and an open gate just ahead of her. Jamie's heartrate quickened as she slowed and read the sign.

Oak Canyon Estates? The development Alex was so concerned about? Jamie and Clay had talked about this place just yesterday, how Alex was still checking up on the REA's headquarters and how he believed this development was next on the group's hit list. So why had Holly given her the address to Oak Canyon Estates, unless ... was this where she worked? Selling exclusively for this one development?

Jamie drove slowly up the hill, giving herself a chance to adjust to the shock. What were the odds that Alex's long-ago love would work at the very custom home site that he feared was in the greatest danger? At the top of the road, a paved street ran perpendicular to the hill, with gorgeous custom estates strategically placed on either side. Each of them was in various stages of construction, and in the middle was a finished home with flags lining the walkway. The address on the front of the house matched the one Holly had given her.

Jamie pulled into the nearest parking spot and checked her look in the mirror. *Please, God, let this be a step in the right direction. Let something come of this meeting that could help both Alex and Holly.* She remembered what Clay had said the night before.

"You're doing your best, and I understand your passion." He smoothed his thumb along the side of her face, looking into the soul of her intentions. "But it's a stretch, Jamie. Finding Alex's old girlfriend, looking her up without telling him."

"She doesn't have to talk to me. I just figure, what if ... what if she can help me understand Alex a little better?"

"It's a bit extreme, honey. Seriously." He kissed her, and his smile put her at ease. "I just hope you're right, that something good will come of it."

She knew Clay well enough to be sure—wherever he was, and whatever he was involved with at work this morning, he was praying for her. The fact gave her the strength to slip her purse over her shoulder, head up the walkway, and knock on the door of the model home. In a matter of seconds, a professional-looking blonde girl answered the door. Her smile stopped short of her eyes. "You must be Jamie Michaels?"

"Yes." Jamie fought back the doubts that rushed at her. She held out her hand. "Nice to meet you."

Holly led her into a formal living room across from what looked to be her office. They took the two chairs closest to each other. "Did you have any trouble finding it?"

"Not really," Jamie gave a light laugh. "I was looking for a real estate office. I didn't realize you worked for Oak Canyon Estates."

"I have for a few years now. This is the developer's third phase."

They talked about the houses for a few minutes, and then Holly slid to the edge of her seat, her eyes intent. "You said we shared a connection?"

"Yes." Jamie wondered if Holly could hear her thudding heart, the way she could hear it herself. She drew a steadying breath. "My husband works with Alex Brady. They're friends."

The reaction happened in her eyes, in the way the muscles beneath them tightened ever so subtly. "You … know Alex?"

"Yes. My husband and I get together every month and barbecue with a few other couples. Alex hasn't missed a dinner."

"Couples?" The guard was up in Holly's eyes. "Alex is married?"

Jamie shook her head. "No, no. My husband invites him because … well, because Alex needs that."

Holly sat back, her eyebrows knit together. "I'm not sure what to say."

The poor girl must've been beyond confused. Jamie didn't want to take up too much of her time — still, she had no choice but to start at the beginning. She told Holly how Alex intentionally kept himself away from people, how he existed in a world of eighty-hour work-weeks where his best friend was his service dog, Bo.

"I know about Alex's father, how he died." Jamie looked down at her hands. "My first husband was a firefighter. He died in the Twin Towers also."

"I'm sorry." Some of the confusion left the young woman's expression. She looked out the window for several seconds, her eyes distant. "It was awful, what Alex went through. He wouldn't let me in, wouldn't let anyone in." Her eyes found Jamie again. "I don't think Alex ever got over it."

"He hasn't, at least not from what we can see." Jamie continued, telling Holly about her time as a volunteer at St. Paul's Chapel. "I look at Alex, how he's going through life broken and hurting, dedicating every heartbeat to getting the bad guys, and my heart breaks for him." She shrugged. "I have to help. To me, Alex's name should be right up there next to the other names on a 9/11 victims' list. Because it seems like the terrorists took his life when they took his dad's." She leaned closer to Holly. "But there is a way for him to live again. I guess … I don't know, somehow because of my experience, I feel like I can help." She paused. "But I need to understand Alex better, the way he was before."

Holly lowered her brow, and for a moment she seemed to struggle with what to say next. But even with no words her face told the story, how much she still felt for the young deputy. Finally, her face darkened with a pain that bordered on anger. "You think I'm part of the solution for Alex?"

"I talked to his mom and …" Jamie scrambled for the right words, "… she said the two of you were very close at one time. I figured maybe if—"

"I can only tell you that the person he used to be no longer exists." Her voice was shaky, marked by sorrow. "Nothing I could say would help you now."

Suddenly Jamie felt ridiculous coming here, making this attempt. She exhaled and moved to the edge of her seat. "I'm sorry, Holly. I can leave."

Unshed tears shone in Holly's eyes. She opened her mouth, but before she could find the words, she shook her head once and released a sound that was part cry, part exasperation. She stood and walked to the window, her back to Jamie. A long moment passed, and Holly made a quiet sniffling sound.

Jamie felt horrible. She stood and collected her purse. "I'll go. I didn't mean—"

"No." Slowly, she faced Jamie again. "I'm glad you came. It's just ... I can't help you."

"Holly ..." Jamie considered whether she should voice her boldest thoughts. She wouldn't have this chance again. She took a quick breath and plunged ahead. "Sometimes ... when he's with us, I have the feeling Alex is thinking about the past, about someone he left behind. Several people, maybe."

"He isn't thinking about me, Ms. Michaels. I can tell you that. It's too late for Alex, for either of us. After he left for LA, I did everything I could." She tossed her hands. "I'm here, right? I went to him and practically begged him to take me back. Of course, I wanted it to work." A tear rolled down her cheek and dropped to the floor. Then the anger left her in a rush. "He doesn't love me. He told me he didn't want anything to do with me. That was years ago."

If Jamie could've disappeared, if she could've undone the entire visit, she would have. What right did she have stirring up old heartache for this young woman? "I'm so sorry." The heat in Jamie's cheeks must've made her guilt obvious. She took a step closer to Holly. "My husband told me something once, something that maybe applies here."

Fresh tears filled Holly's eyes. She gave a light shrug.

"He told me the opposite of love isn't hate. It's indifference." She put her hand on Holly's shoulder and tried to see past her defenses. "And I can only tell you that Alex isn't indifferent."

She angled her head. "So in some small way his resistance to me," she uttered a bitter laugh, "toward every attempt I've made … is all because deep down he still loves me? That's what you think?"

Jamie needed to leave before she made the situation worse. But she had to be honest too. "I think it's possible, Holly." She took a step back. "I came here looking for information, but maybe God wanted us to meet for a different reason. For you and Alex."

Holly exhaled and dragged her hand through her hair, allowing her emotions to ease up. "Thank you, Jamie." She dabbed at the tears caught in her lower eyelashes, and once more her smile lifted the corners of her lips. "I appreciate your effort, but it's just too late." She walked Jamie to the front door. "It was too late a long time ago."

They said good-bye, and Jamie managed to make it to her car before her own sorrow welled up inside her. She slipped on her sunglasses, and by the time she was halfway down the dirt road, her tears came in earnest. So many hurting people, so many broken hearts. Somehow when God let her play a part in bringing healing to a person hurt by the terrorist attacks, the act validated Jake's death, made her feel like some good had come from it.

But stories like Alex and Holly's were proof that the losses of 9/11 were still playing out, that the cost would never fully be realized. Truly, she had believed if she could talk to Holly, she could figure out what had kept Alex so closed off, and that by finding that piece of his past, she could talk to Alex about what he'd left behind. Then, finally, he might let the walls down and realize the one thing Jamie felt sure God was trying to teach him—that he couldn't trade his life for the task of eliminating evil in the world. Because if he gave his life before he truly found it, Alex wouldn't be eliminating the waste the terrorists had created on 9/11.

He'd be adding to it, placing himself forever on the victims' list of those who died on September 11.

TWENTY

The call for backup came just after ten o'clock that night, as Alex was about to circle back west on the Ventura Freeway and park at the base of the road leading up to the Oak Canyon Estates. The Santa Ana winds were back now, and Alex had no doubt the REA would hit that area if Owl and the others had a chance.

"Get ready, Bo," he reached back and patted his dog. "You're helping on this one."

Bo barked a single time, alert and anxious. He could sense the change in the car's speed, the hint of adrenaline already coursing through Alex.

"I know, buddy ... we're almost there." Alex exited at Thousand Oaks Boulevard and forced himself to think about the call at hand. A routine traffic stop by a deputy named Waller, a veteran with the force. The stop took place at the last light at the top of the hill and netted an open container and a drunk guy with an attitude. Waller had told the guy to stay put while he returned to his squad car. An arrest was needed, but Waller needed backup before he would take on the guy by himself.

Alex pressed his foot on the gas and flipped on his siren. The wind whipped through the trees overhead, and a chill ran down his spine. The REA was probably plotting their next fire right now, the same way the terrorists had plotted their horrific deeds in the days before 9/11. He glanced out the passenger window and saw a haze of light-colored smoke in the far distance. It had been a week since the fires at the other developments, and still no arrests had been made. Detectives had questioned Owl and several others, but they'd denied involvement and there wasn't enough evidence to bring anyone in. It wasn't like they carried cards declaring their membership to the REA.

Frustration welled up inside Alex. The guys had to be caught in the act, there was no other way. And he was convinced Oak Canyon Estates was still on the REA's hit list, probably up next. Alex would've liked nothing more than to camp out on the dirt road and catch the cowards in the act.

Waller came over the radio. "Suspect is acting shady, a little too full of motion. He might run."

Not on my shift, Alex thought. He patted Bo again. "He runs and he's yours, Bo. All yours."

This time Bo responded with two barks. He paced across the backseat, ready for whatever was asked of him. Alex reached back and patted Bo, and as he did he caught a glimpse of Bo in the rearview mirror, at his earnest, brave eyes. Such a good dog, such a dedicated partner. Since Alex took the job, that was all he ever wanted—to be a deputy with the same heart and loyalty, the same single-mindedness as Bo, ready at any minute to lay his life down if it meant getting one more thug off the streets of Los Angeles.

Up ahead Alex could see Waller's car, and ahead of it, the dark sedan where the suspect was still sitting. Just as Alex turned off his siren and pulled up behind the squad car, the suspect flung his door open, sprang from his vehicle, and sprinted across the street into a thicket of brush and trees.

Waller's urgent call came over the radio. "Suspect is fleeing on foot, repeat, suspect is fleeing on foot."

Alex barely had time to radio in that he'd arrived and was in pursuit before he leashed Bo, drew his gun, and ran to Waller, who was already out of his car, his gun in his hand. "We'll lead." He started toward the trees. "Cover me."

With even a minute lead, the situation was suddenly danger-ous. The guy could be anywhere in the wooded area, hiding be-hind a tree near the spot where he entered or headed for the other side of the thicket. Alex gave Bo plenty of lead, and immediately the dog picked up the suspect's trail. Bo stopped and barked, his head locked in position, waiting for the command.

"Get 'em, boy!" Alex shouted. "Go get 'em!"

Bo strained against the leash, running as fast as he could with Alex holding the end. Alex tore into the wooded area behind his dog, the ground uneven beneath his feet. Behind him, Waller clicked on a flashlight which helped a little, but the speed of the chase was still such that they were running blind into the dark-ness. If not for Bo leading them, they could never have taken the suspect's trail at this pace.

All at once, there was a blur of motion in a clearing ahead and to the left, but as the suspect jumped out and raised his gun to fire at Alex and the other deputy, Bo ran straight for him. The suspect fired once and Alex felt the bullet blow past him. Before the man could fire a second bullet at the deputies, he seemed to notice the dog running straight at him. He turned his gun on Bo and started to pull the trigger.

"Get him, Bo!" Alex shouted, his sides heaving. *Not Bo. Don't let him get Bo ...*

The suspect tried to finish the shot, but it was too late. Bo leaped at him, leveling the man backward with such a force he flew into a mass of scrub brush. A groan came from him as he hit the brittle bushes, and at the same time he fired his gun again. This time the bullet sailed harmlessly to the side, and before he could raise his weapon another time, Bo quickly identified the suspect's gun-wielding hand and bit hard into that arm, pinning him down and containing him.

Bo was in a frenzy, biting the man's arm and growling at him.

"Hey!" The suspect screamed in pain. "Call him off! Help me! Call off the dog!"

"Throw your gun where we can see it," Alex belted out the command.

The man hesitated, and Bo clearly understood that the fight wasn't over yet. He deepened his growl and bit harder into the man's arm, shaking it like he would a chew toy. The suspect screamed again. "Okay! Here!" He threw his gun onto the ground near where the deputies were standing. "Call him off!"

Alex was still breathing hard. Waller crept up alongside him, his flashlight aimed at the gun on the ground. He picked it up, slid it into his back pocket, and retreated to the spot next to Alex.

"Call him off!" The man's cry was shrill now, desperate.

Next to him, Waller was calling in details of the detainment, instructing backup where to find them.

Alex took a few steps closer to the suspect. "Bo ... release."

Additional deputies were running up behind them, and in the next few minutes the suspect was bandaged, cuffed, and led away. Alex patted Bo's side as he walked next to him back to the street. "Good boy, Bo ... good job." It was one more time when Bo had saved his life. If the suspect hadn't been distracted by the sight of a German shepherd tearing through the brush and coming for him, he would've fired a round of shots before Alex and Waller had a chance to respond.

The wind bent and bowed the trees around them, and as they entered the open street again, Alex thought he could smell smoke. Either the old fires had shifted, sparked to life again by the wind, or something new was burning. He took Bo to the squad car, pulled out the gallon water bottle, and poured some in the dog's blue bowl. Bo lapped it up, stopping just once to cast grateful eyes on Alex.

"'Atta boy, Bo ... good dog." Alex crouched down beside him and rubbed the soft spot by his ear—Bo's favorite.

Waller came up to them. He was still breathing hard, still coming down off the adrenaline rush. He leaned on Alex's car. "First bullet nearly got you."

"Second one would've." Alex kept his eyes on his dog. "Bo knew where he was before the guy stepped out."

He held out his hand and shook Alex's. "Great backup, Brady." He left them alone to go work on the reports.

Alex bent back down and rubbed Bo's ear. "You hungry, boy?" He kept a bag of food in the car for times like this — midway through a shift with a couple of active calls behind them. He scooped a cup of kibble into a second blue bowl and gave it to the dog. Again, Bo lifted grateful eyes his direction. The dog would've died for him, no question about it.

Alex added his comments to the report, dumped out the rest of Bo's water, and opened the door for the dog. "Come on, Bo … back to headquarters." He stacked the two bowls on the floorboard and climbed into the driver's seat. He needed to file his own report before he could go out on patrol again.

He could feel the wind hard against his car as he pulled onto the freeway. He made a quick call to the Lost Hills station. "You have someone checking out the Oak Canyon Estates?" He didn't want to pry, but he couldn't stand the thought of driving the opposite direction from the place where the next ecoterrorist attack could take place.

"Got it. The developer called a few hours ago and asked for extra support."

"Good. Arsonists love nights like this." Alex pictured Owl and the other two clowns trying to make it up the hill and coming face-to-face with a sheriff's deputy.

Halfway to the station, grim thoughts hit him. What if he hadn't had Bo with him tonight? What if the gunman had killed him with that second shot? Alex settled back into his seat. Like a tidal wave, a wall of futility washed over him. If he'd been killed in a thicket by a drunk gunman, then what would his life have mattered? Sure, he'd gotten a number of bad guys, but for every arrest, there were ten that didn't take place, another batch of crooks growing up and taking part in the street war all around them.

He thought about Jamie Bryan, the fact that she'd found a journal entry written by his father, an entry that Alex hadn't let her share with him. In some ways, it might've served as his father's last words for him, but he'd shut them out, refused them. If he had died up there on the brush-covered hill, he never would've had the chance to hear them.

And what about Holly? He'd refused her too, but he still wondered. Was she in New York? Had she fallen in love and married, like he suspected? Had she learned to forgive him, to forget him the way he wanted her to? If the gunman's bullet had hit its mark, Alex would never have those answers, either.

The futility filled him and surrounded him, suffocating him and drawing him into a whirlpool of waste. Wasted time and years and days and effort. He could get a dozen bad guys every day, but would the problem of evil in the city be reduced any, really? He straightened and summoned in himself the courage and determination, the sheer will and sense of justice that lived where his heart had once resided. He might never rid the city of everything bad and dangerous, but with every one, with every chase and every arrest, one more family was spared, one more high school senior didn't have to come home to find his life torn apart.

Gradually, the despair dissipated and he could breathe again. The wind howled overhead as he reached headquarters and went inside with Bo. In the break room, he found Clay and Joe huddled over cups of coffee, their faces lined with concern.

Clay spotted him first. He frowned and motioned for Alex to join them. "We heard about your chase. Good work, Brady."

"Thank you." Alex looked from Clay to Joe and back again. "What's up?"

"A deputy went down." Joe's voice was thick with discouragement. "East LA. Responded to a disturbing the peace and took a bullet in the neck. Suspect was a guy you arrested a few months ago."

Alex's stomach dropped, and he clenched his fists. Gut-wrenching pain took hold of him, the same pain he'd felt when he walked into the house that Tuesday morning and saw his mother watching the television screen, saw the Twin Towers in a heap of rubble with his father somewhere inside them. A pain that consumed him. Alex put his foot on the seat of the nearest chair, dug his elbow into his knee, and hung his head.

"He's been in surgery the last four hours. Critical condition." Clay rarely sounded beaten, but this was one of those times. "If he lives, they don't think he'll walk again. The bullet hit his spine."

A stifled moan built in Alex's chest and came out as an angry cry. He slammed his fist on the table and then stormed to the corner where the coffee was set up. He felt Bo beside him, heard the dog whimper softly. Alex exhaled hard through his nose and leaned down enough to touch his fingers to Bo's head. "It's okay, Bo. Down, boy." His dog kept his eyes locked on Alex as he took a few tentative steps back and then settled down on the cool floor. Alex felt weary, physically beaten. He looked over his shoulder. "The suspect?"

Clay was on his feet coming toward him. "Shot and killed at the scene. Two others were arrested."

The bad guy wouldn't kill again, but still he represented another death, more heartache on the streets. Somewhere tonight the criminal's mother and father, his siblings, maybe even his children would be changed forever because he was gone. He'd arrested the guy a few months ago, but the effort wasn't enough. The guy hadn't changed, hadn't gone home and become an upstanding citizen. So how had Alex's arrest mattered at all? The evil on the streets was still winning if a deputy could make a routine house call and be shot in the process. He hung his head again and gripped the edge of the table where the coffeemaker sat.

"Alex …" Clay put an arm around his shoulders. "There was nothing you could've done. The courts let him back out."

"I know." Alex squeezed the words through a locked jaw. He lifted his head and motioned to the space around him. "But if all this, the department and the deputies and the dogs and the SWAT teams, can't stop that from happening, can't even make a dent in the war out there, then what's it all for?"

Clay's eyes grew hard. "Come on, Brady. We need to talk."

Alex was about to argue, but he wanted to hear Clay out, hear what reasoning his captain could possibly have to justify their work at an hour like this. He gave Bo the command to stay, and he followed Clay outside to a small fenced courtyard with a few empty picnic tables. Clay sat on the edge of the closest one and put his feet on the bench. "This talk's a long time coming." Curiosity disarmed Alex's pain and hopelessness for a moment. He blinked and waited.

"You have it all wrong about the evil around us." Clay's voice was intense, his tone louder than usual. "Now, I know you used to have faith in Christ. You've told me yourself, so what I'm about to say I want you to hear with the ears you used to have. The ears you had before 9/11." The wind swirled around them, pushing through Alex's hair and stinging his eyes. He wanted to run back inside, get his dog, and hit the road. But he squinted against the wind and listened, half hoping Clay would say something that might make sense of everything he was feeling.

"The other day I found a Bible verse that might as well have been written for you." Clay leaned closer, his forearms on his knees. He must've read the reluctance in Alex's eyes because he raised his brow. "Yes, a Bible verse. It's still the best wisdom around, whatever you think."

Alex folded his arms and there was that feeling again, the confusing sense that he was somehow back in his senior year, his dad sitting where Clay sat, talking to him, leading him. Alex stuffed his emotions and waited.

"The verse said, 'There is a way that seems right to a man, but in the end it leads only to death.'" Clay straightened and pointed at Alex. "That's you, Brady. You think you can go out there on the streets of LA and rid the world of everything bad." A sad-sounding laugh came from Clay. "Can't you see? That's never going to happen. You keep thinking like that, and you're going to get yourself killed." He hesitated. "Then we can all sit around and talk about you and wonder what it's all for … because this department needs you. But we need you to be a deputy, not a machine."

Alex couldn't help but let the Scripture Clay had just quoted play again in his mind. *There is a way that seems right to a man, but in the end it leads only to death.* He swallowed hard, trying to think of something to say. He didn't want a Bible verse right now; he wanted real answers. Like how could a felon be back on the streets and able to shoot a deputy? And what had gone wrong in the suspect's life that he was out shooting people in the first place? But the words of the verse wouldn't leave him alone, wouldn't let him go. They were exactly how he'd been feeling earlier, that sense of futility that everything he'd believed was only going to lead to his death. Maybe not today, when Bo had saved him from a bullet. But someday, sometime, when the bad guy at the traffic stop got a shot off a little sooner. Or when he got the routine house call to some ex-felon's place, and ended up being the deputy rushed into surgery, clinging to life.

He cleared his throat, his eyes locked on Clay's. "Then what's the answer?" His tone was bitter, unbelieving. "If the way that seems right leads to death?" His voice rose a notch. "Because the God you serve stands by and watches while firefighters climb sixty flights of stairs to their deaths or," he waved his hand toward the fence at the edge of the property, "while a deputy loses his life. So if God won't take out the evil around us, who will?" He let his voice fall to barely a whisper. "We're the only ones who can."

"No!" Clay's tone was intense again. "You've got it all wrong. Christ didn't die so we could go out and win the fight against evil in the world." He stopped, and his eyes grew softer. He pressed his open hand to the place over his heart. "He died so we might win the fight against evil *here*. Within us."

Alex stared at his friend, baffled. The wind gusted through the patio area, and he had to keep his voice raised just to be heard. "Here? Inside us, Clay? I thought we were the good guys."

"No one's good, Brady. You gotta remember at least that much." He slid closer to the edge of the table, his voice ringing with sincerity. "That's the role of the Holy Spirit ... to change us and mold us so we can be more like Christ—more loving and patient and kind, more forgiving. We'll never be perfect. That's His job. But God wants to work on the evil inside us. Only then can we do things bigger than ourselves." He wasn't finished. "The deputy that got shot? You know him. His name's Jennings. Guy loves God so much he leaks joy everywhere he goes. Whether he lives or dies, people will be changed because of his story, his life story. Not because he was bent on ridding the city of bad guys, but because he stood for everything good and right and true. That's why Christ came. To give people the chance to be like Jennings, joy-filled because he's been forgiven."

Alex had to blink again, because for a moment the voice speaking to him didn't belong to Clay, but to Alex's father. The words were the same his dad would say if he were here today. Before Alex could make a move, the door opened and Joe stepped out. The hope on his face told the story before he said a word. "Jennings is out of surgery. They were able to fix his spine." There was a catch in Joe's voice. "Looks like he could make a full recovery."

Emotions Alex hadn't felt in years came at him from all sides. He held Clay's stare a few seconds longer, and then he nodded to both men as he left. Inside, he rounded up Bo and strode hard and fast for his squad car. Even now he felt eighteen again, and no matter how hard he tried to block out the message Clay had spoken to him, he couldn't do it.

The words had cut through the brick and mortar around his heart and hit their mark dead-on.

He'd been striving for the same goal since he came to LA, but now for the first time he saw the reason for his feelings of futility, the reason why once in a while on his quest to get the crooks, he would simply come to the end of himself. Was it really possible that the only evil he could control was the evil within him? And if he were taken out on the next call, what would people say about him at his memorial service? That he was a talented cop? Was that all his legacy would ever be?

The idea was too sad for him to contemplate. He tried to dismiss everything Clay had said. Whatever evil existed inside him, it was nothing compared to the darkness on the streets. Alex mustered up a determination he'd never felt before. His father would be alive today if it weren't for the evil out there. As long as he had breath, he would fight against crime and terrorism. But in case he died trying, he would do one more thing before the night was up. He'd drive to Jamie Michaels' house, knock on the door, and do the thing he should've done weeks ago.

Read the journal entry.

Twenty-One

Jamie never slept well when Clay worked overtime. She was at peace with his job, the sort of peace she'd never had when she was married to Jake, back when she didn't want to believe in a God who would let firefighters die in the line of duty. After Jake's death, his Bible and his journal had led her into a life-saving relationship with God, one that brought with it a peace that passed all understanding. A peace that wives of police officers rarely felt.

But that didn't mean she slept well.

Sierra and CJ were long since asleep, and she was surfing the Internet looking for a Michael O'Brien CD on iTunes when she heard a knock at the door. For a split second, she didn't move or breathe or allow herself to process the sound. Then, in a rush, the possibilities came slamming into her. Clay wouldn't knock, so if someone was at her door at this hour it could only mean ... She exhaled. *Not again. This couldn't be happening again. God ... whatever it is, You're with me.* Gradually, her panic leveled off enough so she could move through the house to the front door. *Please, God, not Clay ... please ...*

By the time she reached the door, she couldn't feel her legs or her feet, couldn't draw a complete breath. *Help me, God ... whatever this is ...* She reached for the handle and opened the door.

Standing there on the front porch was Alex Brady. He was in uniform and his squad car was parked outside, but he looked wide-eyed and half desperate. "Mrs. Michaels ... I'm sorry, this isn't about Clay. It's just that ... I ..."

"Alex …" Jamie exhaled with relief and clung to the only thing she needed to hear. *This wasn't about Clay.* She took a step back. "Come in." She was in a T-shirt and sweats. The wind was too strong for her to hear him very well. When he stepped inside, she closed the door behind him and tried to imagine what would've brought Alex here at this hour. "What is it?"

"The journal entry." Alex's mouth sounded dry. He ran his tongue along his lips, clearly nervous. "I've changed my mind. I'd like to read it, if that's okay."

Jamie was completely caught off guard. Panic from moments ago became a glimmer of joy, surging through her and giving her hope. If he wanted to know about the journal entry, then God was doing something in his heart. She took a step toward the stairs. "Let me get it. I can make a copy of that page." She was already walking up the stairs. "Would that work?"

"Yes, thanks." He shifted his weight from one foot to another and clasped his hands behind his back. "Sorry to trouble you."

"No trouble." She was at the top of the stairs, and she went to the closet and found the journal. It took her less than a couple of minutes to jog back down to the office printer and make a copy of the correct page. She tucked the journal beneath her arm and handed him the copy. "Here."

"Thank you, Mrs. Michaels." He took the piece of paper, folded it, and slipped it into his back pocket. "I … I know it's crazy of me. Stopping by at this hour."

"Call me Jamie, remember?" She folded her arms across her stomach and tried to look beyond the crumbling walls in his eyes. Her voice was soft, and she prayed he would hear her. Really hear her. "God's doing something in you, isn't He?"

For a long while Alex just stared at her, as if the thought wasn't something he'd actually processed yet. Then he gave a slow shake of his head. "I don't know." He patted his back pocket. "But I couldn't go another night without reading this."

Jamie smiled. "I hope you hear your dad's voice when you read it." She lightly touched his arm. "We're still praying for you."

"Thank you." He nodded to her, his expression closed off again. "Thanks for taking the time." He was already at the door. "See you later." And with that, he shut the door behind him and was gone.

She waited until she heard his car pull away before she returned to the office and called Clay. Once she had him on the phone, she told him about Alex's visit and what he'd come to get. "He looked different. Like something might be starting to change in him."

"Hmmm." Clay sounded thoughtful. "He must've gone straight there after our talk."

Jamie loved this, the way they were working together now on Alex's behalf. "What'd you talk about?"

"Everything I've been wanting to say for a year. I told him about the Bible verses that have been stuck in my mind the last few months and how it wasn't possible for him to rid the city of everything bad." Clay told her everything about their talk, and how he and Joe had prayed for Alex when he left with his dog half an hour earlier. "And then he comes straight to our house."

Chills ran down her arms. Nothing beat the thrill of knowing God was at work around them. "We'll keep praying."

"Definitely." He hesitated. "How's the wind there?"

"Strong." She wandered with the cordless phone to the nearest window. "Stronger than it was earlier. Any new fires?"

"Not yet, but we're waiting. If the REA's going to strike again, it'll be soon. We all know it."

"One more reason to pray." Jamie returned to the phone's base. "Thanks, Clay."

"For what?" His voice was tender, speaking straight to her heart even over the phone lines.

"For helping Alex."

"We're better as a team." There was a smile in his voice. "Now go get some sleep."

She knew better than to make promises she couldn't keep. So instead she told him she loved him, and when the call was over, she went to the window and stared at the wind blowing the trees. Whatever God was doing in Alex's heart, she had a feeling the biggest changes were yet to come. Before another moment passed, she silently lifted her voice to heaven, asking God that between Clay's talk and Jake's journal entry, Alex wouldn't only be ready for the battles he'd face on the streets of LA in the coming days.

He'd also be ready for the one raging in his heart.

Twenty-Two

Alex was desperate for the chance to pull over and read the piece of paper in his pocket, but there was only one place he was willing to park on a windy night like this. The road leading up to the Oak Canyon Estates. He refused to think about what Clay had said or the news about the deputy or about the chase earlier that had almost cost his life. He merely kept his eyes on the road, and one hand on the wheel. With the other hand, he patted Bo. The dog was on edge, sensing something wrong in Alex.

"It's okay, Bo ... don't worry, boy, everything's okay." He said the words again and again, but they never quite sounded convincing. He wasn't okay, not hardly. His very soul felt like it was unraveling. Since 9/11 he hadn't worked this hard to keep himself from feeling. For years he'd gone through life refusing his deepest emotions, driven by a single goal. But now his heart hurt from everything he was trying not to process. He checked the clock on his dashboard. His shift was up at three in the morning, so he still had another couple hours. He sped up some, already picturing the place where he would park to read the journal entry.

Then it happened.

Up ahead, a pale green Honda exited the freeway on the off-ramp before Las Virgenes Road. The same type of car spotted by witnesses leaving the scene of one of the arson fires set last week. Alex ran the plates as he followed the car. The search turned up nothing, but that didn't matter. The REA arsonist hadn't been caught yet, so of course there wasn't a warrant out for the guy. At the base of the exit, Alex flipped on his lights. He expected a chase, so he was surprised when the car's driver slowed down, put on his blinker, and made a safe lane change before pulling into the parking lot of a 7-Eleven.

Alex kept Bo in the car for now. As he approached the vehicle, he had one hand on his gun and a flashlight in the other. The wind beat against his face. For the second time that day, his adrenaline went into overdrive. This was it. The occupants of the car were clearly on their way to set another fire, but he'd caught them before they could do the job. In a few minutes, he would have the leaders of the REA, the arsonists themselves, and that would be that. No more fires, no more threat to innocent families living at the base of a tinder-dry hillside. No more danger to LA firefighters. Alex moved slowly. The occupants of the car were bound to be dangerous. Capable of anything. He circled his fingers tightly around his gun as he made a cautious approach to the driver's side.

About that time, the driver rolled down her window, and Alex aimed the flashlight at her. She was a freckled redhead with blue eyes and an innocent smile. Seventeen, eighteen tops. She squinted against the glare of the light. "Was I speeding?"

Alex's breathing was jagged, his body ready for a fight that was never going to materialize. He straightened and removed his hand from his gun, willing his heartbeat to slow down. He lowered the flashlight a little and thought as quickly as he could. "Your speed was okay." He was scrambling, trying to save face. "But you were weaving between lanes." He crossed his arms, hoping she couldn't tell how awkward he felt. "This one's just a warning."

"Really?" She looked genuinely surprised. "That's so nice of you. I have to pay for my own insurance if I get a ticket." She peered out the windshield. "My parents warned me about the Santa Ana winds, how it's hard to keep control of the car when it's this windy. But I didn't realize I was weaving—"

"Drive safely." Alex was already backing away. He didn't have time to visit.

"I will." She gave him a weak smile, waved once, and then safely left the convenience store parking lot and reentered traffic.

Bo was waiting for him back at the car, his expression slightly bewildered, as if even he was confused by Alex's traffic stop. "I know." Alex slid behind the wheel and slammed the door of the squad car. "That was crazy." He thudded his fist against the steering wheel. He was becoming obsessed. There were more criminals on the streets than just the members of the REA. So what was he going to do? Pull over every pale green Honda Hybrid? The girl hadn't been weaving even a little. He could've gotten more information on the plates and figured out the car was licensed to a teenage girl, right? Or made a note of the vehicle and the owner's address. But pulling someone over for no reason other than the color and make of the car? More than a week after the fires had been set? If he wasn't careful, he'd become a liability to the department.

He pulled out of the parking lot and headed back to the freeway. He would be more careful next time, but still there was just one place he wanted to go, one place where he wanted to park and read the piece of paper in his pocket. He reached back and patted Bo's head. "Get some sleep, Bo … Lie down, boy."

Bo did as he was told. Alex only had a few more hours before they'd be done for the night, and unless he was called for backup, Bo was probably done for the shift. Alex reached the road to the Oak Canyon Estates in ten minutes and noticed a new guard station partway up the drive. Good. The developers finally took the threat of arson seriously. He drove up and introduced himself to the guard.

"Just wanted to spend a little time looking for anything suspicious," he told the man.

"Thank you." The guy was older, retired maybe. He looked alert and concerned. "The extra patrol up here can only help."

Alex agreed. He flipped a U-turn around the guard shack, drove back down to the base of the road, and parked his squad car facing the main street. That way he could get a good look at any vehicle that might come up this way at such a late hour.

The wind had let up a little, but it still howled through the canyon. Alex killed his engine and took the piece of paper from his back pocket. Before he opened it, he stared at the dark, empty road ahead of him, and the flickering lights from the neighborhood at the base of the hill. He shouldn't be here on the West Coast, working as an officer in LA. If life had gone as planned, by now he would've been moving his way up in the FDNY, maybe even working at the same station as his father.

His wonderful, brave dad.

Alex swallowed back the sorrow that suddenly surrounded him. Memories rushed at him, and he was six years old again, sitting in the front row of Mrs. England's kindergarten class, and there was his dad, standing at the front of the class next to the American flag, decked out in his firefighter uniform, talking to the kids about fire safety. And Alex was the proudest kid at Franklin Elementary School.

All he ever wanted in life was to be as good and right and true as his dad, so that people might say, "Alex Brady is doing his father's memory proud, a real good guy just like his dad."

He and his dad would've worked together and fished together, and one day when Alex married Holly, his dad would've stood beside him, his best man. The best man Alex ever knew.

No one understood what he'd lost on 9/11, because the loss had been so great for everyone, the numbers so vast. With hundreds of firefighters dead, there was no way to take a look at each one and let the world know what sort of person had fallen victim to the terrorists. Alex narrowed his eyes. Maybe that's what made the loss even greater. The country hadn't only lost four hundred firefighters and police officers. It had lost four hundred heroes. Four hundred heroes like his dad.

He pursed his lips and let his cheeks fill up with the air from his lungs. As he released it, he forced himself to find the strength to read the journal entry. Whatever it said, the words were sort of a final message from his father. That's why he couldn't wait another day to read it—not when any day on the job might be his last.

The car was too dark, so he flipped on the overhead light and opened the folded sheet. At the top of the page was the journal date—August 7, 2001. Alex tried to remember what he must've been doing that day. It would've still been summer break, and he would've been at football practice, maybe ... or swimming at the city pool a few blocks from their home in Staten Island. Alex steadied himself and started at the beginning.

Sometimes I come across someone in the department who personifies courage and commitment, the sort of firefighter people talk about with words like bravery *and* loyalty, *strength* and *honor. That's the way I feel about my friend Ben Brady from the station a few blocks from mine.*

Alex read the description of his dad once more. Brave and loyal, strong and full of honor. They were words Alex could've written. He blinked back the dampness in his eyes and continued.

We worked a call together yesterday, and I found myself watching him, the way he took charge of the blaze and set an example for the other men from his firehouse. Ben and I know each other. We've talked a number of times. But yesterday we talked on a deeper level, about what drives us. I wasn't surprised when he told me he was a Christian.

Guilt stabbed at Alex. His father had shared his faith as easily as he lived it out. Alex liked to think that somewhere in heaven his dad was proud of his police work, proud that Alex was his son. But what would his dad think about the fact that Alex had walked away from God? Alex pushed the question from his mind and found his place again.

"I take God with me on every call," he said. I liked that. It's the way I feel, the way I live. But I guess I never heard it put that way before. He said something else too. He told me he knows he can only do so much to keep the city of New York safe from fires. "When you live with constant danger," he told me, "you have to remember John 16:33." He winked at me. "That's what keeps me sane. John 16:33." I was familiar with the verse, so I understood. Jesus used that part of Scripture to tell his friends a simple, profound message: "In me you may have peace. In this world you will have trouble. But take heart! I have overcome the world." *He also told me he hoped one day his son would embrace the verse.*

The knife in Alex's conscience went a little deeper. He knew his dad thought about him often, but at work? The fact that his father had talked to another firefighter about his hopes for Alex somehow made his loss even more real. How important the Bible verse must've been to his dad, for him to talk about it with Jake Bryan. Tears burned in his eyes, but he held them off and kept reading the things his father had told Jake.

"So far, my family has had very little trouble. Life is good, love is sweet, and time seems like it'll last forever." His eyes held a bittersweet shine. "We all know that isn't true. Especially working for the FDNY."

His words stayed with me all day and even now, as I write, I can hear them in my heart. He's right. Today is like that for me and Jamie and Sierra too. Life is good, love is sweet, and time seems like it'll last forever. But it won't. It never does. And so we stay strong in the hope of John 16:33 ... because in the end, Christ has overcome the world. That's what I have to tell myself every now and then.

Every now and then.

That was about how often people thought about September 11 anymore. Once in a while, every now and then when an anniversary came along or someone mentioned Ground Zero. Alex allowed himself to focus on his father's words, the thoughts that really did form his final message to all of them. His dad had described their life before 9/11 perfectly.

Alex set the piece of paper down on the seat beside him and stared into the darkness again. Life had been so good ... love, beyond sweet ... and there had been no signs that time as they knew it was about to stop forever. Alex sat unmoving for a few minutes, remembering how great life had been, but gradually a thought came into view, something he hadn't considered before.

His dad had known the life they were living wouldn't last, that by working for the FDNY there was always a chance he could report to the station one day and not come home. But the fact hadn't made his father bitter or driven to conquer every fire in his way; it hadn't made him angry or determined to live cut off from the people who loved him.

Alex picked up the piece of paper and read it again straight through. No, the knowledge of danger and darkness in the world around him only made his father more keenly aware of the truth about life and love and time. And the way he'd kept his focus was not through some fierce determination of his own doing, but through his faith in God, his belief in the Bible. He believed that trouble was a certainty in this world, but he was not to worry because God had already conquered the evil in this world.

The wind had dropped off considerably, and Alex rolled down his window, welcoming the fresh air. No matter what his father wished, Alex didn't think he could embrace God again. But there was something about his dad's faith that pounded at him, pushed him, and made him uncomfortable in his own skin. The talk with Clay earlier tonight came back again. What was that Scripture he'd talked about? There was a way that seemed right for a man, but in the end it would lead only to death, right? Wasn't that it?

More than that, the main thing he remembered from Clay's talk was the part about evil, and how Christ never intended for people to rid the world of all bad things, but for people to deal with the evil inside themselves. Alex tried to breathe, but his chest felt tight. It reminded him of a time when he was doing the bench press at headquarters, running through a few sets alone, without a spotter. Something had him frustrated that day, a drug bust gone awry, maybe. Whatever it was, he piled too much weight on the bar and, as he lowered it, he knew he was in trouble. He was able to hold the bar just high enough off his chest to keep it from crushing him, but he couldn't move it, couldn't get out from beneath it without calling for help.

That's how he felt now.

In the weight room that day, Joe Reynolds must've heard him shout, because he ran in and together they got the bar up and back on the rack. But who could help him now? And what about the evil in his own heart? At first the idea had seemed insane — he was one of the good guys! — but now that he'd had some time to think about it, maybe Clay was right.

He wasn't all good on the inside. What about the way he'd treated his mother, barely calling her and writing her off because she'd remarried? In the back Bo yawned and shifted to a different position. Alex looked back at his dog. He'd treated Bo better than he'd treated the people in his life, so what else could that be but a show of evil?

A car drove past, but it didn't hesitate at the winding dirt road. Alex closed his eyes, and he could see Holly exactly as she looked that day at his house when he sent her away. Her long blonde hair and deep blue eyes, the way they clouded with pain when he told her it was over, that he couldn't love her and that she needed to move on without him.

He blinked and stared at the road again. It was too late for him to make it right with Holly. Too late for any of the buddies he'd left behind. But it wasn't too late for his mother. The phone calls they shared always came from her, and every time he made the conversation brief and strained, with short answers and a sense that he had something pressing he needed to get back to doing.

The piece of paper was still in his hand, and he studied it one more time. His father would've been appalled at the way he'd lost touch with everyone — but especially with his mom. Why hadn't he thought about that before? Again, the pressure built in his chest and he had the sudden feeling that the canyon walls around him were closing in, threatening to crush him.

He looked at the time on his iPhone. It wouldn't be quite five in the morning in New York City, but it no longer mattered. Alex couldn't wait another minute to tell his mom what he should've told her years ago. What he should've told her September 12, 2001.

He found her number and tapped it once. It connected immediately, and on the fourth ring — just when Alex was chiding himself for calling so early — she picked up. "Hello?" her voice was frantic. "Alex? Is everything okay?"

"Yes, Mom, I'm fine." He pressed his fingers to his brow. He should've waited until morning. Any mother of a police officer would be terrified of a call at this hour.

"Alex …" she let go a rush of air. "You scared me. It's five in the morning."

He wasn't sure where to start. "I owe you an apology."

"Son?" she hesitated, calmer now, still trying to catch her breath.

He sighed. "I don't know if I can put it into words." He would tell her the whole story someday, the next time they were together. He held his breath, pressing through the moment. "I … I haven't been the same since Dad died, and … well, I'm sorry. That's all. I just want you to know I'm sorry."

She must've been too surprised to speak because it took her several seconds to respond. "Alex, what … what happened?"

"I don't know." He anchored his elbow on his open window and rested his head in his hand. "It's a long story." His eyes felt damp again. "I couldn't wait another hour to make this call." Alex waited, but there was silence on the other end. He thought maybe they'd lost connection, but then he heard the soft sound of sniffling over the phone line. "Mom … don't be sad … it's all my fault. I can't live like this anymore, pushing everyone away." He paused, his sorrow suffocating him. "Dad would've hated what I've become." He set the piece of paper on the seat beside him again and grabbed the steering wheel. "Can you forgive me?"

"Yes." She sniffed again, although clearly she was trying to hide the fact that she was crying. "I've prayed for this ever since you left."

Alex wasn't sure what to say to that, but something felt different in his heart, the same tenderness he'd felt for the crazy old lady with the imaginary soldiers in her backyard. This time the feeling was almost a welcome one. He squeezed his eyes shut to keep from crying. "I love you, Mom. I do."

"I love you too." Her voice cracked and she couldn't hide her tears.

"Okay, then." Alex's throat felt thick. "Go back to sleep. I'll call you later."

As the call ended, Alex sat back and inhaled fully. He could breathe again, and he took stock of the condition of his heart. On this windy Wednesday night, he had rid the world of one more bad guy, and he'd guarded a development and a neighborhood from the terrorist attacks of the REA. Okay, so what? He couldn't sit up here every night. Besides, the world was no different now than it had been when he woke up. There was no less evil around him.

But he'd told his mother he loved her, and as a result there was less evil inside him.

And that—more than any crime solving—would've truly made his dad proud.

Twenty-Three

Owl felt sick to his stomach. Only one thing could explain his nervousness tonight — the same thing he'd been feeling for the past month. He was having second thoughts. He paced along the front window of the rented house at the base of the foothills. The winds had died down last night, but now it was just past midnight and they were back with a vengeance. The decision was made.

It was Thursday night and the winds were in full force, same as yesterday. But an hour ago the orders had been given by Leo. This was the night the Oak Canyon Estates was going down.

"Listen to this." Steve Simons adjusted his glasses and grabbed a piece of paper off the printer. People thought Steve was the leader among the three of them, but they were wrong. Leo was in control. All three-dozen members of the REA answered to him, and it was Leo who ran the show a few weeks ago when he and Steve masqueraded as brothers and cased Oak Canyon Estates the first time.

A single light reflected off Steve's bald head as he held up the printed document. "We're leaving this at the guard station. If it survives the fire, great. If not, we'll send a copy to the paper." He sat on the edge of the table at the center of the living room. None of them lived here, but they spent more time here than anywhere else. The mission was that demanding.

"Hurry up." Leo was sunk into the sofa along the back wall. Owl tried not to cower. Sometimes he wasn't sure how he got mixed up with Steve and Leo. Somewhere along the way the ideals

Owl prided himself in keeping had distorted so that property, possessions, even people took a lesser role than the environment. But at this point he was committed. He knew too much to back out, and Leo was just psycho enough to kill him if he tried.

Leo waved his hand at Steve. "We need to get on the road. The winds are perfect."

Steve stared at the paper. "We, the members of the REA, committed this act of civil disobedience fully aware of the damage it might exact. In doing so, we take a public stand against the wasteful practices of our society and the materialism that drives industries such as the luxury housing market. Hillsides are better off left alone, in the pristine condition that is their inherent and unerring right. Better to burn the blight of increasing gluttonous materialism now, than to allow it to encroach unchecked into the hills surrounding our city, where continued excess will add to global warming and the demise of our planet. We make a call to all people to reduce, recycle, and respond to the mandate of environmentalism. This is a global war. We stand by our decision. Officially, the REA."

"Perfect." Leo's voice was dry. He stood and slipped his hands into his pockets. "Let's go."

Owl was still looking at Steve, thinking about the letter. "You didn't mention natural resources ... you know, the limited natural resources and how the wasteful habits of overindulgent people are leading to a critical reduction in natural resources whenever—"

"Shut up." Leo walked over to Owl and leaned in close. His breath reeked of stale onions and fresh Diet Coke. He turned to Steve. "The letter's fine. We're out of here."

Owl didn't dare say anything else. After the whole Danny thing, he sort of hoped the guys would kick him out. He wasn't sure how else he could break ties with them now—when he knew so much. His hands shook as he headed for the door. Both Steven and Leo smelled a rat after the meeting with Danny—never mind that the guy said the right things. Leo even thought he might be a cop, of all things. Then there were those detectives sniffing around after the last fire. Owl shuddered and grabbed his bag. If he'd let a cop in on their activities, the guys would kill him and toss his body over a canyon somewhere. Leo, for sure, wouldn't have hesitated to take him out.

"Got everything?" Steve drilled a look at him. They'd been over this a number of times. It wasn't like this was the first fire they'd ever set. But it would definitely be the biggest. Especially with the winds like they were tonight.

Owl definitely wanted to throw up. He thought a moment. The kerosene was in the trunk. He had a dozen rags, six oversized barbecue lighters, and a map of the fire roads around the Oak Canyon Estates—in case they couldn't exit by the gravel road. He nodded at Steve. "Got it."

"What about the gun?" Steve looked at Leo.

"Do you have to ask?" Leo rolled his eyes. "I've got two. Now come on. A couple of our other guys are starting fires tonight. We want to be first."

Owl's teeth began to chatter. He clenched his jaw and made his way to the car before the others. In the beginning he agreed with everything the REA stood for. But now … now they seemed a million miles from their goals of protecting the environment. Like the whole setting fires thing had become an obsession, not a means to an end. Owl took a spot in the backseat. Steve had traded in the green Honda after it was spotted at the last job. Police never got a read on his license plate, so there were no red flags when he made the trade. And with Steve's tech salary, he could afford to trade his car whenever he wanted. Now Steve had a Toyota Prius, a hybrid that could go from city to city on fumes. Owl settled in and tried to calm his pounding heart.

Maybe once they got up there he could take off on foot over the hill and down the canyon, find a footpath or some other way out. After all, he was the firesetter tonight. Steve and Leo would help place the kerosene rags and make sure they'd get the most destruction in the least amount of time on site. But he — Owl — would light the flame.

He wondered what his friends in college would think of him now? Save the earth ... stop global warming ... back then their ideals had been so altruistic, so crucial to the survival of the planet.

But now ...

Up in the front seat Leo was barking orders to Steve, who was behind the wheel, sweat glistening off his smooth head. "Turn off your lights twenty yards before the road turns up to the estates. You remember the place, right?"

"Of course."

"Yeah, but don't forget about the lights."

Owl had heard about Steve and Leo's visit here, how they'd pretended to be a couple of brothers and businessmen on their lunch breaks. Got the whole tour and everything. Now they knew exactly where they wanted to start the fires.

"We're almost there." Leo couldn't sit still. He looked at his watch. "Timing's perfect."

"The wind too."

Five minutes later, the two of them were still talking about the perfect conditions when they approached the gravel road. The main street was empty at this hour, so Steve slowed down and turned off his headlights.

"Don't miss the turn. Take it slow. We don't need any two-bit security guard hearing us at this point." Leo hissed the words. They were only half a minute up the dark hill when he let out a sharp, "Hey! What's that?"

"Looks like a guard station." Steve hovered over the steering wheel and peered into the windy black night. "When did they put up a guard station?"

"Doesn't matter." Leo pulled his gun from his pocket and cocked the trigger. "Looks like a barrier's blocking the way on both sides."

Owl's heart raced. They weren't going to shoot someone, were they? He grabbed hold of the door handle. Maybe he could jump out when the car slowed down. Jump and run for it, because Steve and Leo were crazy if they were willing to shoot a security guard.

"What'ya want me to say?" Steve slowed the vehicle.

"Don't say anything! Drive straight through it."

"He'll call the police." Frustration laced Steve's voice. "We'll be arrested before we light the first fire."

"You drive. I'll take care of it."

Owl's heart beat harder, faster. They never should've brought a gun. He bit at the cuticle on his thumb and waited, looking for his chance. If Leo shot someone, they could all go to prison for a very long time. He sank back in his seat, his eyes wide.

"There's a guard." Steve wasn't slowing down. "You still want me to drive through the barrier?"

"Do it. Gun it!"

Steve did as he was told, pushing the hybrid as best he could. Just as they were about to drive through the gate, the guard stepped out to stop them. Steve almost hit him, but at the last second he swerved and took out the bar instead. The guard had a gun, but before he could fire it, Leo leaned across Steve and clicked off three quick shots.

In the craziness of the moment, Owl forgot to jump. He sat in the back, slack-jawed and stunned. What had just happened? He didn't want to turn around and look, but he had no choice. He had to know if the bullets had hit their mark.

Up front Steve was shouting, "What'd you do that for? Did you hit him?"

"Who cares?" Leo pointed the gun straight ahead. "Let's get this thing burning."

That's when Owl turned, just a quick look over his left shoulder. The road ahead was curving, but in the shadowy light from the guard station he saw a body lying facedown on the ground. Owl felt his heart skip a few beats and then slip into a wild and crazy rhythm. Leo was insane. There was nothing in the REA guidelines that said anything about killing people. Civil disobedience, yes. Arson and vandalism, yes. But murder? His upper lip began to twitch, and he looked at the bag of rags and lighters on the floorboard.

They were going to get caught. He could feel it.

Holly hadn't worked this late in a month, but there had been a burst of activity lately. Mortgage rates had fallen, and more people must've felt confident about the economy. Whatever the reason, she had a mountain of paperwork ahead of her and back-to-back meetings tomorrow. Better to get the extra work done on a Thursday night than let it spill into the weekend. She narrowed her eyes and fought back a yawn. Ron had offered to stay and help, to take care of his own paperwork here with her.

But then his father had experienced chest pains — something that had happened twice in the last week. Ron decided it was better to take him to the emergency room and have him checked. Just in case it was something serious. Dave was worried sick about the threat of arson, and the people who might get hurt if a blaze was set.

Holly didn't blame him, but she figured if the members of the REA were going to hit Oak Canyon Estates they would've done so already. The group had certainly had its chances. For two weeks straight, Holly had avoided working here alone, but with the guard in place, she felt safer than ever before. Tonight — even with the wind — the development felt like an oasis above the Valley floor — safe and serene. The wind howled outside, rattling the windows and beating against the walls, but the forecast was for the winds to die down before morning.

Holly focused on her paperwork. The music playing from her iPod speakers was a country list, and Holly sang along to something by Carrie Underwood. The lyrics reminded her that things weren't going well with Ron. He'd cooled his advances toward her, and she hadn't really minded.

Her mother thought the two of them were being ridiculous. "It's like I told you, Holly. You have to work at love. That means two busy people need to take time from their schedules to date and talk and be together."

Holly still hadn't been able to explain to her mother that a person could only work so hard to find sparks. If they weren't there, they weren't –

Suddenly, from somewhere nearby came three loud, sharp pops—like the sound of gunfire. Holly turned down the music and sat perfectly still. She wasn't sure, but it sounded like a car was coming up the road. She glanced at the clock near the top of the computer screen. Two thirty-five. Who would be coming up the road at this hour, and what were those noises?

She picked up her radio, the one that connected her to the guard at the gate. She pressed down the speaker button. "Michael, come in … this is Holly in the office, come in."

Static sounded on the other end, but nothing else.

"Michael, this is Holly. I heard something, and I need to know what it was." Fear raised the pitch of her voice and she fought back a wave of panic. "Come in, please."

Again there was no answer, but just then she definitely heard the sound of a car. Much closer than before. She stood quickly, rushed to the other side of the office, and flipped off the light switch. Whoever it was, she didn't want them to see her in here alone. The rest of the lights in the house were already off. Without wasting a single second, she hurried across the dark office to the phone and snatched the receiver. Her eyes still glued to the top of the gravel road, she dialed 9-1-1.

In a frantic voice, she told the operator who she was, where she worked, and that she was up at the model house in Oak Canyon Estates by herself. "I think I heard gunshots, and now someone's driving up the private road. It sounds like they're coming very fast."

The operator promised to dispatch a deputy. "Stay put, and call back if anything else happens."

As soon as Holly hung up, the car came into view. It peeled up the hill and onto the paved street. Without hesitating, the car made a sharp right turn and sped toward the far end of the street.

Holly's heart was pounding, and her mouth was dry. She hadn't been able to make out the model or color of the car, let alone a license plate. But what could the people in the car be up to? And why wasn't Michael answering at the gate? Michael should've stopped them, and if he'd run into trouble, he should've called 9-1-1. So what was happening? A gust of wind blew against the house. Were the threats coming to fruition? Were the people in the car about to set fire to the development?

She dialed 9-1-1 again, and this time she spoke in a terrified whisper. "Someone's come up the hill, driving very fast. I can't reach the guard station. I think something very bad is about to happen."

Not until after she hung up did she smell something strange wafting in through the one open window. It wasn't a construction smell—roofing tar or paint or carpet. Rather, this was a smell that paralyzed her with fear.

It was the smell of kerosene.

Twenty-Four

Linda Brady couldn't sleep.

Yesterday around this time, Alex had called her to apologize. The best she could make of his call was that God had been working on his heart. He didn't mention the Lord or what had driven him to call her number in the wee hours of the morning, but in his voice she heard a remorse that hadn't been there since before the terrorist attacks.

God must be answering her prayers.

Now she should've been sound asleep. Alex hadn't called again, and no real reason remained for her to be up alone, wandering through the living room looking at old photographs. Her husband Lee was asleep in their bedroom, and already her restlessness had woken him once. He was concerned for her, aware of the situation with Alex, the way that only now – after seven years – he was finally showing signs of returning to the young man he'd once been.

"Everything okay?" he'd asked her an hour ago. He sat up in bed, half awake, his forehead creased with worry.

"Fine." She smiled at him, grateful for him. "I can't sleep. I'll be out in the living room."

Since then she'd read the Bible and straightened the office. The sun would be up soon, but still she couldn't sleep. She looked over the framed pictures that sat on various shelves and hung on the wall in the living room — photos that reminded her of the old days, pictures that kept her company when Lee was at work and she wanted to reminisce.

Alex as an eight-year-old at work with Ben, both of them wearing the FDNY helmets and sitting in the front seat of a fire truck. A family portrait of the three of them when Alex was fifteen. Ben and Alex fishing in the Adirondacks when he was three years old, and another one when Alex was a high school sophomore. Lee didn't mind the photos. He had a past too, a wife who'd been killed in a car accident the summer after the terrorist attacks. Photos were an important part of the healing process, he'd told her.

So the pictures remained.

Linda moved to the window and looked out over Central Park. Their apartment was on the twenty-first floor, and contained an unbelievable view. Lee bought the place the year before they were married, and it suited both of them. She exhaled and her breath left a circle of condensation on the window.

What was it? Why couldn't she get Alex out of her mind? She watched a single cab make its way down Park Avenue and turn at the first light. Maybe it was his apology from yesterday, a strange and joyful piece still trying to fit in the puzzle of her heart. Hearing him yesterday was like getting a trip back to September 10, when Alex was a happy, carefree teenager whose greatest worry was whether he'd passed his chemistry test. Maybe that was it. The way he'd sounded yesterday had given her hope that she might actually get him back, that he could finally let go of the hurt and pain, the desire to make everything right for his father's sake. Maybe he was about to do what he hadn't done since the Twin Towers came down.

Learn to love again.

She lifted her eyes to the full moon hanging just over the park. If he was close to tearing those walls down, then no wonder God had her walking the quiet apartment tonight. She needed to pray. With that she fell into a familiar routine, asking God for her son's emotional healing and for his physical protection. *Keep him safe, God ... his job is so dangerous that any day ... any day could be his last. So guard him, protect him because he seems closer than ever to finding his way back. Keep knocking on his heart so that soon — maybe even tonight — he might turn and trust You again. Please, Lord ...*

A verse filled her heart and soul as soon as she finished that part of her prayer. *Train up a child in the way he should go: and when he is old he will not depart from it.* It was a promise, one Linda had thought about often in the years since 9/11. But here, in the sacred moment of deep conversation with God, the words almost seemed like an answer. She and Ben had done what God asked of them to the best of their ability. They had trained him up in the way he should go. Now she would pray all night that the rest of the promise would come true, that Alex might return to those ways.

Now, before it was too late.

The call came in just before three in the morning, and Jamie opened her eyes in time to see Clay swing his legs out of bed and snap open his phone. She sat partway up, giving her eyes time to focus. The wind whipped against the house outside, and Jamie felt a chill run down her arms.

Clay listened intently to the caller for a few seconds and then flicked on the light next to his side of the bed. "I know the place. Are the hills burning yet?" He waited a beat. "Okay. I'll be there as fast as I can."

Jamie didn't need Clay to tell her what had happened. He was on call for this very reason — in case there was another fire. The department hadn't received word of more threats from the REA, but this was the sort of night the ecoterrorists liked. A plan was already in place. If another arson fire was set in the hills, SWAT members would go to the scene immediately — to keep order, aid in the evacuation, and help pursue the suspects.

Clay was already at the closet, pulling his uniform off the hanger and slipping into the olive green shirt.

"Where is it?" Jamie couldn't shake the cold feeling surrounding her. The wind was warm, and even at this hour she doubted the temperature had dipped below eighty degrees. Even so she felt a chill in the room, and she pulled the down comforter up around her shoulders. "Oak Canyon Estates." He slipped on his uniform pants and gave her a knowing look. "The place Alex warned us about."

"It's close. A couple of SWAT guys live a few miles from there, right?"

"Right. We might have a chance to catch them. There's no sign of fire yet. The call came from a woman who works at the estates. She was in the office late when she heard gunshots and saw a car speed up and head for the north end of the development. She called us again when she smelled kerosene."

Jamie's head began to spin. "A woman?" She was more awake now than before, as suddenly the details lined up and she gasped. "Clay, that's where she works!"

He was getting into his bulletproof vest now, fastening it and checking the pockets, making sure he had his guns. "Who?"

"The girl. Holly Brooks. The one Alex was in love with before 9/11."

Clay stopped and stared at her. "Alex's old girlfriend works at the Oak Canyon Estates?"

"Yes. She has an office all to herself up there." Jamie smoothed her dark hair and tried to process the information. "The call had to come from her."

"Dispatch thinks she's still up there. They advised a rescue could be necessary."

Jamie brought her hand to her mouth. "Go, Clay. Get her out of there." She went to him, circling her arms around his neck. "Be safe." She kissed him and let her lips linger on his a few seconds longer than usual. "I'm afraid."

"Don't be." They kissed once more. "Pray. God will lead us, Jamie. I already asked Him."

She didn't state the obvious, that Jake also had asked God to lead him, but that time the place where God had led was Heaven. On any given call, that could be true for Clay too. She released him and folded her arms around her chest, still trying to get warm. "I'm praying already. Call me if you get a chance."

He smiled once more at her, then left, running from the room, down the stairs, and along the hallway to the garage. A minute later she heard his car leave the garage and peel down the street.

God ... something big is about to happen, something big and very bad. Please protect Clay and the guys, and protect Holly Brooks.

Peace I leave with you; my peace I give you ... Do not let your hearts be troubled and do not be afraid ...

Jamie stopped shivering. God had heard her; He was with her. Slowly she made her way back to bed and crawled beneath the blankets. The peace of God was stronger than any pill or therapist, more effective than anything she might've found in a bottle or an exercise program. Her body began to relax and warmth came over her. There was reason for concern, no question. But with God's great peace inside her, she had survived before, and she would survive again — whatever the night brought.

She was about to settle back down when an idea hit her. She should call Alex and tell him about the fire, about Holly working at the estates, and that she was possibly trapped on the hillside. Certainly, Alex would want to know. She reached for her cell phone on the table next to her side of the bed and found his number. Then, without waiting another moment, she dialed it.

Two rings ... three ... four. The answering machine picked up. "This is Alex ... leave a message."

Jamie wasn't sure what to say, whether she should tell him about the fire, or about Holly, or neither. She hung up without saying anything and as she did, she prayed again, asking God to help the SWAT guys catch the arsonists and the firefighters stop the fire before houses or lives were in danger. But she also prayed that God would be with Alex Brady, who—if he knew about the fire—would've been the first on the scene.

For better or worse.

Alex had only been awake for a few minutes, but already he and Bo were in his Dodge, headed as fast as they could for the Oak Canyon Estates. Normally he didn't sleep with the police scanner in his room, because he would never get any sleep. But tonight, with the winds stronger than they'd been yesterday, he'd had two choices. Stay parked where he could watch the traffic up to the estates, or sleep with the radio in his room.

He missed the first few words of the call, but by the time the dispatcher got to the part about Oak Canyon Estates, Alex was up and getting dressed. He made the call to headquarters that he was putting in an overtime shift and responding to the possible fire at the estates. As part of the task force, that much would've been expected of him. He considered leaving Bo at home. His dog had worked a lot lately, and rest was important for any service animal.

But Bo stayed at his side while he got dressed and as he headed for his truck, and when he reached for the door that led to the garage, Bo gave a single bark. His look was unmistakable. *Don't go without me.* Alex gave his head a quick pat. "All right, boy. Come on."

They were backing out of the garage when he checked his iPhone and realized he'd missed a call from Jamie Michaels. She must've been calling about the fire. Either way he'd have to call her back later. He needed all his focus on the job ahead—whatever that job was.

Dispatch had said something about a possible rescue, that the woman who had reported the situation at the estates was still in her office—an employee of the developer. Alex pressed his foot down harder on the gas pedal. This was one time when he didn't want his squad car. The Dodge would take him wherever he needed to go—including off-road. With all the warning he and the department had been given about this moment, Alex couldn't live with himself if someone died.

He was already on the freeway, minutes from the scene. The wind gusted against his truck, forcing him to steady the wheel. No traffic stood in the way, so he picked up speed again, blazing toward the exit.

His thoughts swirled in his head, blurring together and rushing at him from all sides. The verse from Clay—*There is a way that seems right to man, but in the end it leads only to death*... and the other thing—how God didn't intend for people to eliminate the evil in the world, but to surrender their lives to Him in order to combat the evil within themselves. In the dark of night, with the wind howling outside, the thoughts surrounded him and mixed with his father's words, the ones captured in Jake's journal, that there would be trouble in this world, but Jesus had overcome the world.

All of it pressed in against his heart and made him glad he'd called his mom, because it was a step. If the first place where evil needed to be conquered was within, then he would check himself from time to time. As for his broken relationship with the Lord, that would have to wait. Right now there were more urgent matters at hand. He squinted at the freeway ahead and moved into the right lane. The exit was a mile up.

Bo must've sensed the seriousness of the call, because he let out a sharp bark. Alex looked at him in the rearview mirror, the loyal eyes, the sense of high alert in the way he held himself. However lonely and driven Alex had become, at least he had Bo. The dog was his most loyal friend. He eased the Dodge onto the exit. Whatever happened tonight, Bo would be part of the solution.

The way he always was.

Twenty-Five

C lay reached the steep dirt road leading up to Oak Canyon Estates just as the first glow of orange appeared from the top of the hill. Firefighters were on the way, but the role of the SWAT team was to check on reports of gunfire and catch whoever set the fires. He and a dozen other officers had been instructed to meet at the entrance to the estates and set up a roadblock. That way, if the arsonists hadn't made their way down the drive, they'd be caught for sure. Clay and Joe could make decisions from there.

Clay was first at the scene and needed to check out the guard station, then establish a roadblock. Why hadn't the person manning the guard booth stopped the car, and what about the possible gunshots the caller had heard? Clay sped the fifty yards up the hill to the small station. As he came closer, his heartbeat quickened. His headlights illuminated a figure lying on the ground, and the gate arm that should've been down was shattered in pieces.

As he pulled up, he saw that the prone figure was in uniform—the security guard. Clay slammed his car to a stop, drew his gun, and climbed out. There was no way of telling how dangerous the situation was, so he stayed low behind his car door. He heard the sound of sirens and the squeal of tires back at the bottom of the road.

The car coming up next was Joe's. He pulled up behind Clay's car and hurried out the same way—gun drawn, low to the ground. "That a body?" he barked.

"Yes. Cover me." With Joe at his back, Clay rushed to the guard's side. He was bleeding from his arm and his side, and Clay felt for a pulse. It was there—faint and fast, same as his breathing. "He's alive," Clay shouted over his shoulder. "Call for an ambulance." He turned back to the guy. "Help's on the way. Don't give up on me now. Come on."

Joe made the call immediately. Wind whipped down the canyon and made it hard for Clay to keep his balance as he hovered over the man. He wanted to get up the hill and check it out, see if the arsonists were still there or if they'd already gone. And there was the woman—was she still trapped up in her office, too afraid to leave? The sirens grew louder still, and a series of squad cars sped onto the gravel road and up to the spot near the booth. As the others climbed out, Joe took charge so Clay could stay with the victim.

"Set up a partial roadblock. The suspects could be coming down any time." Joe had grabbed his bullhorn. "But leave room for the fire trucks ..."

The first fire trucks appeared and roared up the hill. They stopped just long enough for a couple of paramedics to jump off the rigs and hurry over to Clay. "We've got it. The ambulance will be here in a few minutes."

Clay took a last look at the man. There was a circle of red oozing from beneath his shoulder, so he uttered a silent prayer for the guard, for his family. *Let him live, God ... don't let him die here on the roadway. Please, God ...* By now it seemed clear there were no suspects hiding around the booth, looking to ambush them. He ran back to his car and motioned to Joe. "I'm going up."

"Not by yourself." They had to yell to be heard above the sound of sirens and vehicles and gusting wind.

"It'll be fine." At SWAT scenes protocol was to stay in pairs, but this was different. "We don't know if anyone's even up there. But I want it clear before they start on the fire."

Joe hesitated, then nodded. "Hurry back."

"You got it." Clay grabbed his radio and asked that firefighters wait halfway up the road so SWAT could clear the scene of any suspect danger. He was in his car and speeding up the gravel drive even while he was making the order. Word came back from the fire captain that they'd stay a hundred yards shy of the top of the hill until they received word. If the fire moved down into the canyon, they'd fight it from where they were situated.

Clay sped up the hill to the top where the drive intersected the single paved road, then stopped and studied the scene. Three separate houses were fully involved. The lights were off at the model, but the woman who called could still be in there. Another problem became immediately evident. The house at the corner on the right was one of the structures on fire, and already the flames were dancing across the backyard toward a section of the hilly road that Clay had just driven past.

Suddenly, the wind gusted hard, and Clay looked over his shoulder, horrified. In as much time as it took him to breathe, the fire jumped the narrow roadway and lit the brush on the other side, completely blocking the road. There was no way down now, not until the firefighters knocked out the blaze behind him. Clay swallowed hard. *God, this is bad ... I need You. Please, God ... show me what to do.*

He took hold of the radio again and reported what he'd seen. "I need a couple fire units on this thing right away. Clear the road and keep it open. The fire's moving down and to the east, toward the guard booth. We've got three homes on fire, and hillsides catching in each area." His pounding heart pushed him into crisis mode—the place where he could act and react best. He kept his voice clear and calm. "We're gonna need a helicopter drop as fast as possible."

Once more he watched the flames behind him, and a realization hit him hard. The situation had become desperate, the blaze already a monster, pushing up toward the sky, roiling and billowing with the wind, consuming everything in its path. *God, get me out of this, please ... Jamie couldn't stand it if ...*

Clay considered the woman in the model home. For now the fires weren't too close to the place where she must work. Clay was driving toward the model home when something caught his eye off to the left. He turned off his lights and turned slowly in that direction. Down a ways, between two homes, a car sat in the street. Near it, at least two people darted between the buildings. With the sound of the wind, they clearly didn't hear him.

His heart pounded, and he felt the danger rise around him. This was where he should've called for backup, but now that was impossible. The road up to the development was blocked by a wall of flames, so where did that leave him? He radioed to Joe and explained the situation. "There's gotta be another way out, right?"

"I'm on it. What about the woman?" ·

"Still need to check on her, but she's away from the fires for now. I might have the suspects in sight. I need to deal with them first."

Silence shouted across the other end of the radio lines, and Clay understood. With no real warning, Clay had gotten into a situation that no officer wanted to be in. "Michaels ... watch yourself. We're gonna get you out of there. Don't be a hero."

"I won't." Again he thought about Jamie. "Radio the fire captain. Let me know about an alternate exit out of this place."

The roar of the fire was building around him. With every gust of wind, the burning homes sent a cascading wall of flames into the dry brush surrounding the development. Sprinklers had been activated, but they appeared to have no impact on the fire. The speed of the flames was horrifying, beyond anything Clay had seen before. But he could do nothing about the situation now, so he drove slowly down the road, past a burning house on the right, closer, closer, until he could see one of the men pouring something on a pile of towels near the base of another house.

The arsonists weren't finished yet; they were still setting fires. Didn't they know the road was already blocked by flames? They were so zealous in their quest to destroy that they were putting their own lives in jeopardy, and they seemed oblivious to the fact.

Clay radioed again, his mind long since made up. "I've got the suspects in sight. I'm moving in." As he finished his sentence, there was an explosion from the other end of the street. Another house went up, and he saw a third figure dart across the road. This was it. If he didn't take every move with the greatest care, he wouldn't miss only his chance at the suspects.

He would miss his chance at getting out of here alive.

TWENTY-SIX

Alex had just reached the base of the main drive up to Oak Canyon Estates when he heard that Clay was trapped at the top with as many as three suspects. He pictured CJ and Sierra and Jamie waiting at home, and he clenched his jaw. Nothing was going to happen to Clay Michaels. Not tonight. Not if he could help it. Alex saw the roadblock leading up to the estates and made the decision quickly. He sped past the turnoff and drove another half-mile to an unmarked road so narrow it could've passed for a trail.

It was a fire road, one intended as alternate access to the hillsides in case firefighters needed another way up. For now, though, they would certainly be fighting the fire up along the main drive, which meant Alex could get his truck up the hill much faster this way. He would radio his whereabouts later.

He reached the top in time to see four houses fully engulfed in fire. But there was something else. At the far end of the road, there was some kind of activity. One car, or maybe two. It was hard to tell in the wind and smoke that swirled across the paved road ahead. Alex flipped off his lights, slammed his truck into a lower gear, and four-wheeled from the fire road through some brush and between two unfinished houses. Once he touched asphalt, he raced down the street past the burning homes. He saw what he already knew—that the main road was on fire, cut off from emergency vehicles.

Bo released a series of barks as he took in the scene, the flames and wind, the speed of Alex's truck. "It's okay, Bo ... we're almost there."

Ahead Alex saw what looked like Clay's car, and beyond that another vehicle. Alex drew closer, and shock slammed into him when he saw what was unfolding up ahead. One of the suspects was holding Clay facedown against the hood of his car at what looked like gunpoint.

Alex felt rage building, consuming him. This was the REA, setting fires and now threatening to take the life of his friend. He pulled off the road again and hid himself between two houses that weren't burning. They hadn't seen him; he was sure of it. The guy with the gun hadn't looked up or signaled to anyone. With the wind and fire and sirens, the noise of his truck hadn't been loud enough to catch their attention.

When he was far enough between the two houses that he was sure they couldn't see his truck, Alex slammed the gear into park, opened the back door for Bo, and told the dog to heel. Bo lifted his eyes to him, and his look seemed to say he wasn't afraid. He would stay by Alex's side whatever the call, whatever the danger. Alex patted Bo's head. "Good boy, Bo … let's get 'em."

With his gun drawn, he slipped around the back of the house and made his way through the rear yards until he could slide around the corner of one of the houses and get a clear view. A second armed man ran up to the first. In the glow of streetlights, Alex recognized him. It was the bald guy — one of the two REA men with Owl that day at the park.

Alex's desperation grew, and he and Bo moved through the shadows toward Clay. He needed to catch them unaware, order them to freeze at the same time. That way he'd have the advantage and could take both guys out if he needed to before they could fire a shot at Clay.

He flashed Bo an open hand with just his index finger pointing straight out. The sign for Bo to keep quiet, not to bark — no matter what. Clay was in imminent danger, without any time to spare. They weren't going to kill him; Alex wouldn't let it happen.

He stayed low and ran as fast as he could until he was a few feet from the suspects. They still had their backs to him, their focus entirely on Clay.

"Police!" he shouted loud enough to be heard above the sound of the wind and fire around them.

For a few seconds, the two men froze. Now that Alex was closer he could see that one of the guys with Clay was Owl, and that he didn't appear to be armed. It was the taller man who had the gun pressed to Clay's back. Alex raised his voice again. "Get your hands up now, or I'll release my dog." He gave Bo a different signal, and the dog let out a series of barks and loud growling sounds.

Owl's hands came up, just as he turned and looked into Alex's eyes. Clearly Owl recognized him, and he shouted at the bald guy, "He's got a gun and a dog. Do what he says!"

Instead, Owl's accomplice fired wildly at Clay and, in the same motion, spun around and aimed his gun at Alex. It took just one bullet from Alex's gun to level the suspect, knocking him to the ground, motionless. Clay was writhing against the car, holding his shoulder. "I'm okay … it's just my arm," he shouted. Alex was about to signal Bo to watch Owl and the man on the ground so he could go to his friend, when there was a blur of movement behind him.

Before he could cock his gun, Bo barked once and leaped back into the shadows at a man Alex hadn't even seen, a man who had come up behind them unnoticed and now was just a few feet away. With a ferocious second bark, Bo knocked the third man to the grass, but as he did, the man fired once at Bo's chest.

"No!" Alex held up his gun, his knees weak. "No … Bo, come here!"

Bo let out a sound Alex had never heard from his dog. The man's gun flew from his hand as he and Bo fell to the ground. Alex was breathing hard, gasping. "Bo, come here, boy!"

"He's shot." Clay's voice rose above the noise. "Get the suspect's gun."

Alex saw the weapon a few feet from him. He grabbed it and shoved it in his back pocket, his eyes never leaving those of his dog. Bo was lying limp across the suspect's chest, his regal head looking back for Alex. In that split second, Alex saw in Bo's eyes something he'd never seen before, something that told him the situation was terribly serious.

Bo's eyes were glazed with fear.

"Hold on, Bo!"

The suspect's glasses were on the ground and he groped about, pushing Bo off him. Alex wanted to scream at him, ask him why he would set fire to houses and shoot at deputies under the guise of environmentalism. He aimed his gun at the man, but the suspect was no longer armed.

"Freeze!" Alex was shaking, desperate to help Bo. It took every bit of restraint to keep from pulling the trigger, but the suspect did as he asked. He stopped and raised his hands slowly into the air.

Alex gave a quick glance over his shoulder and saw Clay reach into the car and pull out a T-shirt from his passenger seat. "Help me with this." He waved it in Alex's direction. Owl still stood nearby, his face frozen in shock.

Bo was whimpering now, a sick, slow sort of whine. All around them the wind and fire raged, and Alex noticed two more houses now covered in flames that had spread from the other burning structures. "Hold on, boy." He yelled the words at his dog and raced over to his friend, his gun still aimed straight at the third suspect.

He turned just long enough to take the T-shirt from Clay and tie it above the gunshot wound on his upper arm. The wound was bleeding, but not badly enough to be life-threatening. Not yet, anyway, and the tourniquet would help. "You okay?" Alex was breathing hard. He pulled tight on the T-shirt ends and made sure the pressure was in the right place.

"I'm fine." Clay was in pain, but he was handling it. He looked down the street and shook his head. "We're in trouble, buddy. We gotta get out of here."

A quick look at the suspect on the ground told Alex what he suspected from the beginning. The guy was dead.

"What ... what about the fire?" Owl shouted from where he stood, motionless, petrified.

"Don't move," Alex barked at him. But before he could leave Clay and turn the gun back at the third suspect, the guy took off, running down the street toward the model home.

"Let him go." Clay winced, holding his arm against his waist. "Bo needs you."

Alex felt sick as he turned his attention to Bo. The dog wasn't moving, but he still had his head a few inches off the ground, his eyes on Alex, where they had no doubt been since the gun had gone off nearly two minutes ago. Alex slipped his gun back into the holster and fell to his knees at his dog's side. "Bo ... hold on, buddy. It's okay." In the light of the street lamp he could see the dark, wet circle spreading out from Bo's furry chest.

There was no telling where the bullet was, whether it had cleared the dog and maybe only left a wound that could be treated, or whether his injury was much worse. Alex wouldn't let himself think about it. He lowered his face to Bo's and talked calmly against the dog's ear. "It's okay, Bo ... hold on, boy. It's okay." As Alex straightened again, Bo twisted his head back and licked Alex's hand. Like before, his eyes never left Alex's.

Always, Alex had been able to guess what his dog was thinking, and this moment was no exception. Bo's eyes told him of a love and loyalty that couldn't be measured, a care and concern that went beyond his desire to look after himself. In his eyes Alex could see that whatever the outcome, Bo would've done the same thing again. He had taken a bullet intended for Alex, and that was something Bo had been willing to do from the moment the two paired up.

Alex hadn't really cried since right after his dad was killed. The guy he'd been before the terrorist attacks grieved his father long into the night that awful Tuesday, but afterwards buried his pain deep and allowed his determination to drive him. He'd struggled a few times, sure — like when he said his last good-bye to Holly. But he hadn't cried once.

Until now.

With tears hot against his cheeks, he swept his dog into his arms, stood up, and ran him back to his truck. He looked at Clay, and his sick feeling doubled. His friend didn't look good. "Stay here. I'll be right back," he yelled.

"What about me?" It was Owl, his frightened shriek rising above the sound of the fire and wind.

Alex stopped for half a second and stared at the guy through the smoke and blowing embers. "Don't move."

Clay was pale and his skin looked clammy. He leaned against his car and closed his eyes. The sound of a helicopter rose above the sound of the roaring fire, and Alex realized what was happening. Air drops on the fire. That would help, but already the development was an inferno.

Running as fast as he could, Alex carried Bo to the truck and set him carefully across the backseat. "Come on, Bo … you can do this." He spoke the words as calmly as he could, because Bo could sense trouble in his voice. The dog had always been perceptive, and right now he needed to believe that Alex thought he had a chance. And Alex did think so. He refused to think otherwise. Of course, Bo had a chance. He wasn't going to die. He'd survived these last few minutes, so now they only had to get him to a vet hospital.

Alex pulled his truck out of its hiding place and screeched up to the spot where Clay was still leaning against his car. Moving as fast as he could, Alex ran from his truck, grabbed Clay, and walked him to the front passenger seat, helping him inside.

"You!" he barked at Owl. "Get in the back."

Owl didn't need to be told twice. He lurched forward and vaulted himself into the truck bed.

Alex jumped back in behind the wheel and glanced at Clay. "Hang in there."

"How … how are we … getting through the fire?" Clay slumped against the back of his seat, struggling to keep his eyes open. "Everything's burning."

"I know another way." Alex peered down the street. Clay was right. The fire was burning across the main street of the development now, moving closer to the model home. But it didn't matter. They'd have to get through it somehow, because on the other side of the flames, the fire road would still be a safe way down the mountain.

Alex took off and radioed a quick update — one suspect dead, one in custody, one at large. "I've got two victims — Michaels and my dog." He explained that he was heading down the fire road half a mile west of the Oak Canyon turn off. His words were sharp and fast. "I'll need a couple of ambulances."

"Ten-four. Stop at the model home. The woman who made the call is still there. She was trapped by the fire, same as Sergeant Michaels."

Alex looked at Clay and then over his shoulder at Bo. Every minute counted at this point — for both of them. But if a woman was trapped in the model home, he'd have to get her. He was sizing up the extent of the fire ahead of him when he spotted a car parked outside the model, a car he'd missed the first time he'd passed by. It must've belonged to the woman.

Alex dragged his fist over his eyes. No more tears. He couldn't break down now, not when he had so much to do. Again he looked back at Bo, and even now his dog was watching him, looking almost apologetic, like he still wanted to help but his body would no longer let him. Alex shifted his attention to his friend. "You with me, Michaels?"

"I'm here." Clay sounded sleepy, dizzy. He was still losing blood, and he needed to get to a hospital. But Alex had to get the woman first. "I've gotta check the model house. Dispatch says the woman who called in is still in there."

"Check it." Clay lifted his good hand, his voice a little stronger than before. "I'll be fine."

Alex drove up nearly to the front door of the model, jumped out, and raised his gun. He couldn't be too safe. The other suspect had run in this direction, and there was no telling if he'd gotten hold of another gun. Already once today he'd forgotten the possibility of additional suspects. He hurried to the front of the house and tried the handle, but it was locked. He pounded the butt of his gun against the door. "Police ... anyone here?" By now he expected that somehow she'd escaped, run down the street toward the fire road, knowing that her car wouldn't have made it. Certainly, the developer would've told his employees about the alternate way out.

He was about to kick in the door and check the place—just in case some other REA member was holding the woman hostage, when suddenly the door opened and a frantic-looking woman stepped out. "I thought they'd forgotten about—" She stopped, stunned.

For a long moment, Alex couldn't do anything but stare at her, too shocked to act or think or do anything but try to make sense of what he was seeing.

"Alex?" She swayed, confused, terrified. "I ..." she looked over her shoulder. "I didn't know whether it was safe to come out and ..."

"Holly, you ... you made the call?"

"Yes." She was shivering. "I work here."

He tried to find his way back to the urgency of the moment. "Are you by yourself?"

"Yes. They stayed away from the model." She stepped out, and from that vantage point she must've been able to see the full extent of the blaze for the first time. She put her hand over her mouth. "The fire ... it's everywhere!"

Another helicopter was approaching overhead, dropping a load of chemical fire retardant over the part of the street Alex had to get through in order to reach the fire road. "Come on." He put his gun back and grabbed her hand. "We have to get out of here."

He couldn't process everything his heart was feeling. Holly Brooks worked at Oak Canyon Estates? All this time he'd gone by the place and even driven down this street and he'd never known that she—

Another explosion sounded from behind them, and the house next to the model burst into flames. The wind was pushing burning embers in every direction, so it was only a matter of minutes before the model went up too. He raced with Holly to his truck and helped her into the backseat next to Bo. "My dog got shot." He looked at her for half a second, and he knew she could feel the pain in his eyes. Her appearance was still familiar, still the Holly he'd known and loved when he was a boy. She gave the slightest nod as she climbed into his truck, as if to say she'd help the dog, whatever she could do.

Once he was back in the driver's seat, Alex put his hand on Clay's knee. "Talk to me, man. You doing okay?"

"I need ... a doctor."

"You'll get one." Alex refused the feelings that had come instantly to life when he looked into Holly's eyes. The REA wasn't going to kill Clay or Bo, not him or Holly, not while Alex had anything to say about it. He jerked the truck into reverse, and as soon as they were facing the right direction, he shoved the gear-shift into drive. "Everybody hold on."

From the back of the truck, Owl let out a petrified yell. The fingers of fire that blew over the street ahead of them were thinner now, but the road was still covered by a towering fifteen-foot wall of flames. Alex gritted his teeth and slammed his gas pedal hard to the floorboard. In a rush of heat and bright orange, the Dodge passed clean through the blaze and onto the street beyond it. Only then did Alex allow himself to exhale.

He checked his rearview mirror. Owl had his hands over his head, but he was fine. They'd done it; they'd cleared the fire. In that moment he saw the third suspect on the side of the road waving at them, his face stricken. Alex didn't trust the guy. He'd have to come back for him. Up ahead Alex was right about the fire road. The way was clear. But for a few burning houses on the right side of the street, the fire was all headed downhill, away from the fire road.

He reached the end of the street and jerked his truck into four-wheel drive. As he did he looked back at Holly, but she was bent over Bo, stroking his side, whispering to him, comforting him. Alex looked straight ahead and swallowed another wave of tears. He would get them out of here, because he had to get them to safety. He commanded his truck over the rough terrain between the development and the fire road, and once he was on the narrow dirt trail, he flew as fast as he could down the hill.

At the base of the road, a host of emergency vehicles were waiting. He barreled toward them and slid to a stop a few yards from the first ambulance and a group of waiting paramedics with a stretcher. Alex jammed the gearshift into park and tore out of his truck. Clay was his first concern. He waved the medics to the passenger side, and one of them beat him to the door.

"My dog!" Alex shouted at the other paramedics near the second ambulance. "He's in the back."

A pair of them hurried with another stretcher to the back door of Alex's truck. At the same time, two additional medics ran up to Clay with the stretcher and, as Alex reached Clay's side, his friend opened his eyes. "Hey ... thanks." His mouth sounded dry, and he looked drawn and pale. "Can't believe ... you got us out of there. Whole hillside's ... on fire." He looked back toward the truck. "I'm okay." He paused, his breathing harder than before. "Go get Bo."

A pair of SWAT officers took Owl from the back of the truck bed, and Alex shouted at them. "Third suspect's still up there."

"We'll put out an APB," one of them yelled back at him. "But it's too dangerous to go back up."

Alex took a step back, torn. The medics had an IV in Clay and already were assessing his vitals. Alex caught the eye of the first medic, and the guy gave him a slight nod that told him what he wanted to know. Clay was going to be okay. They'd reached the bottom of the hill in time.

"Get ... Bo," Clay sounded as serious as he could, given the situation.

Alex nodded. He turned and ran to the other side of his truck where a couple of guys were lifting Bo carefully and setting him on the stretcher. Holly had stayed beside him, and now she was stooped over him, her long hair hanging against his side as she stroked his head and his ears.

Alex looked at her for a fleeting moment. "Thank you."

She didn't say anything, just brought her fingers to her mouth. That's when he saw that she was crying. He didn't have time to think about her tears, about why she was crying and whether the reason was because of Bo or because of him or because they'd nearly died in a fire. All that mattered right now was Bo. Alex moved in closer to the stretcher, and Holly backed up to make room for him.

"Hey, Bo … it's okay. I'm here." Bo's eyes were closed, and he wasn't moving. Alex put his hand along the side of his dog's face, and at the sound of Alex's voice, at the feel of his touch, Bo opened his eyes and looked straight at him. He tried to lift his head, but this time he could only bring it an inch off the stretcher.

One of the medics was getting an IV into him, but he could hear the two guys whispering and he straightened, his voice stern. "He's gonna make it, right?"

The medics swapped a look, and it made Alex want to scream. The medic at the foot of the stretcher shrugged. "We're taking him to the vet hospital in Calabasas. We'll do everything we can."

Alex took hold of the guy's arm. "He's going to be okay. He would've bled out by now if the bullet had gotten him somewhere bad."

The other paramedic started pushing the stretcher. "We need to go. You coming with us?"

Suddenly, Alex was torn again. The guy who had shot Bo was still up there, still scrambling around in the fire without his glasses. The SWAT deputies were right about the danger of going back up the hill. But what if the guy escaped? He'd walk the streets again until they found a new meeting place and another few members. Next time the wind blew, they'd be setting fires to some other development. Willing to kill people all for the sake of some sick radical environmentalism. Or the guy might die in the fire, and Alex would have to live with that on his conscience, knowing that he'd left the man on the side of the road in his haste to get Clay and Bo to safety.

The ambulance with Clay inside pulled away, its sirens adding to the sound of the relentless wind and the raging fire on the other side of the hill. Alex could feel the urgency again, feel it pushing him back to his truck. Bo would be okay. They would get him to the hospital and take out the bullet, stitch him up, and give him some fluids. He had to be okay. Alex walked alongside the stretcher and watched as they moved it into the back of the ambulance. He crawled up inside and sat as close to Bo as he could, but again Bo's eyes were closed.

"We gave him something for the pain." One of the medics stuck his head in the back. "He'll be asleep in a minute or two."

Alex nodded, but he didn't look at the guy. Drugs were a good idea. Very good. Let Bo sleep. He needed rest after all he'd been through. One of the medics slipped into the back on the other side of the dog. He checked the IV bag and added another medication to the fluid.

"Bo …" Panic edged in around the moment. "Can you hear me, Bo?"

The dog's eyes twitched a few times and then opened. They looked clearer than before, and the fear from earlier was gone. For a long time—Alex wasn't sure if it was a minute or five minutes—Bo looked at him, never blinking, never once looking away. In all their time together, Alex had never seen Bo look sad, but he looked that way now. His dark eyes shone with a sorrow too deep to see the bottom of it.

"You're going to be okay, boy." Alex felt a lump in his throat, and he swallowed hard against it. "You're a good dog, Bo." Alex stroked the dog's head. "Such a good boy, Bo."

"We have to get going." The medic standing outside the ambulance tapped on the open door.

Alex held up his hand and kept his eyes on the dog. The medicine must've been kicking in because Bo blinked a few times very slowly. When it looked like he might be asleep, he struggled one last time to open his eyes and then closed them a final time, knocked out by the drugs.

"Good boy, Bo." Alex eased his dog's head into his arms and cradled him for a few seconds. "You're gonna be okay." Alex pressed his face against Bo's and then set him back down on the stretcher. He had to get the suspect before he could be finished here, but he didn't want Bo to make the trip to the hospital alone.

Alex remembered Holly, and as he stepped out of the ambulance he turned to her. "Could you go with him? In case he wakes up?" He was talking fast, his own fear consuming him, no matter what he wanted to believe about Bo being okay.

"Sure." She wiped the tears on her cheeks as she hurried to the ambulance.

"You know," Alex stepped aside so she could climb in, "so he's not afraid?"

"Of course." She took the place where Alex had been sitting and began petting Bo's head and side. "Why aren't you going?"

He could feel his eyes grow flinty hard. "I'm not finished here."

"Alex ..." her expression changed, and shock filled her eyes. "You aren't going back up? The fire ..."

"I have to." He moved back. "I'll meet you at the hospital as soon as I can." He took a last look at Bo, then found her eyes again and stared for a long moment into those deep blue pools. "Thank you."

The other medic was already in the driver's seat, ready to pull away. Alex slammed the doors shut and hesitated only for a few seconds as the ambulance made a U-turn and headed back toward the freeway. A few SWAT cars were in the area, and as Alex ran back to his Dodge, one of the officers shouted at him. "Where are you going?"

"There's still a man up there — one of the suspects. Somebody has to get him."

"Not you, Brady. You won't have backup," Joe said.

"I don't care." He was already back in his truck, refusing whatever Joe might be saying next. He wouldn't disobey orders, but he had to hear them in order to follow them. And right now he wasn't listening.

Alex felt a sense of purpose as he pushed the truck up the hill, bouncing and skidding around corners and narrow stretches of road. He'd vowed that no one would die at the hands of a fire set by the REA, and already one suspect was dead. But not another one, not when he and the entire headquarters knew this was coming. It wasn't like 9/11, when the country was blindsided by the terrorist attacks. This time they had known, and maybe they hadn't done enough to stop it. Either way, no one else was going to die — not tonight.

He would see to it.

TWENTY-SEVEN

Holly braced herself against the back of the ambulance so she could keep one hand on Bo for the ride to the veterinarian hospital. But as she patted the sleeping dog's side and his head, she was completely absorbed in the task of trying to process what had happened over the last hour. She'd done what she could do ... she had no doubt about that. She'd made the call to 9-1-1 as soon as she had even the slightest clue that something bad was happening.

She leaned her head back and closed her eyes. The estates were gone. Completely gone. Dave Jacobs had insurance, and if he could afford the deductible maybe he'd build again, or maybe not. Either way, her job was no longer a certainty. She had called Ron after she called the police, but by the time he arrived on the scene no one was allowed up. Ron had called her just once to see how bad the situation was. "The houses, are they ... how many are burning?"

"They're gone, Ron. The whole neighborhood's on fire."

In the course of their conversation, she wished she were talking to Dave and not Ron. Someone who might be concerned with her safety. Because Ron definitely seemed more concerned with the buildings than with her, and she knew for sure that she and Ron were finished.

The ambulance bounced and jerked as the driver made his way to the freeway. Holly pictured herself waiting in the dark real estate office for someone to come help her. Early on after the first fires were started, she thought about sneaking out, maybe driving down the dirt road to the guard station and checking in with the officers who were there. But she didn't know if she could make it to her car without attracting attention from the men setting the fires.

Then someone from the sheriff's dispatch called her and ordered her to leave. "You're in grave danger up there," the woman told her.

"What about the arsonists?" Holly had been sitting low at her desk in total darkness, watching fires start at each end of the street.

The dispatcher explained that a SWAT officer was headed up, that he'd make the arrests, and that whether the suspects saw her or not she needed to leave. Holly agreed, but as she hung up, she watched in horror as the fire jumped from the corner house to the brush across the street, closing off the road and trapping her. Trapping all of them. Her next call to 9-1-1 was more urgent, filled with panic.

"What am I supposed to do? Everything's burning up here."

"Stay calm. Is the house you're in on fire?"

"No." Her heart slammed around inside her. "But the wind … it's blowing the fire in every direction."

"Stay put as long as you can. Call if anything changes. We'll have someone come get you as soon as we can."

The next fifteen minutes were the longest in her life. Holly opened her eyes and studied the dog again. The ambulance was getting off the freeway, heading down an off-ramp.

"It won't be long," the medic's eyes looked deeply concerned.

"He's not doing well, is he?" Her voice was thick with tears, and she could barely talk.

"No." He frowned and patted the soft fur around Bo's ears. "He's hurt pretty bad."

Holly sighed and let her forehead rest in her hand. In her wildest dreams, she hadn't imagined the person who would rescue her would be Alex Brady. But seeing him only confirmed what she had wondered about before. She hadn't stopped loving him, not even a little. She would always remember the way he looked on the doorstep of the model home, his eyes wide and worried, features drawn and tense. And then the change in his expression, the half a second when the walls came down and she could see clearly what she'd always believed.

That the Alex she loved was still inside him somewhere. The young man he'd once been had risen to the surface instantly in the shock of seeing her at the door. Just as quickly, the walls were up again, but that was understandable. They had been in the middle of an emergency, a disaster that could've wound up very differently. She patted Bo's side, a couple of long, soft pats. Poor dog. The disaster was still playing out around them. And what about Alex? Holly's heart fluttered about inside her, its rhythm nowhere near normal. Alex was crazy to go back up the hill. The winds could shift at any moment, and the fire would tear down the other side of the development, right across the fire road.

The ambulance turned onto a busy street and sped onto a straightaway.

"The staff knows we're coming." The medic was focused on Bo. "They'll be ready for him."

"Thanks." She sniffed twice. Tears slipped onto her cheeks, and she pressed her finger beneath her nose. What was Alex thinking? He should've stayed with his dog and let another deputy get the suspect. The guy couldn't go anywhere trapped in the fire, so why chase after him? She felt a series of sobs building inside her. The answer was as obvious as it was painful. He had to go for the same reason he'd pushed her out of his life. Because he was driven to save lives—even the life of a bad guy. Every life but his own.

Another wave of tears filled her eyes. Watching him tonight, she realized for the first time that he was right. She couldn't have been in a relationship with someone that driven, that focused on solving crime and saving lives. The terrorist attacks had changed him, and this was the result: Alex's crazy determination to keep other people from going through what he went through, so that no one else would have to be the victim of the attacks of another.

A victim like Alex still was.

He found the suspect trying to get away, stumbling down the hill at the top of the fire road, a wet rag pressed to his mouth. The sight of him assured Alex he'd done the right thing by coming back up. The guy could be killed trying to escape the fire on foot, and if he did make it out, he'd probably be back at his acts of ecoterrorism by next week.

Alex flipped his bright lights on the guy and drew his gun. The suspect froze and raised his hands over his head. Alex ran out, grabbed him, read him his rights, and shoved him into the bed of his Dodge. He didn't have handcuffs, but he wasn't worried about the guy fleeing. Not with his life on the line. Wasting no time, Alex slid back into the driver's seat and hurried up the hill to turn around.

At the same time, he realized what was happening with the firestorm. The wind had shifted, and a towering wave of fire was coming their direction. Alex whipped the truck around as soon as it was physically possible. From the back, the bald guy must've seen the fire coming toward them because he shouted, "Faster!"

Alex tried not to look, tried to stay focused on the road ahead of him because he had to make it down the hill, had to turn the last suspect over to SWAT, and get to the vet hospital. Had to make it back to Bo, back to tell Holly he was grateful for the way she had been there for Bo.

Still he couldn't help but see what was happening.

The fire was spilling down the back side of the canyon at a wicked speed, consuming the brush like a voracious monster and creating an inferno that was now just twenty yards ahead of Alex's truck, pressing its way downhill and edging in on the fire road ahead. He would have to hurry if he was going to make it. Once the fire crossed the road, it would be a sea of flames impossible to drive through.

He gave the truck a little more gas, but as he did, his rear left wheel nearly slid off the narrow road. Alex had to let up on the pedal until he could steer the truck back onto the gravel, and those few seconds were all it took. Ahead, the fire roared across the road and back up the hill on the other side. Before Alex could think of a plan or put his truck in reverse, the flames crossed the road a dozen yards behind him.

"We're surrounded!" The suspect shrieked.

Alex was breathing hard, looking first over his right shoulder, then his left. There had to be an escape. He could drive off the fire road if he had to—at least they'd have some sort of chance that way. But the inferno raged on all fronts, every side, and Alex wondered for an instant if this was what hell felt like, trapped by a mountain of fire with no escape. They were going to die, so maybe he was about to find out, and it occurred to him that Clay was right about the Bible verse. There was a way that seemed right to him, and he'd done that very thing. But in the end it really was going to lead to death.

He hit the brakes and tried to imagine running through the flames or maybe crawling under them. But there wasn't a single space surrounding him that wasn't on fire. He gripped the steering wheel, his heart pounding, his breathing fast and panicky as he reached for the radio. "Brady, here. I'm trapped on the fire road. Flames all around us. I need some help here, guys. Send a helicopter, and hurry."

The flames were closing in, so that they were stuck in a circle maybe thirty yards in diameter and getting smaller with every second, every gust of wind. This was really the end. He could still do one thing, so Alex opened the door and shouted at the suspect. "Get inside the truck. Hurry!"

The tall thin suspect vaulted out of the bed and slid into the backseat, brushing tiny fiery embers from his hair. Gone was the cocky attitude, the larger-than-life bad guy who had shot a bullet through Alex's dog. The suspect was a quivering mass of terror. "Listen … you gotta get us out of here!"

"We're stuck." Alex didn't look back at him, didn't bother to raise his voice. He shut his door and stared at the flames.

In the backseat the suspect was going ballistic now, shouting for him to do something, to drive through the flames, or let him out of the truck. Screaming how they needed to say their prayers, and how he was going to run down the mountainside if Alex didn't do something.

"Go … you won't get far." Alex leaned his forehead on the steering wheel and tuned him out. They were both going to die, and that meant he'd never know about Bo, never see Holly Brooks again. Never have the chance to thank her and tell her what he knew for sure now.

That his love for her had never died, no matter how he'd tried to suffocate it.

He opened his eyes and felt a burst of the fight that was so familiar to him. Maybe he *could* drive through the flames and make it out on the other side. He'd done that once tonight already, so why not at least try? But the fire ahead wasn't a thin wall this time; it was an ocean of flames, an inferno. They'd get a few feet in, his truck would explode, and that would be that.

He never should have come back up the hill after the suspect. If the guy had been killed in the fire, it would've been his own fault. Alex wasn't responsible, and eventually the guy would've been caught—by fire or by the SWAT team when he came down—just like Joe had said. Joe had warned him not to come up here again. So Alex would die because of his own stubbornness, his determination to do things his way. That's what would kill him in the end—just like the Bible verse had said. Alex looked over his shoulder again and saw what he already knew. The flames were closer now, the circle shrinking.

But to sit here and wait for certain death went against everything Alex knew. Suddenly, he remembered what the suspect had said a few seconds ago. How they needed to say their prayers … Whether the guy meant it or not didn't matter. If Alex was going to die in the next few minutes, he had no choice but to talk to God—the God he'd walked away from seven years ago.

Whether it was the fire closing in on him or some divine act of the Holy Spirit, Alex wasn't sure, but in that moment he could finally see with clarity that his father hadn't died because of God's callousness. He died because it was his time, and in a heartbeat he went from the horror of 9/11 to the hallways of heaven. His father never would've blamed God, and now Alex couldn't blame Him either. Not for one more minute.

He opened the truck door, adrenaline flooding his veins, making it almost impossible to breathe or think or feel anything but overwhelming panic. The wind and burning embers gusted overhead, igniting bushes in the shrinking circle that surrounded his truck. The bad guy was still in the back screaming at him, begging him to do something, but there was nothing he could do.

It hit him then that this must be similar to how his father had felt in the moments before his death, trapped by a wall of flames with no way out, knowing that the fire had been set by terrorists. The difference was that his father had gone out with God at his side. Alex had no doubt about that.

So why couldn't he cry out to God even here, minutes before his death? His father had wanted Alex to be a man of faith more than anything else, but all these years he'd refused to think about that. Alex clenched his fists and tried to focus above the roar of the inferno around him. He could almost hear his dad calling to him, telling him to reach out to God—before it was too late.

Alex crouched down beneath the swirling fog of smoke and for a few seconds—like the suspect—he thought about running. But there was nowhere to go. Then, without giving the act another thought, he dropped to his knees. The small gravel and rocks dug into his knees through his jeans, but he didn't care.

"God!" The cry was desperate as it rose above the sound of the firestorm. "I'm sorry!" He shouted the words, but the fire and wind were so loud even he could barely hear them. He had blamed God and in the process he'd lost the life his father had wanted for him. He'd shut out everyone who loved him, and he'd tried to be God, the sort of Almighty he thought God should be. But he could see it all now, the fact that Clay was right. With Christ's strength, the only evil that could ever be conquered was the evil within him.

He lifted his hands and face to the fiery sky. "Help me, God! I'm not ready to die! Please ... forgive me."

A release exploded in his heart and soul, and like a scene from long ago he recognized the feelings, because they were the ones that had defined him before 9/11. Feelings of love and hope and longing, a desire for the kind of life his parents had shared. A favorite Bible verse from long ago came rushing back—*For I can do everything through Christ, who gives me strength.* He'd shared it with Holly one day when the world was his and summer lasted all year long. And suddenly in the midst of the gravest danger he'd ever faced, it was all there again, flooding over him. *Thank You, God ... I feel You here with me.*

He could do this, because with every breath Christ was giving him a strength he hadn't known these past seven years. Alex remembered something his father had told him. That there was a party in heaven whenever one sinner turned back to God. Alex smiled despite the terror around him. *Let my dad be part of the celebration, God ... I see it so clearly. Thank You ...*

He could almost hear the band.

But even as he prayed, the fire moved in closer, sucking the air from the small pocket and making it hard to breathe. Alex wasn't afraid, wasn't panicked anymore. He didn't want to die, but there was no way out. The end could be any moment now, the next gust of wind and the raging inferno would close in on top of them. Alex stayed on his knees and thought again of Bo and Holly and his mom. At least he'd had the chance to tell his mother he was sorry. The heat of the flames was suffocating now, and Alex had a final thought—something good would come from him dying this way.

In a matter of minutes, he would see his dad again.

Twenty-Eight

Jamie was listening to radio updates of the fire as Eric drove her to the hospital. It was still dark outside, and the smoke was thick across the freeway, the orange glow eerie in the western sky, especially since the sun was still hours from rising. Jamie replayed the events of the last half hour. She'd been awake, sitting up in bed when Joe made the initial update. He told her what had happened and how violent the guys from the REA had been. And he told her about Clay.

"You need to get to the hospital, Jamie. As soon as you can."

Jamie's first call was to Eric and Laura, and they had come immediately. Laura was at her house now with the still-sleeping CJ and Sierra, and Eric drove her to the hospital. After Joe's call, Jamie had heard from the doctor. Clay was in critical condition, and she should hurry. But with all the terrible news, Jamie clung to one single hope, something else the doctor had told her.

They expected Clay to pull through.

That alone kept her sane as they sped along the Ventura Freeway to the Los Robles Medical Center; it was the only reason she could listen to the radio for updates. The fire was raging out of control, ripping through the hillsides at incredible speeds and spreading in all directions. The most recent news stated that an entire neighborhood at the base of the mountain had been evacuated. In addition, firefighters were evacuating other neighborhoods—well in advance of the blaze reaching them.

The news reporter kept stating what anyone listening already knew. That the fire was set by members of the REA, and that one of them had been shot and killed by a K9 deputy. The reports didn't say the name of the officer, but Jamie already knew it was Alex. What other K9 officer would've been at the scene of the fire, working to apprehend the suspects?

The number of homes that could burn in the process might reach into the thousands, according to officials. Already—because of the shifting winds and the amount of dry brush in the Las Virgenes hills, the fire had the potential to be one of the area's worst ever—and one of the most violent. The suspects had shot the security guard, then Clay, and finally Bo. Joe had told Jamie all the details he knew. The security guard was in surgery, but he was going to be okay. No one was sure about Bo.

"This just in regarding the deadly fire burning out of control in the Las Virgenes Canyon area," the announcer interrupted Jamie's thoughts. "A spokesperson for the sheriff's department says that at this very moment they have a K9 officer and a suspect trapped on a fire road somewhere on the mountain." Her voice took on a grave tone. "Officials are doing everything they can to make a rescue, but the flames are too intense and the terrain too rugged for emergency vehicles. We'll keep you posted as we receive developments on this tragic story."

"Dear God ... no, please." Jamie whispered the desperate words. "Eric, we need to pray."

Eric kept his eyes on the road, but he reached out and took her hand. "God ... we need a miracle. We think Alex is trapped, but you know right where he is." Eric's voice was tense, and his mouth sounded dry. "Be with him, please ... clear the fire in a way that only you can do."

After the prayer, Jamie wanted to call someone—Joe or another of the SWAT guys, because like before she knew that the officer trapped on the hillside had to be Alex. He must've gone back into the flames after the suspect, and now ... *God, he has so much to live for ... give him a miracle. Put up a hedge of protection around him and stop the flames from reaching him. Get him out, God ... please.*

She pictured Alex trapped in the middle of a firestorm, and the image made her sick to her stomach. She couldn't think about it, not now when she was so worried about Clay. Alex would be okay ... he had to be okay. She'd be at the hospital soon, a few minutes at the most. She was anxious to be with Clay, to touch him and see for herself that he was going to be okay.

Outside her car, the wind felt worse than before, and all along the freeway they were passed by fire trucks and emergency vehicles. A shudder ran through her arms. This moment felt eerily like seven years ago when she raced to a New York hospital in search of Jake. Only that time, the person fighting for life in the hospital bed hadn't been Jake—but Eric Michaels. This was different, everything about it. They'd already been through so much. She couldn't imagine losing Clay now, not Clay or Alex. Eric turned into the hospital parking lot, and she had to blink so she could see the building clearly, that it was Los Robles Medical Center and not the hospital in New York City. *It's not the same ... this is a different day, God, help me hold onto the truth. This isn't 9/11.*

Daughter, breathe ... my peace I give to you ... I don't give as the world gives ...

Eric parked the car, jumped out, and hurried to her side. He helped her to her feet and led her across the parking lot. The whole time she kept thinking about the gentle response to her prayer, the words about peace. God's peace. That was exactly what she needed right now. Whatever happened today, no one could take that away from her. As she walked, she willed herself to believe that very soon God would grant a miracle for her and for Clay.

And especially for Alex.

🌳

The flames were right on top of them now, and Alex wondered if they might die from the heat before the fire reached them. He'd radioed down to the command station, but it hadn't done any good. The inferno was too deep and wide, too all-consuming for any of the firefighters to reach him. His only hope was a helicopter, and so far he hadn't seen a single drop of fire retardant. That wasn't surprising, really. The helicopters were already in use, so after his first call it could've taken fifteen minutes or more to get a drop overhead.

He was still on his knees, his face still raised to the burning sky. He'd lost out on seven years of talking to God, doing the thing his father had taught him to do. Seven years of being angry at the God who had created him and given him his family—even if that wonderful life hadn't lasted as long as Alex wanted. This was only the bus stop, right? Wasn't that what his father used to say? The great and joyous life everlasting was on the other side. His father had taught him that, and now it was what Alex once more believed. What he had always believed, even while he let his pain and sorrow cloud out the truth. Seven years were gone, but every second he had left in this life, he would spend talking to God.

Thank You, Lord ... because I feel You here in this inferno. I feel Your peace and Your forgiveness, Your salvation and certainty. I never should've blamed You, God ... He opened his eyes, and the fire was almost close enough to touch. The suspect in the back was quiet now, uttering only an occasional whimper, too terrified to speak.

Alex could die and be with his dad and his Heavenly Father, now that he had made his peace with God. He would finish well, far better than he would've if this had been a sudden accident or a bullet to his head, the bullet Bo took. But he had one regret, one area where he had failed. And once he was dead he would never have the chance to make it up again.

His regret was Holly.

As her sweet face filled his heart and soul, he used his final breaths to ask God one more time: "Please, Lord ..." he yelled into the roaring fire, "Please save us! Let me have another chance. I have so much time to make up for, God ... please!"

The noise around him grew louder, as if a speeding freight train was bearing down on them, about to crush them. *My son ... I have loved you with an everlasting love ... I know the plans I have for you, plans to prosper you and not to harm you.* The words were in the wind, in the fire, as clearly as if God had stepped down into this terrible moment and spoken them directly to Alex.

He gripped the edge of his truck and lifted himself off his knees so he could see better. A rushing sound added to the noise, and a strange sensation came over Alex, like the atmosphere itself was changing. Something was happening, something with the wind. Around the truck the burning embers swirled and danced and gusted in every direction, and then suddenly, strangely, the fire blew hard to the west and lifted. Alex brought his fist to his mouth. *God, it can't be ... it isn't possible ...*

Ahead of them, the fire road was suddenly and instantly clear again, the blaze raising several stories high on the right side, but reduced to almost nothing on the left. Hope shot straight through him, and Alex didn't hesitate. This was a miracle, nothing less. God had created a path, and this time he was going to take it. He hurled himself behind the wheel and started the engine.

"Go ... drive!" The guy in the backseat must've seen the hole in the flames.

Alex didn't respond. The miracle in front of them was a gift from God, and if the Lord had opened the hole, He would keep it open long enough for them to get down the mountain. Alex drove with a single-mindedness and purpose that he hadn't known since before September 11. God had set him free. Not just from the fire, but from himself—and both kinds of freedom could only have come from the Lord.

It took several minutes to get to the bottom of the hill, and as he did he grabbed his radio again. "We made it through. Have SWAT waiting."

For the first time since the fire lifted, the arsonist fell silent, probably with the realization that for him, things had only just started heating up. The charges that would be filed against him would put him away forever, Alex was pretty sure. He reached the bottom just as Joe stepped out of his squad car.

Alex got the suspect out of his truck as fast as he could and handed him over to Joe. "I already read him his rights, and I'll write my report after I check on Bo." He didn't want to spend another minute being angry or full of rage. The system would take care of Owl and his buddy. Alex had more important matters at hand, desperate life or death matters. He waited until Joe had the suspect cuffed in the backseat of his car, then Alex took hold of his friend's arm. "How's Clay?"

"He's in surgery, but it looks good." Joe hesitated, squinting against the blowing wind and smoke. "What happened up there, Brady? You look different."

Alex laughed just once, the sort of laugh that told his friend there wasn't enough time to explain it all right now. "I'm still trying to believe it." He kept his eyes on Joe but started walking back to his truck. "I shouldn't be here; let's just say that." He climbed into his truck and shut the door. Through the open window he yelled once more to Joe as he peeled off toward the main road. "I've gotta go see my dog."

As he drove, he kept both his windows down. The night wind was smoky and warm, but it was fresher than anything he'd been breathing up on the mountain. He let the wind dust off the grit and ashes that covered his face and tried to get his mind around what had just happened. He should be dead, in heaven with his father. But God had heard his cry and granted him the precious gift he'd begged for.

More time.

It was just after four in the morning, still dark outside. He would get to the vet hospital and see how Bo was doing, and sometime before sunup he would tell Holly everything he should've told her years ago. She had probably moved on by now, and there was nothing he could do about that. But she needed to know what had happened on the hill, how he'd come face-to-face with the same kind of terrorist-set inferno that had killed his father, and in that horrifying moment the impossible had happened.

He'd found his faith in God again.

A wholeness filled his soul, and Alex felt the same freedom he'd experienced in the midst of the fire. He didn't need to be so driven any longer. He could capture the bad guys, because that was his job, and it was one he would always enjoy. But he couldn't capture the evil around him. It was a pervasive part of life, and would be that way until Jesus returned. The only evil he could address—like Clay had told him—was the evil within himself.

Something he planned to spend the next few hours working on.

TWENTY-NINE

Holly had been sitting in the waiting room a long time, too long. By now someone should've come out and told her that the dog was okay, that he was out of surgery and they'd stitched him up. The silence couldn't be a good sign. But since she had no one to talk to, and since she was worried sick that Alex was stuck in the fire at the top of the mountain, she used the time to pray.

Funny how she'd resisted a relationship with God for so many years, how she'd let her faith grow cold to the point that she no longer wanted to go to church and sometimes doubted God even existed, but here ... in the face of intense tragedy, surrounded by the greatest fear she'd known since 9/11, prayer came as easily as her next heartbeat.

She prayed for Bo and for Alex and for Alex's friend—the other sheriff's deputy. Once she'd done that, she felt fresh tears on her cheeks and she did what she should've done long ago. She asked God to forgive her for walking away, for letting her love for Him grow cold.

Of course I believe in You, God ... she uttered the words silently, and as she did they cast a flicker of light in the dark halls of her soul, where the sun hadn't shone for far too long. *I'm sorry, God ... I need You here with me. Please, God ... let me know You're here.*

As she finished that part of her prayer, a janitor entered the otherwise empty waiting room. Holly felt awkward, sitting by herself and crying. She pulled a tissue from her purse and dabbed it beneath her eyes. There was something peculiar about the janitor, something in his stature or mannerisms. Holly watched him, trying to figure it out. The man was small and hunched, with white thinning hair that poked out from beneath a Yankees baseball cap. A name tag on his flannel shirt read only "Max."

Holly was drawn to the man, but she had no idea why. He didn't seem to notice her as he set to work, lifting the mop into a bucket of water, wringing out the excess, and then flinging it onto the floor. She watched him intently, trying to figure out why he looked so familiar, why his actions seemed so peculiar. He was five minutes into the job when he suddenly stopped and looked straight at her. "You ... you're a believer?"

Holly was startled by his question. She was tempted to look over her shoulder, in case he was talking to someone else, but she recovered long enough to point subtly at herself. "Me?"

"Yes." The man smiled, and again there was something different about him, almost otherworldly. "Are you a believer?"

"I am." This time Holly didn't hesitate. "I was just praying." Emotion spilled into her voice. "It's been a long night."

"You were involved in the fire." It wasn't a question. He rested on the handle of his mop, his eyes looking almost through her.

"Yes. I was." Holly wondered how the man could've known that detail. Did she smell that strongly of smoke? Or was her face smudged with ashes? She searched the man's face, trying to figure him out. Maybe she'd seen him before, at the townhouses where she lived or at the market.

He smiled at her, his eyes boring into hers. "The Lord wants you to know something ... He's never going to leave you or forsake you. No matter what happens, no matter how long."

Holly sucked in a quick breath, and it stuck in her throat. A dozen questions came at her, but before she could voice a single one, the janitor tipped the rim of his baseball cap and shuffled off down the hallway.

As soon as he was gone, she realized something had changed —she wasn't afraid anymore. Sad for the injured dog, deeply concerned about Alex, but she could feel the presence of God with her, and she remembered something her mom had told her not long ago. You don't have to feel God to know He's with you. The Bible tells us God is with us, and that's all the proof we need to know. It's a fact. Feelings or no feelings.

For years God had been with her, but Holly hadn't wanted to feel His presence, hadn't sought Him out or thought to talk to Him for any length of time. Even so, God had been with her—the same way He so clearly was with her now. She had asked God to let her know He was here, and he'd sent Max, the janitor.

She glanced at the check-in desk, at the two women and one man in white coats working on various computers. The doctor and his assistant hadn't been seen since Bo was wheeled in, and again that told Holly the situation couldn't be good. There had to be some kind of news on Alex's dog, but still no one had come out to talk to her. She prayed some more, but then her prayers did something she hadn't expected them to do. They took her back to the time before 9/11, when she and Alex were sure about life and love and even forever.

A door sounded at the other end of the waiting room, and Holly looked up to see the doctor enter. He was moving slowly, his face grim, and he stopped a few feet from her. "Ms. Brooks?"

She was on her feet, her heart pounding. Like everyone involved in the fire, she was exhausted and drained. As she watched the doctor she felt faint, and she steadied the back of her legs against the sofa where she'd been sitting. She looked into the doctor's eyes and she knew, she knew before he said a word.

"About Bo ... the news isn't good."

Holly wanted to stop him there, because if something happened to Alex's dog, then maybe Alex would never recover. She remembered the newspaper article, the stoic, cold look on Alex's face and the dog at his side. Holly had no idea how long they'd worked together, but Alex's love for Bo had been obvious tonight. She wanted to run, leave the waiting room and let the news fall on someone else's ears. Because hours ago she'd allowed herself the faintest hope that in finding each other again, Alex might also find himself. That together they would both find the God who would never leave them nor forsake them. But that hope would be gone forever if something happened to Alex's dog.

No matter what Max the janitor had said.

Bo was going to be okay. By the time Alex wheeled his Dodge into the parking lot of the veterinarian hospital, he had convinced himself. Dogs bled out much faster than people, so if the bullet had gotten him in one of his major organs or an artery, he would've died long before they reached the ambulance. As he drove, Alex thought about calling for an update, but he didn't have Holly's number, and there was no time to grab his phone and call information.

Better just to drive and get there.

Alex parked and ran from his car up a few steps to the front door. The place wasn't very big, and the waiting room was empty except for Holly and ...

He stopped and stared at the scene taking place before his eyes. Holly was crying, her fingers covering her face, and the doctor had his hand on her shoulder. *No, God ...* he took a step back, because this couldn't be happening. This wasn't the end. He could run back out to his truck, drive home, and there would be Bo, sleeping near the front door waiting for his return. The whole thing was a mistake, right? It had to be.

Holly must've heard him, because she turned and looked at him, her eyes red and swollen, her face twisted in sorrow.

"No …" he shoved his hands into the back pockets of his jeans and shook his head as he looked from her to the doctor. "Not Bo … don't tell me." He briefly noticed the workers behind the front desk discreetly leave for some back part of the building. They were giving him privacy so that … so that …

"Alex." Holly's arms were crossed and she was gripping her elbows, her whole body shaking.

"Mr. Brady," the doctor was walking toward him.

Alex shook his head again and turned toward the door. He wasn't here, not in a vet hospital with Bo on the other side of the waiting room. He squeezed his eyes closed and grabbed a fistful of his own hair. He wasn't here. He was at headquarters, and his sergeant was ushering him into a small room where a striking young German shepherd was standing at attention, his ears forward, and the sergeant was saying, "Alex, I'd like you to meet your new partner." He blinked and shook his head, refusing to hear anything from anyone, and there he and Bo were at the far end of a grassy field at the training center, seven hundred and ten hours into training. A dozen officers were giving hand signs to their respective K9 partners, and every dog was messing up. Every dog but Bo. Then he was at home a few months later, looking for the TV remote so he could watch the Dodgers game before he went to bed, and there was Bo trotting into the room from the back of the condo, the remote in his mouth, and he was cocking his head, looking at Alex as if to say, "I'm here for you, friend. Anything you need, I'm here."

"Mr. Brady?"

Alex dropped his hands to his side and shook his head one last time. He could feel Bo beside him still, his dog's coat brushing against his legs as they jogged the hills at Pierce College a few weeks ago. He wasn't sure how, but he found the strength to turn around. "I'm sorry …" he looked into the doctor's eyes. "Tell me."

The doctor frowned and his eyes shifted to the floor. When he looked up, there was no question what he was going to say. "We tried everything we could. The bullet pierced one of Bo's lungs and perforated his liver. By the time he got here, he'd lost a lot of blood, but even if we'd operated on him at the scene he wouldn't have made it. Just too much damage. We've been in surgery since he got here, but—" The doctor pressed his lips together, as if he understood that no explanation was needed. No words would help now. He put his hand on Alex's shoulder. "I'm sorry."

Holly was still standing where she had been when Alex walked into the hospital, tears streaming down her cheeks, and quiet sobs shaking her shoulders. She dropped back down to the sofa and put her face in her hands. Alex couldn't think about her, about the conversation he needed to have with her. Right now he had to take care of the matter at hand.

Bo was dead. "Can I …," he swallowed, struggling. "Can I see him?"

"Yes." The doctor moved somberly, the way people moved around in a funeral home, and again the moment didn't feel like it matched the reality. Bo wasn't dead … not his Bo. He was riding in the backseat, barking at the fire and ready for action, and he was heeling at his side, his partner. His friend.

"This way." The doctor walked through a set of double doors to a room at the end of a short hallway. He opened the door and allowed Alex to step inside by himself. "Take as long as you need."

Alex nodded, but already his eyes were on Bo, lying on the table. He heard the door shut behind him, and Alex stayed in that spot, not moving. Because from here, Bo was only sleeping, the familiar blacks and browns and tans that made up his back spread out just the way they'd been a few hours ago at the foot of his bed when Alex first heard the call.

He was probably cold and lonely up there on the sterile examination table. Alex went to him and put his hand on Bo's side. A gathered sheet was pressed against his chest, covering the area where he'd been shot, but otherwise he looked fine and whole, his expression the familiar one of loyalty and trust.

Alex put his hand on the dog's side and patted him, slowly and steadily. He was still warm, still full of the life that had driven him to do whatever Alex asked of him. "Bo ... you're a good dog, boy. Good dog." He moved his hand up to Bo's head and ran his fingers through the softer hair beneath the dog's ear. "Good boy."

A flood of sorrow was rising in his heart, and Alex didn't try to stop it. Alex had been driven to get the REA guys at any cost, and Bo had paid the price. More than that, he had done it willingly, rushing at the suspect with the gun even before Alex had seen him. Bo's heart had beat with one singular concern — the safety and well-being of his partner.

Alex's tears came then, and he was hit by the certain reality that he had failed. He hadn't stopped evil — not in the city of Los Angeles, and not at the Oak Canyon Estates, and not in his own life. Evil had found him, anyway, and now his dog was dead. He wanted to yell, rail at the collective bad in the world that would allow a dog as good and true as Bo to take a bullet. But he couldn't yell here, because the sound would frighten Bo. The dog hated when Alex was angry for any reason, and there was no need to upset him now.

He patted Bo's head again, and once more a host of yesterdays came over him. He was at the beach watching the surf, trying to find himself and failing, but grateful because Bo was his friend anyway, Bo right beside him, his ears back, eyes alert to any danger that might come Alex's way. Bo was there in the middle of every good memory he'd had over the last three years, Bo dashing out along a suspect trail and knocking to the ground one bad guy after another. Bo riding in the backseat behind him for what felt like a lifetime of calls and adventures.

He should've left him home tonight. "Bo," he held the dog's head, cradled it against his chest. "I'm sorry, boy … I'm so sorry."

This wasn't how it was supposed to end. He and Bo had years of calls ahead of them, and when Bo grew too old to be the aggressive, intelligent K9 deputy, he was supposed to retire into Alex's care. Relaxed and doing nothing more demanding than jogging or running hills. They should've had so many years ahead of them.

Alex buried his face against Bo's fur and wept. Of course he couldn't have left his dog at home, because Bo wanted to take the call. He lived for the chance to protect Alex, and if he hadn't jumped at the gunman, if he hadn't taken the bullet, the guy would've shot Alex point-blank in the head. Alex never would've seen it coming.

He pictured Bo's eyes, the way he had looked on the ride down the mountain to the ambulance, the loyal eyes and trusting heart, the look of apology deep within his expression—as if he had known this was good-bye. He hugged his dog once more and then straightened, his eyes too blurred with tears to see clearly.

"Bo … you can't be gone." The words came out with his tears. "I can't let you go, boy." He hated that Bo wasn't moving, that he wasn't lifting his head. Until now there had never been a time when he would talk to Bo and Bo wouldn't look at him. "God … please get me through this, please." He stroked his dog's side one last time. "I hope heaven has dogs, because … because I just want one more chance to run with you, Bo. One more chance."

He couldn't stay. There was no getting Bo back, no turning the hands of the clock the other direction so he could've been standing on the front yard of that house and noticed the suspect himself, so things might've turned out differently. It was too late for any of that. Bo was gone. His partner—his friend—was dead.

One more time he patted Bo's head, the soft place beneath his ears. For all their years together, Bo had desired Alex's praise more than food or water or air. This one last time, Alex took the moment to give his dog what he would've wanted most. He leaned close to Bo's head and whispered, "No better friend ever, Bo ... you saved my life. You did good." He patted his side. "You were a good dog, Bo ... the best. You did everything right."

He couldn't bear to step away, because when he did he would have to believe it was over, and he wouldn't have this chance again. Suddenly, he was mad at himself because he hadn't taken enough pictures. Hardly any over the years, so there would be nothing much to remember Bo by.

As soon as the thought hit his heart, he knew there wasn't an ounce of truth in it. He didn't need photographs. He would remember Bo every time he climbed into his Dodge or whenever he sped off down the streets of Los Angeles after the next crook. He would feel him sitting in the seat behind him and remember the look in his eyes as surely as he knew his own reflection. He stepped back, his fingers still spread deep into Bo's furry side. He needed to say it, because his dog deserved that much.

"Good-bye, Bo ... You were a good friend."

Then, with the weight of the world full against his shoulders, he turned and left the room, closing the door behind him. Out in the hallway, he placed his forearm against the wall and buried his face in the crook of his elbow. The tears came harder, because already he felt lonely and cold and defeated. Bo was dead. How could that be? Couldn't God have spared his dog, when Bo was so full of good?

For a few seconds, the old pain and anger crept back in around the edges of his soul, but then just as quickly he could hear his father's words as they'd been spoken to Jake Bryan. *So far, my family has had very little trouble. Life is good, love is sweet, and time seems like it'll last forever ... We all know that isn't true. Especially working for the FDNY.*

Or working as a K9 officer for the sheriff's department.

He dragged his face against his arm and turned so his back was against the wall. Once more he reminded himself of what Clay had said, that God never intended for man to rid the world of evil, but through God's strength, that man might look at the evil within himself. Bo was gone; there was nothing he could do about the fact. But there was one way he could offset the evil that had taken place over the last five hours.

He could offset it with love.

For a long minute, he examined himself, the heart and soul that had grown cold and hard within him, and he studied the person he had allowed himself to become. His love for Holly Brooks had never wavered. He knew that now. She had been his best friend, the girl who took his breath away every time he saw her. The way he'd treated her these past seven years was, itself, a form of evil.

He opened his eyes and straightened, refusing to give in to the exhaustion and grief that were spinning his head in circles and making his breathing fast and unsteady. He walked down the hall, and he could almost feel Bo there beside him, looking up at him as if to say, "This is the right thing ... let's do this."

She was still on the sofa, where she'd been sitting before, but her head was no longer in her hands. She looked at him, and in her eyes he saw fear, like maybe he would walk past without talking to her, the way he'd done so many ridiculous times that first year after the terrorist attacks. The terrorists who had pulled off 9/11 hadn't only killed his father and the other thousands of people. They'd killed him too.

But God had brought his heart and soul back to life again.

He never stopped, never broke his slow and steady stride as he made his way to her. At first she didn't want to look at him, because the grief was too raw for both of them. But then she must've seen something different in his face, because when he was halfway to her she met his eyes and didn't break contact again. When he reached her, he stopped and held out his arms.

He had so much to say, seven years' worth of words and apologies and questions about how she'd been and why she was still here. He didn't know if she was involved with someone, but it didn't matter anymore. All that mattered was that he loved her the way she deserved to be loved. Not the romantic love that might've come if he'd done things differently, but the love of days gone by, a love that cared for her still—would care for her forever.

But no matter how much he wanted to talk, he couldn't say a word. His sorrow and grief stuck in his throat and stopped him from speaking. So he did the only thing he could. He took her in his arms, slowly, with the greatest care, and he wrapped his arms around her. Alone in the waiting room, buried beneath his sorrow and hers, they stayed that way, clinging to each other until they were both crying again, silently weeping for all they'd lost in the wake of his unrelenting quest to right his father's death.

Please, God … I can't talk … please let her know what I'm feeling.

Her hands pressed into his back and his into hers, and still they stayed in each other's arms, neither of them willing for the moment to end. And it wouldn't end, either. Everything bitter and angry and full of hurt dissolved in wave after wave of love washing over him and leaving him intoxicated by her presence. His Holly, here … impossibly here, where she would stay. Because whatever was happening in her personal life, now that he'd found her, now that he'd found himself, Alex wasn't letting her go. If she was in love with someone else, fine. Alex would be her friend, but he wasn't walking away again.

Not now and not ever.

Thirty

Holly wore dark sunglasses and sat at the end of a middle row in the sea of folding chairs that were lined across the grassy field at the sheriff's headquarters. Jamie Michaels was to her right, and Jamie's kids and in-laws filled out the row. Alex was in front with the other K9 officers. Tissue packets had been handed out as the hundreds of people arrived, and Holly was grateful. It was Alex's friend Clay's turn at the microphone. His arm was in a sling because of the bullet he'd taken to the shoulder, but he was okay. The whole city knew the story by now.

Three days had passed since that awful night, and the fires set by the arsonists were almost completely contained. Oak Canyon Estates was a complete loss, but everyone agreed the damage could've been much worse. The newspapers and local television stations had all remarked that only a miracle could've caused the shift in winds that saved every house at the bottom of the hill below where the fires had been set. "If I didn't know better, I'd say we saw the hand of God at work tonight," one reporter stated. Alex didn't have to wonder. Of course the miracle of the wind shift was the hand of God. Alex had witnessed it firsthand.

No more winds were expected, so the worst of the firestorm was behind them. At least for this season. As Clay made his way up, Holly stared at the picture of Alex and Bo, the one that had run in the newspaper. Someone had enlarged it and framed it on an easel near the platform. Already they'd heard from a dozen K9 and SWAT deputies about Bo's bravery and innate ability to get the crooks. But Jamie had told her before the service that none of them knew Alex and Bo the way Clay did.

Clay took his spot and looked out at the crowd. "This is hard." His voice rang with transparent grief. "Bo was a good dog." He looked down for a few seconds, and when he had composed himself, he continued. "Most of you know … a very unique friendship exists between a K9 officer and his service dog. In the case of Bo and Alex, that dog knew every emotion, every nuance and move his partner made. Everyone who saw them together understood that even among police dogs, Bo was a rare treasure. A dog whose loyalty and commitment to getting the bad guys knew no limits." Clay spoke clearly, and his voice carried across the field. "The same way it was for Alex." He launched into a story, something funny about Bo being lost during a chase, and Alex finding him on the hood of the squad car, waiting and watching for his partner. The story was long, and it gave Holly a chance to fade out for a few minutes. She let her eyes find the back of Alex's head, his dark blond hair and strong shoulders. He had filled out since high school, and he was more handsome than before. More chiseled. But in the days since their hug, he had barely spoken to her.

She'd been busy, of course. There had been the trip back to the site of the fire and the surprise arrival of a dozen contractors with earthmoving equipment. Each of them had taken part in one of Dave Jacobs' charity home-building projects, and now that Dave was in need, they all showed up to help—not expecting anything in return. The story offered beauty amidst the ashes and was picked up by the *Los Angeles Times*.

The next day Holly had a lengthy meeting with Dave and Ron Jacobs, so that she could share every detail about what had happened that fateful night. A debriefing, Ron called it. At the end, Dave came to her and hugged her the way her father used to hug her. "You were very brave, Holly." He pulled back, his eyes shining. "I'm so glad you weren't hurt."

Holly thanked him, and the moment eased the feeling of tension between her and Ron. They had not shared a private moment since the conversation they'd had in the midst of the fire, and it seemed clear to both of them that their dating days were over. Ron was a good man. He and his father would rebound from this and find something new and better to be a part of—whether they rebuilt at Oak Canyon or not.

At the end of the meeting, Holly turned in her resignation. She needed something new, maybe a job with a magazine or a newspaper. Selling houses would never be the same after the horrifying terror of that night, and besides, maybe it was time for her and her mom to sell their condos and move somewhere new. San Diego, or back to New York City, maybe.

Especially now that it looked like she'd lost Alex again.

Holly blinked and focused on him once more. If it weren't for Bo, Alex would be dead now. Clay would be at the podium talking about him and not his dog. Holly couldn't stand the thought. She remembered what it felt like to be in his arms the other night and how she had known with everything in her that she still loved Alex Brady.

She would love him until the day she died. Which was all the more reason why she couldn't stay around. The possibility of running into him was too great. If she was ever going to have a chance to move on, then first she needed to move away from Los Angeles as soon as possible. Her heart would follow in time.

Alex turned his head just enough that she could see the rugged muscles along the side of his face. He hadn't cried during the ceremony, and that was another sign that maybe the Alex she wanted him to be was gone once again, lost even farther than before because of this new injustice in his life.

Be with him, God ... life's too short to spend it angry and driven. She longed for him, ached for him to look at her like he'd looked at her that night in the veterinary hospital, but she hadn't seen him again until an hour ago. In that moment, there wasn't even a flicker of the depth and connection she'd felt in the vet's waiting room. *Help him, God ... let him find the strength to let his feelings show again.*

This was new, this ability to pray as easily as she'd prayed back in high school. It was something good that had come from the terrible firestorm, and Holly was grateful. Whatever the future held, she couldn't imagine taking it on without God's wisdom and protection, His guidance and promise of eternity. If she couldn't have Alex, her faith would sustain her. It was something her mother had prayed about for years, and it would bring the two of them closer, as well.

Clay was finishing up, and after he sat back down, the sergeant of the K9 division said a few more words and then closed the ceremony with a prayer, asking God for continued protection and guidance for Alex and all the deputies in the sheriff's department, and thanking the Lord for the courage of police dogs like Bo.

A quartet of bagpipe players started a haunting rendition of "Amazing Grace" as the procession of officers filed from the seats and back into the meeting room inside headquarters. A reception had been prepared by one of the churches in town, so that the K9 and SWAT guys could talk about the loss and share memories of Bo and his heroic feats. His and Alex's.

"You staying here?" Jamie put her hand over Holly's as she stood with the others in their row.

"For awhile." She looked at Alex and gave a light shrug with one shoulder. "I'm not sure if he wants to talk, but I want to be close ... just in case."

Jamie hesitated, her expression kind and sincere. "Clay and I'll be praying for you."

"Thank you." Holly smiled. "I hope we can see each other again."

"Me too." Jamie took hold of her kids' hands, and together with her family they walked across the grass toward the reception.

While the bagpipers finished up, a few of the deputies stayed and gathered around Alex, talking to him, patting him on the back, hugging him. Holly watched as Jamie came back outside and handed Alex a package. The two talked for a minute, and then Jamie gave him a quick hug and returned to the building with the others.

Eventually, Alex and Holly were the only two left outside. Alex didn't seem to notice she was there. He walked slowly toward the photo and lifted it off the easel. He stayed that way for a long time, looking at the picture.

Suddenly, Holly felt awkward and out of place. She should probably leave now, before he turned around and saw her there by herself. That way he wouldn't feel like he had to come over and talk to her. Because if he'd meant everything she'd felt from him that night in the vet's waiting room, he would've found a way to talk to her by now, maybe not by phone — since he didn't have her number — but here at the service, at least. She started to stand. This was no place for her, here alone with Alex. She'd been rejected by him too many times to let it happen again.

She turned and started to walk silently back toward the parking lot, but she only got a few feet before she heard him call out to her.

"Holly ... wait!"

At the sound of his voice, she turned around. Fifty yards of grass and chairs separated them, but even this far away she thought she could hear a softness in his tone. She stared at him, waiting.

When he seemed sure she wasn't leaving, he set the package from Jamie on a chair and returned the photo back to its place. Then he let his hands fall to his sides, and slowly he walked up the center aisle toward her. The closer he came, the better she could see his eyes, and for a heartbeat she thought they were back to the way they'd been the other night. But in the glare of afternoon sun and through the tint of her glasses, she couldn't let herself believe that, not when her heart was dying inside her.

But with each step, he never once broke eye contact, and when he was only a few feet from her she didn't have to wonder anymore. The man walking up to her wasn't the angry closed-off sheriff's deputy. He wasn't the broken teenager bent on revenging his father's death. He was just Alex. The Alex she wasn't sure she'd ever see again.

THIRTY-ONE

Throughout the service, Alex had refused to let himself think about Holly. He knew she was sitting back there with Jamie, but his heart couldn't process everything happening around him. In the past five years, he'd sat in on memorial services for two police dogs and three deputies from across the state. Always he would sit shoulder-to-shoulder with the other deputies. Always he could picture the service being for him, because that was the sort of cop he was, the type that went all out for every call.

But Bo?

Sure, his dog had a knick in his ear where he'd nearly taken a bullet before, and even in the weeks leading up to his death he had made a number of death-defying captures of bad guys. But Bo was so good, so fiercely determined to take care of the crime scene, that Alex had never imagined him being killed in action.

Never imagined a service like this for his very own dog.

So before he could think about Holly, he had to have this time for Bo. His dog deserved his complete attention, the good-bye he had earned. His remains had been cremated, and Alex planned to let them go on a wave at Malibu beach — where he would always see Bo running along behind him in the shallow surf.

None of that was mentioned at the service, though, because the focus wasn't on Bo's death, but on his life. Alex appreciated every story, every officer who took the time to share about Bo. He could've stood up there and told stories till dark, but those were the moments he'd keep forever inside him. What mattered here is that other people knew about Bo. The people who had come to say good-bye to his dog would leave the service knowing him a little better. And that was worth something.

Strange how the service had played out. He could practically feel Bo lying on the ground at his feet, the way the dogs of the other K9 officers were lying near their partners. If he didn't look down, if he didn't check the photo on the easel or pay too close attention to what was being said, he could pretend for a little while longer that it had never happened, that Bo was still there. If only he didn't look down.

But as the program ended and the bagpipes stopped playing, the truth was as painful as it was obvious. Bo was gone. As the other deputies and the bagpipers cleared out, he talked to God about all he was feeling, and a truth settled in around the broken pieces of his heart.

If — in the minute before his sergeant had introduced him to Bo — someone would've told him that the ride would be far too short, that it would end tragically and before either of them had the chance to work together all the years they should, Alex wouldn't have changed a thing. Working with Bo for the years he did made him one of the lucky ones. Both of them would've done it all again without hesitation.

He'd talked to his sergeant about the next chapter in his life as a sheriff's deputy, and he'd made a decision for now. He didn't want to work with a new K9 partner. Instead, he wanted to work SWAT with Clay and Joe and maybe someday down the road he would think about having another dog. God had spared him from the inferno for a reason, and police work had to be at least part of it. Maybe even K9 work at some point, but it would take time. He would always compare any other dog to Bo, and that wouldn't be fair — not for either of them.

Now, though, the service was over and he was lost in the moment, staring at one of the only pictures of Bo and him, when he heard the faintest sound from the back of the set of chairs. He turned just as Holly was leaving, and panic grabbed at him. What was he doing? He hadn't made his intentions clear to her, hadn't told her that he wanted to stay in her life now that they'd found each other again, or that his faith had been restored. For all she knew, he was the same Alex he'd been before the fire.

And so he set down the picture and the package and went to her, praying as he walked that she might see in his eyes the truth about who he was now, who he had become again. He had learned so much about evil, what he could do about it and what he couldn't. He couldn't stop a bullet or rid the city of every crook or terrorist that came along. He would get rid of as much evil as he could, but he would also remember that evil won most when it won in his heart.

Something he would never let it do again.

He came to her slowly, and with every step the walls and years and distance between them faded away. When he was so close he could smell the scent of the shampoo she used in her hair, he stopped and looked at her, looked into the deepest parts of her.

"Alex … is it really you?" Her words came out as a whisper. She took off her sunglasses, and unshed tears made her eyes sparkle in the sunlight.

They'd hugged the other day, but they hadn't held hands since the day before 9/11. Sometimes Alex would be driving in his squad car, patrolling the streets of LA, and he'd remember the sensation of her hands in his with such force that it took his breath. He still didn't have any idea whether she had a boyfriend or even a fiancé, but no one could touch what they'd shared all those years ago. So now, when words could never capture the extent of his feelings, he did the only thing he knew to do.

He held out his hands.

Holly made a soft sound that was more cry than laughter, but she must've understood what he was feeling because she took a step closer and slowly, tenderly wove her fingers between his. The sensation was magic, and it lifted everything he had ever felt for her to a higher degree that almost frightened him. He didn't want to ask, but he couldn't wait much longer. He could feel himself falling beyond anything he'd ever felt before. "Is ... is there someone in your life, Holly?"

She kept looking deeper into his eyes. "No." She seemed tentative, as if she didn't believe this was really happening here, now. "You?"

"No one. Never."

Her fingers pressed in a little deeper between his. "Me neither."

He could smell the sweetness of her skin, and all he wanted was to take her in his arms and kiss her, so she would know without a doubt how he felt about her. But first he had to at least try to make himself understood. "I ... I became someone else after my dad died in that tower."

"I know." A well of sadness rang in her voice, and she smiled through fresh tears. "I watched it happen, remember?"

He eased one of his hands free, and with his thumb he brushed back a piece of her blonde hair. "I'm sorry, Holly. I was blinded by what happened." He put his hand over his chest. "But in here, you never left me." He placed his fingers along the side of her face. "You were always in my heart."

"Right next to you." With her free hand, she gently touched the muscles in his jawline. "Because you — the Alex I knew — were always inside your heart too. No matter how hard you tried to become someone who didn't care." She tilted her head, her eyes beyond tender now. "I never stopped loving you, Alex. I always believed someday I'd find you again."

"Holly ..." Bittersweet joy rushed through his veins and swelled his heart, filling him with feelings he hadn't known before this moment. But he didn't celebrate just yet. "It would've been so easy for you to forget me, move on. I'm sorry." He worked his fingers into the soft hair at the nape of her neck. "Can you ever forgive me?'

There was only the two of them and nothing else. Not the planes overhead or the traffic on the busy streets outside headquarters. Not the chairs or the memorial service or any of it. Holly's sad smile was as familiar as home. "No, Alex."

"No?" His heart pounded, and her nearness made his breathing faster than before.

Her smile faded, but her eyes had never loved him more. "No, you could never have been easy to forget." She blinked back the shine in her eyes. "And, yes, I forgive you."

It was going to happen. He was going to kiss her like some scene from a distant dream. Alex searched her eyes, her face. His body trembled from the intense love he felt in that moment. "I've never loved anyone but you. I tried, but a part of me never stopped." Then, because he couldn't force his brain to think of another coherent word until he did what he was longing to do, he touched his lips to hers and, in a dance as old as time, they came together, lost in the moment, lost in each other.

The kiss lasted a long time, but it wasn't one of crazy passion or physical desire—although that place wasn't far off. Instead, it was a kiss that erased the years and doubts and told of a love neither of them had forgotten. He tasted her tears as the kiss grew, and when finally they eased back and caught their breath, his cheeks were wet too.

She wiped them with the softest touch of her thumb. "I'm sorry ... about Bo."

Alex sucked in a quick breath and lifted his chin, his eyes on the blue sky overhead. "He was a good partner."

"I wish I'd known him longer." She sniffed and hugged him, swaying just a little as they allowed the memory of the dog to stand with them for a moment.

Again Alex wished he had more tangible ways to remember Bo, something he could've shared with Holly. Then he remembered Jamie's gift. She'd given him a package and said something about not being sure if Alex had anything like it. "Wait," he eased free of her embrace and took hold of her hand. "Come with me. I need to open Jamie's package."

Holly kept up with him, her fingers still laced between his, the feeling something Alex never wanted to lose again. They reached the first row, and Alex let go briefly so he could open the gift. Holly stayed by his side, watching, waiting.

He lifted the lid of a white box, and inside, beneath a few pieces of tissue paper, was a framed collage that made Alex catch his breath. The pictures in the frame were several beautiful shots of him and Bo on the Michaels' front porch, and one amazing photo of Bo all by himself. Regal and loyal, his eyes exactly as Alex would always remember them. The moment came rushing back, Jamie's awkward picture-taking so she could find a way to talk to him about his past. He had been grateful since then for the risks she'd taken, for giving him the copied page from Jake's journal, and playing a part in helping him find his way back to the Lord.

But he'd forgotten about the pictures until now.

"He looks so strong, so beautiful." Holly touched the side of the frame. "These are amazing."

"I ... I didn't think there were any pictures like this." Alex covered the frame with the tissue papers again. He would thank Jamie later, Jamie and Clay, and Joe and his wife — because all of them had prayed for him to find his way back. He knew that from conversations he'd had with Clay in the last few days.

As he fit the lid back on the box, his fingers brushed against hers, and electricity shot through him. He framed her face with his hand and kissed her again. "I can't believe this is happening."

"Only God could've done this." She kissed him again, more slowly than before. Then they collected the gift from Jamie and the framed photo on the easel and headed inside.

As they walked, Alex marveled at the goodness of God, who had given him the most wonderful parents, and a dog he would remember forever. God who had helped him understand that the condition of his heart was far more critical than the condition of the world, and who had spared him from certain death in the midst of towering flames. But beyond all that, he marveled that God would give him this.

A second chance with Holly.

THIRTY-TWO

Linda held her son's elbow as he led her down the center aisle of the stunning little chapel on the hill at Pepperdine University, the one that overlooked the beach where Alex and Bo used to go on their rare days off. A hundred or so deputies and their families, and a handful of Holly's friends filled the pews. The air smelled of salt and sunshine and seawater.

They reached the front right pew and Alex kissed her cheek. "I love you, Mom."

"Love you too, Son." She held on a few seconds longer, still amazed at the transformation in him. "I'm so happy for you."

"Thanks." Alex leaned past her to his stepfather, Lee, who was already seated. Alex shook his hand. "Good to see you, sir."

"Yes," the two shared a sincere smile. Lee's voice filled with pride. "It's all so very good."

Alex patted his mother's hand and then left them and went to stand at the front of the church next to the pastor. Linda sat down and tried to catch her breath. If it was all just a dream, she wanted to wake up now before they went any further. But that was the most amazing part of the story. It was real. She sat back against the hard wooden bench and remembered again how she'd found out the news. It had been Veteran's Day — November 11 — just before dinner. The buzzer sounded, and Lee pushed the button to open the apartment building door. But when Linda asked who it was, Lee only smiled and said, "Delivery."

Five minutes later, Lee opened the front door and Alex walked in holding the hand of Holly Brooks. Linda still had to allow a quiet laugh when she thought of the way she must've looked. "Alex," her mouth stayed open and she turned to Holly. "What ... how could ...?"

Lee came to her and steadied her until she was able to form a complete sentence. In the meantime, Alex explained that after the fire and losing Bo, he and Holly had found common ground again. "The two of us and God too." He came to her and hugged her. "I've missed so much, but no more, Mom. Not after this."

After a month of seeing each other every day, Alex had done what Linda had always hoped he would do. He had asked Holly's mother for permission and then purchased an engagement ring for her. They had a lot of years to make up for, and they wanted counseling from the pastor who would marry them, so the wedding was set for Saturday, March 7.

"We wanted to tell you in person." Alex moved back, and Holly took his place, with hugs of her own.

Linda laughed and cried and told Alex and Holly and Lee over and over again that she had prayed for this and believed for this all along. Alex and Holly stayed for dinner, and the truth came out—Lee had known about the surprise for a week. The next morning they all took a trip to Ground Zero and St. Paul's Chapel, and Alex talked about how he had connected with Jamie Bryan, and how she had worked in the church for three years after 9/11 and showed him the journal entry about his father.

Before Alex and Holly left for Los Angeles again, Linda and Lee prayed with them, asking God to protect them and thanking Him for this new chance at love. Now Linda smiled at her handsome son as the music began to change. That November weekend was one she'd remember forever.

But it wouldn't come close to the one that was about to play out.

❧

Alex still couldn't believe Holly had said yes. After how he'd treated her, she could easily have told him no or asked for more time. But she stuck with what she'd told him that tender day of Bo's memorial service. She had always believed that the Alex she had fallen in love with as a teenage girl was still in his heart somewhere.

He clasped his hands behind him and watched the door at the back of the church. So much had changed in the last four months. He was moving ahead in his SWAT training, but he wasn't working overtime anymore. His time at headquarters was rich and fulfilling, the way it always would be. But it was a job. His faith, his love for Holly, his friends — those were his life now. Six times already, he and Holly had met up with Clay and Jamie and the others for dinner at the Michaels' house.

Life was good at Clay and Jamie's house. Sierra's cat Wrinkles wasn't sick like before, and the kids were well — so their times together had been happy and full of laughter. Alex smiled to himself. Laughter, of all things, something he wouldn't have believed would ever be part of his life again. During their counseling sessions with the pastor, he and Holly had even talked about having kids of their own.

They'd also taken a day and gone down to the beach where Alex had scattered Bo's ashes in the foam of a particularly powerful wave, the kind of wave Bo would've barked at had he been there.

Through Christmas and the New Year, Alex grew so close to Holly he couldn't understand how he'd lived seven years without her. They had both agreed to wait until they were married to begin the physical relationship they were both aching to experience. Some days Alex wondered why they'd scheduled the wedding so far out, but other times he enjoyed the wait, enjoyed watching Holly register for wedding gifts and get excited about going with her mom to pick out a dress.

Alex looked out over the faces in the church, the deputies and sergeants he'd worked with and grieved with, the family that made up the sheriff's department. But more than that, his eyes found those of Jamie, Joe and Wanda, and Eric and Laura Michaels. These were friends he'd have for life, he was sure. Holly already loved them, and right now he felt a little like his father had told Jake Bryan he felt. Life was good, love was sweet, and time felt like it would last forever.

He understood John 16:33 better now, the verse his father had wanted him to take hold of. Yes, in this world there would be trouble. But God had overcome the world. Otherwise, Alex never would've been standing here. Alex looked at Clay standing beside him — his best man. The two shared a smile, and for a few seconds Alex imagined what it would be like if his father were standing beside him now. A fleeting, familiar pain seared the surface of his heart, but it came with no rage, no sense of driven determination. Sure, he still thought about 9/11, the way he always would. But at this point, the crippling sorrow was far less all-consuming and only hit him as often as it did other victims of the terrorist attacks.

Every now and then.

Again the music changed, and this time the organist began to play the "Wedding March." Across both sides of the pews, people rose and faced the back of the church. The doors opened and Holly appeared, a vision of white lace and tanned arms, so stunning that an appreciative hush fell over their friends and family. Alex's heartbeat quickened and he stood straighter, not believing she was really about to be his. This was what he'd waited all his life for, even in the years when he had lied to himself. Holly Brooks, walking up the aisle, about to be his wife. *My dear God ... I can't believe You've brought us here ... thank You ... I'll never have enough days to thank you.*

He remembered to breathe as she came closer. Holly had never looked more beautiful, but not so much because of her pretty dress. That wasn't what captured Alex's attention. Her veil was thin enough that Alex could see the only thing that mattered in this moment.

Holly's eyes, and an undying love that would stand the test of time.

❧

Holly couldn't take her eyes off him. Of all the miracles God had worked on their behalf, this was the most unbelievable. The change in Alex. Because looking at him now, it was impossible to think of him the way he'd been only five months ago — hard and cold, closed off to love or life or any feelings other than the quest for revenge. She smiled as she came closer.

Alex standing at the front of the church waiting for her was everything she had always wanted — and he was everything she had known he could be. A man full of faith and a love that shone through in their beach walks and late-night talks, a love that was as transparent as the spring breeze outside their wedding chapel.

She had never dreamed she'd feel this happy again, but here she was — about to marry Alex Brady. They had written brief vows for this moment, a reflection of the pure richness of their love. The way they felt about each other wouldn't take a lot of words. They loved each other more than life, and they trusted God to take them through whatever the years held.

That was all.

As she reached him, as their hands touched and her body felt the now familiar desire, she could only think of one thing. Her mother was wrong. It wasn't only in the movies that love came at people all at once. Because what she and Alex shared really was a stunning rainbow across an otherwise dreary sky. When they'd found each other again, their intense feelings of a love that had never died hadn't taken time or work or any sort of effort.

They came all at once, in a rush, because they simply were, the way they would always be.

❦

Jamie watched the wedding through teary eyes.

Clay was completely healed now, and he looked rugged and full of joy as he stood beside Alex during the ceremony. She thanked God every day that he hadn't been killed, but she had to hold on lightly. The way any living person had to hold on if they understood the fleeting nature of life. She and Clay had spent more time together than ever before, and she couldn't possibly love him more. In the past months he'd become a mentor to Alex, helping him understand what it meant to really love a woman the way Christ intended her to be loved.

On a couple occasions, he had even drawn from excerpts in Jake's journal and favorite Bible verses to talk about love languages, and the danger of going to bed angry with each other. Clay had confided in Jamie last night that he was happy with how their talks had gone.

"Alex is going to be an amazing husband. The transformation in him is something only God could've done."

"Yes." Jamie looped her arms around his neck. "Because Alex finally understood that any move toward being a 'good guy' had to start with a hard look in the mirror."

Clay looked at her now and their eyes held. His lips curved into a subtle smile before he turned his attention back to the vows. Jamie dabbed at her eyes and listened to the words being said.

"Holly, I've loved you since the first time I saw you, and I'll love you until the last time." Alex smiled at his bride, his eyes damp. "I promise to respect and love you, to honor and cherish you." Alex was holding Holly's hands, lost in her eyes. They might as well have been the only two people in the room. He was finishing up, and the last part was the most poignant. "There will be hard times, as there have been before. But when they come, I promise never to put walls between me and you, and I will share with you whatever pain comes my way, because you are a part of me, Holly. As long as we both shall live."

Holly sounded choked up when it came to her turn. Her vows were the same as his until the very end. "Alex, I've watched what hurt and loss can do to you, and I promise you one more thing here, before our family and friends. I promise that when life hurts so much you're tempted to forget who you are, you can always come to me. I will be your mirror, Alex ... for the real you will always live here, inside my heart."

They were about to exchange rings when Jamie felt a tap on her shoulder.

"Mom," Sierra leaned in close to her. "Why are you crying?"

"Because I'm happy." Jamie sniffed. "Love makes me feel this way."

She wrinkled up her nose. "I'm glad I'm not in love." She stifled a giggle and then leaned her head on Jamie's shoulder.

CJ was on her other side, but he was too sleepy to notice much about the wedding. Jamie was glad for the chance to really focus on what was being said, because somehow the wedding between Alex and Holly was symbolic. It was a sign that beauty could rise from brokenness as many times as God was allowed to work in their lives. But beyond that, seeing this couple get married brought Jamie that final bit of closure where Jake was concerned.

She had devoted three years to helping victims of September 11, and when she moved here she thought that job was done. But with Alex and Holly, God had given her one more chance to help. Her prayers, the words from Jake's journal, Clay's talks with Alex—God had used all of it to bring about a dramatic healing in Alex's heart. Jamie smiled, and as she did, she was almost certain of something else.

Somewhere in heaven, Jake was smiling too.

Author's Note

Dear Friends,

Writing about Alex Brady was an emotional journey for me. In him I saw so many of you who write and tell me about broken relationships or lost loves, strained friendships and hurt feelings between siblings. I can relate, of course, the way anyone breathing can relate.

Sometimes—as with Holly—we can clearly see what happened to turn the person we love away from us. But other times, we aren't so sure. There have been very good friends in our lives who have turned away, and we may never know the reason they have chosen to no longer love.

But the message of Alex's life is one we can all draw hope from. Broken relationships can be healed. More than that, it is simply impossible to think we can solve the pain and evil in the world, or even the pain in someone's life. When I outlined this book, I planned to show how Alex would eventually reach the end of himself in his quest to rid Los Angeles of crime. But then God showed me something I didn't expect.

One weekend in the middle of writing this book, through a sermon from the book of John by our wonderful Pastor Matt, I realized there was an even deeper truth in Alex's misguided determination. The fact that God never intended for us to eliminate the evil around us. But rather, through Christ's strength, to take a hard look at the evil within us. Wow. That message hit hard and became a driving force for the theme behind this story.

I really liked Alex, the way that he wanted so desperately to do good. We're a lot like him at times, but we all need to remember the Scripture Clay shared with Alex. *There is a way that seems right to a man, but in the end it leads only to death.* It's so important as we choose our way each day that we look to Jesus for wisdom and direction. When we're driven by emotions—healthy or hurtful—we can easily get distracted from the true work God has for us.

And what about Holly? Her love for Alex was a lot like Christ's love for us—no matter where we are now or how far we've moved from a faith in God, Christ loves us. He knows who we are on the inside—the person He made us to be. Even if we've allowed time and tragedy to make us into someone different.

No one and nothing can separate us from the love of God—isn't that amazing? It's the same way Holly felt about Alex, and it will leave me with an example I'll think back on years from now.

I'm sad to see this story end, really. Alex was a special character for me, and so was Holly. In addition, I've loved writing about Jamie Bryan Michaels and remembering once more the incredible guy Jake Bryan was. I enjoyed spending time again with Clay, reminding myself of his godly qualities and his great love for Jamie and Sierra and CJ. It was nice to spend more time with Joe and Wanda, and to check in with Eric and Laura since *Beyond Tuesday Morning* four years ago.

Always, as I finish a book, I spend many hours praying for you—my reader friends. Sometimes God needs to take us to the middle of a towering inferno before we let go of our own ways and grab onto Him for life. But for most of us, we'll never wind up trapped on a hillside in the middle of a firestorm. Most of us will hear the voice of God calling us back or drawing us closer some other way. Through a conversation with a friend or a sermon on the radio.

Maybe even through Life-Changing Fiction ™.

If during the course of reading this book you, like Alex Brady, found yourself crying out for God to forgive you, for Him to find you again, for the chance to become the person deep inside your heart that once upon a yesterday you used to be ... then I pray that you will connect with a Bible-believing church in your area. There, you should be able to find a Bible—if you don't already have one. That life-saving relationship with Christ is always rooted in His truth, the Scriptures.

If you are unable to purchase a Bible or find one at your local church, and if this is the first time you are walking into that relationship with Jesus, then write to me at my website—www.KarenKingsbury.com. Write the words "New Life" in the subject line, and I will send you a Bible. Because between the covers of that precious book are all the secrets to a new life.

For the rest of you, I'd love to hear your thoughts on *Remember Tuesday Morning*, how Alex's story spoke to you, and how it maybe even changed you. Contact me at my website, and while you're there, take a moment to look at the ways you can get involved with the community of other Karen Kingsbury readers. You can leave a prayer request or pray for someone else, tell me about an active military hero or a fallen one, and send me a picture so that all the world can pray for your soldier. You can also join my club and chat with other readers about your favorite characters and books.

If this is your first time with me, thank you for taking the time to read. My website lists my other titles in their order, as well as by topic—in case you're looking for a specific type of Life-Changing Fiction ™.

Again, thank you for your prayers for me and my family. We are doing well and trying to keep up with our kids—all of whom are growing way too fast. We feel your prayers on a daily basis, and please know that we pray for you too.

Until next time,

In His light and love,
Karen Kingsbury

www.KarenKingsbury.com

DISCUSSION QUESTIONS

Please share these with your book clubs, church groups, friends, and family. Discussion makes the experience of reading so much richer!

1. How would you explain the change in Alex after the terrorist attacks on September 11?

2. Have you ever experienced a tragedy that made you doubt God or feel angry toward God? Explain.

3. Alex's father wanted him to have a firm understanding of John 16:33 — *In this world you will have trouble. But take heart! I have overcome the world.* What do you think Alex's father wanted him to get from that verse? What might have been his father's concerns for Alex?

4. How has that Scripture applied in your life? Tell about a time when you might've relied on that truth to get you through a certain situation.

5. Explain why Holly was still in LA years after she'd been turned away by Alex. What signs made it clear she hadn't forgotten him?

6. Was there a time in your life when you were stuck in a certain phase, unable to move forward? Tell about that time and why it left you feeling stuck.

7. What did you learn about ecoterrorists in *Remember Tuesday Morning*? Share your thoughts on this new criminal phenomenon.

8. Dave Jacobs was a developer, but he was also a bird-watcher and a generous friend to the homeless population in Los

Angeles. What did the members of the REA probably think about Dave Jacobs? Why is it important not to view builders, environmentalists, or anyone else only as stereotypes?

9. Jamie wanted desperately to fix the problems in Alex's heart. What did she finally have to do in order to see that happen?

10. Are there people in your life who you'd love to step in and help? Is God giving you direction on how you can do that? What do you feel He wants you to do? Share the situation, if possible.

11. What did Clay mean when he explained the difference between the evil outside a person, and the evil within?

12. Read John, chapter 16, and discuss what the Bible says about the evil within and without. What is Christ's plan for his people in regards to this issue?

13. Police dogs exhibit a very great loyalty and sense of courage and protection. Do you know anyone who has worked with a police dog? Tell about their experience.

14. In what ways is our relationship with Jesus like that of Alex's relationship with Bo?

15. A lot of people were praying for Alex as he traveled this difficult and challenging time in his life. What people's prayers stood out as making a difference?

16. Who are you praying for right now? What can you focus on so that you'll be encouraged to continue to pray? Tell about a time when a prayer in your life was answered after someone spent time praying for you.

17. The tragedy of September 11 is more of a distant memory for many Americans. Kids in high school today were in grade school when the terrorist attacks happened. What must we, as a nation, do to never forget the losses experienced that day?

18. The loss of his father will always be difficult for Alex. But as he marries Holly he realizes he will no longer be weighed down by that grief on an hourly basis. Instead he decides to

allow himself to feel the pain only every now and then. What situation in your life are you better off visiting only every now and then?

19. Holly's mother told her that real love takes work, that it didn't come at a person all at once like a blazing rainbow across an otherwise dreary sky. How do you feel about love?

20. Many different types of love were illustrated in this book. Talk about a few of them and explain what types of love are illustrated in your life.

One Tuesday Morning

Karen Kingsbury

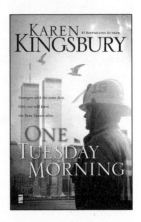

The last thing Jake Bryan knew was the roar of the World Trade Center collapsing on top of him and his fellow firefighters. The man in the hospital bed remembers nothing. Not rushing with his teammates up the stairway of the South Tower to help trapped victims. Not being blasted from the building. And not the woman sitting by his bedside who says she is his wife.

Jamie Bryan will do anything to help her beloved husband regain his memory. But that means helping Jake rediscover the one thing Jamie has never shared with him: his deep faith in God.

Beyond Tuesday Morning

Karen Kingsbury

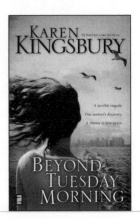

Winner of the Silver Medallion Book Award

Determined to find meaning in her grief three years after the terrorist attacks on New York City, FDNY widow Jamie Bryan pours her life into volunteer work at a small memorial chapel across from where the Twin Towers once stood. There, unsure and feeling somehow guilty, Jamie opens herself to the possibility of love again.

But in the face of a staggering revelation, only the persistence of a tenacious man, the questions from Jamie's curious young daughter, and the words from her dead husband's journal can move Jamie beyond one Tuesday morning ... toward life.

BAILEY FLANIGAN SERIES

Leaving

Karen Kingsbury,
New York Times *Bestselling Author*

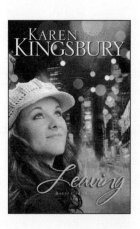

The Bailey Flanigan Series begins with Bailey leaving Bloomington for the adventure of a lifetime. She has won an audition for the ensemble of a Broadway musical in New York City. She's determined to take advantage of this once-in-a-lifetime opportunity, but is she really ready to leave family and friends for the loneliness of the city? And what of Cody? His disappearance has her worried about their future and praying that their love can survive.

In order to be closer to his mother in jail, Cody takes a coaching job in a small community outside Indianapolis. New friends, distance, and circumstances expose cracks in his relationship with Bailey Flanigan.

Love, loneliness, big opportunities, and even bigger decisions highlight the first book in the new Bailey Flanigan Series that features members of the popular Baxter family and finally completes the Bailey Flanigan/Cody Coleman story.

Available in stores and online!

BAILEY FLANIGAN SERIES

Learning

Karen Kingsbury,
New York Times *Bestselling Author*

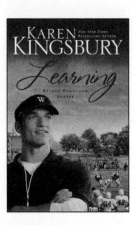

Learning, book two in the Bailey Flanigan Series, picks up where Leaving ended. Bailey Flanigan and Cody Coleman are not only separated by physical distance, they are also faced with great emotional distance. While Bailey grows closer to her dream to be an actress and dancer in New York, Cody coaches a small high school football team ... on and off the field. But neither feels complete without the chance to share their dreams with one other.

Can distance truly make the heart grow fonder? Or will Cody learn to turn to others to share in his happiness? And in the face of tragedy, who will be there to provide comfort?

As Cody's past catches up with him, he must learn to reach out for help or risk withdrawing permanently inside himself. Both Bailey and Cody find themselves learning significant life lessons in this poignant love story, featuring members from Karen Kingsbury's popular Baxter family.

Available in stores and online!

ABOVE THE LINE SERIES

The four novels of the bestselling Above the Line Series follow dedicated Hollywood producers, as they seek to transform the culture through their film. The books also feature characters from the much-loved Baxter Family. Follow Chase Ryan and Keith Ellison as they journey through the world of moviemaking and learn all that glitters is not gold, and that success could cost them everything— their relationships and their ideals. Each book in the series focuses on a different part of the process and the various struggles they face to reach their goals of making a movie that changes lives.

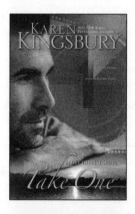

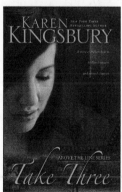

Available in stores and online!

Unlocked

A Love Story

Karen Kingsbury,
New York Times *Bestselling Author*

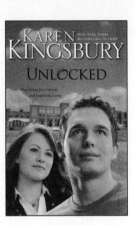

Before You Take a Stand ...
You've Got to Take a Chance.

Holden Harris is an eighteen-year-old
locked in a prison of autism. Despite his quiet ways and quirky be-
haviors, Holden is very happy and socially normal — on the inside, in
a private world all his own. In reality, he is bullied at school by kids
who only see that he is very different.

Ella Reynolds is part of the "in" crowd. A cheerleader and star
of the high school drama production, her life seems perfect. When
she catches Holden listening to her rehearse for the school play,
she is drawn to him ... the way he is drawn to the music. Then, Ella
makes a dramatic discovery — she and Holden were best friends as
children.

Frustrated by the way Holden is bullied, and horrified at the indifference of her peers, Ella decides to take a stand against the
most privileged and popular kids at school. Including her boyfriend,
Jake.

Ella believes miracles can happen in the unlikeliest places, and
that just maybe an entire community might celebrate from the sidelines. But will Holden's praying mother and the efforts of Ella and
a cast of theater kids be enough to unlock the prison that contains
Holden?

This time, friendship, faith, and the power of a song must be
strong enough to open the doors to the miracle Holden needs.

Available in stores and online!

ZONDERVAN®
.com

LOST LOVE SERIES

Even Now

Karen Kingsbury

Sometimes hope for the future is found in the ashes of yesterday.

A young woman seeking answers to her heart's deepest questions. A man and woman driven apart by lies and years of separation ... who have never forgotten each other.

With hallmark tenderness and power, Karen Kingsbury weaves a tapestry of lives, losses, love, and faith — and the miracle of resurrection.

Ever After

Karen Kingsbury

2007 Christian Book of the Year

Two couples torn apart — one by war between countries, and one by a war within.

In this moving sequel to *Even Now*, Emily Anderson, now twenty, meets the man who changes everything for her: Army reservist Justin Baker. Their tender relationship, founded on a mutual faith in God and nurtured by their trust and love for each other, proves to be a shining inspiration to everyone they know, especially Emily's reunited birth parents.

But Lauren and Shane still struggle to move past their opposing beliefs about war, politics, and faith. When tragedy strikes, can they set aside their opposing views so that love — God's love — might win, no matter how great the odds?

Available in stores and online!

Shades of Blue

Karen Kingsbury,
New York Times *Bestselling Author*

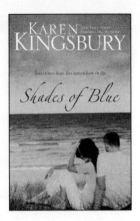

In between a checkered past and a fairytale future, a decision awaits.

Brad Cutler, twenty-eight, is a rising star at his New York ad agency, about to marry the girl of his dreams. Anyone would agree he has it all — a great career, a beautiful and loving fiancée, and a fairy tale life ahead of him ... when memories of a high school girlfriend begin to torment him. Lost innocence and one very difficult choice flood his conscience, and he is no longer sure what the future will bring except for this: He must go back to the shores of Holden Beach in search of his first love, and a forgiveness neither of them has ever known.

Three people must work through the repercussions of a decision made long ago before any of them can look toward a new future.

Available in stores and online!

Between Sundays

Karen Kingsbury,
New York Times *Bestselling Author*

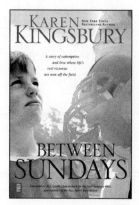

Aaron Hill has it all—athletic good looks and the many privileges of a star quarterback. His Sundays are spent playing NFL football in front of a televised audience of millions. But Aaron's about to receive an unexpected handoff, one that will give him a whole new view of his self-centered life.

Derrick Anderson is a family man who volunteers his time with foster kids while sustaining a long career as a pro football player. But now he's looking for a miracle. He must act as team mentor while still striving for the one thing that matters most this season—keeping a promise he made years ago.

Megan Gunn works two jobs and spends her spare time helping at the youth center. Much of what she does, she does for the one boy for whom she is everything—a foster child whose dying mother left him in Megan's care. Now she wants to adopt him, but one obstacle stands in the way. Her foster son, Cory, is convinced that 49ers quarterback Aaron Hill is his father.

Two men and the game they love. A woman with a heart for the lonely and lost, and a boy who believes the impossible. Thrown together in a season of self-discovery, they're about to learn lessons in character and grace, love and sacrifice.

Because in the end, life isn't defined by what takes place on the first day of the week, but how we live it between Sundays.

Available in stores and online!

Share Your Thoughts

With the Author: Your comments will be forwarded to the author when you send them to *zauthor@zondervan.com*.

With Zondervan: Submit your review of this book by writing to *zreview@zondervan.com*.

Free Online Resources at
www.zondervan.com

Zondervan AuthorTracker: Be notified whenever your favorite authors publish new books, go on tour, or post an update about what's happening in their lives at www.zondervan.com/authortracker.

Daily Bible Verses and Devotions: Enrich your life with daily Bible verses or devotions that help you start every morning focused on God. Visit www.zondervan.com/newsletters.

Free Email Publications: Sign up for newsletters on Christian living, academic resources, church ministry, fiction, children's resources, and more. Visit www.zondervan.com/newsletters.

Zondervan Bible Search: Find and compare Bible passages in a variety of translations at www.zondervanbiblesearch.com.

Other Benefits: Register to receive online benefits like coupons and special offers, or to participate in research.

ZONDERVAN®

ZONDERVAN.com/
AUTHORTRACKER
follow your favorite authors